W9-BLA-993

Praise for
The Hundred Days

"*The Hundred Days* has all the elements that O'Brian's fans have come to love. . . . And, as always, there's the language—ornate and orotund, coarse and common, and more magically evocative of another era than it seems possible mere words could be."

—*San Francisco Chronicle*

"Not one of those overweening lists and counterlists of 100 greatest novels that provoked such harrumphing a few months ago mentioned the remarkable British novelist Patrick O'Brian. This, his beguiled readers could argue, demeans not O'Brian but the lists."   —*Time*

"As usual, it is O'Brian's rendering of the internal lives of the characters—his loving and apt portrayal of their rich mix of feelings and experiences—that gives *The Hundred Days* distinction."

—*Chicago Tribune*

"O'Brian matches Forester in the excitement, details and bloody realism of his reconstructions. But these naval tales are blended into a larger panorama of Georgian society and politics, science, medicine, botany and the whole conspectus of contemporary Enlightenment knowledge about the natural world. . . . O'Brian's works abound with captivating descriptions. . . . There is no doubt that fans will like [*The Hundred Days*]."

—Paul Kennedy, *New York Times Book Review*

"Both newcomers and enthusiasts of the series will relish the entertaining evidence that 'The Hundred Days' demonstrates no diminution of [O'Brian's] literary powers or his obvious affection for his enduring, attractive dual characters. . . . The Aubrey-Maturin books, ultimately, are the 6,300-page unfolding of the characters, personalities and tastes of two very different men as they struggle with the challenges, threats and temptations of a tough, very imperfect and predominantly masculine world. That they preserve their loyalties and civilized values through the many successes and failures of their 19 installments is both Patrick O'Brian's triumph and a voluminously humanistic treat for his readers." —*Cleveland Plain Dealer*

"Master storyteller Patrick O'Brian continues to deliver, in the 19th book in the series, what most people value in great fiction: clear, seemingly effortless writing and character-driven stories. . . . His characters seem real, and he obviously delights in them. They are of their time, but so familiar in their behavior that they remind readers how little human nature has changed in 200 years." —*Minneapolis Star Tribune*

"*The Hundred Days* . . . is a wonderful novel, full of brisk battles and devious plots, sweet sailing and livid storms, bright laughter and terrible tragedy. . . . [O'Brian is] better than anybody at historical fiction. . . . [He] is as able and graceful with the English language as a writer can be." —*Denver Post*

"Using all the craftiness of a veteran knuckleball pitcher, [O'Brian] delivers the expected unexpectedly. And then tosses in the truly unexpected." —*Seattle Weekly*

"Colorful historical background, smooth plotting, marvelous characters and great style. . . . O'Brian continues to unroll a splendid Turkish rug of a saga." —*Publishers Weekly* (starred)

"O'Brian's is the finest depiction of sailing warfare since C. S. Forester's in the Hornblower tales, and he also brings to life the society of Napoleonic Europe like no one else since Georgette Heyer laid down her writing brush. Not supplying Aubrey-Maturin fandom with this volume would be the equivalent of wantonly stopping the crew's grog, and loud protest, if not outright mutiny, would certainly be the result."   —*Booklist*

"If you have read O'Brian's work, then you are probably addicted to him. To this group of readers, I offer reassurance: the master has turned another great performance."   —*Book Page*

"O'Brian is not that hard a taste to acquire, but he is very tough to shake. . . . [The Aubrey/Maturin series] is a great work."
—*Boston Globe*

"Fresh and compelling . . . a first-class read."
—*The Virginian-Pilot*

David Furniss
6/00

THE HUNDRED DAYS

The Works of Patrick O'Brian

Biography

PICASSO
JOSEPH BANKS

The Aubrey-Maturin Novels
in order of publication

MASTER AND COMMANDER
POST CAPTAIN
HMS SURPRISE
THE MAURITIUS COMMAND
DESOLATION ISLAND
THE FORTUNE OF WAR
THE SURGEON'S MATE
THE IONIAN MISSION
TREASON'S HARBOUR
THE FAR SIDE OF THE WORLD
THE REVERSE OF THE MEDAL
THE LETTER OF MARQUE
THE THIRTEEN-GUN SALUTE
THE NUTMEG OF CONSOLATION
THE TRUELOVE
THE WINE-DARK SEA
THE COMMODORE
THE YELLOW ADMIRAL
THE HUNDRED DAYS

Novels

TESTIMONIES
THE GOLDEN OCEAN
THE UNKNOWN SHORE

Collections

THE RENDEZVOUS AND OTHER STORIES

THE HUNDRED DAYS

Patrick O'Brian

W · W · NORTON & COMPANY
NEW YORK · LONDON

Copyright © 1998 by Patrick O'Brian
All rights reserved
Printed in the United States of America

First published as a Norton paperback 1999

For information about permission to reproduce from this book, write to Permissions,
W. W. Norton & Company, Inc., 500 Fifth Avenue, New York, NY 10110.

Library of Congress Cataloging-in-Publication Data
O'Brian, Patrick, 1914–
The hundred days / Patrick O'Brian. —1st American ed.
p.   cm.
ISBN 0-393-04674-5
1. Napoleon, I, Emperor of the French, 1769–1821—Elba and the Hundred Days,
1814–1815—Fiction. 2. Great Britain—History, Naval—19th century—Fiction.
3. Maturin, Stephen (Fictitious character)—Fiction. 4. Aubrey, Jack (Fictitious
character)—Fiction. 5. Napoleonic Wars, 1800–1815—Fiction. I. Title.
PR6029.B55H86   1998
823'.914—dc21   98-35866
CIP

ISBN 0-393-31979-2 pbk.

W. W. Norton & Company, Inc., 500 Fifth Avenue, New York, N.Y. 10110
www.wwnorton.com

W. W. Norton & Company Ltd., 10 Coptic Street, London WC1A 1PU

1 2 3 4 5 6 7 8 9 0

FOR MARY
WITH LOVE

The sails of a square-rigged ship, hung out to dry in a calm.

1 Flying jib
2 Jib
3 Fore topmast staysail
4 Fore staysail
5 Foresail, or course
6 Fore topsail
7 Fore topgallant
8 Mainstaysail
9 Main topmast staysail
10 Middle staysail
11 Main topgallant staysail
12 Mainsail, or course
13 Maintopsail
14 Main topgallant
15 Mizzen staysail
16 Mizzen topmast staysail
17 Mizzen topgallant staysail
18 Mizzen sail
19 Spanker
20 Mizzen topsail
21 Mizzen topgallant

Illustration source: Serres, Liber Nauticus.
Courtesy of The Science and Technology Research Center,
The New York Public Library, Astor, Lenox, and Tilden Foundation

Chapter One

The sudden rearmament that followed Napoleon's escape from Elba had done little to thin the ranks of unemployed sea-officers by the early spring of 1815. A man-of-war stripped, dismantled and laid up cannot be manned, equipped and made ready for sea in a matter of weeks; and the best vantage-points in Gibraltar were now crowded with gentlemen on half-pay who with others had gathered to watch the long-expected arrival of Commodore Aubrey's squadron from Madeira, a squadron that would do something to refurnish the great bare stretch of water inside the mole – an extraordinary nakedness emphasized by the presence of a few hulks, the *Royal Sovereign* wearing the flag of the Commander-in-Chief, and a couple of lonely seventy-fours: no stream of liberty-boats plying to and fro, almost no appearance of true wartime life.

It was a wonderfully beautiful day, with a slight and varying but reasonably favourable breeze at last: the sun blazed on the various kinds of broom in flower, upon the Rock, upon the cistuses and giant heath, while an uninterrupted stream of migrant birds, honey-buzzards, black kites, all the European vultures, storks both black and white, bee-eaters, hoopoes and countless hirundines flowed across the sky amidst a general indifference; for all eyes were fixed upon the middle distance, where the squadron had come about on the starboard tack. Among the earlier of the watchers, both carrying well-worn telescopes, were two elderly naval lieutenants who could no longer bear the English climate and who found that their £127 15s. od a year went much farther here. 'The breeze is veering again,' said the first. 'It will be abaft the beam directly.'

'They will be in on this leg, sure.'

'In at last, after all these weary days, poor souls. *Briseis* kept them hanging about in Funchal until they almost grounded on their own beef-bones. She was always over-masted; and even now I cannot congratulate her on that botched-together bowsprit. Marsham has always over-steeved his bowsprits.'

'Nor on her new foretopmast: their bosun must have died.'

'Now they have steadied, and the line is as clear as can be. *Briseis* . . . *Surprise* – she must have been called back into service – *Pomone*, wearing Commodore Jack Aubrey's broad pennant – that must have put poor Wrangle's nose out of joint. *Dover* . . . *Ganymede. Dover* . . . *Ganymede. Dover* was fitted as a troopship and now she is changing herself back into a frigate as fast as ever she can. What a shambles!'

The breeze came aft and the whole squadron flashed out studdingsails, broad wings set in a thoroughly seamanlike manner: a glorious sight. Yet now the current was against them and in spite of their fine spread of canvas they made but little headway. They were all of them sailing large, of course, all of them getting the last ounce of thrust from the dying breeze with all the skill learnt in more than twenty years of war; a noble spectacle, but one that after a while called for no particular comment, and presently the old lieutenant, John Arrowsmith, two months senior to his friend Thomas Edwards, said, 'When I was young I always used to turn to the births and marriages in the *Times* as soon as I had done with the promotions and dispatches; but now I turn to the deaths.'

'So do I,' said Edwards.

'. . . and with this last batch that came with the packet I found several names I knew. The first was Admiral

Stranraer, Admiral Lord Stranraer, Captain Koop that was.'

'Oh, indeed? I sailed with him in the old *Defender*, a West Indies commission where he taught us the spit and polish of those parts. Gloves at all times, whatever the weather; Hessian boots with tassels, on the quarterdeck; up lower yards and cross topgallant yards in under five minutes or watch out for squalls; no reply allowed to any rebuke. If it were not that he is dead, I could tell you many a tale about him in Kingston.'

'Indeed, he was not a well-liked man at all, at all. They say his surgeon and another medico killed him with a black draught or something of that kind: but slowly, you understand me now, like the husband of one of those arsenic wives eager to be a widow but not choosing to swing for it.'

'From my acquaintance with his lordship, what you say does not surprise me in the least. On reflection, I believe I should offer each or either of the physical gentlemen a glass of brandy, were the occasions to offer. Do you see *Surprise* start her stuns'l sheet not to outrun her station?'

'Aye. She was always a wonderfully swift sailer; and now they have done her proud, as trim as a royal yacht. Webster saw her in young Seppings' yard where they were fitting her out regardless, diagonal bracing and everything you can think of — fitting her out for a hydrographical voyage. A lovely little craft.'

For some time they discussed the ship's perfections; their practised hands holding her steady in their telescopes; but then, the line being perfectly re-established, a cable's length apart, Arrowsmith clapped his glass to and said, 'Another death was of quite a different kind of man: Governor Wood of Sierra Leone. He was a fine fellow, very popular in the service, and he kept a noble table — invited whole wardrooms when the King's ships came in; and youngsters too.'

'I remember him very well. John Kneller and I and nearly all our messmates dined with him after some cruel weather

off the River Plate and weeks of damned short commons –
a sprung butt had drowned the bread-room. Lord, how we
ate, and laughed, and sang! So he is dead. Well, God rest
him, say I. Though when everything is said and done, we
must all come to it; which may be some comfort to those
that go before. A very handsome wife, as I recall, but on
the learned side, which made her neighbours shy.'

'The breeze is strengthening out there. *Dover* has let fly
her foretop-gallant sheets.'

The gust – the series of gusts – disturbed the picture-book
regularity for a while, but it was restored after a remarkably
short interval (all hands knew that they were being watched
not only by an uncommonly exigent commodore and the
even more formidable Commander-in-Chief Lord Keith,
but also by an increasingly numerous band of highly-
informed, highly-critical observers on shore) and presently
the two lieutenants' conversation resumed.

'And then there was another what you might call naval
death, a good deal earlier than the others but only now
reported. Did you ever meet Dr Maturin?'

'I don't know that I did, but I have often heard of him.
A very clever doctor, they say – called in to treat Prince
William – always sails with Jack Aubrey.'

'That's the man. Well, he has a wife. They live with the
Aubreys at his big place in Dorset – but of course you know
it, being a Dorset man.'

'Yes. Woolcombe; or Woolhampton as some say. It is
rather far for us and we do not visit, but I have been to one
or two of the Blackstone's meets there and we used to see
Mrs Aubrey and Mrs Maturin at the Dorchester assembly.
Mrs Maturin breeds Arabs: a very good horsewoman and
an uncommon fine whip.'

'Well, yes . . . so they said. But do you know a place called
Maiden Oscott?'

'Only too well, with its damned awkward bridge.'

'The report gives no details, but it seemed she pitched

over – the whole shooting-match, coach, horses and all, pitched over right down into the river, and only the groom was brought out alive.'

'Oh, my God!' cried Edwards: and after a pause, 'My wife disliked her; but she was a very beautiful woman. Some people said she was a demi-rep . . . she had some astonishing jewels . . . there was some talk of a Colonel Cholmondeley . . . and it is said the marriage was not a happy one. But she is dead, God rest her. I say no more. Yet I doubt I ever see her like again.'

They both reflected, gazing out over the brilliant sea with half-closed eyes as the squadron drew inshore and the watching crowd increased; and Edwards said, 'When you come to think of it, on looking about our shipmates and relations, can you think of any marriage that could be called a happy one, after the first flush? There is something to be said for a bachelor's existence, you know: turn in whenever you like, read in bed . . .'

'Offhand I cannot think of many – poor Wood in Sierra Leone for example: they entertained without a pause, so as not to have to sit down at table alone. It is said that Wood – but he is dead. No, I cannot think of many without some discord or contention; but unless it is very obvious, who can tell just where the balance lies? After all, as a philosopher said, "Though matrimony has its pains, celibacy can have no pleasure".'

'I know nothing about philosophy, but I have met some philosophers – we often used to go to Cambridge to see my brother the don – and a miserable set of . . .' He checked the word at the sight of his friend's daughters – the elder charming, though rather shabby – pushing through the crowd towards them, and went on in a disapproving tone, '. . . though you always were a bookish fellow, even in *Britannia*'s cockpit.'

'Oh Papa,' cried the elder girl, 'which is the *Surprise*?'

'The second in the line, my dear.'

5

The leading ships were now close enough for people to be seen – blue coats and red on the quarterdeck, white-trousered seamen taking in topsails and courses together with jib and staysails – but scarcely to be distinguished. The young lady gently took her father's telescope and trained it on the *Surprise*. 'Is *that* the famous Captain Aubrey?' she asked. 'Why, he is short, fat and red-faced. I *am* disappointed.'

'No, booby,' said her father. 'The Commodore is where a Commodore ought to be, aboard the pennant-ship, of course: *Pomone*. Come, child, don't you see the broad pennant, hey?'

'Oh yes, sir, I see it,' she replied, training her glass on *Pomone*'s quarterdeck. 'Pray who is the very tall fair-haired man wearing a rear-admiral's uniform and holding his hat under his arm?'

'Why, Lizzie, that is your famous Jack Aubrey. Commodores dress like rear-admirals, you know: and they receive a flag-officer's return to their salute, as you will hear in about ten seconds.'

'Oh, isn't he *beautiful*? Molly Butler had a coloured engraving of him in action with the Turks – of his boarding the *Torgud* sword in hand, and all the great girls at school . . .'

What all the great girls said or thought was lost in the *Pomone*'s exactly-spaced seventeen-gun salute to the Commander-in-Chief; and the echo of the last report and the drift of powder-smoke had not disappeared before the towering flagship began her fifteen-gun reply. When that too was done, Mr Arrowsmith said, 'Now in another ten seconds you will see the signal break out *Commodore repair aboard flag*. His barge is already lowering down.'

'Who is that little man beside him, in a black coat and drab breeches?'

'Oh, that will be his surgeon, Dr Maturin: they always sail together. He can whip off an arm or a leg quicker than any man in the service; and it is a joy to see him carve a saddle of mutton.'

'Oh fie, Papa!' cried the girl: her younger sister gave a coarse great laugh.

Aboard *Pomone* the proper ceremony for the occasion was well under way, and as Jack walked out of the great cabin, stuffing a fresh handkerchief into his pocket and pursued by Killick with a clothes-brush, flicking specks of dust from the back of his gold-laced coat, he found his officers present on the quarterdeck, together with most of the midshipmen, all either wearing gloves or concealing their hands behind their backs.

The side-boys offered him the sumptuous man-ropes, and following the reefer on duty he ran down into his barge. All the bargemen knew him perfectly well – they had been shipmates in many a commission, and two of them, Joe Plaice and Davies, had served in his first command, the *Sophie*; but neither they nor Bonden, his coxswain, gave the least sign of recognition as he settled in the stern-sheets, shifting his sword to give the midshipman more room. They sat there in their formal bargeman's rig – broad-brimmed white sennit hat with ribbons, white shirts, black silk Barcelona handkerchiefs tied round their necks, snowy duck trousers – looking solemn: they were part of a ceremony, and levity, winking, whispering, smiling, had no place in it. Bonden shoved off, said 'Give way', and with exact timing, rowing dry with long grave strokes, they pulled the barge across to the starboard accommodation-ladder of the flagship, where an even more impressive ceremony took place. Jack, having been piped aboard, saluted the quarterdeck, shook hands with the ship's captain and the master of the fleet, while the Royal Marines – scarlet perfection under a brilliant sun – presented arms with a rhythmic clash and stamp.

A master's mate led the *Pomone*'s youngster away, and Captain Buchan, who commanded the *Royal Sovereign*,

7

ushered Jack Aubrey below, to the Admiral's splendid quarters: but rather than the very large, grim and hoary Commander-in-Chief, there rose a diaphanous cloud of blue tulle from the locker against the screen-bulkhead – tulle that enveloped a particularly tall and elegant woman, very good-looking but even more remarkable for her fine carriage and amiable expression. 'Well, dearest Jack,' she said, they having kissed, 'how very happy I am to see you wearing a broad pennant. It was a damned near-run thing that you were not out of reach, half-way to Tierra del Fuego in a mere hydrographical tub, a hired vessel. But how we ever came to miss you on Common Hard I shall never understand – never, though I have gone over it again and again. True, Keith was in a great taking about the naval estimates, and I was turning some obscure lines of Ennius in my head without being able to make any sense of them frontwards or backwards; but even so . . .'

'Nor shall I ever understand how I came to be such an oaf as to walk in here, ask you how you did, and sit down by your side without the slightest word of congratulations on being a viscountess: yet it had been in my head all the way across. Give you joy with all my heart, dear Queenie,' he said, kissing her again; and they sat there very companionably on the broad cushioned locker. Jack was taller than Queenie and far more than twice as heavy; and having been in the wars for a great while and much battered, he now looked older. He was in fact seven years her junior, and there had been a time when he was a very little boy whose ears she boxed for impertinence, uncleanliness and greed, and whose frequent nightmares she would soothe by taking him into her bed.

'By the way,' said Jack, 'does the Admiral prefer to be addressed as Lord Viscount Keith like Nelson in his time or just as plain Lord K?'

'Oh, just plain Lord, I think. The other thing is formal court usage, to be sure, and I know that dear Nelson loved it; but I think it has died out among ordinary people. Anyway he does not give a hoot for such things, you know. He values his flag extremely, of course, and I dare say he would like the Garter; but the Keiths of Elphinstone go back to the night of time– they are earl marischals of Scotland, and would not call Moses cousin.'

They sat smiling at one another. An odd pair: handsome creatures both, but they might have been of the same sex or neither. Nor was it a brother and sister connection, with all the possibilities of jealousy and competition so often found therein, but a steady uncomplicated friendship and a pleasure in one another's company. Certainly, when Jack was scarcely breeched and Queenie took care of him after his mother's death, she had been somewhat authoritarian, insisting on due modesty and decent eating; but that was long ago, and for a great while now they had been perfectly well together.

A cloud passed over her face, and putting her hand on Jack's knee she said, 'I was so happy to see you – to have recovered you from Cape Horn at the very last moment – that I overlooked more important things. Tell me, how is poor dear Maturin?'

'He looks older, and bent; but he bears up wonderfully, and it has not done away with his love of music. He eats nothing, though, and when he came back to Funchal, having attended to everything at Woolcombe, I lifted him out of the boat with one hand.'

'She was an extraordinarily handsome woman and she had prodigious style: I admired her exceedingly. But she was not a wife for him; nor a mother for that dear little girl. How is she? She was not in the coach, I collect?'

'No. The only other one on the box was Cholmondeley; my mother-in-law and her companion inside, and Harry Willet, the groom, up behind – happily Padeen did not go that day. And Brigid does not seem very gravely upset, from what I understand. She is very deeply attached to Sophie, you know, and to Mrs Oakes.'

9

'I do not believe I know Mrs Oakes.'

'A sea-officer's widow who lives with us, a learned lady – not as learned as you, Queenie, I am sure – but she teaches the children Latin and French. They are none of them clever enough for Greek.'

A pause. 'If he does not eat, he will certainly grow weak and pine away,' said Lady Keith. 'We have a famous cook aboard *Royal Sovereign* – he came back to England with the Bourbons. Would an invitation be acceptable, do you think? Just us and the Physician of the Fleet and a few very old friends. I have a crux in this passage of Ennius I should like to show him. And of course he must have a conference with Keith's secretary and the political adviser very soon . . . Oh, and Jack, there is something I must tell you, just between ourselves. Another Mediterranean command would be too much for him, so we are only here until Pellew comes out; though we shall stay in the Governor's cottage a little while to enjoy the spring. Do you get along well with Pellew, Jackie?'

'I have a great admiration for him,' said Jack – and indeed Admiral Sir Edward Pellew had been a remarkably dashing and successful frigate-captain – 'but not quite the veneration I have for Lord Keith.'

'My dear Aubrey,' cried the Admiral, walking in from the coach, 'there you are! How glad I am to see you.'

'And I to see you, my Lord Viscount, if I may so express myself. My heartiest congratulations.'

'Thankee, thankee, Aubrey,' said the Admiral, more pleasant than quite suited his wife. 'But I must say that I deserve to be degraded for having put in that foolish proviso in your orders about waiting for *Briseis*. I should have said . . . but never mind what I should have said. The fact is that at that time I merely wanted your squadron to guard the passage of the Straits: now, at the present moment, the situation is much more complex. Six hundred thousand people cheered Napoleon when he entered Paris – Ney has joined him – a hundred and fifty thousand King's troops, well-equipped, drilled and officered, have done the same – he has countless seasoned men who were prisoners of war in England and Russia and all over Europe at his devotion, flooding to the colours – the Emperor's colours. There is the Devil to pay and no tar hot. Is Dr Maturin with you?'

'Yes, sir.'

'Is he up to talking about all this with my secretary and the politicos?'

'I believe so, my Lord. Although he shuns ordinary company he is dead set on the war and seizes upon any means whatsoever of informing himself – newspapers, correspondence and so on – and I have known him talk for three hours on end with a French officer – royalist of course – whose brig was in company with us during a flat calm off Bugio.'

'He would sooner not dine aboard *Royal Sovereign*, I gather.'

'I believe not, sir. But he will discuss the international situation and the means of bringing Napoleon down with the utmost vigour. That is what keeps him alive, it seems to me.'

'I am glad he has so great a resource at such a dreadful time, poor dear man. I have a great regard for him: as you will remember, I proposed he should be Physician of the Fleet at one time. Aye, aye, so I did. Well, I shall not pain him with an invitation he might find difficult to refuse. But if, in the course of duty, you could require him to report aboard just after the evening gun, when I hope for an overland packet by courier, he may learn still more about the international situation. A damned complex situation, upon my word. As I said, when first I sent for you I thought your squadron would be enough, at a pinch, to guard the passage of the Straits – at a pinch, for you see how pitifully little we have here. But now, *now*, you will have to cut yourself in three to do half the things I want you to do. Heugh, heugh, a damned complex situation as the Doctor will learn when he comes here: he will be finely amazed. I will give you the broadest view just for the now . . .'

Lady Keith gathered up her belongings and said, 'My dear, I will leave you to it. But do not tire yourself: you have a meeting with González this evening. I will send Geordie with a dish of tea directly.'

The broadest view, stripped of the Admiral's great authority and of his distinctive northern accent, generally pleasing to an English ear though sometimes impenetrably obscure, was very roughly this: Wellington, with ninety-three thousand British and Dutch troops, and Blücher, with a hundred and sixteen thousand Prussians, were in the Low Countries, waiting until Schwarzenberg, with two hundred and ten thousand Austrians, and Barclay de Tolly, slowly advancing with a hundred and fifty thousand Russians, should reach the Rhine, when in principle the Allies were to invade France. For his part Napoleon had about three hundred and sixty thousand men: they were made up of five corps along the northern frontier, the Imperial Guard in Paris, and some thirty thousand more stationed on the southeast frontier and in the Vendée.

Both men made their additions: both made their allowances for unity of command, the great value of a common language, and the stimulus of fighting on one's own soil under the orders of a man who had battered Prussians, Austrians and Russians again and again, fighting with extraordinary tactical skill against odds far greater than these.

Jack could not with propriety ask about the zeal or even the good faith of the Austrians and Prussians at this juncture, still less about the efficiency of their mobilization and equipment; but the Admiral's worn, anxious face told him a great deal. 'Still,' said Lord Keith, 'this is all the soldiers' business: we have our own concern to deal with. How I wish Geordie would come along with that tea – why, Geordie, put the tray down here, ye thrawn, ill-feckit gaberlunzie.'

A pause. 'How I value a cup of tea,' he said. 'May I pour you another?'

'Thank you, sir,' said Jack, shaking his head. 'I have done admirably well already.'

The Admiral reflected, carefully put more hot water to the teapot, and went on, 'In the first place there is the difficulty about the French Navy, their attitude varies from port to port, ship to ship. They are of course extremely susceptible and any untoward incident – so easily brought about – might have disastrous results. But far worse is this building of French men-of-war in the obscure Adriatic ports: obscure, but filled with prime timber and capital shipwrights – country *you* know very well. This continued building, more or less disguised, is a great evil; and all the greater as Bonapartist officers and men are said to be standing by to take them over.'

'But payment, sir? Even a corvette costs a very great deal of money, and there is talk of frigates, even of two or three heavy frigates.'

'Aye. There is something very odd about it all. Our intelligence people see a Muslim influence, possibly Turkish, possibly the Barbary states, or even of all of them combined. At this very moment there is much greater activity in Algiers, Tunis and down the Moroccan coast, fomented by Napoleonic renegadoes with native craft and vessels up to the size of a sloop of war: it is almost impossible to deal with it, our naval strength being so reduced and so tied up. Already it is most harmful to Allied trade, particularly to ours, and it is likely to grow worse.'

The Admiral stirred his tea, contemplated, and said, 'If Napoleon Bonaparte with his three hundred thousand very well trained men and his usual brilliant cavalry and artillery, can knock out say the Russians or part of the Austrians, the French navy may sweep us out of the Mediterranean again, above all as the Maltese and the Moroccans are so ungrateful as to hate us and as there is a real possibility of a French alliance with Tunis, Algeria and the other piratical states, to say nothing of the Emperor of Morocco and even the Sultan himself. For you know, Aubrey, do you not, that Bonaparte turned Turk? During the Egyptian campaign I think it was; but Turk in any case.'

'I heard of it, sir, of course; but no one has ever asserted that he recoiled from swine's flesh or a bottle of wine. I put it down to one of those foolish things a man says when he wishes to be elected to Parliament, such as "give me your votes, and I undertake to do away with the National Debt in eighteen months." I do not believe he is any more a Mussulman than I am. You have to be circumcised to be a Turk.'

'For my own part I have no knowledge of the gentleman's soul, or heart, or private parts: all I am sure of is that the statement was made, and that at this juncture it may be of capital importance. But we are prating away like a couple of old women . . .' He was interrupted by his secretary, who said, 'I beg pardon, my Lord, but the courier is just come aboard with his budget.'

Jack had started to his feet, and now he said, 'May I wait upon you later, sir, when you are less engaged?'

'Is there anything urgent, Mr Campbell?' asked Lord Keith, with a temporizing wave.

'Tedious and toilsome, rather than immediate, apart from one enclosure that I have already sent on.'

'Very good, very good. Thank you, Mr Campbell. Sit down, Aubrey. I will just run through the heads of these, then attend to your statements of the squadron's condition, and give you some notion of what I should like you to do.' A pause, during which the Admiral's long-practised hand ran through the dockets, already marked with Campbell's secret mark of importance: none rated above c3, and putting them down he said, 'Well, Aubrey, in the first place you must allot a force adequate for the protection of the Constantinople trade. Convoys have been re-introduced, you know

– one is due within the week – and the Algerians in particular have grown very bold, though some vessels are also to be expected from Tripoli, Tunis and the rest, while other corsairs push up from Sallee and pass the Straits in the dark of the moon. Then you must prevent any unauthorized outward or inward movement to the best of your ability. But your most important task by far is to look into those Adriatic ports you know so well. Even the small places are capable of building a frigate, and we have reports of actual ships of the line on the stocks in four places whose names Campbell will give you. If any of the two-deckers have openly declared for Napoleon you must not venture upon an action but send to me without the loss of a moment. Where frigates, corvettes or sloops are concerned, particularly if they are unfinished, you must endeavour to stop the building and obtain their disarmament, all of which requires the utmost degree of tact: I am so glad you have Maturin with you. An incident would, as I have said, be disastrous: though of course if there is a clearly-expressed intent of joining Bonaparte, you must burn, sink or destroy as usual.'

'Aye-aye, sir,' said Jack, and then, 'My Lord, I believe you spoke of a courier. If he is not already gone, may I beg for my tender *Ringle* to be sent out immediately? William Reade, master's mate, handles her very well indeed – an uncommon fast and weatherly Chesapeake clipper – and I shall have the utmost need for such a craft.'

'William Reade, the young gentleman that lost an arm with you in the East Indies?' asked the Admiral, scribbling a note. 'Certainly. Should you like to send him a message – things to be brought out? Or Maturin? Well, I think that is the essential: you will of course receive detailed orders and some estimate of what you can expect from Malta when you are in Mahon.' The Admiral stood up. 'I hope you will dine with us tomorrow?' Jack bowed, said, 'Very happy,' and Keith went on, 'I do not wish to be importunate, but if you feel you could convey some sense of our feeling – our concern

– our sympathy – to Maturin, pray do so. In any case, I look forward to learning his views on the situation this evening, when he will have been closeted with Campbell and the two gentlemen who came down from Whitehall. Do not ask him to come aboard the flag: they will go to see him in *Pomone*.'

A little before the evening gun Preserved Killick, Captain Aubrey's steward, an ill-faced, ill-tempered, meagre, atrabilious, shrewish man who kept his officer's uniform, equipment and silver in a state of exact, old-maidish order come wind or high water, and who did the same for Aubrey's close friend and companion, Dr Stephen Maturin, or even more so, since in the Doctor's case Killick added a fretful nursemaid quality to his service, as though Maturin were "not quite exactly" a fully intelligent being, approached Stephen's cabin. It is true that in the community of mariners the "not quite exactly" opinion was widely held; for although Stephen could now tell the difference between starboard and larboard, it still called for some reflection: and it marked the limit of his powers. This general view, however, in no way affected their deep respect for him as a medical man: his work with a trephine or a saw, sometimes carried out on open deck for the sake of the light, excited universal admiration, and it was said that if he chose, and if the tide were still making, he could save you although you were already three parts dead and mouldy. Furthermore, a small half of one of his boluses would blow the backside off a bullock. The placebo effect of this reputation had indeed preserved many a sadly shattered sailor, and he was much caressed aboard. A little before the evening gun, therefore, Preserved Killick walked into Stephen's cabin and found him sitting there in his drawers, a jug of now cold water and an unused razor in front of him, together with a clean shirt, neck-cloth, new-brushed black coat, new-curled wig, clean breeches, silk stockings and a respectable handkerchief, reading the close-written coded message from Sir Joseph Blaine, the chief of naval intelligence that had just arrived by courier.

'Oh sir,' cried Killick: but even as he exclaimed he choked the inborn shrew, lowering the 'sir' to the gentlest tones of remonstrance.

'One moment, Killick,' said Stephen, resolving a particularly intractable group: he wrote it in the margin, covered it close, and said, 'I am yours.'

Apart from the words 'Which the gentlemen have been waiting ten minutes – called twice for wine, and was you quite well?' Killick dressed him silently, efficiently, and led him to the captain's cabin, where the Admiral's secretary and the two gentlemen from Whitehall rose to greet him. One of them, Mr William Kent, was a familiar figure, his high office sometimes required him to resolve difficulties between the various departments of government and the services so that confidential work might be carried on in official silence: the other, Mr Dee, he knew only from having seen him at a few restricted conferences at which he spoke rarely or not at all, though he was treated with deference as an authority on eastern matters, particularly those concerned with finance – he was connected with some of the great banking-houses in the City. Sir Joseph's coded message had only said 'You will of course remember his book on Persian literature'.

Stephen did indeed remember it: he had had his own battered second-hand copy rebound – a first edition – and he recalled that the binder had put the date of publication at the bottom of the spine: 1764.

As they all sat down again, Stephen, with his back to the light, looked at Mr Dee with discreet curiosity, as at one whose work had enriched his youth: Mr Dee's face, alas, showed little but discontent and weariness. He did not see fit to open the conversation, so after a hesitant glance or so William Kent it was who addressed himself to Stephen, saying, 'Well, sir, since you have been windbound for so long – quite out of touch – perhaps it would not be improper to give a brief sketch of the present situation?'

Stephen bowed, and leant towards him. Kent's summary was essentially the same as Lord Keith's; but Stephen, being unaffected by considerations of rank, tact, ignorance or particular respect, had no hesitation in asking questions, and he learned that the Netherlanders were by no means happy about the presence of Wellington's and Blücher's armies; that the various rulers, commanders, and war offices were indeed at odds upon a very wide variety of subjects; that secrecy about plans, orders and appointed meetings scarcely existed in the Austrian army, with its many nationalities, rivalries and languages; and that as opposed to the effervescent sense of returning glory in France, there was a total lack of enthusiasm in many of the Allied regiments, and something worse, not far from mutiny, among the Russians, particularly the units from the wreck of divided Poland. Barclay de Tolly was doing all that a good soldier could do with his ill-equipped and discontented forces, but he could not make them move fast and they were already sixteen days behind the agreed timetable. They had an immense distance still to travel, and the rearguard had not yet even left its distant barracks. There was also mutual distrust, a fear of betrayal on the part of other members of the coalition or on that of some one or another of the many subject nations that made up the eastern powers.

Mr Dee coughed, and leaning forward he spoke for the first time, reminding Kent of an ancient Persian war in which a more numerous army made up of different nations had behaved in much the same way, being utterly shattered by the united Persian force on the banks of the Tigris: his account went on and on but as his voice was weak Stephen could not follow at all well – he was ill-placed for listening – and gradually he sank deeper and deeper into his own reflections, all necessarily of a kind as painful as could well be imagined. From time to time he was half aware that Mr Campbell was trying to lead them back to the matter in hand by mentioning Carebago, Spalato, Ragusa and other ports on the Adriatic shore – if once the French were out they would represent a great danger – few sea-officers reliable, if any . . .

He had some success, and in time Stephen was conscious that all three had in fact returned to naval matters; but much of his mind was still far down in the recent past when the voice of Kent pierced through with remarkable clarity. '. . . a very important point is that eventually one or another of these ships might protect or even carry the treasure.'

'The treasure, sir?'

He saw the three faces turned towards him and at almost the same moment he saw their expressions of surprise, even displeasure, turn to the grave, unobtrusive consideration that now surrounded him – that must in decency surround him, like a pall, ever since his loss became public knowledge. It could not be otherwise: his presence was necessarily a constraint: levity, even good-fellowship, certainly mirth, were as much out of place as reproof or unkindness.

Kent cleared his throat, and the Admiral's secretary, excusing himself, withdrew. 'Yes, sir, the treasure,' said Kent; and after a slight pause, 'Mr Dee and I were discussing a scheme planned by Dumanoir and his friends – a scheme to drive a Muslim wedge between the suspicious, slow-moving Austrian forces and the lingering Russians, preventing their junction and thus disrupting the planned meeting of the Allies on the Rhine.' Another pause. 'You will recall that Bonaparte professed himself a Muslim at the time of the Egyptian campaign?'

'I remember it, sure. But am I mistaken when I say that it was of no consequence at all, apart from damaging his reputation still farther? No Mahometan I ever met or heard of was much elated. The Grand Mufti took no notice whatsoever.'

'Very true,' said Dee, his old voice stronger now. 'But Islam is a world as varied as our own miserable congeries of hostile sects, and some of the more remote did in fact hail the news of his conversion with delight. Among these were people as widely separated as the Azgar, on the edge of the desert, and certain heretical Shiite fraternities in European Turkey, particularly Albania, Monastir, and a region close to the northern frontier, whose interpretation of the Sunna, read without the usual glosses, points to Napoleon as the Hidden Imam, the Mahdi. The most extreme are the descendants and followers of the Sheikh-al-Jabal.'

'The Old Man of the Mountains himself? Then they are the true, the only genuine Assassins? I long to see one,' said Stephen, with a certain animation.

'They are indeed; and although they are by no means so prominent as they were in the time of the Crusades, they are still a very dangerous body, even though the fedais, the experts, the actual killers, amount to only a few score. The rest of the mercenaries in the plan we are discussing, the rest of the potential mercenaries, though willing and eager to massacre unbelievers, are not moved by so pure a religious fervour that they will venture their skins free, gratis and for nothing. The three related fraternities throughout European Turkey all agree: the men are there, and as soon as they see two months' pay laid out before them, they will move. But not otherwise.'

'Is the sum very great?'

'Enormous: in the present state of affairs, when gold is at such a very shocking, unheard of premium, and credit is virtually dead. Far beyond anything the French can put down immediately: for, do you see, this sudden incursion must be very well-manned, with former Turkish auxiliaries, bashi-bazouks, tribal warriors, bandits and the like, all members of the Muslim fraternities or provided by them – a very formidable body indeed if it is to succeed in its aim – if it is to wreck the Allied plans and to give Napoleon the chance of engaging the weakest of the opposing armies and destroying it, as he has done before.'

'Certainly,' said Stephen. 'But am I right in supposing that the Assassins' role is something more subtle than the wild impetuous assault of the bashi-bazouks?'

'Yes: and a truly devoted band of fedais might do Napoleon's cause an incomparable service by removing Schwarzenberg or Barclay de Tolly or an imperial prince or indeed any of the thinking heads. Yet even so there would have to be the massive intervention, preferably by night, and some truly bloody fighting for the full effect of panic, mutual distrust and delay.'

'Where is the money to come from?'

'The Turk reluctantly shakes his head,' said Mr Dee. 'The Barbary states will provide volunteers and one tenth of the total when they see the rest. Morocco wavers. Their real hope is the Shiite ruler of Azgar, in whom they put all their trust. It is reported on very good authority that the gold has been promised and that messengers are to be sent – perhaps have been sent – to arrange the transport, probably from Algiers.'

'I speak as a man wholly ignorant of money-matters,' said Stephen. 'Yet I had always supposed that even moderately flourishing states like Turkey, Tunis, Tripoli and the like, or the bankers of Cairo and a dozen other cities could at any time raise a million or so without difficulty. Am I perhaps mistaken?'

'Wholly mistaken, my dear sir, if you will forgive me: wholly mistaken where the present juncture is concerned. You must understand that several of my cousins are bankers in the City – one of them is associated with Nathan Rothschild – and that I act as their consultant where eastern affairs are concerned. So I think I may confidently assert that at this point no bank in those parts could without long notice raise so much – let alone advance a single maravedi on such security. While as for the governments . . .' Leaning forward and speaking in a much clearer, younger voice, his eyes full of life, he launched into an account of the economic basis of each Muslim country from the Persian Gulf to the Atlantic, its income and liabilities, its banking practice and forms of credit: he gave the impression of immense competence and authority – the old man's quavering prolixity of earlier on disappeared entirely, and when he ended '. . . their only hope is Ibn Hazm of Azgar,' Stephen cried, 'I am sure of it, sir: would you have the great kindness to tell us something of the place and its ruler? For I blush to say that I know nothing of either.'

'To be sure, it is small, and it has almost no history: but it is happily placed at the junction of three caravan routes, where one of the very few springs in that vast area rises pure and cool from the rock, watering a remarkable grove of date-palms. It is defended by its position, by the shrines of three universally-acknowledged Muslim saints, by the aridity of the surrounding country, and by the sagacity of a long-continued series of rulers. By immemorial custom the little state is run on lines not wholly unlike those I have observed in a well-run man-of-war: every man has his place and his duty; the day is divided by the blast of a ram's horn, signifying assembly, prayers, meals, diversion, and the rest, while except in Ramadan there is daily exercise with cannon or small-arms. Furthermore, you must know that the customary dues and tolls levied on all caravans are paid, and always have been paid, in the form of very small ingots of pure gold. These are publicly weighed and publicly divided according to established shares, often being cut or reduced to powder and weighed again with extraordinary precision to the required amount. Clearly the ruler gets most, and in the course of several generations this must amount to a very great deal, in spite of the family's proverbial charity. Where it is kept there is no telling – curiosity in Azgar would be sadly out of place – but since the Sheikh spends most of his time in the wilderness with the famous herds of Azgar camels he may have banks of an impregnable security in any one of the innumerable caverns that are to be found where the limestone rises above the sand. At all events he possesses the means and the zeal to carry out this operation.'

'In economies of this kind, would letters of credit, drafts on a banking-house or the like have any existence, sir?'

'They are not unknown, as between merchants in high credit who have dealt with one another for many years: but in the present case the gold itself would have to travel to the coast and then take ship – no great matter, with a well-armed troop of Azgar camels and the swift Algerine xebecs or galleys. But with the pace at which the Russians are moving there is no furious hurry, although from our latest information the fraternities' messengers may be on their way to Azgar by now; and in the intervening time, well before Barclay de Tolly and Schwarzenberg can meet, it is to be hoped that the Royal Navy will have made it impossible for any disaffected French man-of-war to help the gold over the water, or for any vessel from the African shore to enter an Adriatic port.'

Mr Dee paused: the colour that had risen into his face while he was speaking faded. He was old and remote once more, and seeing Kent glance at him with evident concern he said, 'Pray go on, Mr Kent.'

'Very well, sir,' said William Kent. 'Dr Maturin, when we were speaking of this matter with Sir Joseph and his colleagues, it was suggested that with your knowledge of these parts and of the at least nominally Turkish officials governing them – of many important private and ecclesiastical persons – that you might bring pressure to bear – in a word, that you might cause this conspiracy to fail. The Ministry attaches great importance to the matter and you could draw on the Treasury for very large sums indeed if for example arbitrary arrests and the like were called for.' He looked earnestly into Stephen's face, coughed and went on, 'One of those present said that you might decline, for

23

personal reasons and on the grounds that your Turkish and Arabic did not meet your very high standards . . .'

'Arabic?'

'Yes, sir: it might be necessary to intervene in Africa – in Algiers or one of the other ports for example, or conceivably in Azgar itself. Others observed that your command of languages had already allowed you to deal admirably with Turks, Albanians and Montenegrins before: but Sir Joseph, though agreeing most emphatically, was of opinion that a lieutenant capable of writing both these languages might take a great deal of the strain off your shoulders. He said that Mr Dee –' a bow to the old gentleman who nodded '– and he were acquainted with just such a person, whose discretion could be guaranteed, whose parts and conversation were usually thought acceptable, and whose presence might induce you to agree – a physical gentleman.'

'There is indeed a great deal to be said for a literary as well as a merely colloquial knowledge of both those languages: and of Hebrew,' said Stephen. 'Would it be possible to see him, at all?'

'He is in Gibraltar at this moment, Doctor,' said Kent. Then, 'I believe I gathered from Sir Joseph that you might possibly be acquainted with him already.'

'May I ask, sir,' said Mr Dee, reviving, 'whether you have any strong feeling against Jews?'

'I have not, sir,' replied Stephen.

'I am glad of that,' said Mr Dee, 'for the gentleman, the physical gentleman in question, is a Jew, a Spanish Jew. That is to say he was brought up as an orthodox Sephardi, which gave him not only the curious Spanish the Sephardim speak in Africa and the Turkish dominions, but Hebrew too and Arabic, together with an equally fluent Turkish. But with age and the influence of the Enlightenment – he studied in Paris before the Revolution – his principles grew more . . . liberal, as one might say. Very much more so, indeed: he quarrelled with the synagogue, and this had a disastrous effect on his practice, which, from the paying point of view, was entirely among its members. He was reduced to sad straits; but in earlier days, and out of mere kindness, he often used his linguistic skill to help one of our friends; and some time ago it was suggested that this assistance should be put on a more formal basis. Since then he has carried out several missions for us, usually as a merchant in precious stones, of which he has a considerable knowledge; and with his wide acquaintance, relations, medical skill and so on he has given very great satisfaction. We have of course repeatedly tested his – his *discretion* – in the usual way.'

'Tell me, sir, is the gentleman married?'

'I believe not,' said Kent. 'But if it is tomorrow's unhappy affair that prompts your question, I can assure you he is perfectly orthodox in those respects. For a while he resided in Algiers on our behalf, and the reporting agent mentioned two mistresses, one white, one black. But apart from these ladies he had many connexions in Algiers, his musical abilities making him particularly welcome among the Europeans of the better sort: and these connexions may prove of the utmost value if Algiers is the chosen port, which seems . . .'

'Very true,' said Mr Dee. 'But I must insist that the Adriatic harbours and dockyards come first: a great show of force, the elimination of potential enemies and the presence of the Royal Navy will necessarily have a great effect upon the fraternities – so great an effect that their conspiracy may well prove abortive. All our efforts should be directed towards that end. I am too old and infirm to take an active part: but my cousins have a banking-house in Ancona, just across the water, and from there I can correspond with my Turkish friends in the Ottoman provinces and co-ordinate our operations. I can also communicate with London by the bankers' couriers.'

During the time of this conference, Jack had been very much occupied with the rest of his squadron: on the way down from Madeira he had had all the captains to dinner, he had been aboard them repeatedly, and he had a fair notion of their abilities; but it was still not clear how he should divide the ships for their separate duties. As far as the Adriatic was concerned, he would certainly shift his pennant into the *Surprise*, with her wonderful sailing qualities, her old, trained, thoroughly reliable ship's company, capable of such a deadly rate of fire: but for his consort he could not decide between *Pomone* and *Dover*. The difference in broadside weight of metal was very great: no less than a hundred and forty-four pounds. But the thirty-gun *Pomone* was the unhappy ship whose captain was laid up in Funchal with a badly broken leg, unlikely to recover, and whose second lieutenant was confined to his cabin to await trial for an offence under the twenty-ninth Article of War, which dealt with 'unnatural and detestable sin' – a ship to which Lord Keith had appointed a young man, very recently made post, the only qualified officer at hand. Whatever the outcome of tomorrow's ugly trial, the *Pomone*'s people would be very upset – new officers, new ways . . . mockery.

'Larboard, sir?' asked Bonden in an undertone.

Jack nodded. The gig hooked on and he ran up the frigate's side, still lost in thought. He had seen the flagship's barge carrying the civilians away long before and he expected to find Stephen in the cabin. 'Where is the Doctor?' he cried.

'Which he is in the other doctor's cabin,' said Killick, appearing as if by magic, 'discoursing of physical matters and drinking rare old East India sherry. Dr Glover called for another bottle a quarter of an hour ago.'

In fact at this moment they were discoursing of impotence. Their conversation had begun when, having dismissed the Sick and Hurt Board as a parcel of incompetent Ascitans, fit only to dance round an inflated wineskin, Dr Glover asked Stephen whether he had heard of the death of Governor Wood of Sierra Leone.

'I have, alas,' said Stephen. 'A most hospitable man: he and his wife entertained us nobly when we were there in *Bellona*. I am about to write . . . the most difficult kind of letter in the world, however highly you esteem the person to whom it is addressed, and however much you sympathize. I grieve for her extremely.'

Dr Glover did not reply for some time: then, having finished his glass, he looked sideways at his old friend and said, 'I was in Freetown the best part of a year, and they were both my patients. I can tell you as one medico to another that in this case formal expressions of regret would be perfectly adequate: more indeed might be offensive. It was not anything much of a marriage, you know. Indeed legally I believe it was no marriage at all. The Governor was impotent. I took the ordinary measures, and some out of the ordinary: but nothing answered. How the connexion came about in the first place or what they made of it I do not know: but they slept in separate rooms and I had the strong impression that it was but a sad cohabitation – guilt and resentment just under the surface. He of course was a busy man, and very fortunately she had her anatomical studies – a most uncommonly gifted lady. No. Condolence by all means; but tempered, tempered . . . Besides, one very usual and genuine source of grief is wholly lacking: she is well-off in her own right. I know the family in Lancashire.'

'So much the better. Now reverting to this question of impotence: was it physical?'

'Not evidently so.'

'Was the patient an opium-eater?'

'Certainly not. I once had occasion to administer a very moderate dose, and he was astonished by the effects. No, no: it was all in the head – and what innumerable strange surprising fancies the head of a physically normal, active, intelligent man can hold, quite apart from anxiety, that most . . . what is it?'

'Commodore's compliments, sir,' said a midshipman, 'and when Dr Maturin is at liberty, should be happy to see him. But I am to add that there is no hurry at all.'

'Another glass before you go . . . or rather let me call for another bottle, since there is no hurry.'

'You are too kind,' said Stephen, shaking his head; and to the boy, 'Pray tell the Commodore that I shall wait upon him directly.'

'Why, Stephen, there you are,' cried Jack. 'I do beg pardon for interrupting you. But since I am sure you have heard of poor Governor Wood's death, I thought you would like to know that there is a Guineaman sailing this evening, in case you chose to send . . . Then again, the Admiral has a courier setting off for England within the hour: I have asked for William Reade to bring *Ringle*, and since she will need a day or two's readying, he could ride over to Woolhampton, taking messages and bringing things back.'

'I had indeed heard of Captain Wood's death, God rest his soul, and I have been composing a letter to his widow in my mind – perhaps I may be able to dash something off by this evening, though I am a slow, dry and barren creature with a pen. As for William Reade, if he will buy a fine bold hoop in Portsmouth and give it to Brigid with my love, together with this crown piece, I should be infinitely obliged to him. And if he would bring back my narwhal horn, or rather tusk – the tusk you so very kindly gave me a great while since – I should be most uncommon grateful. I was contemplating on it in the night, for I am told that in Mahon we are likely to meet that eminent engineer, metallurgist and natural philosopher James Wright, and I hope that he will be able to tell me – do you see the horn in your eye, at all clearly?'

'Fairly well.'

'To tell me whether those whorls, or perhaps I should say those torsades or undulations, and those spirals running from the base almost to the very tip add strength or possibly elasticity to the whole improbable structure.'

'Beg pardon, sir,' said Killick, 'but your number one scraper ain't fit to be seen aboard the flag.' He held up a gold-laced hat, very fine, but strangely dented. 'Which you trod on it last Thursday and put it back in its case without a word: but there is still just time to have it reblocked at Broad's.'

'Make it so, Killick,' said Jack. 'Ask Mr Willis for a boat.' And to Stephen, 'I shall add your requests in my letter to Reade: hoop and a crown for Brigid, with your love, and the narwhal horn.'

'Love to dear Sophie too, of course, and the kindest of wishes to Clarissa Oakes. The horn is in a bow-case, hanging in one of the cupboards in the gunroom. Brother, I am afraid you are low in your spirits.'

'I do so hate a court-martial, above all one of this kind. Will you attend?'

'I will not. In any case I have an appointment ashore.' They gazed out of the great broad sweep of stern-lights at the tawny Rock itself, soaring away as unlikely and as impressive as ever. 'Jack,' he went on, with a significant expression familiar to them both, 'it is not impossible that I may bring an assistant surgeon back with me. If I am not mistaken entirely, it would not be fit that the gentleman should mess with the midshipmen and mates, so if he cannot be admitted to the gunroom, perhaps I might be indulged in his company as a guest?'

'Of course you may,' said Jack. 'But if he is a gentleman of a certain age and standing, as I suppose, I am sure the gunroom would stretch a point, particularly as you are almost never there: he could take your place.'

'As far as standing goes, he is as much of a physician as myself – a doctor of medicine. We studied in Paris together for a while: he was some years junior to me, but already highly considered as an anatomist. That would certainly be the best arrangement; for although he is a tolerable musician, and you might very well consider inviting him on occasion . . . that would certainly be the best arrangement.'

Feeling Stephen's embarrassment, Jack cried, 'Oh, I have not told you: tomorrow is going to be a day of hellish turmoil. I am shifting my pennant into *Surprise* and there are going to be some important changes: apart from anything else the squadron is promised two new drafts to bring us up to something like establishment.'

The hellish din began before eight bells in the middle watch, when, in the complete darkness, the people who were to remove into other ships began packing their chests and manhandling them along the narrow, crowded passages and up the steep, steep ladders to strategic corners from which they could be hurried on deck as soon as the boats came alongside. These corners were often occupied, which led to disagreement, very noisy disagreement sometimes, and then to renewed thumping as the defeated chest was humped away. At eight bells, or four in the morning, that part of the starboard watch which had managed to stay asleep was roused with the usual shattering din and mustered on deck: then a little later the idlers were called and for the next two hours they and the starboard watch cleaned the decks with water, sand, holystones great and small, and swabs. Barely were the spotless decks quite dry before hammocks were piped up, and in the midst of the frantic hurry boats from *Dover*, *Rainbow*, *Ganymede* and *Briseis* approached: unhappily, the officer of the watch, Mr Clegg, was some way below the deck, stilling a quarrel about chests dangerously near the sacred cabin, and the master's mate, misunderstanding his cry, allowed the boats to come alongside. The seamen swarmed aboard with their belongings, and it called for all the authority of a tall, furious, nightshirted Captain Aubrey to restore anything like order.

'I am very sorry for the pandemonium, Stephen,' he said

as at last they sat down to their breakfast, brought by a now silent, timid Killick. 'All this mad rushing up and down, bellowing like Gadarene swine . . .'

The breakfast itself was adequate, with quantities of fresh eggs, sausages, bacon, a noble pork pie, rolls and toast, cream for their coffee; but there was little to be said for it as a fleshly indulgence, since every other bite was interrupted by a message from one ship or another, often delivered by midshipmen, washed, brushed and extremely nervous, presenting their captain's compliments and might he be favoured with a few, just a few, really able seamen, with heavy carronades instead of nine-pounder guns, or any of the countless variety of stores that the Commodore's good word with the dockyard officials might provide. Even more irritating was Killick's unceasing concern with the splendid uniform in which Jack was to appear at the court-martial – his intolerable twitching of the napkin that guarded breeches and lower waistcoat, his muttered warnings about egg-yolk, butter, anchovy paste, marmalade.

At last the mate of the watch came, with the first lieutenant's duty and compliments, to announce that *Royal Sovereign* had thrown out her signal for the court-martial. A last cup of coffee and they both went on deck: over the smooth water of the bay captains' barges could already be seen converging on the flagship. Jack's was waiting for him and after a momentary hesitation he nodded to Stephen, stepping forward to the gangway stanchions as the bosun and his mates piped their captain over the side and all his officers saluted.

'Sir. If you please, sir,' said a boy's voice for the second time, now with a certain impatience, and turning from the rail Stephen saw a familiar face, young Witherby, formerly of the *Bellona*. The shifting of officers and ratings since Jack's appointment to the *Pomone* had never been clear to Stephen. He knew that *Surprise*'s coxswain and the bargemen had followed their captain, but what this boy was doing here he could not tell. Indeed, there were many, many things that remained obscure unless he made a determined effort of collecting his mind and concentrating upon the present. 'Mr Witherby,' he said, 'what may I do for you?'

'Why, sir,' said the boy, 'I understood you were for the shore, and I have the jolly-boat under the stern, if you please to walk this way.'

Witherby landed him at the Ragged Staff steps, and once he was through the Southport Gate he found the familiar surroundings a comfort: the move into the unknown *Pomone*, though wholly unimportant in itself, had for once been strangely disturbing. He made his way steadily along to Thompson's comfortable, unpretentious hotel, glancing right and left at shops and buildings he had known these many years. Many red-coats, many sea-officers, but nothing to touch the hive-like multitudes of Gibraltar in full wartime.

He turned in at Thompson's door. 'Dr Jacob, if you please,' he said. 'He is expecting me.'

'Yes, sir. Should you like him to come down?'

'Oh no. Tell me the number of his room and I will go up.'

'Very good, sir. Pablito, show the gentleman to the third floor back.'

Pablito tapped; the door opened, and a well-known voice said, 'Dr Maturin, I presume?'

The door closed. Pablito's feet echoed on the stairs. Dr Jacob seized Stephen, kissed him on both cheeks and led him into a cool, shaded room where a jug of horchata stood on a low table and smoke from the hookah hung from the ceiling down to eye level.

'I am so exceedingly happy that it *is* you,' said Jacob, guiding him to a sofa. 'I was so nearly sure of it from Sir Joseph's calculated indiscretions that I brought you an example of the palmar aponeurosis and the contractions which so interested you and Dupuytren.' He slipped into his bedroom and came out carrying a jar: but realizing that

32

his gift could not be fully appreciated in the half-light he thrust open the balcony doors and led Stephen out into the brilliant sun.

'You are altogether too good, dear Amos,' said Stephen, gazing at the severed hand, clear in its spirits of wine, the middle fingers so hard-clenched against the palm that their nails had grown into the flesh. 'You are too good entirely. I have never seen so perfect an example. I long to make a very exact dissection.'

But Jacob, taking no notice, turned him gently to the full sun and looked hard into his face. 'Stephen, you have not made some cruel self-diagnosis, I trust?'

'I have not,' said Stephen, and in as few words as possible he explained the situation – his personal situation. Amos did not oppress him with any sympathy other than a deeply affectionate pressure on the shoulder, but suggested that they should walk out high on the Rock, where they could speak about their present undertaking in complete safety. '. . . that is to say, if you still feel concerned.'

'I am wholly concerned, wholly committed,' said Stephen. 'If it were not so wicked, I could almost be grateful for this very evil man and his odious system.'

They walked out of the town, up and up to the ridge itself, where the cliffs fall down to Catalan Bay and where Stephen saw, with a muted satisfaction, that the peregrine eyrie was occupied again, the falcon standing on the outer edge, bating and calling. All the way along they walked, with the migrant birds passing overhead, sometimes very low, and on either side, Stephen mechanically noting the rarities (six pallid harriers, more than he had ever seen together), right out to the far end overlooking Europa Point, and back again; and all the time, with a much more conscious, concentrated mind, Stephen listened to all that Jacob, with his remarkable sources of information, had gathered about the Adriatic ports, the Muslim fraternities and the progress of their urgent request for money to pay their mercenaries. Jacob

33

also spoke, and with equal authority, of the probable donor and of the pressure that might be brought to bear on the Dey of Algiers. 'But where Africa is concerned,' he said, 'it seems to me that little or nothing should be attempted until we have had at least some success in the Adriatic.'

Stephen agreed, his eyes following a troop of black storks as they passed over the flagship; and quite suddenly he realized that the *Royal Sovereign* was no longer flying the court-martial signal. Indeed, the captains' barges were already dispersing.

On the way down they walked almost in silence. They had said all that could usefully be said at this point, though more intelligence was to be expected at Mahon – and Stephen very often glanced at the flagship's main yardarm. In these waters the Commander-in-Chief was all-powerful: he could confirm a court's sentence of death without the least reference to the King or the Admiralty. In naval courts-martial sentence was pronounced at once: it was final, with no appeal: and Lord Keith was not one for delay.

By the time they reached the town there was no man hanging from the yardarm; but on the battlements this side of the Southport Gate there were several officers, including Jack Aubrey and some of the *Pomone*'s people, looking earnestly southward along the strand. Stephen joined them, saying, 'Sir, may I introduce Dr Jacob, the assistant surgeon of whom I told you?'

'Very happy, sir,' said Jack, shaking Jacob's hand. He would obviously have said more, but at this moment a strong murmur all along from the bastion increased immensely as two boats left the flagship, pulling for the shore and towing a bare grating, the soaked and wretched prisoners upon it. A few minutes later the grating was cast off: a small surf brought it in and the men scrambled in the shallows. There was some sparse cat-calling from the crowd, but not much; and half a dozen people helped them to dry land, dragging their belongings.

'Dr Jacob, sir,' said Jack, 'I hope that you will be able to come aboard without delay. I am eager to be out of sight of this place.' And privately to Stephen he said, 'I repeated your "No penetration, no sodomy", which floored one and all; though I must say that most of them were glad to be floored. I persuaded the others to find no more than gross indecency.'

'And is being towed ashore on a grating the set penalty for gross indecency?'

'No. We call it the use and custom of the sea: that is the way it has always been.'

Chapter Two

For several years now Stephen Maturin had been perfectly
aware that a life at sea, above all in a man-of-war, was not
the waterborne picnic sometimes imagined by those living
far inland; but he had never supposed that anything could
be quite so arduous as this existence between the two, neither
floating free nor firmly ashore, with what conveniences the
land might provide.

The squadron, necessarily gathered together in a hurry
and necessarily short-handed, had to be thoroughly reorgan-
ized, above all the unhappy *Pomone*: a ship always suffered
from a trial for sodomy and although her people had not
been in her for anything like an ordinary commission it was
long enough for them to feel their position acutely – to resent
the calls they heard ashore or the smiles and meaning silence
when a group of them walked into a bar. After all, one of
their officers had been dismissed from the service in the
most ignominious fashion possible and towed ashore on a
grating in the view of countless spectators; and some of
the discredit clung to his former shipmates. This corporate
shame had a thoroughly bad effect on discipline, which had
never been the *Pomone*'s strongest point; and a new captain,
with a second lieutenant who knew nobody aboard, was
unlikely to remedy this state of affairs in the near future.
She did have a good bosun, however, and the gunner, though
discouraged, was willing and knowledgeable. He and Captain Pomfret were suitably shocked when the Commodore
invited them to accompany *Surprise* well out into the Strait,
off Algeciras, so that both ships might exercise the great

guns, firing at towed targets. The Pomones brought their ship out creditably and they were reasonably brisk at the dumb-show of running the eighteen-pounders in and out, but some of the gun-crews were hesitant about firing them. Only three or four in the starboard battery had much notion of anything but point-blank aim or of judging the roll. The first and second captains were competent upon the whole, but the midshipmen in charge of the divisions left much to be desired and some of the ordinary hands belonging to the gun might never have seen an eighteen-pounder fired in earnest before. The fury of the recoil shocked them extremely and after the first wavering, ragged broadside several had to be led or carried below, hurt by iron-taut tackles and breechings or even by the angles of the carriage itself. The Marines who took their places did at least stand clear, but on the whole it was a most lamentable exhibition, and the Surprises had no compunction in making it even more obviously ludicrous by destroying, utterly destroying, the hitherto unscathed target with three broadsides in five minutes and ten seconds.

'Captain Pomfret,' said Jack before he left the ship, 'I can foresee a very great deal of great-gun exercise, morning and afternoon, as well as at quarters: the team *must* know their pieces through and through, so that they never have to think, as I am sure you are very well aware.'

'Yes, sir,' said Pomfret, trying to master his distress. 'The only thing I can advance is that we are cruelly short-handed, and the people have not been together long.'

'You have enough right seamen to man your pinnace and launch?'

'Yes, sir.'

'Then let your first lieutenant and the second when he joins – I know the Admiral means to let you have an excellent young man – take them out in the middle watch and lie off Cape Spartel till dawn. If they do not press a score of hands out of the passing merchantmen who have not yet heard the news I shall be amazed. But above all keep your people hard at it, the young gentlemen especially – idle young dogs, sauntering about with their hands in their pockets – hard at it: yet do not blackguard them. Praise if ever you can; you will find it answer wonderfully. Next week you may fire live – nothing pleases them more, once they are used to the din.'

Returning to harbour, Jack visited the other ships and vessels of his squadron, requiring each to beat to quarters and at least to cast loose their guns. The exactness of the coiled muzzle-lashing, made fast to the eye-bolt above the port-lid, the seizing of the mid-breeching to the pommelion, the neat arrangement of the sponge, handspike, powder-horn, priming-wire, bed, quoin, train-tackle, shot and all the rest told a knowing eye a great deal about the gun-crew and even more about the midshipman of the sub-division. The *Dover*, still actively reconverting herself, was in rather a sad way, but not very discreditably so; the others would do at a push, and the little *Briseis*, one of that numerous class called coffin-brigs from their tendency to turn over and sink, was positively brilliant. He told her captain so, and the hands within earshot visibly swelled with satisfaction.

Back to *Surprise* and her great cabin, familiar, elegant, but in spite of its conventional name not really spacious enough for all the administrative work he had to do. There were no more than six ships or vessels in the squadron, but their books and papers already overflowed the Commodore's desk: not much more than a thousand men were concerned, but all those of real importance in the running of the squadron had to be entered on separate slips together with what comments he had so far been able to make on their abilities; and to house these slips he had called upon his joiner to make temporary tray-like wings to his desk, so that eventually he should have all the elements at his disposal laid out, to be rearranged according to the tasks the squadron might be called to undertake. In these quite exceptional circumstances, with no settled ships' companies apart from those in *Surprise* and to some extent *Briseis*, he would have an equally exceptional free hand.

But Jack Aubrey was a neat creature by temperament and rigorous training, and he had set no more than one foot in the cabin before he saw that order was confounded, that some criminal hand had merged at least three complements into one unmeaning heap, and that this same hand had spread out several manuscript sheets of music, the score of a pavan in C minor.

'Oh I do beg your pardon, Jack,' cried Stephen, walking quickly in from the quarter-gallery. 'I had a sudden thought to be set down – but I trust I have not disturbed anything at all?'

'Not in the least,' said Jack. 'And Stephen, I believe I have solved your problem. I believe I have found you a loblolly-boy you will thoroughly approve of.'

Stephen, concerned though he was with his music – only two bars yet to write, but the magical sound already fading from his inner ear – and filled though he was with a conviction that Jack's mild 'not in the least' concealed an intense irritation, made no reply other than a questioning look. He owed his survival as an intelligence-agent to an acute ear for falsity, and Jack's last words were certainly quite untrue.

'Yes,' Jack went on, 'together with a draft of hands turned over to the squadron out of *Leviathan*, refitting, Maggie Cheal and Poll Skeeping have come aboard; and Poll was trained at Haslar. She is up to anything in the way of blood and horrors.'

'You are speaking of *women*, brother? You who have always abominated so much as the smell of a skirt aboard ship? The invariable cause of trouble, quarrelling, ill-luck. Wholly out of place in any ship, above all in a man-of-war. I have never seen a woman aboard a man-of-war.'

'Have you not, my poor Stephen? Did you never see them helping with the guns and passing shot in *Bellona*?'

39

'Never in life. Am I not always shut up in the cockpit during an action?'

'Very true. But if Jill Travers, for example, the sailmaker's wife who helped serve number eight, had been wounded, you would have seen her.'

'But seriously, Jack, are you obliged to take these women aboard? You who have always inveighed against the creatures.'

'These are not creatures, in the sense of whore-ladies or Portsmouth trollops: oh no. They are usually middle-aged or more, often the wife or widow of a petty or even of a warrant-officer. One or two may have run away like the girl in the ballad, wearing trousers, to be with her Jack when he sailed; but most have used the sea these ten or twenty years, and they look like seamen, only for the skirt and maybe shawl.'

'And yet I have never seen one, apart from the odd gunner's wife who looks after the very little fellows: and apart, of course, from that poor unhappy Mrs Horner on Juan Fernandez.'

'To be sure, they do keep out of the way. They don't belong to any watch, of course, and they don't appear at quarters, no, nor anywhere else, except when we rig church.' At any other time he would have added that for all his botanizing and stuffing curious birds, Stephen was a singularly unobservant cove: he had not even noticed the brilliant flint-locks that now, by grace of Lord Keith, adorned *Surprise*'s guns, doing away with those potential misfires when the linstock wavered over the touch-hole or was doused by flying spray – misfires that might make those few seconds' difference between defeat and victory. Yet they blazed with all the splendour of guinea-gold, the pride of the crews, who surreptitiously breathed upon them, wiping off the mist with a silk handkerchief.

'A loblolly-*girl*, for all love? I wonder at it, Jack.'

'Come, come, Stephen: you say a loblolly-boy for an

ancient of sixty or even more: it is only a figure of speech, a naval figure of speech. And speaking of figures, Poll's is very like a round-shot; she is a kind, cheerful, conscientious soul, but she is not likely to stir the amorous propensities of the sick-berth. Besides, she is perfectly used to seamen, and would instantly put them down. Will you at least have a word with her? I said I should mention her name. We were shipmates once, and I can answer for her being kind – no blackguarding, no bawling out orders, not topping it the ship's corporal; kind, honest, sober, and very tender with the wounded.'

'Of course I will see her, brother: a kind, honest and sober nurse is a rare and valuable creature, God knows.'

Jack rang the bell and to the answering Killick he said, 'Tell Poll Skeeping the Doctor will see her directly.'

Poll Skeeping had been at sea, off and on, for twenty years, sometimes under harsh and tyrannical officers; but for her 'directly' still allowed latitude enough for putting on a clean apron, changing her cap and finding her character: thus equipped she hurried to the cabin door, knocked and walked in, a little out of breath and obviously nervous. She bobbed to the officers, holding her character to her bosom.

'Sit down, Poll,' said Captain Aubrey, waving to a chair. 'This is Dr Maturin, who would like to speak to you.'

She thanked him and sat, bolt upright, the envelope of her character held like a shield.

'Mrs Skeeping,' said Stephen, 'I am without a sick-berth attendant, a loblolly-boy, and the Captain tells me that you might like the post.'

'That was very kind in his honour,' she said, bowing to Jack. 'Which I should be happy to be your sick-berth attendant, sir.'

'May I ask about your experience and professional qualifications? The Captain has already told me that you are kind, conscientious, and tender to the wounded; and indeed one can hardly ask more. But what of amputation, lithotomy, the use of the trephine?'

'Bless you, sir, my father, God rest his soul' (crossing herself) 'was a butcher and horse-knacker in the wholesale line, down Deptford way, and my brothers and me used to play at surgeons in the jointing house: then when I was at Haslar they put me almost straight away into the theatre. So, do you see, sir, I am hardly what could be called squeamish. But may I show you my character, sir? The surgeon of my last ship, a very learned gentleman, tells what I can do better than ever I could manage.' She passed the somewhat aged cover, and begging Jack's pardon Stephen broke the seal. The elegant Latin testimonial to Mrs Skeeping's worth, capabilities, and exceptional sobriety was written in a remarkably familiar hand but one to which he could not give a name until he turned the page and saw the signature of Kevin Teevan, an Ulster Catholic from Cavan, a friend of his student days and yet another Irishman who saw the Napoleonic tyranny as a far greater and more immediate evil than the English government of Ireland.

'Well,' he said, patting the letter affectionately, 'anyone so highly spoken of by Mr Teevan will certainly answer for me; and since I do not yet have an assistant surgeon – he will be coming aboard this afternoon – I will show you the sick-berth myself, if the Captain will excuse us.'

'There,' he went on at last, having displayed the neat arrangements of the *Surprise*, 'that deals with the ventilation system: no ship of the line can show a better. Now pray tell me how Mr Teevan was when last you saw him.'

'He was brimming full of joy, sir. A cousin with a practice in some grand part of London and with too many patients, offered him a partnership, and he left Mahon that very evening in *Northumberland*, going home to pay off and lay up. For that was when we thought it was all over, the pity and woe . . . that Boney.'

'The pity and woe indeed,' said Stephen. 'But with the

blessing we shall soon settle *his* account.' And running his eye over the neat shelves of the forward medicine-chest, he said, 'We are short of blue ointment. Do you understand the making of blue ointment, Mrs Skeeping?'

'Oh dear me yes, sir: many is the great jar I have ground in my time.'

'Then pray reach me down the little keg of hog's lard, the jar of mutton suet, and the quicksilver. There are two mortars with their pestles just below the colcothar of vitriol.'

When they had ground away companionably at their ointment for perhaps half a glass Stephen said, 'Mrs Skeeping, in my sea-time I have seen few, very few women at all, although I am told they are not in fact so very rare. Will you tell me how they come to be aboard and why they stay in a place so often damp and always so bare of comfort?'

'Why, sir, in the first place a good many warrant-officers – like the gunner, of course – take their wives to sea, and some captains allow the good petty-officers to do the same. Then there are wives that take a relation along – my particular friend Maggie Cheal is the bosun's wife's sister. And some just take passage, with the captain's or first lieutenant's leave. And there are a few in very hard times by land that dress as men and are not found out until very late, when no notice is taken: they speak gruff, they are good seamen, and there is not much odds after forty. And as for staying aboard, it is not a comfortable life to be sure, except in a first or second rate that does not wear a flag; but there is company, and you are sure of food; and then men, upon the whole, are kinder than women – you get used to it all, and the order and regularity is a comfort in itself. For my part it was as simple as kiss your hand. At Haslar I was put to look after an officer, a post-captain that had lost a foot – there had been a secondary resection and the dressing was very delicate. His wife, Mrs Wilson, and the children came to see him every day, and when the wound was healed and he posted to a seventy-four in Jamaica she asked me to go with them, looking after the little ones. It was a long, slow voyage with no foul weather and everybody enjoyed it, most of all the children. But they had not been there a month before they were all dead of the Yellow Jack. Luckily for me, the officer who took over Captain Wilson's ship brought a great many youngsters aboard, more than the gunner's wife could deal with; so we having made friends on the way over, she asked me to give her a hand – and so it went, relations in ships – I had a sister married to the sailmaker's mate in *Ajax* – friends in ships, with a spell or two in naval hospitals – and here I am, loblolly-boy in *Surprise*, I hope, sir, if I give satisfaction.'

'Certainly you are, particularly as I learn from Mr Teevan that you do not play the physician, puzzle the patients with long words or criticize the doctor's orders.'

Mrs Skeeping thanked him very kindly; but having taken her leave she paused at the door, and blushing she said, 'Sir, might I beg you to call me just Poll, as the Captain does, and Killick and all the others I have been shipmates with? Otherwise they would think I was topping it the knob; and that they will not abide, no, not if it is ever so.'

'By all means, Poll, my dear,' said Stephen.

He read a couple of pages on leeches and their surprising variety in the *Transactions*, and then, judging his time, summoned their common steward and said, 'Preserved Killick, I am going to fetch Dr Jacob, my assistant surgeon, who as you know is to mess in the gunroom.'

'Which the Captain told me,' said Killick with a satisfied smile. 'So did Mr Harding.'

'And I should like you to find him a stout boy to be his servant and to bring his sea-chest down from Thompson's in their little two-wheeled cart. You will give the gunroom cook good warning, I am sure.'

The introduction went as well and easily as Stephen could have wished. Harding, Somers and Whewell were hospitable, civilized men, and the quiet, unpretentious Dr Jacob, willing to please and to be pleased, succeeded in both: he was somewhat older than the lieutenants, which ensured a certain respect; his friendship with their much-esteemed Doctor gave rise to more; and when Woodbine, the master, hurried in he found the gunroom in a fine buzz of conversation. He excused his lateness to the president: 'That sudden gust took Elpenor the Greek over the side, and we have been fishing him out – a very strong and sudden gust indeed: north-east. How do you do, sir?' – this to Jacob – 'You are very welcome, I am sure. A glass of wine with you, sir.'

With shore supplies at hand it was a pleasant meal, with a steady flow of talk, much of it about the sea and its wonders – the enormous rays of the West Indies, albatrosses nesting on Desolation Island (one of the many Desolation Islands) and their tameness, St Elmo's Fire, the Northern Lights. Woodbine belonged to an older generation than the lieutenants: he had travelled even more widely, and encouraged by the close attention of the medical man he spoke at considerable length about some pools or natural resurgences of pitch in Mexico. 'Not to be compared to the Pitch-Lake in Trinidad for size, but much more interesting: there is one where the tar comes bubbling up in the middle, so liquid you can take it with a ladle; and every now and then a white bone comes surging up in the great bubble. Such bones! People may prate about their Russian mammoths, but these creatures – or some of them – would make mammoths look like pug-dogs. The gentleman that took me there, a natural philosopher, collects the most curious, and he showed me great curved tusks, oh, three fathoms long and . . .' Another of those curious furious blasts came down from the face of the Rock, ruffling the whole bay and heeling the *Surprise* so that all hands automatically reached for their glasses and the mess-servants grasped the backs of the chairs. The master, an unusually truthful, scrupulous man, an elder of the congregation of Sethians in Shelmerston, checked himself and said, 'Well, perhaps ten foot, to be on the safe side. And I tell you what, gentlemen, I have known this gust or warning foretell a seven-day blow out of the north-east four or even five times when my ship has been lying here.'

'In that case, God help the poor fellows in *Pomone*'s boats,' said Somers: he spoke facetiously, but the master shook his head, asking, 'Did you ever know a bad omen to be wrong, Mr Somers?'

There did indeed follow a series of strong, steady winds, scarcely varying a point in direction from north-east day after day, nor in force from full to close-reefed topsails: and during all this time Jack and David Adams, his clerk on and off these many years but now styled his secretary (and paid as such) – for although on this occasion it had been agreed that Jack, with a small squadron soon to be split up for various duties while he himself was to have such a particular mission, should not have a captain under him, he was certainly allowed a secretary – during all this time they rearranged the forces at hand and the recent drafts, the Commodore exercising them at gunnery whenever it was at all possible and dining regularly with his captains. Two of them he liked very well: young Pomfret in acting command of *Pomone* and Harris of *Briseis*, both excellent seamen and both of his own mind entirely about the capital importance of rapid, accurate fire. Brawley and Cartwright of the corvettes *Rainbow* and *Ganymede*, though somewhat lacking in authority, were agreeable young men; but they were not fortunate in their officers and neither ship was in first-rate order, which was a pity, since both were Bermuda-built, dry, swift and weatherly. Ward of the *Dover* on the other hand was the kind of man Jack could not possibly like: heavy, graceless, dark-faced; rude, domineering and inefficient. He was said to be rich and he was certainly mean: a very rare combination in a sailor, though Jack had met it before – a man generally disliked is hardly apt to lavish good food and wine on those who despise him; and Ward's dinners were execrable.

The wind, which at times was strong enough to send small pebbles flying through the air on the upper reaches of the Rock, did not interrupt Stephen's habit of visiting the hospital every morning: he generally went there with Jacob, and on two separate occasions he had the pleasure of carrying out his particular operation of suprapubic cystotomy in the presence of the Physician of the Fleet and of Poll, who comforted the patient and passed the sutures. She told Jacob in private 'that it was the neatest, quickest job she had ever seen – should never have believed it could have been done so quick, and with scarcely a groan. I shall light a candle for each of them, against the infection.'

Yet although the wind did not interfere with his work, which included a very minute dissection, with Jacob's help, of the anomalous hand, it did away with his outdoor pleasure almost entirely. The migrant birds, always averse to crossing wide expanses of sea and wholly incapable of making headway against gales of this nature, were pinned down in Morocco; and in the sheltered hollows behind Cape Spartel twenty booted eagles might be seen in a single bush. He turned therefore to an occupation that fell into neither category and, it having been turning in his mind for some time, particularly at night, he quickly finished the second part of his suite, a forlan, copied it fair that afternoon and showed it to Jack in the evening.

Sitting there with the score tilted towards the lamp and what little light there was, with the small rain sweeping in swathes across the sea, his mouth now formed for whistling (but silent), now for a very deep humming where the 'cello came in, Jack came to the end of the saraband, with its curiously reiterated melody. He gathered the sheets and reached for the forlan: 'It is *terribly* sad,' he observed, almost to himself – words he wished unsaid with all his heart.

'Do you know any happy music?' asked Stephen. 'I do not.'

Embarrassment hung there in the great cabin for no more than a moment before it was dissipated first by a measured series of small explosions and then by Salmon, master's mate, bursting in as the ship, heeling before a fresh blast, shot him through the door. 'Beg pardon, sir,' he cried, 'beg pardon. *Ringle*'s come in. That was her, sir, saluting the flag.'

Divided between fury that the schooner could have come in unseen and unhailed and delight at her presence, Jack gave Salmon a cold glance. He saw that the young man was dripping to a most uncommon degree and called for his boat-cloak. As soon as he was on deck he saw why no lookout had reported a sail: even with this short fetch, the unceasing wind had built up a wall of broken water against the towering mole, a wall made even more impenetrable at deck-height by the fog-like rain and the disappearance of the sun's faint, faint ghost behind the Rock. Furthermore, to shoot between the moles *Ringle* had shown no more than a scrap of storm-jib right in, which her people were now stowing in a seamanlike fashion.

Her one-armed captain was already half-way up the frigate's side, extraordinarily nimble with his hook. He carried a packet of letters in his bosom. 'Come on board, sir,' he said, saluting as he reached the quarterdeck.

'How in God's name did you get here so quick, William?' cried Jack, shaking his one hand. 'I had not looked for you this week and more. Come below – have a tot of brandy – you must be destroyed.'

'Why, sir, you would not believe our run – this splendid breeze right aft or on our quarter day after day. But sir, before I say anything more than all's well at home – much love from all hands' – here he put down his packet – 'I must tell you we saw *Pomone*'s boats being attacked by smallcraft under the lee of Spartel, where they were lying-to after a cruel long pull. We soon dealt with the Moors and offered the boats a tow. But *Pomone*'s first lieutenant said no, we must carry straight on and tell the flag that there were half a dozen Sallee rovers in Laraish waiting for the East-Indiamen lying-to just down the coast. He said he could certainly look after the local Moors if they came back, with the small arms we had given them, and he bade us shove off instantly – there was not a moment to lose.'

'Very true,' said Jack. 'Mr Harding, strike topgallant-masts down on deck; take a warp out on to the mole; throw out the signal *Squadron prepare to unmoor*. I am going across to the flag in Mr Reade's boat.'

It was not a long pull to the *Royal Sovereign*, but in spite of their hooded boat-cloaks both Jack and William Reade came up the side as wet as drowned rats. Waterlogged officers were by no means rare in the Royal Navy, however, and their appearance excited no comment: but when Jack, in a very few words, had outlined the position, the Captain of the Fleet whistled and said, 'By God, I think you must see the Admiral.'

Jack repeated his statement to Lord Keith, who looked grave and asked, 'What measures do you propose?'

'My Lord, I propose leading the squadron out directly, making for Laraish. If the corsairs are still there I shall just make a show of force and stand on until I find the Indiamen, presumably still lying under the Sugar Loaf. If I find them engaged, clearly I disengage them: if not, I escort them westward and as near north as they can lie, leaving *Dover* to see them home.'

'Make it so, Captain Aubrey.'

'Aye-aye, sir. My best compliments to Lady Keith, if you please.'

On his way back the boat passed *Dover* and *Pomone*, both of which he hailed, directing them to make sail, to shape a course for Tangier, and to attend to his signals. It was not really night when he reached the *Surprise*, but the weather was so thick that he sent his orders by word of mouth to the rest of the squadron, adding that signals would now be made by lights and guns.

It gave him the liveliest pleasure to see how naturally the frigate came to life: battle-lanterns fore and aft, the signal midshipman and his yeoman overhauling the flares, the blue lights and apparatus, the ease with which the warp moved the ship's six hundred tons and all her people towards the mole, and the totally professional, even nonchalant manner in which, edging round its head with barely steerage-way, they flashed out headsails, carried her clean through the gap and into the open sea, where she lay a-try, waiting for the others to join her. This they did, creditably enough on the whole, though their moorings had been ill-placed for this uncommon wind, while the mole itself and its overlapping neighbour, in the course of construction, were singularly awkward. But in the event they all came through, though *Dover*, setting a trifle too much sail at that unhandy turn, grazed the new stonework with enough force to wound her forward starboard mainchains. Her captain's voice, cracked with fury, could be heard a great way downwind; yet even so he had enough right sailors, officers and ratings, aboard to make sail and steer the course shown by the Commodore's signal, while the excellent bosun and his mates made good the worst of the damage, so that the frigate, though disfigured, did not disgrace herself as the squadron formed the line, heading for a point west of Tangier at no more than eight knots to give the *Dover* time to reinforce the main shrouds before their southward turn for Laraish.

They had scarcely cleared the Straits, leaving the glow of Tangier on the larboard quarter, before the rain stopped and the wind lessened, though it was still capable of a powerful gust from the same direction. 'Mr Woodbine,' said Jack to the master, 'I believe we may send up the topgallantmasts and spread a little more canvas.'

This, with the help of a clearing sky over the main ocean, the light of a splendid moon and a more regular sea, was soon done; and the squadron, well in hand, at the proper cable's length apart, ran down the Moroccan coast under courses and full topsails with an easier following sea and the wind on their larboard quarter; they were still in the order of their leaving, *Ringle* lying under *Surprise*'s lee, as became a tender.

This was pure sailing, with a fine regular heave and lift, an urgency of the water along the side, and sea-harping in the taut sheets and windward shrouds, the moon and the stars making their even journey across the clearer sky from bow to quarter, pause and back again.

At eight bells in the first watch the log was heaved and a very small and sleepy boy reported, 'Twelve knots and one fathom, sir, if you please.'

'Thank you, Mr Wells,' said Jack. 'You may turn in now.'

'Thank you very much, sir: good night, sir,' said the child, and staggered off to get four hours' sleep.

Beautiful sailing, and it was with some reluctance that Jack, having re-arranged his line by signal, so that they sailed *Surprise*, *Pomone*, *Dover*, *Ganymede*, *Rainbow*, *Briseis*, left the deck: he had an overwhelming desire to read his letters again, thoroughly digesting every detail.

The cabin had not yet been fully cleared for action and Stephen was sitting there with the light of an Argand lamp focused by a concave mirror on to the dark purple of that terrible hand, now stretched out by clamps on a board; and he was making an extraordinarily exact drawing of a particular tendon, in spite of the frigate's motion.

'What a sea-dog you are become,' said Jack.

'I flatter myself that a whole pack of sea-dogs could not have improved upon the forward starboard aspect of this aponeurosis,' said Stephen. 'I do it by pressing the underneath of the table with my knees and the top of it with my elbows so that we all, paper, object, table and draughtsman,

51

move together with very little discontinuity – one substance, as it were. To be sure, a fairly regular motion of the vessel is required; and for regularity this slow, even swing could hardly be bettered; though the amplitude calls for such tension that I believe I shall now take a spell.'

They both returned to their heaps of letters – small heaps, since William Reade had kept nagging at the writers about his tide, and since they had had so little notice that many things of the first importance flew out of their heads. Clarissa Oakes wrote by far the best, least flustered account of the household and its return towards something like a normal existence, much helped by the unchanging ritual of the countryside – of Jack's estate and his plantations in particular – and by the children's steadily continuing education. Sophie's two hurried, tear-blotted pages did her heart more credit than her head, but it was clear that the company of Mrs Oakes was a great relief to her; though of course their neighbours far and near were very kind: she asked Jack's advice about the wording of her mother's epitaph – the stone was ready and the mason eager to begin – and she referred to the window-tax.

'Sophie and the children send their love,' he said, when Stephen laid down the letter he was reading. 'George tells me that the keeper showed him a sett with young badgers in it.'

'That is kind of them,' said Stephen. 'And Brigid sends you hers, together with a long passage from Padeen that I cannot make out entirely. He told it her in Irish, do you see – they generally speak Irish together – but although she is perfectly fluent in the language she has no notion at all of its orthography, so she writes as it might sound, spoken by an English person. In time I shall find out the meaning, I am sure, by murmuring it aloud.'

He fell to his murmuring, and Jack to a closer study of Sophie's hurried, distracted words: both were interrupted by the sound of seven bells in the middle watch. Jack tidied his papers, reached for his sextant and stood up. 'Is anything afoot?' asked Stephen.

'I must look at the coast, take our latitude and have a word with William: we should be quite near the height of Laraish by now.'

On deck he found the sky clearer still, with the outline of the shore plain against it. Both wind and sea had been diminishing steadily, and if it had not been for his doubt about the solidity of *Dover*'s mainmast he would have increased sail some time ago: he glanced down the line – all present and correct – and to leeward, where the schooner was running goose-winged on a course exactly parallel with his, well within hail for a powerful voice. Jack had a powerful voice, strengthened by many, many years of practice; but for the moment he contented himself with looking at the log-board, with all its entries of course and speed, doing some mental arithmetic, and taking the exact, double-checked height of Mizar, a star for which he had a particular affection.

'Mr Whewell,' he asked the officer of the watch, 'what do you make our position?'

'Just at seven bells, sir, I had a very good observation and found 35° 17' and perhaps twelve seconds.'

'Very good,' said Jack with satisfaction. 'Let us signal *Squadron diminish lights, reduce sail.*' Then, leaning over the rail, '*Ringle?*'

'Sir?'

'Close to speak pennant.'

'William,' said Jack in a conversational tone, some minutes later, looking down at the young man who stood there, smiling up, his steel hook gleaming in the foremast ratlines. 'William, you have been in and out of Laraish pretty often, I believe?'

'Oh, a score of times at least, sir. There was a young person – that is to say, quite frequently, sir.'

'And are we near enough for you to recognize the shore-line?'

'Yes, sir.'

'Then be so good as to look into the harbour, and if you see more than two or three corsairs – big xebec-rigged corsairs and galleys – stand half a mile offshore and send up three blue lights. If less, then red lights and rejoin without the loss of a moment.'

'Aye-aye, sir. More than three, stand off half a mile: three blue lights. Less, then red lights and rejoin without the loss of a moment.'

'Make it so, Mr Reade. Mr Whewell: *Reduce sail in conformity with pennant*.' And directing his voice upwards, 'Look afore, there!'

Eight bells: all round *Surprise* the sentinels called 'All's well' and prepared to go below, but without much conviction, they knowing the general situation and their captain's tone of voice. How right they were. As soon as the muffled thunder of the watch below hurrying up on deck had died away, Jack said, loud and clear, to Somers, the relieving officer, 'Mr Somers, we may pipe to breakfast at two bells or earlier, and then clear. It is not worth going below. Look out afore, there.'

He swung over the rail to the larboard ratlines and ran up to the maintop. 'Good morning, Wilson,' he said to the lookout, and stood gazing away eastward, gazing, gazing.

Two bells, and almost at once three red lights appeared, spreading like crimson flowers one after another, fading and drifting away fast downwind. Before the second had reached its full Jack called down, 'Pipe to breakfast.'

On the quarterdeck he gave orders to increase sail, to steer south by south-south-west, and to prepare for action: these of course were signals, but by word of mouth he sent to tell the cook to use a bucket of slush to get the galley stove right hot right quick.

'Stephen,' he said, walking into the cabin, 'I am afraid we must disturb you. William has just let us know that Laraish has no corsairs: since the wind has been dropping this last watch and more, the likelihood is that the Indiamen will very soon leave their shelter under the lee of the Sugar Loaf, sailing for home, and that the corsairs mean to cut them off. So we are pelting down to stop their capers – we shall be setting close-reefed topgallants presently – and quite soon we shall have to turn you out to clear for action. But at least there is this consolation: we shall have an uncovenanted pot of coffee. It is always far better for the people to have something in their belly before a fight, even if it is only hot burgoo; and since the fires are lit, we may as well profit by the situation.'

'It is our obvious duty,' said Stephen, with a pale smile. In the earlier crises of his life he had often, indeed generally, taken refuge in laudanum, or more recently in coca leaves: on this occasion he had entirely forsworn them, together with tobacco and anything but the merest token of wine to avoid singularity; yet he had always despised the stylite or even hair-shirt kind of asceticism and he was still drinking the last of the pot with something not far from relish – Jack had left him ten minutes earlier – when the thundering drum beat to quarters.

He swallowed the remaining grouts and hurried down to the orlop, where he found Poll and Harris, the ship's butcher: seamen had already lashed chests together to form two operating tables and Poll was making fast the covers of number eight sailcloth with a practised hand – she had already laid out a selection of saws, catlings, clamps, tourniquets, leather-covered chains, dressings, splints; while Harris had lined up buckets, swabs, and the usual boxes for limbs.

To them, after a long pause, entered Dr Jacob, led by an irascible boy – not a ship's boy, but a nominal captain's servant, entered as a first-class volunteer and looked after by the gunner until he should be rated midshipman and join their berth – one of those useless little creatures who had been wished on Jack Aubrey in Gibraltar by former shipmates, men he could not refuse, though the original hydro-graphical *Surprise* had carried no learners, only thoroughly trained midshipmen capable of passing their examination for lieutenant in a year or two.

'There, sir,' said the first-class volunteer, 'it was as simple as I told you the first time. First left, second left, down the ladder and second on your right. Your *right*.'

'Thank you, thank you,' said Jacob; and to Stephen, 'Oh sir, I do beg you to forgive me. I am no great seaman, as you know, and this great dark wandering labyrinth con-founded me – darkness visible. At one time I found myself by the seat of ease in the head, spray dashing upon me from the rising wave.'

'No doubt it will become more familiar in time,' said Stephen. 'What do you say to putting a true razor's edge on our implements? Poll, my dear, there are two coarse and two very fine oilstones on the bottom shelf of the medicine chest.'

Each of the surgeons valued himself upon his skill in sharpening knives of all kinds, scalpels, gouges – almost everything indeed except saws, which they left to the armourer – and they ground away by the light of the power-ful lamp. There was some degree of silent competition, avowed only by the slightly ostentatious manner in which each shaved his forearm with his finished blade and his evi-dent complacency when the skin was left perfectly bare. Stephen was uniformly successful with the scalpels, but he had to return the largest catling, a heavy, double-edged, sharp-pointed amputating knife, to the coarse stone again and again.

'No sir,' cried Harris, who could bear it no longer. 'Let me show you.' Stephen was not a particularly sweet-tempered man, above all at this moment when Jacob had scarcely a hair left to show; but Harris's professional auth-ority was so evident that he let the heavy catling be taken – he let the stone be spat upon, the spittle smoothed with an even rapid drawing movement, heel to tip, then transferred to the fine stone and finished with an emulsion of spit and oil. 'There, sir,' said the butcher, 'that's how we do it in Leadenhall Market, asking your pardon.'

'Well damn you, Harris,' said Stephen, having tried the superlative edge. 'If ever I have to operate upon you, I shall do so with an instrument of your own preparing, and . . .' He was about to add something more likely to please when all present raised their heads, listening intently, ignoring the sound of the hull in a fairly heavy sea, the whole complex voice of the ship; and after a few seconds there it was again, not thunder but the sound of guns.

On deck Jack had not only the advantage of hearing more clearly but of seeing too. The squadron had been sailing close inshore, heading for a point beyond which there rose the modest hill called the Sugar Loaf: at the first remote sound he had thrown out the signal *Make more sail*, and when they came round the point at twelve or even thirteen knots they had the battle spread out full before them in the little leeward bay, rosy with a burning ship and lit by innumerable flashes. The East India convoy, under sail, was being attacked by at least a score of xebecs and galleys, while smallcraft crammed with Moors waited to board any disabled merchantman.

The convoy, escorted only by a sixteen-gun brig-sloop, had formed in something of a line and it was protecting itself moderately well against the xebecs, powerfully armed though they were. But it was almost helpless against the galleys, which could race downwind of the line under sail, turn, take to their oars and come up from leeward, raking the hindmost ships from right aft or on the quarter, where their guns, though comparatively small and few, could do terrible slaughter, firing from so low and near, right along the deck, while the galley itself could not be touched by its victim's cannon.

The rearmost Indiaman it was that lit the bay – an enemy

57

shot having no doubt traversed her light-room and powder-magazine – but even without that, the moonlight, the clear sky and the flashes made the position perfectly evident. Jack made the signal for independent engagement, emphasized it with two guns, and he launched the *Surprise* at what seemed to be the commanding xebec, the corsairs' leader: the Moors had no distinct line of battle, but this one wore some red and tawny pennants.

They met, sailing with the wind on the beam, *Surprise* on the starboard tack, the Moor on the larboard. When each was five points on the other's bow, Jack backed his fore-topsail, and called, 'On the downward roll: fire from forward as they bear.'

All along the deck the gun-crews crouched motionless, the captain with the linstock in his hand, glaring along the barrel. Officers and midshipmen exactly spaced.

Some desultory musket-fire, two or three well-directed round-shot from the xebec; the tingling sound of a gun hit full on the barrel; and immediately after the height of the wave *Surprise* fired a long rippling broadside from forty yards. The wind blew the smoke back, blinding them, and when it cleared they saw a most shocking wreckage, half the xebec's ports beaten in and her rudder shot away. They also heard Jack's roaring 'Look alive, look alive, there: run 'em out!' his order to fill the topsail and the cry 'Port your helm!'

He took the *Surprise* right under the xebec's stern. The frigate stayed beautifully and ran up the enemy's side. The next slower, even more deliberate broadside shattered the Moor entirely. Xebecs were fine nimble fast-sailing craft, but they were not strongly built and she began to settle at once, her people crowding the deck and flinging everything that would float over the side.

Jack saw the whole of the rest of the squadron engaged, and *Ringle* playing long bowls with a half-galley that was trying to get into position to rake an Indiaman: even *Dover* had come up, in spite of having lost her main topmast; and the bay resounded with the bellowing of guns. But already the issue was decided. The convoy and its escort had mauled the corsairs quite seriously in the first phase and the arrival of six brisk men-of-war made it absurd to stay. Those xebecs that could spread their huge lateens on either side, in hare's ears, and raced away at close on fifteen knots southward home to Sallee, where with their slight draught they could lie safely inside the bar; while the uninjured galleys pulled straight into the wind's eye, where no sailing ship could follow them. There were some stragglers, wounded xebecs and such, but there was no point in chasing them: they were useless as prizes and in any case there were more important things to do, such as succouring the ship on fire.

The blaze having been mastered by sunrise, and the combined bosuns and carpenters of the convoy having set about rerigging and repairing the ship, the commodore and senior captains of the Indiamen waited on Jack to express their acknowledgements and to hope that his squadron had not suffered very grievous loss.

'Two of our men were killed, I regret to say, in the very first exchange, when a gun was struck on the muzzle. Otherwise there were only musket-ball and splinter wounds – perhaps a score of hands in the sick-bay. The rest of the squadron are in much the same case. But I am afraid your losses must have been more considerable?'

'Nothing to touch theirs, sir, I do assure you: the three galleys that *Pomone* destroyed or cut in two would have manned a heavy frigate.'

Killick uttered a theatrical cough and when Jack turned, he said, 'Beg pardon, sir: which coffee is up, and a little relish.'

The relish consisted of Gibraltar crabs, lobsters, crayfish, prawns and shrimps and the captains ate them with the keen appetite of those who had had a long, wearisome, and ultimately extremely dangerous voyage on short commons from Cape Town on. They looked upon their host with more than usual benevolence, and with the intention of making an obliging remark one of them said he was very glad that Commodore Aubrey should have suffered so little, in what might have been a most bloody engagement.

'It is true, as the gentleman observes, that we lost few men,' replied Jack, 'but then we had very few men to lose. The squadron is sadly short of hands, *Pomone* above all; and I will tell you frankly that before I knew of your plight I had intended that her boats should have visited you in the hope of some right seamen. And for my own part I should be thankful for two or three upper-yard hands and above all for a steady, reliable master's mate. When you sailed none of you can have known that the war had broken out again, so I dare say there are two or three score men in the convoy who would like to enter voluntarily and take the bounty.'

In the short pause that followed the captains looked at their chief with a studied want of expression: but he, knowing them well, gathered the sense of the company – everyone present knew that Jack could press if he chose – everyone knew how much they owed him – and he replied, 'I am sure you are right, sir; and I am sure that none of us would be so wanting in his duty as to make the slightest difficulty. Word will be passed in all ships belonging to the convoy, together with a promise that any man joining you will have his pay-docket to the present date countersigned by me. As for your two or three active young upper-yard men, I shall certainly send you four of my own. But where master's mates are concerned, we are all very poor indeed – guinea-pigs by the dozen, but nothing that would answer for you, sir. On the other hand, I could offer you a bright, well-qualified, gentlemanly purser. As a volunteer, sir,' he added, seeing the doubt in the Commodore's eye, a doubt caused not only by the strangeness of the offer but even more so (for the offer in itself was by no means unwelcome, though inexplicable) by the countless formalities surrounding the appointment of a purser in a ship of the Royal Navy – the sureties, the guarantees, the verbiage, the paper-work. 'Purely as a volunteer, just for a few months or so if so desired; or at least until his domestic affairs are settled. There is a question of children born when he was on a three-year China voyage. The first he heard of it was at the Cape on the way back, and he does not like to go home until the lawyers have dealt with it all: he cannot face going into his own house with the little bastards running about in it, if I may so express myself without offence. He is used to the Navy, sir: was captain's clerk in *Hebe*, then purser in *Dryad* and *Hermione*, before joining the Company, where his brother has a China ship.'

For the hydrographical voyage Jack had intended to act as his own purser: yet even by Funchal he had found it a very wearisome task indeed, and now that he had this present command some relief was essential. Three times he had meant to speak of it aboard the *Royal Sovereign* and three times he had lost the opportunity.

'Do you guarantee your man?' he asked.

'Without the least reserve, sir.'

'Then I should be happy to see him; and his fellows, of course. Now for my part, I do not believe for a moment that those villains are going to lie in Sallee wringing their hands and lamenting their loss. So in case they come out again when the squadron is gone, I shall send *Dover* to strengthen your escort. They will not face your artillery again, backed up with that of a thirty-two gun frigate. And there is always the possibility of French privateers or even men-of-war in the Channel.'

'Very good – hear him – hear him,' cried the captains, beating on the table.

When they had buried their dead – an expeditious matter at such a time – and repaired the worst of their damage, the convoy and squadron parted on the best of terms, the Indiamen and their escort steering north-west and the squadron beating up tack upon tack for Gibraltar.

Stephen and Jacob had some very seriously injured patients as well as the routine strains, common fractures, contusions and powder-burns; and it was now that Dr Maturin came to appreciate the full value of good female nursing. Both Poll Skeeping and Mrs Cheal had that devotion peculiar perhaps to their sex and a lightness of hand, a dexterity where dressings were concerned that he had not seen equalled outside a religious order. He was busy, but not desperately so (as he had been after some much bloodier fights), and he was quite able to accept Jack's invitation to dine with several of the captains and other officers. He was placed between Hugh Pomfret and Mr Woodbine, the master, an old acquaintance who was eagerly engaged in an argument with Captain Cartwright of *Ganymede* about lunar observations, an argument that had started before dinner and that did not interest Stephen in the least. Captain Pomfret, though obviously unwell and in very low spirits, was a civilized man and he provided a proper amount of conversation; yet their end of the table could hardly have been described as outstandingly cheerful or amusing and it did not surprise Stephen when, as the party broke up, Pomfret asked in a low voice whether he might beg for a consultation, a medical or quasi-medical consultation, at any time that suited Dr Maturin.

'Certainly you may,' said Stephen, who very much liked what he had seen of the young man and who knew the limits of *Pomone*'s surgeon. 'But only with the concurrence of Mr Glover.'

'Mr Glover is no doubt a very clever doctor,' said Pomfret, 'but unhappily we are barely on speaking terms, and this is a wholly personal, confidential matter.'

'Let us take a turn upon deck.'

There under the open sky, with the ship close-hauled on the larboard tack, he explained the rudiments of medical etiquette. 'I quite take your point,' said Pomfret, 'but this is more what might be called a moral or spiritual rather than a physical matter – not wholly unlike the distinction between right and wrong.'

'If you would be a little more specific, I might perhaps tell you whether I could properly be of any use.'

'My trouble is this: *Pomone*, under my orders, beat one Moorish galley to pieces by gunfire and deliberately rode down two others in the mêlée, cutting them in half so that they sank within the minute. And I perpetually see those scores of men, Christian slaves chained to their oars, looking up in horror, looking up perhaps for mercy; and I sailed on to destroy another. Is it right? *Can* it be right? I cannot sleep for those faces gazing, straining up. Have I mistaken my profession?'

'On the face of it,' said Stephen, 'I do not think you have. I feel extremely for your very great distress, but . . . no, I should have to summon more powers than I can call upon at present, to justify a war, even a war against a dictatorial system, an open denial of freedom; and I shall only say that I feel it *must* be fought. And since it *has* to be fought it is better that it should be fought, at least on one side, with what humanity war does allow, and by officers of your kind. I shall play the doctor so far as to send you a box of pills that will give you two nights' heavy sleep. If, having slept, you wish to hear my reasons, I hope I shall have them fairly well arranged; and after that you must be your own physician.'

Chapter Three

That night the wind backed steadily until by two bells in
the graveyard watch it was a little south of west, where it
steadied, strengthened and carried them right through the
Strait – no more piping of all hands every other glass or two,
but a sweet passage to the Rock itself and their accustomed
moorings.

Stephen and Jacob were heartily glad of it because three of
their badly injured men had taken a serious turn for the worse:
in one case a leg could no longer be saved, in another a resection was imperatively necessary, and in the third trephining
on a solid table was preferable to the same operation on a
moving deck. They and all but the slightly wounded men were
taken to the hospital, where in any event more surgeons were
called for, one of the immense cranes on the new mole having
collapsed, very heavily loaded, on a gang of workmen.

They had finished, they had taken off their bloody aprons
and they were washing their hands when a midshipman from
the *Surprise* arrived with a note from the Commodore desiring them to come aboard at once.

It was a quiet, serious, hurried boat that carried them out,
and the midshipman, young Adams, looked particularly
grave: both surgeons were silent too – they were sadly worn –
but Stephen did notice the Blue Peter at *Surprise*'s masthead
and he did notice the curious, bedraggled appearance of the
usually trim and more than trim *Pomone*, with yards all
uneven, sails drooping, sagging in the breeze, rope-ends here
and there. He had never seen a man-of-war look so desolate.

As they approached the pennant-ship they saw a captain's

barge at the starboard gangway and so pulled round to the other side. By the time Stephen reached the deck – a slow process, with no side-ropes – the officer had taken leave of the Commodore and his barge was shoving off.

'There you are, Doctor,' said Jack. 'Come and take a draught. How are our people?'

'The usual reply, I am afraid, my dear: "as well as can be expected", after that cruel bucketing of going about in a heavy head-sea. But poor Thomas could not keep his leg. We had it off in a trice, with barely a moan.'

'Well done. It will be a cook's warrant for him, if I and my friends have any influence. I wish my news were as good. While you were in the hospital there was a shocking accident aboard *Pomone*. Most unhappily poor Hugh Pomfret was cleaning his pistols – we are ordered to sea directly – and by some wretched mischance one was loaded. It blew his brains out. Then the Admiral sent for me. He commended what the squadron had done very handsomely indeed and he will do us full justice in his dispatch, sending it by the same courier that brought him orders to send the squadron to sea immediately – the Ministry are much perturbed by the attitude of the Balkan Muslims. He was deeply concerned about Pomfret's death; but he has a young man of his own at hand, John Vaux, who distinguished himself at the taking and above all the arming of the Diamond Rock in the year four and who should have been made post long ago – that was the man you saw leaving the quarterdeck when you came aboard. His barge will carry Pomfret's body to the cemetery but our orders are so urgent that the Admiral and his staff will take care of the funeral. As soon as the barge is back we unmoor and proceed to Mahon, where we shall ship our Marines. Captain Vaux will already have *Pomone* out of mourning and shipshape – you have seen her yards all a-cockbill, I am sure, and her scandalized mizen? Very proper, of course, but horrible to see.'

*   *   *

65

The squadron had received no more damage than the bosuns and carpenters, with some help from the dockyard, could repair within the day; and by early evening, with the shattered gun aboard *Surprise* replaced, they took advantage of the kind north-wester to make sail for Mahon, where they would refit more thoroughly, take in stores, and above all learn the most recent intelligence from the Adriatic, the eastern Mediterranean and the convoys to be protected. By the time they had sunk the land, the full-topsail gale was so steady from the west-north-west that the ship was making ten knots and more, never touching a sheet or brace; and after retreat the smoking-circle formed in the galley, the only place where smoking was allowed.

Although most of the Surprises had sailed together long before this, there were many who preferred to chew their tobacco, there were some who liked fishing over the side, and there were some who were too bashful to attend; for this was not an assembly for just any boy, landman or ordinary seaman – not that there were many aboard – nor for those who were not at ease in conversation, particularly cheerful conversation, enlivened by anecdotes.

Yet this particular evening began in a positively lugubrious fashion. Mrs Skeeping, though professionally neat as a wren, contrived to trip over the cheese of wads that served as her chair and flung her fresh-filled boiling teapot into Joshua Simmons' lap and bosom. She begged his pardon, mopped him more or less dry, hung his waistcoat in the ratlines and assured him with a laugh that now he was at least clean in places, while the waistcoat was as good as new: but Joshua Simmons – commonly known as Old Groan and tolerated only because he had served at the Nile with Jack Aubrey, under Nelson again at Copenhagen, and finally at Trafalgar – was not to be amused, nor comforted; no, nor mollified neither. After a while he said, 'Well, this is a fine beginning – an unlucky squadron if ever there was one. Those bloody Indiamen never gave so much as a brass farthing between us, though we saved their lives and fortunes; and now there is this wicked self-murder in *Pomone*. How can there be any luck in such a commission? Which is doomed from the bleeding start.'

'Balls,' said Killick.

'Now then, Preserved Killick,' cried Maggie Cheal, the bosun's wife's sister, taking her short clay pipe from her mouth so that her words were mixed with smoke. 'None of your coarse Seven Dials kind of talk, if you please, with ladies present.'

'How do *you* know it was self-murder?' asked the cook, jerking his chin at Simmons. 'You was not there.'

'No, I was not; but it stands to reason.'

'Gammon,' cried Killick. 'If it had been self-murder he would have been buried at the crossroads with a stake through his heart. And was he buried at the crossroads with a stake through his heart? No, mates, he was not. He was buried in a Christian grave in the churchyard, with the words said over him by a parson, the Admiral in attendance, the union flag on his coffin, and a volley fired over him. So be damned to Old Groan and his bad luck.'

Simmons gave a bitter sniff, unpinned his waistcoat and walked off, deliberately feeling in its pockets and glancing back at his companions.

'In any case,' Killick went on, 'even if he had done himself in a dozen times over, we have a gent aboard that brings in luck by wholesale. Luck? I never seen anything like it. He has a unicorn's horn in his cabin, whole and entire – a unicorn's horn as is proof against all poisons whatsoever, as some people know very well –' glancing at Poll, who nodded in a very emphatic and knowledgeable manner '– and which is worth ten times its own weight in guinea-gold. Ten times! Can you imagine it? And not only that, mates, not only that. He likewise has a Hand of Glory! There's luck for you, I believe.'

A shocked silence, but for the even song of the ship.

'What's a Hand of Glory?' asked a nervous voice.

'Why, you lemon: don't you even know what a Hand of Glory is? Well, I'll tell you. It is one of the hangman's prime perquisites.'

'What's a perquisite?'

'Don't you know what a . . . ? You're ignorant, is all. Dead ignorant.'

A voice, 'The same as vails.'

Another, 'Advantages on the side, like.'

'There is the rope, of course. He can get half a crown an inch for a rope that hanged a right willain. And there are the clothes, bought by them that think a pair of pissed and shitten breeches . . .'

'Now then, Killick,' cried Poll, 'this ain't one of your Wapping ale-houses or knocking-kens, so clap a stopper over that kind of talk. "Soiled linen" is what you mean.'

'. . . are worth a guinea, for the sake of the luck they bring. But most of all it is the Hand of Glory that makes the hangman so eager for the work. Because why? Because it too is worth its weight in gold . . . well, in silver.'

'What's a Hand of Glory?' asked the nervous voice.

'Which it is the hand that did the deed – ripped the young girl up or slit the old gentleman's throat – and that the hangman cuts off and holds up. And our Doctor has one in a jar which he keeps secret in the cabin and looks at by night with his mate, talking very low.'

The uneasy silence was broken by a hail from the forecastle lookout: 'Land, ho. Land fine on the starboard bow.'

It was the island of Alboran, almost exactly where it ought to be but slightly earlier than Jack had expected. He altered course a trifle and stood straight on for Mahon.

There were some rather dull sailers in Jack Aubrey's squadron, and it was not until Tuesday afternoon that they rounded Ayre Island, standing for Cape Mola and the narrow entrance, with the breeze just before the beam and the larboard tacks aboard.

The Commodore knew Port Mahon intimately well and he took the lead, beginning his salute at exactly the right distance from the great batteries and sailing on until the port-captain's boat hailed him, desiring him to take up his old moorings with the others astern of him.

'How very little it has changed,' he said, gazing about with lively pleasure as they glided down the long, long inlet and raising his voice to carry above the prodigious reverberations of the fort's reply, echoing from shore to shore.

'It is even finer than I had remembered,' said Stephen.

On, past the lazaretto, past the hospital island: but now the warm breeze, meeting the flank of La Mola, hauled aft, blowing so gently that even with topgallants abroad the squadron took just over an hour to reach the moorings at the far end of the port, just under the steep-pitched town and a cable's length from the wharf, where the Pigtail Steps ran down from the main square, sailing all the way under a pure sky, intensely blue at the zenith and passing through imperceptible gradations to a soft lapis lazuli just above the land.

It was as beautiful a run, or rather a living glide, as could be imagined. Ordinarily the northern side of the great harbour was somewhat harsh, even forbidding, but now in the very height of Mediterranean spring it was green, countless varieties of green, all young and delightful – even the grim scrub-oak looked happy. And if they turned to contemplate the much nearer, much more cultivated land to larboard, there were orange-groves, with the round-topped, exactly-spaced little trees like the most charming embroidery imaginable; and from them wafted the scent of blossom – fruit and blossom on the tree together.

They did not speak, except to point out a known house or inn or once, on Stephen's part, an Eleonora's falcon, until they were very near the man-of-war's end of the great wharf, when Jack, exchanging a happy smile with Stephen, said to the master, 'Let us moor ship, Mr Woodbine.'

'Aye-aye, sir,' said Woodbine, and he roared to the bosun, just at hand, 'All hands to moor ship.'

The bosun and his mates repeated the order louder still, emphasizing it with an extraordinarily shrill piping, as though the entire ship's company had not been poised for the exercise ever since the mooring buoys were seen – a roaring and piping repeated right down the squadron's line and even aboard the little *Ringle*, a biscuit-toss to leeward.

'We will furl in a body, if you please, Mr Woodbine: and let us square by the lifts and braces.'

Meeting Bonden's questioning look, Jack nodded, and said to Stephen, 'I hope you will accompany me? I must pay my respects to the Spanish commandant.' It was known throughout the *Surprise* – always had been known – that the Doctor spoke foreign to a remarkable extent, and was always called upon to do the civil thing in case of need: today he was to present the Commodore's ceremonial compliment to the senior officer who represented his country's sovereignty, a purely nominal sovereignty at present, since with the full agreement of her Spanish ally, Great Britain's Royal Navy carried on with the unrestricted use of the great naval base.

While his barge was lowering down, Jack lingered on the quarterdeck, watching the other ships as they too furled in a body and squared their yards. It was toilsome, but it did look trim; and, he hoped, would to some extent redeem the slowness of his passage.

'Now, sir,' said Killick at his side, 'all is laid along, together with your presentation sword. But, sir,' – lowering his voice – 'the Doctor can't go ashore in that there rig. Which it would bring discredit on the barky.'

Stephen was in fact wearing an old black frock-coat in which he had obviously been either operating or dissecting without an apron; and although late last night Killick had privately taken his shirt and neck-cloth from beside his cot, the Doctor had obviously found where they were stowed.

Some years before this, the Sick and Hurt Board had ordained a special uniform for surgeons, a blue cloth coat with blue cloth lapels, cuffs and embroidered collar, three buttons on cuffs and pockets, white lining, white cloth waistcoat and breeches: the garments existed, they having been made by the naval tailor who had always looked after Jack, but Stephen had doggedly resisted hints that he should wear them, even when the gunroom gave a ceremonial dinner to welcome Mr Candish, their new purser.

Now, however, Jack's argument that for the sake of the Adriatic cruise and all that it entailed they must both look like grave, responsible beings, after their call on the Spaniard, when they waited upon Admiral Fanshawe, his secretary and his political adviser, good relations being of the first importance – an argument that was expressed with great earnestness – overcame Stephen's reluctance, and they both went over the side soberly magnificent.

'Lord,' said Jack, pausing for breath at the top of the Pigtail Steps, 'I must get back to my way of running up to the masthead at least once every morning. I am growing old, unsound in wind and limb.'

'You are growing obese: or rather you *have* grown obese. You eat far too much. I particularly noticed the shameless way you indulged in the soused pig's face at our feast to welcome Mr Candish.'

'I did so deliberately, to encourage him. He is somewhat bashful, though he is a very fine fellow. I am delighted to have him: though how Mr Smith ever came to propose him, I cannot tell.'

'When the convoy's captains came aboard there was a certain lack of candles, as you may recall.'

'Well, what of it?'

'And perhaps Mr Smith may have heard one of our sailors call out "if only we had a real purser, there would not be all this Bedlam running about and shouting every single time we want a bloody dip". And one of the Indiamen's officers asked "What, ain't you got a real purser?" '

'Well, whatever you may say I am very glad to have him. And if only I had a master's mate of the same competence I should be gladder still. Poor Wantage. He was one of the most promising young men I have ever had – a born navigator – had the Requisite Tables by rote, so that he could give you your position without looking at them. And he had a very good feeling for *Surprise*'s likes and dislikes. How I regret him. And all because of that vile wench.'

In the peace of 1814, the *Surprise*, setting out on what was ostensibly an expedition to survey the coasts of Chile, had sailed with a very moderate ship's company – no ordinary midshipmen and no youngsters at all. On her first leg she had carried Sophie Aubrey and her children and Diana Maturin and her daughter as far as Madeira for a holiday, the plan being that the women and children should return to England in the packet when the *Surprise* carried on to South America. But during this stay, young Wantage, exploring the mountains, had met a shepherdess. Then, Napoleon having escaped from Elba, the frigate was at once ordered to Gibraltar. Parties were sent out for stragglers, guns were fired, the Blue Peter flew to the very last minute before she sailed, all her people aboard except for Wantage; and it was generally believed that the shepherd, coming back untimely to the mountain hut, had killed him.

'He was indeed a most amiable young man,' said Stephen. 'But I believe that the great house with two sentinels before it is where Don José lives.'

It was, and Don José was at home. He received them very kindly: Stephen and he went through the graceful Spanish ceremony of compliments presented and returned, Jack bowing from time to time, and Don José accompanied them to the outer door itself.

They were equally well received by Admiral Fanshawe and his secretary. Jack introduced Stephen: the Admiral said, 'How do you do, sir? I remember you well after that horrible affair off Algeciras, when you were so good to my brother William.'

Stephen asked after his former patient. 'Very well, I thank you, Doctor,' said the Admiral. 'He can get along quite well without crutches now, and he has had a saddle made that allows him to take leaps that would astonish you.'

Very soon after this the secretary said, 'I believe, sir, that I should take Dr Maturin to see Mr Colvin.'

'Do, do, by all means; and the Commodore and I will talk about convoys.'

'Forgive me, sir,' said Jack to the Admiral, and in a discreet undertone to Stephen, 'In case your conversation takes a great while, let us meet at the Crown.'

As he walked along the corridors with the Admiral's secretary, Stephen wondered how Colvin came to be here rather than in Malta. He was a man with whom Stephen had quite often had dealings, almost always in London or Gibraltar, and without being friends they were necessarily well-acquainted. Colvin had probably meant to restrict their conversation to intelligence, to the question of the Adriatic, but he could not prevent a certain earnestness from making part of his 'I hope I see you well?' or from giving a slightly more than usual pressure as they shook hands.

When the Admiral's secretary had left them they sat down and with an artificial cheerfulness Colvin began, 'I am happy to say that although the Ministry is growing more and more worried about the Russians' procrastination, the passing of time, and the possibility of this shocking intervention, we have at least made a beginning with the Adriatic yards. From Ancona and Bari our banking friend, a man of extraordinary energy for his age, has not only called in the loans made to the small and out-of-the-way shipwrights concerned with French vessels but he has also warned all suppliers to insist on cash: no notes of hand, no promises. He and his associates along the coast are closely allied to what few local banks there are on the Turkish side of the water: they will make no difficulties, nor, of course, will any of the beys or pashas. Mr Dee knows perfectly well that these small yards have almost no capital of their own – they work on borrowed money – and that when pay-day comes round and there *is* no pay, the workmen are likely to turn ugly, very ugly. These places rely for a large part on itinerant skilled labour, most of it Italian. Now I do not know, sir, whether you have any moral scruples about having dealings with the Carbonari . . . or even Freemasons: as it were allying yourself with such people. Or perhaps I should say making use of them.'

Both Colvin and Stephen were Catholics and like most of their kind they had been brought up with some curious notions: in childhood they had been assured by those they loved and respected that whenever Freemasons held a formal gathering one of their number was invariably the Devil himself, sometimes more or less disguised; and after a short pause Stephen replied, 'As for the Carbonari, Lord William had no hesitation about treating with them in Sicily . . .'

'In these parts they are said to be strangely allied to the Freemasons: some of their rites are similar.'

Stephen shook his head. 'I have known only one avowed Mason,' he said, 'a member of my club: and when he voted for the execution of the King, his brother, he was asked to resign. Such things sustain a largely irrational prejudice. However, a scruple would have to be very moral indeed for me to reject any means of bringing this vile war to an end. I take it that you feel these people might be useful to us?'

'Indeed they may. Many of the Italian craftsmen in the yards and even some of the natives are Carbonari. At the same time our friends in Ancona and Bari have great influence with their fellow-Masons in the Adriatic ports – the bankers and money-men, I mean – and will prevent them from relieving the shipwrights. Now wood is by its nature inflammable, and when two pay-days have gone by with no wages, it would not be surprising if the yards were to go up in flames. The Carbonari are much given to an incendiary revenge – I believe it has to do with their mystic beliefs – and a very little prompting or tangible encouragement of the more enthusiastic would certainly earn brilliant results. I might almost promise a blazing success.'

Stephen's dislike of Colvin increased, but with no change of tone or expression he went on, 'In some yards, as I understand it, the French officers who oversee the construction are strongly Bonapartist, in others hesitant or downright for the King. Only the first are potentially dangerous, either as privateers on their own or as renegadoes with the Barbary pirates, preying on our trade. Quite apart from any other point of view, a general conflagration would be wholly against our interests: you are to consider that some vessels may come over to us voluntarily, joining the King of France; and at this juncture even a few *allied* French men-of-war would be of the utmost value here in the Mediterranean. Then again, a wholesale burning would do away with the possibility of cutting out any nearly completed or repaired vessels commanded by resolute Bonapartists, and making prizes of them. It is difficult for a landsman to have any conception of the sailor's delight in a prize or of the prodigies of valour and enterprise he will display to gain it. But as to these differing loyalties, have you any information?'

'I am very sorry to say I have not. Because of a gross indiscretion committed by an agent belonging to the other firm just before I arrived, it was not thought desirable that I should cross to the Turkish side. On the other hand, we have all the details you could wish about the geographical and financial position of the yards, and the presents expected by the beys, pashas and local officials for various accommodations and forms of blindness.'

The *other firm* was an intelligence service of sorts, or rather a collection of services, run by the army; and its agents often poached on naval preserves, sometimes doing serious damage and always causing a very high degree of resentment.

'If you would let me have this information, I should be very much obliged,' said Stephen.

'Of course. You shall have it this very evening . . .' Colvin hesitated and then went on, 'Though now I come to reflect, I am by no means sure that I have the papers with me.' Another pause, and he said, 'I dare say you were surprised at finding me here rather than in Malta or Brindisi?'

'Not at all,' said Stephen.

'There was a certain amount of unpleasantness over that indiscretion I mentioned and I am on my way either to Gibraltar or even perhaps London to clear it up; and knowing that Commodore Aubrey's squadron must touch here I thought I should wait, in order to tell you about the general aspect of affairs in the Adriatic. Those particulars will of course be at your disposal as soon as you reach Malta.'

Stephen made the necessary acknowledgements and they talked for a while about colleagues in Whitehall before he took his leave, saying that he must rejoin the Commodore without delay – it was death to keep the Commodore waiting.

'Well, sir,' said Jack Aubrey, looking up from his notes and counting the slips that would enable the officers in charge of the base to revictual and refit the squadron with all the astonishing variety of objects it might need, from musket-flints to dead-eyes, hearts and euphroes. 'I think that sets us up very handsomely: many, many thanks. And now, sir, if I may I will beg leave to retire. I have an appointment with my surgeon at the Crown, and it would never do to vex a man you next meet in the cockpit, with you flat on your back and he standing over you with a knife. He is not ordinarily an irascible creature, but I know that today he is with child to call upon your engineer.'

'James Wright, that prodigy of learning? I would give a five-pound note to see them together.'

In fact the sight was not worth nearly so much, particulàrly at first. Dr Maturin, holding his visiting-card in his hand, was about to knock at the door of Mr Wright's house when it flew open from within and an angry voice cried, 'What do you want with me? Eh? What do you want with me?'

'Mr Wright?' asked Stephen, with a hint of smiling recognition. 'My name is Maturin.'

'It might just as well be Beelzebub,' said Mr Wright. 'Not a brass farthing will you firk out of me before the end of the month, as I told that pragmatical bastard, your chief.'

'My dear sir,' cried Stephen, 'I have ventured to call upon you as a fellow member of a learned society, not, upon my soul and honour, as a dun: bad luck to them all.'

'You belong to the Royal?' asked Wright, bending from the uppermost step and peering into Stephen's face with narrowed, suspicious eyes.

'Certainly I belong to the Royal,' said Stephen, now somewhat warm. 'Furthermore, Mr Watt did me the honour of introducing me to you. I was sitting next to him, and old Mr Bolton was on the other side. It was the evening you read the paper on screwing.'

'Oh,' said Wright, taken aback. 'Pray walk in – I beg pardon – I have lost my spectacles. And from what little I could make out your uniform looked like that of a bailiff's man. I beg pardon. Pray walk in.' He led Stephen into a large, well-lit room with exactly-drawn plans on the walls, on high tables and on a pair of rollers that could bring any corner of the port or dockyard before the viewer's eye. He found his spectacles, one of the pairs that lay about on chairs and desks, and putting them on he gazed at Stephen. 'Sir,' he said, rather more civilly now, 'may I ask what that uniform is? I do not believe I have seen it before.'

'Sir,' replied Stephen, 'it is the uniform that was laid down for surgeons of the Royal Navy some time ago: it is rarely worn.'

Having considered this, cocking his head like an intelligent dog, Mr Wright asked how he might serve his visitor, whom he now remembered from their meeting at the Royal Philosophers' Club, before the formal session.

'I have presumed to wait upon you, sir,' said Stephen, 'because some of our more eminent colleagues, particularly those distinguished in the mechanical and mathematical sciences, have assured me that you know more than any man living about the physical properties of substances – their inherent strength and the means of increasing it – their resistance to the elements – and if I may I should like to ask whether in the course of your studies you have ever been brought to reflect upon the narwhal's horn?' During his last few words Stephen noticed a total absence of attention come over the aged face before him and he was not surprised to hear Mr Wright cry, 'Dr Maturin, Dr *Maturin* of course: I grow more forgetful day by day, but now I recall our meeting even more perfectly. And what is of much greater consequence, I recall a letter from my young cousin Christine – Christine Heatherleigh as she was, but now the widow of Governor Wood of Sierra Leone. It was her usual birthday letter, and among other things she said she had prepared the articulated bones of some creature that interested you – she was always a great anatomist, even as a child – and would it be right to send the specimen to Somerset House?'

'How very kind. I have the fondest recollections of dear Mrs Wood. It was no doubt my tailless potto, one of the most interesting of the primates: but alas short-lived.'

'So I said Somerset House by all means: Robertshaw and his people take the greatest care of Fellows' specimens. But I believe, sir, that you mentioned a narwhal. Pray what is a narwhal?'

'A cetacean of the northern, the far northern seas, a moderate whale of about five yards long; and the male possesses a horn that may be half as long again. I say "horn" sir, because that is the term commonly used; but in fact the object is made of ivory.'

'And only the males wear it?'

'So I am told by whalers and by those few who have had the happiness of dissecting the creature.'

'Then they share our fate: for with us too it is the males alone that wear the horns.' After a moment Mr Wright began to laugh – a low, creaking sound that went on and on. 'Forgive me,' he said at last, taking off his spectacles and wiping them. 'I am facetious at times. You were speaking of ivory?'

'Yes, sir: a particularly hard and dense ivory. The infant narwhal has but two teeth, both in his upper jaw. That on the right usually remains in a rudimentary state: the other develops into a tapering column that may protrude for six or seven feet and weigh a stone or more.'

'What is its function?'

'That appears to be unknown. There are no reports of its use as a weapon – no boat has ever been attacked – and although sportive narwhals have been seen to cross their tusks above the surface, no fighting ensued, and it was thought to be done in play. As for its alleged use as a fish-spear, an animal with no hands would be puzzled to transfer its transfixed prey from tusk to mouth: besides, the females are tuskless: yet they do not starve. There are innumerable suppositions, all based upon very little knowledge indeed; but there is one undoubted, instantly observable phenomenon – the very curious shape of the horn. Not only does it bear a large number of parallel spirals ascending in half a dozen left-hand turns from the base almost to the bare, smooth tip, but it also has several much larger tori or undulating turns, rising in the same direction. All this puzzles me extremely, though I am something of a physiologist, devoted to comparative osteology; and I should very much like to ask whether these adaptations of the tusk are designed to strengthen it, without adding to its already considerable bulk, and whether the much larger tori help the animal, a very rapid swimmer, to diminish the turbulence it must encounter at every stroke. I am aware sir, that turbulence is one of the chief studies among gentlemen of your profession.'

'Turbulence. Aye, turbulence,' said Mr Wright, shaking his head. 'Any man that means to build a lighthouse, or a bridge, or a jetty, must think long and hard upon turbulence, and the enormous force exerted by water in violent motion. But oh the wearisome calculations, the uncertainty! On the face of it, sir, your suppositions seem reasonable: surface corrugation does often increase resistance to certain forms of stress; and conceivably your tori might have a favourable effect in directing a spiral flow past the advancing body and in counteracting the rotary force – for your animal is propelled by his tail, is he not?'

'Just so. A horizontal tail, of course, like the rest of his kind.'

'It is an interesting problem: but any suggestion that I might put forward, based solely on a verbal description, however well-informed, would scarcely be worth the air expended. If I could see the horn, measure the depth and angle of the spiral and of the larger processes, my opinion might possibly have some slight value.'

'Sir,' said Dr Maturin, 'if you would honour me with your company at dinner, let us say tomorrow, I should be delighted to show you my tusk, a small but perfect specimen.'

Jack and Stephen met again, almost on the very steps of the Crown. 'Well met, brother,' cried Jack from a little distance. Stephen considered the Commodore's face and his gait: was he sober? 'You look uncommon cheerful, my dear,' he said, leading him in the direction of the Pigtail Steps. 'I wish you may not have met with some compliant young person, overwhelmed with all the gold lace upon your person.'

'Never in life,' said Jack. 'Aubrey the Chaste is what I am called throughout the service. I did indeed meet a young person, but one that shaves, when he can afford it. Stephen, you may remember that I have told you about our grievous lack of master's mates, and how I yearned to replace poor Wantage?'

'I do not suppose you have mentioned it much above ten times a day.'

'It is not a question of those midshipmen who are promoted master's mate merely so that they may pass for lieutenants at the end of their servitude – you know of course that they have to show certificates proving that they have served in that rating for two years – no, no, it is your true master's mate, the mate to the master of the ship, if you follow me, whose only ambition is to become a master himself, an expert navigator and ship-handler, but as an officer with a warrant from the Navy Board rather than the King's commission. Admittedly we have Salmon, but how I longed for another, if only to second poor tired old Woodbine! Our mids are good young fellows, but they are not mathematicians, and their navigation is brutish, brutish.'

A vigilant eye aboard *Surprise* had caught the Commodore's broad gestures, designed to illustrate the brutishness of the ordinary midshipman's navigation, and his boat set off across the harbour at once. It took some time to thread its way through the crowded shipping and smallcraft – the whole squadron was refitting at the utmost speed – and Jack went on, 'Well, the young person I met was John Daniel.' He looked into Stephen's face for some gleam of intelligence, recognition of the name: no gleam of any kind whatsoever. 'John Daniel,' repeated Jack, 'we were shipmates for a short while in *Worcester*. And he was in *Agamemnon*: Woodbine knows him well, and many other officers. He was paid off at the peace and joined a privateer . . .'

'Sir, sir, oh sir, if you please,' called a shrill boy, purple in the face from running, 'the Admiral's compliments and desires you will hand this to Dr Maturin.'

'My compliments and duty to the Admiral,' said Jack,

taking the letter and passing it to Stephen, 'and you may tell him that his orders have been carried out.'

They walked down the steps to the waiting boat, and as they walked Stephen turned the letter over and over, looking thoughtful. 'Do not mind me, I beg,' said Jack; but already bow-oar, an old seaman who knew Stephen well, was at hand to ensure that he cleared the gunwale with one firm stride.

Bonden shoved off the moment the Commodore was settled, cried 'Give way,' and the launch weaved through the mêlée with never a bump until he brought it alongside with his usual perfection.

In the cabin Stephen said, 'Jack, I fear I have been so indiscreet as to ask Mr Wright to dine aboard without consulting you. I particularly wish to hear his view on the action of water flowing the whole length of the horn you so very kindly gave me long ago, upon the nature of the turbulence set up by the whorls or convolutions, and upon the effect of the more delicate ascending spirals.'

'Not at all, not at all,' said Jack. 'I should very much like to hear him: no man more. Although I have been waterborne most of my days, I am sadly ignorant of hydrostatics except in a pragmatic, rule-of-thumb kind of fashion. We could invite Jacob too, and have some music. I know that Mr Wright, like some of the other mathematical Fellows, delights in a fugue. Oh, and Stephen, let me go back to John Daniel, Wantage's replacement: he is so prodigiously shabby it would be cruel to introduce him to the berth. He is a poor, short, bent, meagre, ill-looking little creature, very like . . . that is to say, you are the only grown person aboard whose clothes would fit him. You shall have them back of course, as soon as he can whip up something to appear on the quarterdeck in.'

'Killick,' called Stephen, barely raising his voice, since he knew that their valuable common servant was listening behind the door – Killick had something of a cold in his chest and his heavy breathing could have been heard at a far greater distance. 'Killick, be so good as to bring a respectable white shirt, the blue coat whose button you were replacing, a neck-cloth, a pair of duck trousers, stockings, shoes – buckled shoes – and a handkerchief.'

Killick opened his mouth: but to Captain Aubrey's astonishment he shut it again, paused, said, 'Aye-aye, sir: respectable white shirt it is, the blue coat, neck-cloth, ducks, stockings, buckled shoes, wipe,' and hurried away. Stephen was not surprised: it was but another example of that singular deference that attended not only his state but also that of men condemned to death. 'Jack, pray tell me about your master's mate,' he said.

'His name is John Daniel, and he comes from Leominster, where his father was a bookseller in a small way of business: he had a fair amount of education in his father's shop and at the town school. But Mr Woodbine, whose family lived there, tells me that it was not a reading town at all, and with trade declining, the customers did not pay their bills. The shop was in a sad way, getting worse and worse, and to preserve his father from being carried off to the debtors' prison, young Daniel took the bounty and went aboard the receiving ship at Pompey. He was drafted with such a hopeless set of quota-men to *Arethusa* that he was the only one who could write his name. Nicholls, Edward Nicholls, who was first of *Arethusa*, looked at him without much love – no seaman, too feeble to haul, no handicraft, and he was about to rate him landman and waister when he happened to ask him what he thought he could do that might be useful aboard a ship. Daniel said he had studied the mathematics and that he could cast accounts. Nicholls set him a few questions, saw that he was telling the truth, and said that if Daniel wrote a neat hand, he could be of some help to the purser or the captain's clerk and perhaps the master. This he did to their satisfaction, but once they were clear of the Channel purser and clerk had little employment for him and he spent most of his time with the master, Oakhurst. You remember Oakhurst, Stephen? He was in *Euryalus* off Brest, a great lunarian. He dined with us once, and cried out against those ignorant idle swabs who would depend on chronometers.'

'I remember him as a somewhat passionate, even an irascible companion.'

'Yes. But he was kind to Daniel, who was entranced with the whole idea of navigation – the celestial clock – the circling stars – the planets among them – the moon – and who, being lent an old quadrant, perpetually took altitudes or measured the distances between the moon and various stars. He was a young man who delighted in the beauty of mathematics: who delighted in number itself . . . Furthermore, when *Arethusa*'s people were all turned over into *Inflexible*, he was rated ordinary and, being small and light, he was stationed in the maintop.'

'He must have found that very hard.'

'I am sure he did, and I cannot imagine what the premier was about – to be sure, they were cruel short-handed, yet even so . . . But, however, he survived it. He had been at sea for some time, turning out whenever all hands was piped and he was used to the ways of the Navy: he was not a stranger, but a well-liked man surrounded with shipmates, and they helped him. After a year or so of this – for he was a quick learner – he had a fair notion of sailing a ship as well as navigating her. But he was very happy when *Inflexible* went into dock for repair and Oakhurst asked his captain to rate Daniel master's mate in the old *Behemoth*. And then, of course, like most men-of-war *Behemoth* was paid off in the peace; and after a while on the shore – anything for a berth – he joined a privateer fitting out to pursue and take pirates on the Barbary coast, but in no way suited for the task. One of the first pirates they met, a Tangerine, so battered her that she only just reached Oran, where she grounded and bilged. A Genoese tartan let him work his

passage back to Mahon, where he hoped he might find someone he knew, but they stripped him of all he possessed. He
had barely a shirt to his back when I saw him sitting under
the arcades. But now returning to our dinner, I shall have
a word with my cook; and if Mr Wright agrees, we could
play him the Zelenka fugue that the three of us ran through
again on Sunday – a most uncommon piece.'

The frigate's dinner for Mr Wright was surprisingly successful: the captain's cook, with all the delights of Minorca
at hand, had put himself out, and they ate nobly, drinking
a great deal of a light local red from Fornells and then some
ancient Madeira; but what particularly pleased Stephen was
the way in which the great engineer, ordinarily a difficult
guest and apt to be sullen, took to Jack Aubrey and even
more to Jacob. They had a lively discussion on the local
varieties of modern Greek and the curious versions of
Turkish that had come into being among the subject nations
of the immense Turkish empire. 'I was a fair hand with
Homer at school,' said Wright, holding up his glass,
'– athesphatos oinos, by the way – but when I was desired to
build the wharves and breakwater at Hyla I found to my
dismay that my Greek was no good to me, no good at all,
and I was obliged to employ a dragoman at every turn.
No doubt you, sir, were better prepared for the Eastern
Mediterranean?'
    'Why, sir, it was not so much prescience or virtue on my
part as the pure good fortune of having spent my tender
years – the years when a language flows into your mind with
no intellectual effort – among Turks, Greeks and people
speaking many varieties of Arabic and Berber as well as the
archaic Hebrew of the Beni Mzab Jews. My people were
jewel-merchants, based mostly in the Levant but travelling
very widely indeed, even to Mogador on the Atlantic coast
on the one hand and Baghdad on the other.'
    'Surely, Doctor,' said Jack, 'it must be a perilous business,

rambling about mountains and deserts with a parcel of jewels in your pocket or your saddle-bag? I mean quite apart from the wild beasts – lions ravening for their prey – there are likely to be bandits, are there not? One hears sad tales of the Arabs: and I well remember that in the Holy Land, where people were no doubt a great deal better than they are now, the Good Samaritan came upon a poor fellow beaten, wounded and robbed on the highway. While a little later in this watch I am going to send off two convoys, heavily armed, to see some merchantmen safe into London river, laden with no more than Smyrna figs and the like – never so much as a pearl or a diamond between the lot of them. For my part I should never dare wander about a desert carrying a stock of gem-stones without a troop of horse at my back.'

'Nor, unless I had a soul triply bound in brass, should I ever dare to put to sea in a frail wooden affair drifting as the wind chooses: but as you know, sir, better than I, a little use makes it seem almost safe, even commonplace. To be sure, both mountain and desert can be mortal for one not brought up to them; but after some generations they seem little more dangerous than a journey to Brighton.'

A midshipman came, walked to Commodore Aubrey's side and discreetly conveyed Mr Harding's duty together with the news that the officer commanding the convoy desired leave to part company.

'Forgive me, gentlemen,' said Jack, rising. 'I shall not be long.'

Long he was not, but already the talk had flowed on, and Jacob was repeating the word 'Mzab' with some emphasis to Mr Wright, who leant forward, one hand cupping his ear.

'Forgive me, sir,' said Jacob, 'I was just explaining how generations of nomadic jewel-trading teach one to survive – the network of trusted associates, often related – the custom of travelling in small family groups – middle-aged women, young children – few guards and those few at a distance –

a modest drove of indifferent horses or camels as ostensible property. I particularly stressed the young and preferably dirty, shabby children: they do away with any idea of wealth. And I did so partly to explain to Dr Maturin how I came to be acquainted with the Zeneta dialect of Berber and the archaic Hebrew of Mzab.'

'An acquaintance I envy you,' said Jack.

Jacob bowed and continued, 'I had been taken along by some Alexandrian cousins, playing the part of unwashed child to perfection; but when we came to their usual resting-place among the Beni Mzab a camel gave me so severe a bite – a bite that would not heal – that they were obliged to leave me and a great-aunt and travel on to an important rendezvous a great way off. It was there that I learnt the double guttural of the Beni Mzab Hebrew and that I became thoroughly at home with the triliteral roots of the Berber.' He gave a good many examples of the Hebrew in question and of Berber grammar, illustrating them with quotations from Ibn Khaldun.

'By your leave, sir,' cried Killick, to Jack's relief, for not only was he thoroughly set-up for a reasonable quantity of spotted dog, but he was afraid that Mr Wright's interest in archaic Hebrew, never very strong, was waning fast.

His interest in food, however, was as eager as Jack's, in spite of his age; and after a while he said in a voice of real authority, 'The French may say what they please, and Apicius, with his slave-fed moray eels, was no doubt very well; but it seems to me that civilization reaches its very height in the glistening, gently mottled form of just such a pudding as this, bedewed with its unctuous sauce.'

'How wholly I agree with you, sir,' cried Jack. 'Allow me to cut you a slice from the translucent starboard end.'

'Well, if I must, I must,' said Mr Wright, eagerly advancing his plate.

Gradually the pudding diminished; the decanters made their stately round; and Jack Aubrey brought up the subject of music. 'Until a little while ago,' he observed, 'I had never heard of a Bohemian composer called Zelenka.'

'Dismas, I believe.'

Jack bowed and went on, 'But then I was given a copy of his Ricercare for Three Voices, which we have now played several times and which I thought we might offer you with your coffee: unless indeed you would prefer the Locatelli C major trio.'

'To tell you the truth, dear Commodore, I *should* prefer the Locatelli. There is something truly dispassionate and as it were geometrical in the trio that touches me, in something of the same manner as your paper on nutation and the precession of the equinoxes, considered from the navigator's point of view, in the *Transactions*. But before that, may I beg Dr Maturin to show me his horn? Then while I am listening, being at the same time in physical contact with the problems posed by this improbable tooth, perhaps intuition may lead me to the solution, as it has done on three or four very happy occasions.'

Jack Aubrey had spoken of coffee, and to be sure it was as inevitable as the setting of the sun; but at present the stronger constitutions were still engaged with the remains of the spotted dog, and all hands were still drinking madeira – most emphatically *all hands*, since Killick, his mate and the boy, third class, who helped him in the background, were very fond of this ancient and generous wine and had perfected a way of substituting a full for a half-emptied decanter at the end of each passing: the dwarvish third-class boy wafted the first decanter out, emptied it entirely into tumblers which the three then drained in hurried gulps as opportunity offered.

Stephen had been aware of their motions for some little while – he was, in any case, well acquainted with Killick's tendency to finish anything that was left and indeed to encourage the leaving, though rarely to this remarkable extent: Stephen had little to say about it on moral grounds, but it appeared to him that the third-class boy, a weedy little villain of about five feet, was very near his limit – he had had more opportunity than the other two and of course much less stamina. It was therefore something of a relief to Stephen when the last decanter, which had furnished the loyal toast, was removed, and Jack, Mr Wright and Jacob looked expectantly at him. 'Killick,' he said, 'pray be so good as to step into my cabin and bring the bow-case hanging behind the door.'

'Aye-aye, sir,' cried Killick, paler than Stephen could have wished, and apt to stare. 'Bow-case it is.'

But bow-case it was not. Killick had seen fit to take the horn out and now he could be seen for a moment in the light of the open door, making antic gestures with its point at the third-class boy, who was draining the last of the wine. 'Oh, oh,' cried the boy, choking, and he plunged forward in a paroxysm of adolescent drunkenness, spewing improbable jets of madeira, grasping Killick's knees and bringing him down. He fell flat on the deck, holding the horn close to his chest. It broke in the middle with a sharp crack, sending off a long sliver that shot into the great cabin.

These things took place in the coach, the small apartment forward and to larboard, generally used on such occasions. Jack strode through it over the two bodies, calling very loud and clear for his bosun, swabbers and the master-at-arms.

Bonden took in the situation at once and in a cold, silent fury he ran the now speechless Killick away forward, while the master-at-arms dragged the limp wretched boy to the nearest pump. The swabbers, old hands at this job, set to without a word: and with extraordinary speed – no comments whatsoever – the frigate's people cleaned up, cleared away, and even before the deck was quite dry, restored the cabin to a wholly clean and civilized condition.

Mr Wright was sitting on the broad locker that ran across the *Surprise*'s great cabin, just by the sweep of stern windows, when Stephen came back, carrying his 'cello and the scores. The old gentleman had the pieces of narwhal horn carefully arranged by his side, the broken parts set together and the eighteen-inch splinter laid so exactly in place that at first sight the horn looked whole. 'Dear Dr Maturin,' he said, 'I fear you must be grievously distressed.'

'No, sir,' said Stephen. 'I do not mind it.'

Wright hesitated for a moment and then went on, 'But believe me, this is one of the few things I can do really well. The providential splinter has shown me the nature of the inner substance; the breaks are perfectly clean; and I have a cement that will knit them so firmly that the tooth will retain all its original strength: a cement that would make dentists' fortunes, were it less noxious. Pray let me take it home with me, will you?'

'I should be infinitely obliged to you, sir, but . . .'

'I used to do the same for Cousin Christine's skeletons many years ago. And while you are playing I shall muse with the other half of my mind on the lower shaft, in which those whorls and spirals are so startlingly obvious. A very extraordinary puzzle indeed.'

'You mean to play, Stephen?' Jack murmured in his ear.

'Why, certainly.'

'Bonden,' called Jack, 'place the music stand and light along my fiddle, d'ye hear me, there?'

'Aye-aye, sir: music stands and light along the fiddle it is.'

Chapter Four

Once again the thunder roared from the saluting batteries as Jack Aubrey's squadron made its painful and dangerous way out of Mahon harbour: short boards down the narrow Cala de San Esteban against an irregular gusting southerly breeze and what tide the Mediterranean could summon up at its worst. A small squadron now, since *Briseis, Rainbow* and *Ganymede* had been sent off to protect the eastern trade and *Dover* was still escorting the Indiamen on their homeward run.

Ringle, leading the way, was nimbler and brisk in stays, as became a schooner of her class, and she was tolerably at home in such waters; so was *Surprise,* handled by a man who had sailed her for the finest part of his life at sea and who loved her dearly – a ship, furthermore, that was blessed with an uncommonly high proportion of truly able seamen, thoroughly accustomed to her ways and to her captain's. Not that theirs was a happy lot as the channel grew even narrower, the cries of 'Hands about ship' more frequent, and the recently-shipped Marines (at least one in each gun-crew) more awkward still: for in common decency the batteries' salutes to the broad pennant had to be returned, returned exactly: and this called for wonderful activity.

Yet the sufferings of the Surprises, though severe and often commented upon, were not to be compared to those of the Pomones, a huddled-together ship's company with a captain who had never commanded a post-ship before, a disgruntled first lieutenant and a new second lieutenant – he was now officer of the watch – who did not know a single man aboard and whose orders were often confused, often misunderstood and sometimes shouted down by exasperated, frightened bosun's mates, far too busy with their starters: and all this in an unhandy, heavily-pitching frigate with far too much sail set forward, pressing down her forefoot.

The Commodore and his officers watched from the quarterdeck: often and often their faces assumed the appearance of whistling and their heads shook with the same grave, foreboding motion. Had it not been for the frenzied zeal of *Pomone*'s aged gunner and his mates she would never have contributed a tenth part of her share of salutes, and even so she cut but a wretched figure.

'Shall I ever be able to use her heavy broadside in the Adriatic?' murmured Jack to himself. 'Or anywhere else, for that matter? Three hundred blundering hopeless grass-combing buggers, for all love,' he added, as the *Pomone* very, very nearly missed stays, her jib-boom brushing the pitiless rock.

Unlikely though it had seemed at times, even the Cala de San Esteban had an end: first *Ringle* cleared the point, stood on and brought the wind abaft the beam; and she was followed by the others. Yet although against probability he had escaped shipwreck, young Captain Vaux (a deeply conscientious officer) did not, like some of his shipmates, give way to relief and self-congratulation. 'Silence, fore and aft,' he cried in a voice worthy the service, and in the shocked hush he went on, 'Mr Bates, let us take advantage of the guns being warm and the screens being rigged and make the signal *Permission to fire a few rounds.*'

Fortunately Mr Bates, whose talents would never have recommended him anywhere, had a thoroughly efficient master's mate and yeoman of the signals: between them they whipped the flags from the locker, composed the hoist and ran it aloft. It had barely broken out before another intelligent young master's mate, the recently-joined John Daniel, murmured to Mr Whewell, *Surprise*'s third lieutenant, 'I beg pardon, sir, but *Pomone* is asking permission to fire a few rounds.'

Mr Whewell confirmed this with his telescope and the yeoman; then stepping across to Jack Aubrey he took off his hat and said, 'Sir, if you please, *Pomone* requests permission to fire a few rounds.'

'Reply *As many as you can afford: but with reduced charges and abaft the beam.*'

Captain Vaux was of a wealthy, open-handed family and he dreaded having the appearance of one who owed his early promotion to his connexions: he wanted his ship to be a fighting-machine as efficient as the *Surprise*, and if a few hundredweight of powder would advance her in that direction he was perfectly willing to pay for them, particularly as he could renew his supplies in Malta.

A few minutes after the Commodore's signal, therefore, the gunfire began again, starting with single chasers, the occasional carronade, and then fairly regular broadsides that surrounded the frigate with a fine cloud of smoke – broadsides that grew perceptibly more regular as time went on.

The stabbing flame and the heart-shaking din of a great-gun exercise of this kind nearly always spread cheerfulness and high spirits – the noise alone was exhilarating, and exhilaration has some affinity with joy. Yet although *Pomone*'s cannon roared and bellowed prodigiously, there was precious little joy aboard her near neighbour the *Surprise*.

Even after dinner (two pounds of fresh Minorcan beef a head) and dinner's charming grog, and even after supper, the general gloom persisted. Killick's misfortune was known to the last detail; the wretched boy's capers were recounted again and again; and the dreadful fall, the shattering of the precious horn.

It was much the same the next day, and the next; and even when Mahon was far astern, beneath the western horizon from the main royal masthead, the squadron holding its course for Malta with a steady, gentle topgallant breeze on the starboard quarter.

No joy among the people of *Surprise*, for the luck had gone out of the ship together with the broken horn: for what could be expected of a broken horn, however expertly repaired? Many a time did the older hands mutter something about virginity, maidenhead; and this, with a melancholy shake of the head conveyed all that was to be conveyed. No joy among those of *Pomone*, either; for not only did their new skipper prove a right Tartar, keeping them at the great-gun exercise morning, noon and night, stopping the grog of a whole gun-crew for the least trifling mistake, but some of those badly hurt by recoil, powder-flash or rope-burn, had to be taken across to the pennant-ship, their own surgeon being so far gone with the double-pox that he did not choose to risk his hand on the delicate cases, and aboard *Surprise* the Pomones soon learnt what had happened. Nor among the Ringles, their captain having dined with the Commodore and his boat's crew having spent the afternoon among their friends and cousins. No joy.

Yet the officer in command of the *Surprise*'s Royal Marines, Captain Hobden, had a long-legged, rangy, limping yellow dog, Naseby, whose mother had belonged to the horse-artillery and who absolutely delighted in the smell of powder, even that which came wafting faintly across from *Pomone*, the laborious *Pomone*. He was a friendly young creature, used to shipboard life and scrupulously clean, though somewhat given to theft: but he at least was thoroughly cheerful, the animal. He was fond of Marines and their familiar uniform, of course, but he also liked seamen; and as Captain Hobden was much given to playing the German flute (an abomination to dogs) while his other ranks spent their free time cleaning their weapons, polishing, brushing and pipeclaying their equipment, Naseby very soon found out the smoking-circle in the galley. It was not a very jovial, lively place at present, but they were kind to him and the women might give him a biscuit or even a piece of sugar; and in any case it was company.

'Well, Naseby, here you are again,' said Poll, when they were far and far from land, the stars beginning to prick. 'At least it wasn't you.' She gave him an edge of cake and went on '. . . there they were, the Doctor and his mate, or rather the two doctors as I should say, stamping up and down in a horrid passion and uttering words which I shall not repeat them in mixed company, like a pair of mad lions.'

At this point Killick came in with an improbable pile of shirts in his arms, kept there by his pointed chin – linen to be aired in the galley when the fires were drawn. He had been washing, ironing and goffering (where appropriate) all Jack's and Stephen's shirts, neck-cloths, handkerchiefs, waistcoats, drawers and duck trousers, and polishing the great cabin's silver to an unearthly brilliance in the hope of forgiveness: but from the great cabin to the galley and even to ship's heads he was still looked upon with a sour, disappointed dislike: and none of the women, nor even the ship's boys, called him Mr Killick any more.

But even in a pitch of distress that had cut his appetite, his pleasure in tobacco and his sleep, his intense curiosity lingered on and now he asked why the doctors were swearing so.

'Well, Killick,' said Poll Skeeping. 'I am surprised *you* should not know, being it was your so-called Hand of Glory, that was to make us all so rich.'

'Oh no,' whispered Killick.

'Oh yes,' cried Poll, tossing her head. 'As *you* know very well, the doctors kept it in a jar of double-refined spirits of wine so that it should stay fresh and clean: and what happened? I'll tell you what happened, if you really *need* to be told. Some God-damned villain or villains had been drawing off the spirit and replacing it with water, so now it's just bloody water and damn all else, while the Hand has grown gamy, like. It is all up with the finer tissues, but at least

95

they have put it out to dry and they hope to draw the tendons and wire the bones together tomorrow evening.'

Alas for their hopes. When in one of their few free moments (*Pomone*'s working-up was proving quite exceptionally bloody; and a surprising crop of boils, disturbingly like the Aleppo button, had broken out in *Surprise*) the medical men approached the table next to a scuttle where the poor hand had been left to dry – indeed to desiccate – they found nothing but a very faint bloody trace, the wooden dissecting board and the print of a large dog's right forefoot on the padded stool.

'Your beautiful present utterly desecrated, deep in the maw of that vile mongrel' – 'All our work wasted,' they cried, and they cursed the dog with extreme violence in Berber and Gaelic.

Stephen found Hobden in the gunroom, fingering his unlucky flute while the two off-duty lieutenants played backgammon. 'Sir,' he said, pale with anger, 'I must have your dog. He has stolen my preserved hand and I must either open him or exhibit a powerful emetic before it is too late.'

'How do you know it was my dog? There are all the ship's cats, thieves to a man.'

'Come with me to the galley and I will show you.'

Naseby was indeed in the galley, comfortably installed among the women, who started up. Stephen seized the dog, raised his deeply-scarred right fore-paw, showed it to Hobden and said, 'There's your proof.'

'You never stole anything, did you, Naseby?' asked Hobden. Naseby was a clever dog: he could find a hare and do all sorts of things like counting up to eight bells and opening a latched door; but he could not lie. Perfectly aware of the accusation, he drooped ears and body, licked his lips and confessed total guilt.

'I must either cut him and recover my hand or give him a very strong emetic: and if the emetic does not work, then it must be the knife.'

'It was your own silly fault for leaving it about,' cried Hobden. 'You shall not touch my dog, you pragmatical bastard.'

'Will you stand by those words, sir?' asked Stephen after a short pause, his head cocked to one side.

'Until my dying day,' said Hobden, rather too loud. Stephen left the room, smiling. He found Somers, the second lieutenant, standing on the forecastle and gazing up at the beauty of the headsails, brilliant in the sun and scarcely less so in the white shadow. 'Mr Somers,' he said, 'I beg pardon for interrupting you – a glorious sight, indeed – but I have had a disagreement with Captain Hobden, who used, and stood by, a very blackguardly insult, made in public – in the galley itself, for God's sake. May I beg you to be my second?'

'Of course you may, my dear Maturin. How very much I regret it. I shall wait upon him at once.'

'Come in,' cried Jack Aubrey, looking up from his desk.

'I beg pardon for interrupting you, sir,' said Harding, the frigate's first lieutenant, 'but I have some awkward, pressing things to tell you.' He said this in a low voice, and Jack led him aft to the locker under the stern windows, where he could speak in perfect safety – in a ship a hundred and twenty feet long with two hundred men crammed into her, privacy was a rare commodity, as he knew from very long experience.

'Well, sir,' Harding went on, obviously disliking the role of informer, 'Dr Maturin has challenged Hobden, Hobden's dog having eaten a preserved hand; and Hobden, having been told that the hand must be recovered by knife or purge, gave Maturin the lie. I tell you this because the people are very much upset. I do not have to tell *you*, sir, that seamen or at least our seamen, are as superstitious as a parcel of old women: they looked upon the horn, sir, as the surest possible guarantee of luck: and next to the horn, or even before it, this Hand of Glory . . . you know about it, sir?'

'Of course I do. Thank you for telling me all this, Harding: it was very proper in you. Now pray be so good as to tell Hobden that I wish to see him at once. He will waste no time with uniform.'

A minute later he called 'Come in' again, and a shirt-sleeved, duck-trousered Hobden appeared.

'Captain Hobden,' said Jack in a tone of the deepest displeasure, 'I understand that your dog ate Dr Maturin's preserved hand, and that when he checked you with the fact you gave him the lie or something worse. You must either withdraw the insult and let him retrieve the hand as best he may, or you must leave this ship at Malta. I cannot give you more than five minutes to reflect, dogs' powers of digestion being what they are. But while you are reflecting, remember this: in the heat of the moment any man may blurt out a blackguardly expression: yet after a while any man worth a groat knows he must unsay it. A note of apology would answer, if you find the spoken word stick in your gullet.'

Hobden changed colour once or twice – a variety of emotions appeared upon his face, all of them wretchedly unhappy.

'If you choose to write it now, here are pens and paper,' said Jack, nodding to his desk and chair.

For some time Jacob and Stephen Maturin had been talking about the pleasanter sides of their evening with Mr Wright as they sharpened their instruments on a variety of hones and oilstones by the Argand light in the orlop. When they had finished discussing their dispassionate and geometrical treatment of the Locatelli, Jacob said, 'Yet earlier on I fear I was somewhat too loquacious, with my examples of the Zeneta dialect and the double gutturals of the local Hebrew; but at least I did not bore the company with an account of what is perhaps the most curious thing about the Beni Mzab – curious, but difficult to explain in a few words.

I mean the fact that not only are the Moslems Ibadite heretics, but many of the Jews are Cainites, equally erroneous according to the orthodox.'

Stephen reflected, grinding still, and then said, 'I do not think I know about Cainites.'

'They derive their descent from the Kenites, who themselves have Abel's brother Cain as their common ancestor: furthermore, the initiated still bear his mark; though discreetly, since they do not choose to have it generally known, there still being so many vulgar prejudices against him. This shared mark of Cain forms the strongest bond imaginable, far outdoing that between Freemasons, and of infinitely greater antiquity.'

'So I should imagine.'

'In early Christian times some of them formed a Gnostic sect; but those belonging to the Beni Mzab have returned to the ancient ways, maintaining that Cain was brought into being by a superior power and Abel by an inferior; and that he was the ancestor of Esau, Korah and the Sodomites.'

'Come in,' called Stephen.

Captain Hobden came stooping under the lintel. 'I beg pardon for interrupting you, Doctor Maturin. I beg your pardon. Here is my apology' – handing his letter – 'and here is my dog.'

'You are very good, sir,' cried Stephen, starting up and shaking his hand. 'Do not fear for Naseby: these are very simple operations, and I would not hurt him for the world.'

Seamen, according to Dr Maturin's experience, were even fonder of remedies that could be seen and felt to work at once than most people; and the *Surprise*'s medicine-chest was well stocked with powerful emetics.

'There is little hope,' said Stephen as he slid the dose down Naseby's unresisting throat. 'At this late hour there is little hope, at all.'

'On the other hand, the animal's early detection and

99

subsequent evident guilt may well have diminished or even arrested his digestive secretions.'

'Hold the bucket and belay, there. Stand back.'

Sick, sick as a dog he was: but indeed it was too late. 'Yet at least we have virtually all the bones,' said Stephen, stirring with a pair of retractors. 'And they are almost untouched. All the rest is now meaningless, but once the bones are boiled clean we can wire them together: the hand will be even more emphatically hand-like, and that will comfort the crew. Poll. Poll there! Be so good as to call for a couple of swabbers, and I will take this poor fellow back to his master.'

The wiring-together with the help of the carpenter's finest drills, the very convincing wiring-together, which was completed before the end of the last dog-watch, did indeed comfort the crew. They waited in files to see the dead-white fingers rising tall and high from the neat pattern of carpal-bones set in black-gleaming pitch, the whole enclosed in a stern-lantern glass. Each group, having gazed upon it for the regulation minute, hurried back to the beginning of the line to see it again; and it was universally agreed that a more Glorious Hand did not exist. No one was foolish enough to mention luck, but the Surprises wore a deeply satisfied look that said much more than any open exultation.

At quarters the next day they were still unusually lively and cheerful in spite of the falling breeze, backing so far easterly that it might come foul before the end of the exercise, and that also carried drifting swathes of mist, and sometimes rain. But even downright snow would neither have chilled or damped their spirits, and they ran their guns in and above all out with a fine hearty thump.

Then, just before the drum beat the retreat and hammocks were piped down, an extremely shrill and piercing voice from the foretopmast cried, 'On deck, there. On deck, there. Two sail of ships, four points on the starboard beam. Standing south-east. Just about hull-up.'

'Mr Daniel,' called Jack to the master's mate. 'Follow me

aloft with my night-glass from the cabin, will you?' He was settled in the topgallant cross-trees by the time Daniel and the telescope reached him; but whereas the Commodore was puffing, Daniel, in spite of his recent hardships, was not.

'There, sir,' called the lookout some way along the yard. 'Just abaft the preventer-stay.' And there indeed, just for a moment, was a white blur: perhaps two white blurs. Then the low cloud hid them entirely.

'Joe,' said the Commodore, who had known the lookout from childhood, 'what did you make of them at best?'

'Just when I hailed, sir, they were pretty clear. I should have said a right man-of-war, a medium frigate: trim, though foreign. And maybe a merchantman in her wake. Under all plain sail. But when I see them again they had altered course, working to windward; and I am reasonable sure the frigate heaved a white flag aboard, as though for a parley, like.'

Jack nodded, smiling: the white flag, showing either submission or an absence of hostile intent or a wish to speak was often used as a ruse de guerre to obtain intelligence or even sometimes a tactical advantage: in any case he was not going to present his squadron on the lee-bow of any potential enemy. Yet before he called down the orders that would do away with such an uncomfortable situation, a tear in the low cloud and a certain diffused moonlight showed him the two strangers fairly clear. They were not indeed under a press of sail, but they had more abroad than *Surprise* or *Pomone*, and they were certainly steering a course that would presently give them the weather-gage, with all the advantages it conferred – power to attack or to decline battle as they saw fit, and a sense of general comfort. He also saw, though only as a squarish pallor, the white flag that Joe Willett had mentioned; but he paid little attention, his mind being taken up with ensuring that in these variable airs and currents and *Pomone*'s imperfections, first light would find the squadron well to windward of the strangers.

Below him, as he revolved the possibilities, the Marines

beat the retreat, hammocks were piped down, and at eight bells the watch was mustered: all these operations were carried out correctly, but with a most uncommon degree of levity – jocose remarks, open laughter, antic gestures with the hammocks.

It was the master, Mr Woodbine, who had the first watch: Jack told him that the squadron should very gradually increase sail – no appearance of anxiety or hurry – and perpetually work to windward, so that at dawn they should certainly have the weather-gage. He then summoned the *Ringle*, and to her captain he said, 'William, I am not going to ask *Pomone* to come within hail in this head-sea, so you run down, lie under her larboard quarter and tell Captain Vaux with my compliments that there are two strange sail in the east-north-east – did you see them?'

'Yes, sir: we caught just a couple of glimpses through the murk.'

'What did you make of them?'

'I thought they might be frigates. One was wearing a white flag for a parley.'

'Parley be damned, William. Those wicked brutes are edging away to gain the weather-gage. Obviously we must do the same, and Devil take the hindmost.'

'Amen, sir: so be it.'

'So you run down and tell *Pomone*, will you? She is a fairly weatherly ship, in spite of bows like a butcher's arse. Then crack on and bear away to windward and see if you can learn anything of them to tell us at first light.'

The *Ringle* filled and spun about: Jack walked into his cabin and leant over the charts, considering the probable local currents in this weather and at this time of the year. He had had a very good noon observation and both his chronometers agreed admirably: with the present wet obscurity he could hope for no external confirmation, but he was reasonably certain of the ship's position; and in any event there were no cruel coasts nor uncomfortable shoals in this part of the sea. With the present breeze or even with twice the present breeze he had sea-room enough to manoeuvre against the potential enemy until noon tomorrow: his only anxiety was the *Pomone*, with her unhandy crew. He was unwilling to use top- or even stern-lanterns, which might so easily betray his motions; but in order that poor Vaux with his band of boobies should not lose the pennant-ship altogether he had a stout, well-provisioned boat veered astern, carrying Bonden and half a dozen of his shipmates, who were to guide the frigate with a fisherman's light if ever she offered to stray.

This accomplished he took a last look at traverse-board and log-readings, pencilled a tentative disk on his chart, with the exact time, returned to the deck and the familiar, welcome task of driving his ship to windward, taking advantage of every very slightly favourable shift in sea or wind. With his own people round him, keenly attentive to his orders and expert in carrying them out intelligently, with the utmost speed, he made such excellent way that two bells later and with the utmost hesitation Harding, his first lieutenant, begged his pardon and observed that *Pomone* was dropping far behind, while there was real danger that the cutter astern might tow under.

His words aroused displeasure, strong displeasure among all within earshot: but on looking round Jack cried, 'By God, you are right, Harding . . . I am driving her altogether too hard.' He raised his voice and gave the orders that deadened her way – orders that were obeyed slowly, with sullen looks, but that nevertheless changed the voice of the sea on her cutwater, down her sides and under her rudder from a thrilling urgency to something quite commonplace in a matter of minutes.

'Beg pardon, sir,' said Killick, 'but supper will be on table whenever you please.'

Stephen was already in the cabin, trying to play a half-forgotten tune pizzicato on Jack's second-best sea-going fiddle. 'I heard this long ago at a crossroads meeting something north of Derry and perhaps just in the county Donegal, the kind of gathering for music and song and above all for dancing that we call a ceilidh; but there was a dying fall near the end that I cannot recapture.'

'It will come to you in the middle of the night,' said Jack. 'Pray draw up your chair and let us fall to: I am fairly wasted with hunger.'

They ate a large quantity of ox-tail soup, Jack fairly shovelling it down like a boy, then half a small tunny, caught by trolling over the side, and then their almost invariable toasted cheese, a Minorcan formatge duro, not unlike Cheddar, that toasted remarkably well.

'What a joy it is to satisfy desire,' observed Jack when all was done. He emptied his glass, threw down his napkin, and said, 'Will you not turn in now, Stephen? It is very late. I shall be doing nothing but work steadily to windward: there will be no excitement until well on in the morning watch, when I hope to find these skulking villains under our lee.'

Comfortable words: but scarcely had hammocks been piped up (at six bells, this being a Sunday morning) and scarcely had the sound of stowing them in the nettings been superimposed upon that of the decks being thoroughly cleaned, than something very like a battle broke out, starting with fairly distant gunfire, then deep-voiced cannon no great way off.

Yet there was no interruption in the steady swabbing overhead, the flogging of the spotless quarterdeck to spotless dryness, no excited cries, no orders, and above all no beating to quarters; and as the *Surprise* began to fire Stephen's mind arose, not without difficulty, still somewhat bemused from an extraordinarily vivid, *and coloured* dream of wiring a small primate's skeleton together, Christine Wood directing or performing the more delicate movements, and he realized that this was not an engagement at all but the leisurely, regular, and perfectly dispassionate return to a salute.

A young gentleman darted in, stood by Stephen's cot and in a very shrill voice he cried, 'Sir, if you please: if you are awake the Captain desires you will come on deck, *in uniform.*' He had obviously been told to emphasize the last words, and this he did with such force that his voice broke an octave above its usual pitch.

Messages about uniform and respectability had also reached Killick, who now, opening the door, called out, 'By your leave, Mr Spooner, I have to attend to the Doctor. Captain's orders. Not a moment to spare – the Devil to pay and no pitch hot.' Quite what he meant by this was far from clear, but he hustled the boy out, and with a zeal to be equalled only by his desire for forgiveness he plucked Stephen's nightshirt from him, sponged and soaped his face, shaved it as close as a bridegroom's, clothed him in clean drawers, a cambric shirt and his regulation garments, hissing the while as though to soothe a restive horse, arranged his cravat, clapped on and smoothed his best wig – all without a word in answer to Stephen's now peevish enquiries but with an intensity that compelled respect – and so led him up to the quarterdeck, delivering him to Harding by the capstan with a final tweak.

'There you are, Doctor,' cried Jack, turning from the starboard rail, 'a very good morning to you. Here's a glorious sight.'

Blinking in the glare of the early sun, Stephen followed his pointing hand, and there rode a fine proud frigate together with a smaller, shabbier companion, probably a twenty-two-gun corvette: they were both wearing the Bourbon ensign, a white flag with a white cross; and rather more than half-way between the two French ships and *Surprise* a captain's barge was rowing with an even stroke.

Stephen had been quite extraordinarily far down in his dreaming sleep, and even after his brisk handling and the brilliant dawn all round he found it hard to fix his mind on Jack's explanation: '. . . so there he is in his barge, coming across to breakfast. Do not you recognize him, Stephen? Surely you recognize him? Take my glass.'

Stephen took the glass. He focused it, and there, sharp and clear in the early sun, was the happy, familiar face of Captain Christy-Pallière, their captor a little before the Algeciras action in 1801 and then their host in Toulon during the brief peace that followed. 'How happy I am to see him,' he cried.

'Yes. He declared for the king at once, and so did all his officers – they had almost finished refitting in a little yard south of Castelnuovo, bar some spars and a certain amount of cordage – but many of the other sea-officers up and down the coast were all for Bonaparte or for setting up on their own account, and some are preparing for sea. He had meant to head straight for Malta, where he had friends, but the wind would not serve (as it does not serve for us) so he came by Messina, and in the straits he picked up that corvette, commanded by a cousin of his.'

Already the Marines were beginning to form on the quarterdeck; the bosun had his ceremonial whistle, the sideboys were fiddling with their gloves. Stephen was gathering his wits, but not as quickly as he could have wished – the dream still hung heavily about him. He glanced aft, where the *Pomone* lay with a backed foresail, heaving on the swell; and the sight of her, though she was not a vessel he could like, brought him more nearly into the present world. The *Ringle*, with a tender's modesty, rode under the Commodore's lee.

The French barge hooked on: the side-boys ran down with their padded man-ropes, and the moment Captain Christy-Pallière set foot upon the steps the bosun raised his call and piped him aboard in style.

'Captain Christy-Pallière,' cried Jack, taking him most affectionately by the hand, 'how very happy I am to see you here, and looking so uncommon well – I do not have to introduce Dr Maturin, I am sure?'

'Never in life,' said Christy-Pallière in his perfect English. 'Dear Doctor, how do you do?' They too shook hands, and Jack went on, 'But you will allow me to present my first lieutenant, Mr Harding. Mr Harding, this is Captain Christy-Pallière, of His Most Christian Majesty's frigate *Caroline.*'

'Very happy, sir,' said each, bowing; and Jack led his guest below.

'First, Commodore,' said Christy-Pallière, taking his seat at the breakfast table, 'let me congratulate you on your broad pennant. I have never saluted one with half so much pleasure in all my life.'

'How kind you are to say so: and may I say how very agreeable it is to have you sitting here as a friend and an ally. Apart from anything else, I know how short-handed or rather short-shipped poor Admiral Fanshawe is in Mahon. He will greet you with open arms, if only to convoy a few merchantmen to the chops of the Channel.'

'Might I beg you to give me an introduction?'

'Of course I will. May I help you to another sausage?'

'Oh, if you please. I have not smelt this divine combination of toast, bacon, sausage and coffee since last I was with my cousins in Laura Place.'

They talked about the cousins and about Bath for a few moments and then settled to really serious eating. Grimble, Killick's mate, had been a pork-butcher by land, and given a bold, thriving hog he could turn out a Leadenhall sausage of the very first order.

Eventually they reached toast, marmalade and the third pot of coffee, and Jack Aubrey said, 'My orders take me to the Adriatic. With a favourable wind I shall look into Malta for possible but improbable reinforcements and the latest intelligence from those parts, and then proceed to Durazzo and beyond for the purpose of strengthening royalists and of capturing or destroying Bonapartist or privateering ships. Would it be indiscreet to ask you how the land lies along the coast? I mean the places where there are shipyards that would concern me one way or the other?'

'It would not be in the least indiscreet, my dear Aubrey,' said Christy-Pallière, 'and I will freely tell you all I know. But the situation there is so extremely complicated, with doubtful loyalties, concealed motives, blunders in Paris, that I should have to collect my wits – recollect myself . . . and I think I could best give you a fairly clear notion of things as they were when I left Castelnuovo if I were to be looking at your charts.'

It was clear to Stephen that Christy-Pallière felt that matters to do with intelligence were no proper subject for general conversation. He agreed most heartily, and presently – two cups of coffee later – he excused himself: not only were there his morning rounds but he also had a minor operation to perform.

'We shall see you again in the sick-bay towards the end of divisions,' said Jack to him, and to his guest, 'I am so glad that you are here on a Sunday. I shall be able to show you one of our Navy's particular ceremonies: we call it divisions.'

'Oh indeed?' cried Christy-Pallière. 'Then in that case may I beg that *Caroline*'s secretary may be present? He takes the utmost interest in these matters, and he is writing a comparative study of the different nations' naval economies, disciplines, ceremonies and the like.'

'Does the gentleman speak English?'

'Not a word,' cried Christy-Pallière, laughing at so wild a notion. 'Richard speak English? Oh dear me no. Wonderfully fluent in Latin, but English . . . oh, ha, ha, ha!'

'Then perhaps Dr Maturin could join us at the beginning of divisions,' said Jack, with a questioning look at Stephen.

'Very happy,' said Dr Maturin, perfectly at ease, since Jacob would be present, with everything perfectly in order when the Commodore and his guest came to inspect the sick-bay. So when five bells in the forenoon watch resounded there he was, so unnaturally trim that he almost did the frigate credit. The bosun piped divisions, and in the howling of the long-drawn notes the Commodore, with his guest and Mr Harding, walked up to the quarterdeck, followed by Stephen and Richard.

Here, as exactly arranged as the men on a chess-board in spite of the swell, stood the *Surprise*'s Royal Marines, drawn up athwartships right aft, with their officer, sergeant, corporal and drummer. They were in their fine scarlet coats, white waistcoats, tight white breeches and gaiters; their black stocks were as trim and tight as was consistent with breathing at all, their muskets, side-arms, buttons gleaming. Ordinarily, when they were helping with the work of the ship or making part of a gun-crew, they wore seaman's slops, sometimes with an old Marine jacket or cap. The high pitch of military splendour was reached only when they were on guard-duty or at this climax of the week; and out of Christian charity Jack inspected them first, so that they could be dismissed and no longer suffer in the sun.

This done, with a fine stamp, a dismissive clash of arms and a roll on the drum, the Commodore turned to the purely nautical side.

'As you see,' murmured Stephen, 'the various divisions, each under a particular lieutenant, with sub-divisions under his midshipmen or master's mates, are already standing along predetermined lines upon the deck. They are in their best sea-going clothes, they are newly-shaved, their pigtails have been tied afresh. This has taken them two and a half hours; and they have been closely inspected by their lieutenant and his midshipmen. And now, as you see, the Commodore inspects them all over again – see, he checks a midshipman for not wearing gloves. But on the whole there are very few reproofs . . . very little occasion for reproof in so seasoned and competent a ship's company.'

'Is nobody to be flogged?'

'No, sir. Not at divisions.'

'I am glad of that. It is a spectacle that I find extremely painful.'

Jack had finished with the first division: he said something kind to the lieutenant and the senior midshipman and moved on. The group he had just inspected was made up of the afterguard and waisters, but in such a ship as the *Surprise* almost all of them were right seamen, though some might be a little less nimble than they were: Stephen knew every soul present except for those who replaced the casualties in the recent action; and even of these one had been shipmates with him in the *Worcester*. He had a word with most, particularly those he had treated, calling them by name, until half-way along the line, when he came to a face, a perfectly distinct, typical middle-aged seaman's face, brown, wrinkled, gold-earringed, yet one that baffled him again and again, as the waister knew very well: he was used to it and he called out, 'Walker, sir, if you please; and much better for the bolus.' They both laughed: Stephen said, 'I must take one myself, to jog my memory.'

'Is this familiarity usual in the service?' asked the *Caroline*'s secretary.

'Only in ship's companies that have served long together,' said Stephen.

'In a Russian ship, such a remark . . .' began the secretary, but he checked himself as they came to the next group, under Whewell, the third lieutenant, and three comparatively mature midshipmen or master's mates. These hands, all prime seamen, managed the midship guns in a way and at a speed that gave Jack the utmost satisfaction: many of them came from that curious little port Shelmerston, when the *Surprise* was a letter of marque. Stephen knew them and their families, had treated them again and again for everything from the cruellest wounds and scurvy to piles, with the usual seamen's diseases in between. Many, if not most of them he had always called by their Christian names. 'Well, Tom,' he said, 'how are you coming along?' The

Commodore, the French captain and Mr Harding were well ahead, so some of Tom's wittier companions answered for him, in hoarse whispers – Tom had got a young woman with child again – and there was a good deal of stifled mirth.

The ceremony carried on, past the forecastle-men, the oldest, most highly-skilled seamen in the ship, then to the boys – the few ship's boys – under the master-at-arms, and so by way of the galley with its gleaming cauldrons and coppers, which Jack ritually wiped, looking at his spotless handkerchief, and so to the sick-berth, which Poll Skeeping and her friends had reduced to such a supernatural state of cleanliness that the two patients (bloody flux), pinned in their cots by tight-drawn, unwrinkled sheets, dared neither speak nor move, but lay there as though rigor mortis had already reached its height.

The sick-berth, however gratifying, was only a preliminary to the climax of divisions; and when Jack, Stephen and Christy-Pallière returned to the quarterdeck they found everything set out, with chairs for the officers and a kind of lectern made of an arms-rack with a union flag draped over it for the captain.

'Shipmates,' said he, with a significant look, 'this Sunday I am not going to read a sermon. Let us just sing the Old Hundredth. Mr Adams' – to his clerk – 'pray give the note.'

The clerk drew a pitch-pipe from his bosom, blew the note loud and clear, and the ship's company fearlessly joined their captain in the psalm, a fine deep body of sound. The frigate had a moderate breeze on her larboard quarter, with *Pomone* no great way astern; and when the Surprises had uttered their full-throated amen, the Pomones' hymn reached them over the water, admirably clear. Jack stood listening for a moment, then he squared to the lectern, opened the book the clerk had brought him, and in a strong, grave voice he read the Articles of War, right through to XXXV: 'If any person who shall be in actual service and full pay in his Majesty's ships and vessels of war, shall commit upon the shore, in any place or places out of his Majesty's dominions, any of the crimes punishable by these articles and orders, the persons so offending shall be liable to be tried and punished for the same, to all intents and purposes, as if the same crimes had been committed at sea, on board any of his Majesty's ships or vessels of war.' And to XXXVI, the catch-all: 'All other crimes, committed by any person or persons in the fleet, which are not mentioned in this act, or for which no punishment is directed to be inflicted, shall be punished according to the laws and customs in such cases used at sea.'

During this familiar series of articles (twenty-one of which included the death penalty) Stephen had been reflecting on his quite unusually happy morning and the evident good will that surrounded him as he walked along the decks. He rarely saw many of his shipmates at any one time; and for a long while now those that his duties or his leisure had brought him into touch with had been grave and if not reserved then something like it – concerned only with the matter in hand, unwilling to speak at length, even embarrassed – no open expression of sympathy, still less of condolence, until the horn was broken, when Bonden and Joe Plaice and a few others he had known for a great while, said 'it was a cruel hard thing – they were very sorry for his trouble.'

That day Stephen dined in the gunroom, with Richard as his guest. The sense of well-being continued. Black desolation underlay it, as he knew perfectly well; but the two could exist in the same being. Some part of the gunroom's friendliness would certainly have been caused by the presence of his guest, part of his happiness to the fact that he was speaking French most of the time (a language in which he had been wildly happy, amorous and even politically enthusiastic when he was a student in Paris), and part to the excellence of the dinner; but there remained an overplus that he had to attribute to his return to what was, after these many years, his own village, his own ship's company, that complex entity so much more easily sensed than described: part of his natural habitat.

The long pause after the gunroom's dinner, while Jack and Christy-Pallière carried on with their conversation in the cabin, was filled, as far as Stephen and Richard were concerned, with medical consultation. 'I do not in any way mean to criticize the Royal Navy's food,' said Richard, when they were alone. 'An excellent dinner, upon my word, and remarkably good wine. But what was that ponderous mass, glutinous and yet crumbling, enveloped in a *sweet* sauce, that came at the end?'

'Why, that was plum duff, a great favourite in the service.'

'Well, I am sure it is very good if you are used to it: but I fear that such very *heavy* cooking does not suit my digestion, delicate from childhood. Frankly, sir, I think that I may die.'

After the usual questions, palpations and other gestures, Stephen suggested a comfortable vomit: this was rejected with a shudder, but a moderate glass of brandy was exhibited with some small beneficial effect, and they spent the rest of their time playing a languid series of games of piquet for love, keeping themselves awake with coffee.

At last however they heard the bosun's call and the watch on deck manning the side; and a midshipman came below with the Commodore's compliments: *Caroline*'s barge was pulling across.

It was an affectionate farewell between the two commanders, but both were hoarse with talking; and when Jack Aubrey turned from the side after a last wave to Christy-Pallière he looked tired and worn. 'Can you spare me a minute?' he asked Stephen.

'How I wish you had been with us,' he went on as they sat by the stern windows, watching the French ship haul her wind and head for Mahon, followed by her shabby consort.

'It would never have done.'

'No. I suppose not . . . but if only someone could have

taken notes. He is a dear fellow and a capital seaman, but he does tend to ramble in his speech and start false hares: and in any case it is, as he often said, an extraordinarily complicated situation in the Adriatic – divided loyalties – some good men on either side, but more waiting to see which way the cat jumps, or as Christy put it "trying to reinsure themselves" in either event. And some of course are just out for the main chance, privateering on their own account or with Algerine renegadoes. Most of them think that Boney will win; and to be sure he had collected an extraordinary number of followers . . . One of the things that struck Christy most was the utter confusion in Paris. He went there last year, and having made the proper declarations and sworn the same oaths all over again at their Admiralty, and having complained in the right quarters about the continued delay in payment for the repairing and refitting of *Caroline* in Ragusa, he attended a levee. There were many people there, several of them men he had never seen who were wearing naval uniform, sometimes of high rank, who stared at him: it was a curious atmosphere of caution and jockeying for position – it was known that he had come up from the Adriatic and some of his service acquaintances avoided him. But when the king spoke to him quite kindly and told a naval aide-de-camp to ask Monsieur Lesueur to receive him that day, there was a singular change – he was no longer potentially dangerous to know. Yet the change had not reached the Ministry: there he found a different set of officials who did not know him, who did not know anything at all about him or his ship – what was her name? What type of vessel? – and who, looking at him with narrowed eyes, made him go through all the earlier formalities once more. Monsieur Lesueur was not available, they said; but he might be the next afternoon. So he was, and although he kept Christy-Pallière waiting for an hour and three quarters he did say that he was sorry for it – that Christy would understand that at such times he was not master of his movements – that the Ministry would very much appreciate a detailed report on the position in the Adriatic, where it was feared that irregularities might be taking place – and that Captain Christy-Pallière would be well advised to wait on Admiral Lafarge.

'Christy-Pallière had served under Lafarge in his youth: they had neither of them liked one another then and they neither of them liked one another now. Lafarge's face was still scarlet from his last interview and in the same angry tone he asked Christy-Pallière who the devil had given him leave to come up to Paris, and brushing aside his explanation told him that His Majesty did not pay him for whoring about in the capital and making interest for himself: his clear duty was to return to his ship directly, to attend to her repair and refitting, and to await further orders. The Admiral wished neither to listen to his excuses nor to see him again.

'Christy also told me that this Admiral Lafarge had a half-brother and a cousin in the Adriatic, both of whom were said to have been in communication with Bonaparte when he was on Elba; and that may be an explanation. Just what it might explain I do not know: but I tell you what, Stephen, my wits are strangely muddled – not only am I afraid of forgetting half what Christy told me, but I am as far out of my depth in this devious kind of business as he was: more so, indeed. When we had brought him back to his ship – and a horrible journey he had of it, poor fellow – he said it would be easier for him to explain the situation in the Adriatic, as far as he understood it at all, if we were standing at the chart-table. Shall we do the same?'

'By all means.'

'Well, here is Castelnuovo, on the northern tip of the Bocche di Cattaro: *Caroline* was being repaired and refitted in a perfectly reputable yard just round the headland. Inside the bay there were two brigs of war not far from completion. Now up to Ragusa Vecchio, and there is a thirty-two-gun frigate almost ready for sea after a long refitting in two different yards – almost ready but for some of the shortages that I had and a near-complete lack of cables and hawsers: she is commanded by a fervent Bonapartist. He is called Charles de La Tour, an odd sort of fellow – Christy rather likes him, in a way. A pretty good seaman, and not at all shy: several creditable actions, and it was he who made that dash at *Phoebe*, very nearly cutting her out. But extremely romantic and a great admirer of Byron: he learnt English on purpose. The only thing Christy cannot bear is this passion for Bonaparte. La Tour knows the campaigns through and through and he is said to carry one of the imperial gloves in his bosom. Yet he is of considerable family and perfectly well bred. By the way, I should have said that although most of the sea-officers up and down the coast are reasonably sure that Bonaparte will win, not many have openly declared for him. This Ragusa Vecchio ship, which according to rumour is paid for in part by a group of Algerines, is moored up against the ruined castle. Now moving northward up the islands, there are at least half a dozen small yards building cutters, xebecs and brigs, obviously intended for privateering: yet recently work has almost stopped for want of funds and material. But moving up to Spalato, there lies the *Cerbère*, pretty well ready for sea, whose commander, never happy with the Empire or the Emperor, would be perfectly willing to surrender to Louis XVIII's allies if they appeared in face-saving force and made a great deal of noise. On the other hand, Christy was really anxious about the number of people who were sitting on the fence and the amount of damage they could do if things looked just a little better for Bonaparte – the havoc they could work on the supplies for the Valetta yards: timber, cordage and everything that came down from the Dalmatian shore.'

He paused. 'And he was even more concerned with some kind of a plot that he had heard of at third or second hand but that neither he nor his best, most trustworthy informant thoroughly understood – the informant's English was most imperfect in any case and Christy's Greek and lingua franca worse. Yet imperfect though it was, the account impressed him very deeply. It appears that the Mussulmans of the country are preparing to send a very powerful, seasoned force of mercenaries north to prevent the junction of the Austrian and Russian armies – if possible to make each side believe in the treachery of the other – but in any case to delay their united march westward, giving Napoleon time to bring up his reserves from the south-east and to establish himself in a very strong position for battle. He felt that there was an extreme urgency. That is why he put to sea, with most of his water and half his cables still on shore.'

'I am sure he is right,' said Stephen. 'So is the Admiralty: that is why we are here. I think you know that Jacob, my nominal assistant, was assigned to me by Sir Joseph? He has worked in our department for years. He speaks the languages of these parts with extraordinary fluency. What I should like you to do is to put him aboard the *Ringle* and desire William Reade to carry him with all possible speed to Kutali – we have true friends in that fine city, I believe – there to learn all that Sciahan Bey and his vizier, the Orthodox bishop and the Catholic bishop, and all the private connexions he may have can tell him, and then to return to us with the same extreme rapidity, either in Malta or if I may suggest it, on our way up the Dalmatian coast.'

Jack Aubrey gazed earnestly at his friend for a minute; then he nodded and said, 'Very well. Give Dr Jacob his orders and what introductions you think fit, and I will summon *Ringle*.' He touched the bell, and to Killick he said, 'My compliments to Dr Jacob, and should like to see him as soon as it may be convenient.'

'Dr Jacob,' he said, a few moments later, 'pray sit down. Dr Maturin will tell you the reason for this somewhat abrupt summons; and in the mean time I shall go on deck.'

On deck he said to the signal midshipman, 'To *Ringle*: *Captain repair aboard.*'

117

William Reade came up the side, his hook gleaming and with something of the look of a keen, intelligent dog that believes it may have heard someone taking down a fowling-piece. Jack led him below. 'Now, William,' he said, guiding him to the chart-table, 'here is Kutali, a fine upstanding city, going up like the stairs inside the Monument; or it was when I last saw it. The approaches are straightforward and you have good holding ground in fifteen to twenty fathoms from here to here: only you want to have two anchors out ahead almost to the bitter end if the bora sets in. And you are to take Dr Jacob there. In all likelihood you will outsail us, so unless you receive orders to the contrary you will proceed to Spalato the moment Dr Jacob is aboard again: still with the utmost dispatch.'

'To Kutali it is, sir, and then to Spalato, with the utmost dispatch in both cases,' said Reade. 'Is the gentleman ready?'

Ready or not, Jacob was hurried aboard the schooner with what letters Stephen had had time to write to his friends in Kutali, with a clean shirt wrapped up by Killick and his best coat, and with Stephen's words nestling in his ears: 'The whole essence is to learn whether the Brotherhood's messengers have been sent, and if so whether they can still be intercepted. Money is of no consequence whatsoever.'

Ringle did indeed outsail *Surprise* and *Pomone*, but not to such an extent as she might have done if Captain Vaux had not grown more used to the ways of his ship and had not so changed her trim, bringing her by the stern, that even in these moderate breezes she gained nearly a knot on a broad reach. The schooner was indeed just in sight from the masthead when they rounded Cape Santa Maria at dawn, but she soon vanished with the coming of the sun. It rose over the Montenegrin heights, and for a while the far coast remained sombre though the zenith was already a brilliant, quite light blue. This eastern shore was a coast familiar to

Jack and Stephen: in the very same ship they had sailed up from the Ionian Sea reasonably far along the Adriatic.

They drew in with the land – a fine topgallant breeze on the larboard quarter – and presently the sea grew more and more populated with feluccas, trabaccaloes, merchantmen of various rigs and sizes making for the Bocche di Cattaro or emerging from the splendid great harbour, and with fishermen, some in fast xebecs with twenty-foot-long trolling rods out on either side, like the antennae of some enormous insect.

One hailed the *Surprise*, and drawing alongside, pointed to their catch, a single tunny, but so huge that it filled the bottom of the boat – a fish that would feed two hundred men. The master, a jovial soul, called out to Jack, 'Cheap, cheap, oh very cheap,' and made the gestures of eating – of eating with delight.

'Pass the word for the cook,' said Jack, and to the cook, who stood there wiping his hands on his apron, 'Franklin, nip down into the boat: look whether it is a today's fish, and if so, set a fair price.' Franklin was considered a judge of fish and a competent hand with the lingua franca.

'Dead fresh, sir,' called Franklin, looking up from the boat. 'Still warm.'

'Do you speak figuratively?' asked Stephen.

'Anan, sir?'

'Do you mean warm *warm*, as who should say a rabbit was so fresh killed that it was still warm?'

The cook looked anxious, and made no reply; so Stephen scrambled down the side, tripped over the xebec's gunwale and fell on his knees in the tunny's blood.

'Well, sir,' said the cook, setting him upright, 'now you've fair wrecked and ruined your trousers – which it will never come out – so you might as well put your hand in the place where they gaffed him and where all this blood is coming out of.'

'By God, you are right,' cried Stephen, rising and shaking

Franklin's reluctant hand. 'It is against nature – I am amazed – amazed and delighted.'

The cook fixed the price in a passionate five-minute argument, referred it to the purser, who nodded, and then said to Stephen, 'By your leave, sir, by your leave,' as a double whip came down from the mainyard to hoist the great fish aboard.

Stephen came up the frigate's side again, leaving traces all the way. 'That was wonderful, wonderful,' he cried, disengaging himself from Killick's officious hand. 'I must run downstairs for a thermometer.'

The whole ship's company dined on that enormous fish; and this being Thursday, a make-and-mend day, they sat about on deck, some quite stertorous, all delighting in the gentle breeze that tempered the sun.

'I can scarcely remember a more agreeable day,' said Stephen, looking up from his notes, '– and there, just above the high land behind Castelnuovo, is a pair of spotted eagles, almost exactly where I saw my first. I only regret that Jacob was not here to view, to experience the tunny's blood. But I shall read such a paper to the Royal, ha, ha . . .' He dipped his pen, took another draught of coffee, and wrote on.

'Mr Harding's duty, sir,' said a midshipman, 'and the cutter is alongside.' Jack followed him, and looking down at the squalor he said, 'Well done, Mr Whewell. I do not think anyone would connect the boat with the Royal Navy.'

'I hope not, sir,' said Whewell, surveying the grease, slime, plain filth and tawdry ornament fore and aft, the knotted rigging and the crew of flashily undressed criminal lunatics. 'I did not like to come aboard in quite this shape.'

'The gunroom might have blushed at quite so much rouge,' said Jack. 'Well, shove off now, Mr Whewell, if you please. Fortunately the breeze is veering, and I do not think you will have to pull back.'

Nor did they. The cutter was seen coming round the point at dawn, close-hauled and making a good five knots: her crew had spent much of their time cleaning the boat and themselves, and although neither sails nor rigging could do the *Surprise* any credit until the bosun and the sailmaker had taken her in hand again, Whewell did not hesitate in coming aboard, nor indeed in breakfasting with the Commodore and his surgeon.

'Well, sir,' he said, 'there she was, lying in front of the old castle, as you said: but there were two armed polacres with her, or rather a polacre and a polacre-settee: both Algerines, I take it.'

'How many guns did they carry?'

'It was very difficult to make out, sir, the ports being closed and great heaps of sailcloth and cordage dangling over the sides, but I should say probably twelve for the one and perhaps eight for the other. Nine-pounders, I should imagine, though I cannot assert it. A great many people aboard.'

'Shore batteries, I dare say?' Jack was not good at dissembling: Stephen noticed the artificial lightness of his tone, but gazed steadily at the coffee in his coffee-cup.

'Yes, sir: one at each end of the mole. I did not like to be too busy with my glass, but I thought I could make out six emplacements in each. I could not speak to the nature of the guns.'

'No, of course not.' A pause. 'Mr Whewell, pray help yourself to bacon: it stands at your right hand – the covered dish.'

Chapter Five

When Captain Vaux came aboard the pennant-ship in response to a signal he found the great cabin still comfortably scented with bacon, coffee and toast.

'Good morning, Vaux,' said the Commodore, offering him a chair. 'Mr Whewell had just given me his report on Ragusa Vecchio, where that Bonapartist frigate is lying. As you know, she is moored by the mole in front of the old castle. She has been very short of stores and cordage, but now it seems probable that she has been supplied with them by her Algerian friends: there are two of them with her at present, a polacre and a polacre-settee, both armed and mounting perhaps a score of guns between them, nine- or at the most twelve-pounders. There are also two shore-batteries with six gun-emplacements each: how armed I cannot tell. Now if, as it seems probable, she has the cables and hawsers to allow her to put to sea, she is very likely to go off cruising with her Algerian companions: the present situation makes some people think that Napoleon will very soon be restored. So I think we should deal with this frigate at once. We will sail up the coast prepared for action and summon him: if he does not comply, why so much the worse for him. Or conceivably for us: he carries eighteen-pounders. But since today is a banyan day I have ordered beef to be served out instead of the dried peas, as being a better foundation for battle. You might consider of it.'

'I too shall certainly order beef, sir,' said Vaux.

'With this breeze and a steady glass, I believe we should raise Ragusa Vecchio at four or five bells in the afternoon watch. But there is this question of shore-batteries: Mr Whewell reports one at each end of the mole – come and look at the chart. Here we are. He could not tell what guns they mounted, but even nine-pounders intelligently fired – and generally speaking the French artillery is very good – could annoy us in our approach, knocking away spars and even masts. You have your full complement of Marines, I believe?'

'Yes, sir: under a very capable, experienced officer, Lieutenant Turnbull.'

'Well, that makes sixty-five between us: and it occurs to me that if we land them here' – he pointed to a small bay just south of Ragusa Vecchio – 'they can cross the slight rise to the next beach and take the batteries from behind. The mole will protect them from the frigate's guns, once they reach it. Let our Marine officers consider the plan and tell us what they think. Your Mr Turnbull is the senior, I believe?'

'Yes, sir: and he has led some remarkably dashing attacks by land.'

'Very well: they will turn it over in their minds while we are filling cartridge and rousing out our dreadnought screens. I think we should weigh at about four bells: that will give us plenty of time to have dinner quietly and clear for action with no mad frenzy.'

So little frenzy was there, indeed, that when somewhat before the appointed time Stephen walked aft from the bows, where he had been watching a flight of Dalmatian pelicans, presumably from the Scutari lake, he found Jack Aubrey playing his violin in the cabin – a cabin that was already pretty bare, but by no means really stripped for action.

Jack listened to his account of the pelicans, of the hundreds and hundreds of pelicans and their curious evolutions, no doubt associated with the mating season, and then said, 'I know little of birds, as you are aware; but let me tell you of a remarkable instance of humanity in our own kind: the Royal Marine officers waited on me to give their opinion of my suggested attack on the shore-batteries. They thought it an excellent scheme – were much pleased with the idea of tearing along under the shelter of the mole – but they proposed that just for this occasion, it being so uncommon hot, their men might be indulged in trousers rather than tight breeches and gaiters, and that they might take off their stocks.'

Four bells, loud and clear; and Mr Harding could be heard, louder and clearer, giving the order to ship capstan bars. From that time on there was little point in playing the violin or even conversing, for although the capstan on the quarterdeck was not directly overhead, its bars, now in place, swept back almost to the wheel, and once the messenger had been made fast to the cable, once it had taken the strain and the bosun had cried 'Stamp and go' and a little wizened old forecastle-hand had leapt onto the capstan-head with his fife and played the tune of 'Round and round and round we go, step out my lads and make your feet tell 'em so', the whole space below was filled with a huge confusion of sound dominated by the rhythmic tread of the men at the bars and punctuated by innumerable cries, and by the indescribable sound of the great sodden cable coming in, attached by nippers to the messenger, and then, they being cast off, plunging heavily down to the tiers in the orlop where very strong men coiled it and stowed the great coils away.

The frigate glided over the water quite briskly, then slower, slower until the bosun called 'Right up and down, sir,' and the officer of the watch replied 'Thick and dry for weighing,' a cry instantly echoed from the depths by the extraordinarily penetrating voice of Eddie Soames, the ship's eunuch, always good for a laugh.

The Surprises, who had done this hundreds of times before, catted and then fished the anchor: this accomplished, they hurried to their stations for making sail: but no order came from aft. Both Jack and Somers had seen that the less skilled Pomones were having difficulty with passing the cat-hook: indeed, some had fallen from the cathead into the sea.

'Thick and *wet* for weighing,' called Eddie Soames, 'Ha, ha, ha.'

However, it appeared that they were soon fished out, for presently *Pomone* spread most of the canvas she possessed and somewhat later she assumed her proper position a cable's length astern of the Commodore: and thus they sailed easily along the coast, both ships now completely cleared for action – everything peaceable struck down into the hold, shot-garlands filled, screens in place over the magazines, deck sanded and wet, cutlasses sharpened and ready to hand, together with boarding-axes and pistols; while down below Stephen's operating-table (the midshipmen's sea-chests lashed together and covered with tight-drawn number eight sailcloth) was ready, the lantern hanging just so, and dressings, pledgets and coil upon coil of bandages tactfully covering the leather-bound chains necessary for some operations. To one side there lay the grim saws, retractors, tenacula, scalpels, bistouries (sharp and blunt-pointed), forceps, trephines, single-edged amputating knives and catlings, arranged with loving care by Poll and her friend the bosun's wife's sister, both of whom wore starched aprons, bibs and sleeves, and white caps. Buckets, and the usual lavish supply of swabs.

They were sailing almost directly before the wind – not *Surprise*'s best point of all, but one that nearly did away with any strong sense of motion; and the perfect regularity of the slight following swell added much to the dreamlike impression. Time scarcely existed, except for the succession of bells, and in spite of their martial appearance the remarkably well-fed crew tended to stare at the even, deserted coast as it passed slowly by quite close at hand, and doze. There was little sound from the ship at this gentle pace, and Naseby, shut up in the hold, could be heard howling from boredom.

Jack, the master and Stephen were in the bows, the master holding an azimuth compass. 'It is my impression,' said Jack, 'that when we round this point we shall be in a shallow bay whose farther side overlooks Ragusa Vecchio. What do you say, Doctor? You have been here twice.'

'If it has a low island in the middle of it, swarming with terns at this time of the year, then I am sure you are right,' said Stephen, 'since even from half-way up the further slope the tower of the ruined castle – the very top of it – can be seen.'

'My instrument is not as accurate as I could wish,' said Mr Woodbine, 'but I am inclined to agree with you.'

The two ships rounded the point, and there before them, to starboard, lay a shallow bay with a low island in the middle; and even from here the coming and going of innumerable birds could be made out, while Stephen, borrowing the Commodore's telescope without so much as a 'by your leave', and resting it on the cathead, named the species: 'Gull-billed ... Caspian, what joy! Another ... Sandwich ... many, many common terns, dear creatures ... little tern ... black ... I believe, yes, I believe he must be a white-winged black tern. I am amazed.' He turned to share his amazement, but found that he was alone. Boats were already lowering down from both ships, and the Royal Marines, their muskets gleaming and their red coats brilliant in the sun, were about to embark.

The boats pulled away, loaded to the gunwales – *Pomone*'s pinnace had ludicrously muffled its oars – steering for the shore immediately below the point where the tower of the ruined castle just broke the even skyline.

They landed their men – scarcely more than a ripple on the strand – and then as the boats made for the northern tip of the bay, Jack made sail to recover them and so stood on. Five minutes later Ragusa Vecchio came into view, a decayed straggling village north of the ruined castle; and at the bottom of the bay the frigate in question, with the two Algerian vessels. Boats passing to and fro over the smooth water: the fine topgallant breeze still at south-south-west.

Surprise and *Pomone* both beat to quarters. Jack ordered colours to be hoisted and said to the master, 'Mr Woodbine, lay me twenty-five yards from her larboard bow and then back topsails. Doctor, be so good as to stand by to translate.'

There was great activity aboard the French frigate, and they seemed to be casting off their moorings. The polacre had already won her single anchor and her companion was slipping her cable.

The *Surprise* sailed between them and the Frenchman, backed two of her topsails and lay there rocking gently.

Jack hailed the Frenchman with the usual cry of the sea, 'What ship is that?' his words echoed by Stephen Maturin.

A remarkably handsome young man on the quarterdeck – post-captain's uniform and cocked hat, which he raised – replied, '*Ardent*, of the Imperial Navy.'

At this there was a universal and singularly impressive cry of 'Vive l'Empereur!' from the *Ardent*'s company.

'My dear sir,' Jack went on, returning the salute, 'France is now ruled by His Most Christian Majesty Louis XVIII – by my master's ally. I must ask you to hoist the appropriate colours and accompany me to Malta.'

'It grieves me to disappoint you, sir,' said the *Ardent*'s captain, now very pale with anger, 'but it would be contrary to my duty.'

'It grieves me to insist, but if you do not comply we shall be obliged to use force.'

During this time, lengthened by the need for translation, the Algerians had been making short boards: they now lay on the *Surprise*'s larboard bow and quarter and their people were shrieking orders or advice.

'Port-lids, both sides,' called Jack.

The gun-crews had been waiting for the word, and now

the red-painted lids all flew up as one, while two seconds later the guns ran out with a deep echoing thump.

The same happened aboard the Frenchman. 'Messieurs les Anglais,' called the *Ardent*'s captain, 'tirez les premiers.'

Who in fact fired the first shot was never decided, for once there had been a chance explosion aboard the polacre-settee, both sides went to it as fast as ever they could, a most enormous shattering din that echoed from the castle and the mole, gunfire that covered the immediate shore with a dense cloud of white smoke shot through and through with stabbing orange jets of flame.

At first *Surprise*'s fire was rather slow – she had not enough hands to fight both sides at once: but very soon the slight-built Algerines found they could not bear the weight of her shot and they retreated out of range.

At first the roar of gunfire on the *Ardent*'s side had been much increased by the shore-batteries, firing eighteen-pounders; but even in the tumult of battle the Surprises caught the rapid decline, and those with the odd seconds to spare nodded to one another, smiling, and said, 'The Jollies.'

And scarcely had the Marines silenced the last of the batteries' guns than three well-directed shot, fired from *Surprise*'s aftermost guns on the downward roll, pierced the *Ardent*'s side, striking her light-room. There was a small explosion, the beginning of a fire, and then some seconds later a second explosion, enormously greater. A vast column of smoke and flame shot into the sky, darkening the sun.

The aftermost third of the frigate was wholly shattered: the wreckage sank directly and the rest followed in a slow hideous lurch, settling on the bottom with only her foretopmast showing. Yet even before she had settled the sea was torn and lashed by falling debris – her whole maintop with several feet of the mast, many great spars, scarcely broken, countless blocks and unrecognizable great smouldering lumps of timber: most of it fell somewhat inshore, but smaller pieces were still raining down minutes later, some trailing smoke.

'Avast firing,' cried Jack in the unnatural deafened silence that followed. 'House the guns. Mr Harding, lower what boats we have left' – the launch on the booms was pierced through and through – 'and bid *Pomone* come within hail.'

He ran below, where Stephen was just straightening after having placed a splint on a torn and broken arm that Poll was quickly, expertly bandaging. 'The Doctor will soon put you right, Edwardes,' he said to the patient, and drawing Stephen aside he asked him privately how urgent he thought their mission to Spalato. 'Of the very first urgency,' said Stephen. Jack nodded. 'Very well,' said he. 'What is our damage?'

'Harris shot dead with a musket-ball. Six splinter-wounds, one dangerous; and two men hurt by falling blocks.'

A very, very modest butcher's bill. Jack said a word to each of the men waiting to be treated and returned to the deck. *Pomone* had already come abreast. 'Captain Vaux,' he called, 'have you suffered much?'

'Very little, sir, for such a brisk turn-to, short though it was. Four powder-burns; one gun overset, four pair of shrouds cut and damage to the running rigging. Some men hurt by falling blocks and timber. But our boats are all sound.'

'Then pray lower them down. Pick up what survivors you can and recover our Marines. Land the prisoners at Ragusa – the *new* Ragusa up the coast – and then follow me to Spalato without the loss of a minute.'

During the later part of their voyage to Spalato, rendered tedious by capricious winds varying from a furious bora, shrieking down from the north and blowing the foretopmast staysail from its boltrope to very gentle breezes right aft that often died away to a flat calm, and by the hazardous nature of the Dalmatian coast with its many islands, not to say vile reefs, Stephen spent much of his time aloft, at the topmast cross-trees. With practice he had grown used to the climb to the maintop, though nobody liked to see him make the attempt, however smooth the calm; and he asserted that he could certainly rise even higher, to the cross-trees, with perfect safety. This however was never countenanced, and Jack required John Daniel to accompany the Doctor if ever he showed an inclination to view anything from a greater height than the carriage of a bow-chaser.

Daniel had sailed these waters in a ship belonging to Hoste's squadron and once he had overcome his shyness he not only told Stephen the names of the various headlands, promontories and islands but also described some of the actions in which he had taken part, often giving an exact account of the number of round-shot fired and the weight of the powder expended.

Stephen liked the young man, open, friendly and candid, and one day, as they were sitting up there, he said, 'Mr Daniel, I believe you attach a particular importance to number?'

'Yes, sir, I do. Number seems to me to be at the heart of everything.'

'I have heard others say so: and one gentleman I knew in India told me that there was a very special quality in primes.'

'To be sure,' said Daniel, nodding. 'They give one great pleasure.'

'Can you explain the nature of that pleasure?'

'No, sir: but I feel it strongly.'

'Number as the perception of quantity is no doubt a pitifully limited aspect of its true nature; but how many feet, would you say, is it from here to the deck?'

'Why, sir,' said Daniel, glancing down, 'I should reckon a hundred and twelve. Or shall I say a hundred and thirteen, which is prime?' He looked at Stephen's face, expecting the pleasure he felt himself; but Stephen only shook his head.

'There are some unfortunates to whom music brings no sort of delight: I fear that I am excluded not only from the joy of prime numbers and surds but from the mathematics as a whole. I could wish it were otherwise. I should like to join the company of mathematicians, of people like Pascal, Cardan . . .'

'Oh, sir,' cried Daniel, 'I am no mathematician in that glorious sense. I just like to play with numbers – fix the ship's position from a quantity of observations, with as small a cocked hat of error as possible, calculate the rate of sailing, the compound interest on ten pounds invested at two and three quarters per cent a thousand years ago, and games like that.'

'In an early bestiary,' said Stephen after a long pause, 'an antiquarian of my acquaintance once showed me a picture of an amphisbaena, a serpent with a head at each end. I forget its moral significance but I do remember its form – its immensely enviable power of looking fore and aft' – he slightly emphasized the nautical term and went on, 'All this bell I have been twisting and turning like a soul in torment, trying to make out the *Pomone* behind and the *Ringle*, God bless her, together with the fabled city of Spalato in front. My buttocks are a grief to me.'

'Well, sir,' said Daniel. 'I believe I could suggest a solution, was you to tell me which you had rather see first.'

'Oh, *Ringle* without a doubt.'

'Then I will turn about, facing aft; and should *Pomone* heave in sight before sunset, or whenever you choose to go down on deck, I will give you the word. But before I turn let me beg you to look at Brazza again, the big island well beyond the point of Lesina: then to the left of Brazza you have some low-lying land: and when we are a little closer you will see a narrow passage between it and Brazza. Indeed, you could see it now, with your glass.'

'So I can: very dark and very narrow.'

'Well, from the way he is trimming sail, I believe Mr Woodbine means to take us through in spite of the wind abeam. He knows these waters uncommon well. It is not very long, thanks be, and we are a weatherly ship: and when you are through, there is Spalato right before you.'

There indeed was Spalato right before them, the horrors of the very dark and very narrow passage forgotten and the setting sun casting an indistinct but wonderfully moving glory on the enormous rectangle of Diocletian's palace.

And before *Surprise* was wholly clear of the channel the immense voice of the lookout at the foremasthead called, 'On deck, there. On deck. *Ringle* fine on the starboard bow.'

Jack instantly gave a series of orders: before she reached the open water the frigate was under bare poles, riding to a kedge in the gentle outward current. By the time *Ringle* was alongside and Reade aboard *Surprise* with Dr Jacob, darkness had fallen, and fireflies could be seen drifting across the strait.

Jack took them both below, but Jacob was bleeding so profusely from a wound that he had contrived to inflict upon himself as he came up the side, probably on a shattered length of the gunwale, that Stephen had to lead him away, send his breeches to be soaked in cold water at once, sew up the gash, and then ask Poll to bandage it and to find a pair of clean duck trousers that would fit. While this was doing, Jacob asked, 'You did not receive my dispatches, I suppose?'

'Never a one. Have the Brotherhood's messengers left?'

'Three days ago. Your friends in Kutali received me nobly and told me a great deal: let me summarize. In the very first place the Sheikh of Azgar has promised the sum required for the mercenaries: the news came more than a week ago. The Russians and Austrians are still dawdling – there is said to be suspicion, ill-will, on both sides. Zeal among the Moslem Bonapartists reached a feverish point when a pilgrim back from one of the Shiite shrines in the farther Atlas reported seeing the gold being weighed out in the presence of Ibn Hazm as he passed through Azgar. The heads of the

Brotherhood met in a Moslem village, resolved all difficulties to do with personal dislikes and rivalries and appointed five of their most considerable members, two of them influential figures in Constantinople. They are riding by the pashas' relays to Durazzo and there they will take one of Selim's fast-sailing houarios for Algiers. There they are to beg the Dey to transport the money, the treasure, promised by the Sheikh. It may be possible to intercept them between Pantellaria and Kelibia.'

Jack opened the door of the sick-bay and looked in. 'Forgive me for interrupting you,' he said, 'but I just wanted to ask Dr Jacob where the French frigate is lying.'

'Over by the Marsa, sir, the broad northern end. There are some merchantmen from the Barbary Coast fairly near.'

'How many guns does she carry?'

'I am sorry to say that I never noticed, sir, but so many, according to his secretary, that he could not decently surrender to a little nine-pounder frigate.'

'I see,' said Jack. 'Thank you, Doctor.'

'I am afraid I offended him,' said Jacob, when the door had closed.

'Never in life, colleague,' said Stephen. 'Pray go on.'

But Jacob had been so shaken by that cold look of dislike that it took him some moments to collect his ideas. 'Yes,' he said, 'well, I took it upon myself to send word to our friend in Ancona and to arrange a meeting with the heads of the Carbonari as soon as you should appear. I hope this does not embarrass you?'

'Not in the least. Has a time been named?'

'Just after the rising of the moon.'

'At what o'clock would that be?'

'I took it to be at night, of course, but I am sorry to say I cannot be more precise.'

'I *have* seen the moon by day, looking very whimsical in the presence of the sun. However, I shall ask the Commodore.'

'Commodore, dear,' he said some moments later, 'would you know when the moon rises tonight?'

'At thirty-three minutes after midnight; and she is just five degrees below the planet Mars. And Stephen, let me tell you something: *Pomone* is in this channel, no great way astern. If I were on my own I should send a French-speaking officer aboard the French frigate to tell her captain that *Pomone*, a thirty-gun eighteen-pounder frigate, and the twelve-pounder *Surprise* would enter the harbour at first light tomorrow, that they would fire half a dozen blank broadsides at close range, to which he would respond, also with blanks; and that then, decencies preserved, we should all make sail, leaving by the broad north-west passage if this leading wind holds as I expect, and proceed to Malta. But would this interfere with your plans?'

'Not in the least: and if you wish I will carry your proposal over to the *Cerbère*.'

'That would be very kind of you, Stephen. Should you like me to write it down?'

'If you please.'

Jack scratched for a while, and passing the list he said, 'You will see that I have underlined *blank* every time: but in his agitation the poor man might not think to draw all his guns before the first exchange. You will put him in mind of it, if you please . . . but tactfully, *tactfully*, if you know what I mean.'

'What would be a proper time for this visit?' asked Stephen without the least sign of having heard but reflecting upon his friend's large, clear, somewhat round and feminine hand, his instant reaction in time of nautical crisis, and his not uncommon ineptitudes.

'As soon as you have put on your good uniform and Killick has found your best wig. A boat and a bosun's chair will be ready.'

The captain and the officers of *Cerbère* were an intelligent set, and since captains usually collect men of a like mind, they were all thoroughly dissatisfied with the present state of affairs. They longed to be out of this ambiguous posture, and it was with a general satisfaction that they saw the light of a boat pulling, man-of-war fashion, from the narrow mouth of the Porte di Spalato. They all of them studied it with their night-glasses and when its obvious intention was to come aboard them, the officer of the watch ordered a bosun's chair to be rigged: they had already experienced Dr Jacob's almost fatal attempt at coming up the side.

They hailed the boat as a matter of form, and they were somewhat shocked when the reply 'a message from the English commodore', though in French, was not in Jacob's French. However, they lowered the chair and Stephen came aboard with what grace could be managed with such a vehicle but at least dry, clean and orderly.

He returned the first lieutenant's salute, said that he should like to speak to the captain, and was shown into the great cabin.

Captain Delalande received him with a grave courtesy and listened to what he had to say in silence: when Stephen had finished he said, 'Be so good as to tell the Commodore, with my compliments, that I agree to all his proposals, and that I shall reply to his and his consort's blank broadsides with an equal number, equally blank, that I shall follow him through the Canale di Spalato, and then proceed to Malta.' He coughed, unbent a little, and proposed coffee.

When they had drunk two cups and eaten two Dalmatian almond biscuits, the tension had so far diminished that Stephen asked whether the captain had ever known the firing of a salute or the like to be accompanied by the involuntary discharge of a ball, the drawing of the cannon having been overlooked.

'No, sir,' said Delalande, 'I have not. When we fire a salute or anything of that nature, we like the gun to make as much noise as possible. And to this end we withdraw the ball – in itself precious enough, I assure you, and much regarded by the Ministry – and replace it with more wads and sometimes a disk or two of wood as well.'

Stephen thanked him and took his leave, escorted by a lieutenant; and not only on the quarterdeck but also in the waist of the ship among the hands he noticed approving, even friendly looks. It was not only in the Royal Navy, he concluded, that secrecy was the rarest commodity aboard a ship.

'My dear William,' he said, safely on the tender's deck, 'I dare say the moon will be up presently?'

'In about half an hour, sir,' said Reade.

'Then if it can be spared, would you be so very kind as to lend me your little boat and a reliable, grave, sober man to carry Dr Jacob and me ashore in let us say twenty minutes?'

'Of course I will, sir: should be very happy.'

'Jack,' he said, walking into the cabin where the Commodore and his clerk were busy with book after book of accounts, 'I do beg your pardon for this untimely . . .'

'Tomorrow morning, Mr Adams.'

'. . . but I have first to tell you that Captain Delalande wholly accepts your proposals: he will expect you at first light tomorrow.'

'Oh, I am so . . .'

'On the other hand the Brotherhood's messengers have already left for Algiers. Now I must write a minute for Malta and then go to a conference ashore. Until tomorrow, brother.'

'The doctors are going ashore,' said Joe Plaice to his old friend Barret Bonden.

'I don't blame them,' said Bonden. 'I should like to see the sights of Spalato myself. I dare say they are going to burn a candle to some saint.'

'That's a genteel way of putting it,' said Plaice.

At six bells in the middle watch, when all the larboard and most of the starboard guns had been drawn and reloaded with powder that Jack kept for saluting, the doctors came back. They were kindly helped up the side by powerful seamen and they crept, weary and bowed, towards their beds.

'Wholly shagged out,' said the gunner's mate. 'Dear me, they can't hardly walk.'

'Well, we are all of us human,' said the yeoman of the sheets.

'There you are, gentlemen,' called the Commodore from by the wheel. 'You have come aboard again, I find. Let me advise you to get what sleep you can, for presently there may be too much noise for it.'

'Kedge up and down,' cried Whewell from the bows.

'Win her briskly, Mr Whewell,' said Jack, and directing his voice aft, 'Are you ready, Master Gunner?'

'Ready, aye ready, sir,' replied the gunner, that bull of Bashan.

'Mr Woodbine,' said Jack to the master, 'we will take her in now: just topsails. You can make out the Frenchman's lights, I believe?'

'Oh yes, sir.'

'Then steer for a point a cable's length astern of her and then run up her larboard side within fifty yards. But I shall be on deck again by then.' He walked aft and called over the dark water, '*Pomone!*'

'Sir?' replied Captain Vaux.

'I am about to get under way.'

'Very good, sir.'

'Hands to make sail,' said the master to the bosun, who instantly piped the invariable call. 'Topsails,' said the master. In almost total silence the hands appointed to gaskets, sheets, clewlines and buntlines, ties, halyards and then braces carried out their tasks with barely a word, at great speed: a pretty example of exact timing, co-ordination and long-established skill, if there had been anyone there who did not take it for granted.

The topsails rose; they filled and they were sheeted home: the ship began to move, with the warm breeze steady on her larboard quarter. Within moments she had steerageway, and the water spoke down her side, as gently as the breeze in the rigging: out of the shelter of Brazza she began to roll and pitch just a little – it was life renewed after that lying-to.

Light there was none, apart from the faint blur of the moon behind very high cloud – never a star – and here and there remote top-lanterns on the shipping far on the starboard bow and the odd cluster of lights on the distant quay. Dark and silent: so dark that even the topsails grew faint towards the height of the cross-trees.

All along the starboard side the gun-crews stood mute, some just visible above their shaded fighting-lanterns: midshipmen or master's mates behind them: lieutenants behind each division.

Mr Woodbine kept his eyes fixed on the *Cerbère*'s lit stern from the moment they cleared the channel: it grew larger, brighter and brighter. He glanced across at the Commodore, who nodded. 'Round to,' said Woodbine to the man at the wheel, and then, as *Surprise*'s turn laid her parallel to the *Cerbère*, 'Dyce, very well dyce,' and he steadied her on this course. When her bows came level with the Frenchman's quarter the master backed the main topsail, taking the way off her, and Jack cried 'Fire!'

Instantly the ship's side shot forth an enormous volume of sound and an immense smoke-bank lit with brilliant flashes – smoke that drifted evenly over the *Cerbère*, which replied through it with an even greater roar – greater, though as Jack noticed with satisfaction, not quite so exactly uniform.

Stephen Maturin, worn limp as an old and dirty pair of stockings after countless hours of negotiation, mostly in Slavonic languages that he understood no more than Turkish and that had to be translated, all in a stifling atmosphere, with people playing shawms outside to prevent the possibility of eavesdropping – shawms in no key known to him or range of intervals – had lain flat on his cot the moment he reached it, plunging instantly into a stupor rather than a Christian sleep.

From this his body leapt up at the first prodigious crash, leaving its wits behind it: and when the two came together he found that he was sitting by the door, his body as tense as a frightened cat's. Understanding and recollection came with the next roaring broadside; he recognized his dimly-lit surroundings and groped his way on deck.

He arrived for the Frenchman's next reply. Above the smoke the whole low arch of the sky was brilliantly lit – the Algerine merchantmen could be seen frantically making sail, innumerable lights on shore running about, the whole city clear in a momentary blaze of light.

Surprise drew ahead and now it was *Pomone*'s turn, her eighteen-pounders making an even more shocking din, improbably loud: again and again, on both sides, the almost simultaneous flashes lit the sky – astonished sea-birds could be seen, flying in a wild, uncertain fashion.

'Well, Doctor,' said the Commodore, just beside him, 'I am afraid you had but a short nap of it: but we shall soon have done – Mr Woodbine, I believe we may go about.' And aside to Stephen, as the bosun piped *All hands about ship*, 'There is that big Kutali xebec, flying in a state of dreadful concern, as though this were the end of the world, ha, ha.'

'It sounds very like it, and looks very like it,' said Stephen, and he muttered, '. . . *solvet saeclum in favilla.*'

Now they were on the other tack, running gently down the side of *Cerbère*: it was the turn of the larboard guns and this time they were so close that some of the Frenchman's smouldering wads came aboard, to be put out with a great deal of laughter, and indignant, often very cross cries of 'Silence, fore and aft' from the midshipmen.

Yet another tack, yet another apocalyptic series of shattering broadsides – renewed screeching, howling and running about on shore – distant drums and trumpets, church bells ringing – and having given the order to reload with right cartridge and ball, and to house the guns, Jack carried straight on, shaping a course for the Canale di Spalato, followed by *Cerbère* and *Pomone*, with *Ringle* under his lee. He called for stern-lanterns and top-lights, desiring Mr Harding to dismiss the starboard watch once courses had been set, and went below himself, ludicrously walking on tiptoe. In the cabin – the bed-place – that they had shared for so many years, he found Stephen, not dead asleep – far from it – but writing.

'I hope I do not interrupt you,' he said.

'Not at all. I am only setting down a succinct account of my conversation in Spalato with certain organizations for the benefit of the Admiral's intelligence officer in Malta; and as soon as it is done, my duty, as I see it, is to go to Algiers as fast as ship will fly.'

'What do you think we should do?'

'Obviously I cannot dictate to a Commodore; but as far as the single aim of defeating this intervention by Bonapartist mercenaries, this potentially "extremely dangerous intervention" as the Secretary of State put it, I think we should run down the coast, looking attentively into the yards that contain vessels in any state of forwardness – and then as soon as we have examined Durazzo, straight away for Algiers, keeping the sharpest possible watch for a houario between Pantellaria and Kelibia. Then, it being assumed that we do not catch the vessel, I should go on in *Ringle* to dissuade the Dey from carrying the promised treasure across, while you remain, a very present threat on the horizon, a powerful, famous frigate, seen by all shipping that comes and goes.'

'No *Pomone*?'

'Her eighteen-pounders are very well, but this is no longer a matter of direct physical strength. We have already dealt with the two dangerous heavy frigates and I have – at *enor*-

mous expense, I may say – set in train a series of measures that will rid us of several smaller but still dangerous vessels repairing or nearing completion – brigs-of-war, corvettes, three gunboats. Letting *Pomone* return to Malta with her companion seems to me a master-stroke.'

Jack considered. 'Very well,' he said. 'We shall do as you say. As soon as you have finished your account I will send it across to *Pomone*, who will carry it to Valetta.'

A violent ten-minute downpour had cleared the sky without much deadening the prosperous topgallant breeze: day was breaking fair and clear in the east and looking southward at his companions he saw that *Cerbère* had hoisted the French royal ensign. 'Mr Rodger,' he said to the signal midshipman, 'to *Ringle*: *Send a boat aboard pennant*, if you please.'

The young man had seen much great-gun exercise, but he had never been in anything so very like action as this and he was still at least three parts deaf, as well as stupid from lack of sleep. Jack repeated the words somewhat louder, but the grizzled yeoman had heard the first time and he had the hoist not exactly ready, but clearly evident.

'Stephen,' said Jack, 'I do not mean to hurry you in the least, but as soon as you have finished a boat will carry it to *Pomone*. Shall I send word too, stating our aims?'

'It might be as well: just "it has been agreed that . . ." Yours will be a separate cover.' He drew the candle towards himself, melted wax, and sealed his brief account: as a matter of course he wrapped it in oiled silk, thrust the whole into a sailcloth pocket, sealed that too, and passed it over.

'I wonder that so fumble-fisted a companion can be as neat as a seamstress when it comes to parcels: or opening your belly, for that matter,' reflected Jack, watching him.

'Use makes master,' observed Stephen.

'I never said a word,' cried Jack. 'I was as mute as a swan.'

Ringle's boat came alongside. The young officer received the parcel reverentially, and Jack put his ship about, heading back to the coast with the wind two points free, followed by the *Ringle*. As they passed those bound for Malta they exchanged greetings, some formal, others, from the open gunports, facetious and even bawdy. The Commodore had it in mind to observe an already ancient naval tradition and throw out a signal consisting of book, chapter and verse: 'Oh that my words were now written, oh, that they were printed in a book' was the quotation that had been addressed to him in the Baltic by Admiral Gambier when he was very slow with a return of stores; but before he could think of the references, a truly heavenly smell of coffee and kippered herrings wafted along the quarterdeck.

'Mr Rodger,' he said to the signal midshipman, 'should you care to breakfast in the cabin?'

'Oh yes, sir, if you please.'

'My compliments to Mr Harding, and should be happy if he were to join us.'

It was a cheerful breakfast, and copious, as Jack Aubrey's breakfasts always were whenever he was anywhere near a civilized shore; and his present cook Franklin was an old Mediterranean hand, with a genius at shopping in lingua franca, gestures, and cheerful repetition growing louder and louder until the poor foreigner (Dalmatian in this case) understood. The kippers had of course been brought from home, but the perfectly fresh eggs, butter, cream and veal cutlets were from the island of Brazza itself and the new sack of true Mocha from a friendly Turkish ship encountered off the Bocche di Cattaro.

Harding had been in the Adriatic with Hoste in 1811, serving as second in *Active*, 38, and since they could now see the island of Lissa through the stern windows, on the starboard quarter, with very little prompting he gave a vivid account of that famous action, one of the few frigate-battles of the war, with ten of them engaged, besides smaller vessels, illustrating the movements of the squadrons with pieces of crust.

Breakfast was necessarily late that day and the very exact

account of an engagement with so many ships in constant motion made it later still. *Favorite* had only just run aground in shocking confusion when a midshipman came in, and begging the Commodore's pardon, asked if he might tell Dr Maturin that Dr Jacob would like to speak to him.

'I hope not to be a moment,' said Stephen. 'I would not miss a single manoeuvre.'

'Have I done wrong in calling you?' asked Jacob. 'I thought you would like to see the first results of our conversations in Spalato.' In the bright sun flames could not be seen to full advantage, but the great trail of smoke drifting west-north-west was very eloquent. 'Bertolucci's yard, of course,' said Jacob. 'It had half-completed *Néréide*, a . . . what is smaller than a frigate?'

'A corvetto.'

'Just so: a corvetto. The men have not been paid these three weeks and more . . . I believe I see French sailors trying to put the fire out.'

'Should you like to climb into that platform up there, with a perspective glass?'

'Not at all, not at all. Besides, there are our morning rounds, and it is already late. Surely you have not forgotten young Mr Daniel, your guardian spirit?'

So practised a body of men as the Surprises could ordinarily fire a rapid series of broadsides without doing themselves much harm, but this time, almost entirely because of levity and mirth, there were three or four hands in the sickberth, some from rope-burns as they tried to check the gun's recoil, and some from getting in the way of the carriage itself. The exception was John Daniel, the only true casualty: Captain Delalande, like his opponent, preferred that his gunfire, however formal, should make a great deal of noise, and he too had the charge rammed home with wooden disks. One of these, flying out ahead of the wad, had struck poor Daniel in the chest, breaking his collar-bone and making a great livid bruise.

Stephen had certainly not forgotten him; but later in the morning, with all the patients dressed, bandaged and treated (in Daniel's case with a comfortable dose of laudanum), he was glad to be able to make his way into the maintop unescorted as the frigate ran (or rather crept, the breeze dying on them) between Sabbioncello and Meleda.

Papadopoulos' yard on the one and Pavelic's on the other had already been destroyed: only a little smoke rose from the sail- and rigging-lofts, ropewalks and blackened hulls. He stared fixedly at the southern end of Sabbioncello, where according to his list there was a small yard belonging to one Boccanegra: but as Boccanegra, a Sicilian, had a father-in-law of importance among the Carbonari and their sometimes very curious allies, Stephen was not sure that his yard was part of the bargain. He stared with increasing intensity as the frigate moved gently across the placid Adriatic, focusing and refocusing Jack's telescope, some remote part of his mind was aware of the striking of eight bells, the assembly of officers making the noon observation, the cheerful sound of hands being piped to dinner; and then at one bell the fife's squeaking out the expected but still very welcome news that grog was ready.

The cheers and the beating of wooden plates on mess-tables that greeted its arrival were still quite audible from far below when a nervous ship's boy in a bright blue jacket, nominally Dr Maturin's servant, nipped into the top and said, 'Oh sir, if you please . . . oh, sir, if you please . . . which Mr Killick bids me remind you that the Commodore, his honour, is to dine in the gunroom and you are all filthy. Which he has powdered your best wig.'

'Thank you, Peter; you may tell him that you have delivered the message,' said Stephen. He looked at his hands. 'Not as who should say *filthy*,' he murmured. 'But it is true I had forgotten.'

Although he led Peter a hard life, Killick had not yet recovered the power, consequence or esteem that had been his before he broke the horn, nor anything like it, either in the cabin or on the lower deck, he could still point out, in a tolerably shrewish voice, that the gentlemen were all assembled, that they were only waiting for the Commodore, and that Dr Maturin's *clean* breeches, his *brushed* best coat, and his *newly-powdered* wig were on that there chair: there was not time to more than just sponge his face in this here warm basin and how did he manage to get into such a pickle? 'We shall never do it in the time, oh dear, oh . . . dear.'

They did do it in the time, however, and five or even ten seconds before the Commodore walked in, Stephen was already in his place between Whewell and the master, his servant behind his chair, and Dr Jacob opposite him. They exchanged a calm, unconscious look as the door opened and the Commodore walked in. Everybody stood up.

'Be seated, gentlemen, I beg,' cried Jack. 'I was so very nearly late that I do not deserve such courtesy. For one who tends to cry up timeliness more than faith, hope or charity it is a very shocking performance. Absurdly enough, I was looking for my glass: I looked in every conceivable place – no glass. But here is consolation' – draining his admirable sherry.

A chill fell upon Stephen's heart: without leave he had taken the telescope, and slinging it about his neck in a sea-manlike or fairly seamanlike fashion, had carried it up into the maintop. And there, shocked by Peter's news, he had left it, lying on a neat heap of studdingsails. To cover his guilt he said, 'We often hear of people calling their daughters Faith, Hope, Charity, or even Prudence; but never Justice, Fortitude or Temperance; nor yet Punctuality, though I am sure it has its charms.' He helped himself to soup, and the talk flowed on. Nobody said anything particularly witty or profound or really memorable for foolishness but it was agreeable, friendly conversation, accompanied by acceptable food and more than acceptable wine.

*   *   *

When they had drunk the loyal toast Stephen excused himself: there 'was something he had forgotten', he told the president, avoiding Jacob's eye. There was indeed: but he had completely overlooked the difficulty, for those unrelated to the more nimble kind of ape, of climbing in tight breeches, buckled shoes, and a fine long-tailed coat. In his hurry he slipped again and again, for the ship, now almost becalmed in the lee of a headland, was rolling, wallowing, in a very disgraceful and uncharacteristic fashion. Sometimes he hung by both hands, writhing to get his feet back onto the ratlines, sometimes by one. He was in this ludicrous posture, much disturbed in his mind, when Bonden came racing up the shrouds, seized him with an iron grasp, wheeled him round to the outboard side and at his faint, wheezing request, propelled him into the top, where he gave him the buckled shoe that had dropped on deck. He asked no questions, he gave no advice; but he did look very thoughtfully at the Commodore's telescope: he was, after all, Jack Aubrey's coxswain.

'Barret Bonden,' said Stephen, when he had recovered his breath, 'I am very much obliged to you indeed. Deeply obliged, upon my word. But you need not mention that telescope to the Commodore. I am about to carry it down to him myself, and explain . . .'

'Why,' cried the Commodore, heaving his powerful frame over the top-brim, 'there's my glass. I had been looking for it everywhere.'

'I am so sorry – I should not have made you uneasy for the world – thank you, Bonden, for your very timely help: please be so good as to tell Dr Jacob that I may be a few minutes late for our appointment.' When Bonden had disappeared, Stephen went on, 'That dear good fellow gave me a hand when a hand was extraordinarily welcome: I found breeches and shoes a sad embarrassment. The truth is . . .' He hesitated for a moment. 'The truth is,' he went on with more conviction, 'that there was something on the shore that interested me extremely: I could not be certain of the object without bringing it closer, so seeing your glass on its usual peg, and you not being in the way, I took the perhaps unwarrantable liberty of seizing it and running aloft as fast as my powers would admit; and upon my soul it was worth the journey. And, although it is scarcely decent in me to say so, the liberty.'

All this time – and it was not inconsiderable, for diffidence reduced Maturin's ordinarily rapid canter to a hobbling walk with frequent pauses – Jack had been examining his precious telescope, one of Dollond's achromatic masterpieces, with a jealous eye: but finding it quite undamaged he said, 'Well, I am glad you saw your object. A double-headed Dalmatian eagle, I make no doubt.'

'Do you see the blur of smoke over the headland, somewhat to the left?'

'Yes. It looks as if they were burning the furze on the far side: though spring is an odd time of year to be doing so. Cape San Giorgio, I believe. Have you noticed how foreigners can never get English names quite right?'

'Poor souls: yet I hope this name, though distorted, may be a good omen. On the far side of that little projection lies the village of Sopopeia, with its chalybeate springs; and in a deep, sheltered inlet let us say a furlong south of it, the shipyard of Simon Macchabe, a sordid wretch, but one who was building a gunboat until his unpaid hands laid down their tools. I believe they burnt the yard some hours ago, and this wafting smoke, much diminished since first I saw it, rises only from the calcined ashes.'

He was by no means sure how Jack would take this form of warfare, and when the ship rounded the cape, opening Macchabe's creek, whose dismal blackened ruins Jack surveyed through his glass with his closest attention before closing it and saying, 'Whewell saw a newly-burned yard on the coast of Curzola. It was not on our list, but that one over there is, and at this point I should have looked into it, sending *Ringle* or the boats if necessary.'

'In the nature of things you would have burnt the half-finished gunboat in that event. Even if we had time to spare, which we have not, most certainly not, such a miserable prize would not have been worth the while. Jack, I must tell you in your private ear that we have some allies ashore, rather curious allies, I admit, who look after these operations: I hope and trust that you will see many another yard burnt or burning before we reach Durazzo. I am aware that this is not your kind of war, brother: it is not glorious. Yet as you see, it is effective.'

'Do not take me for a bloody-minded man, Stephen, a death-or-glory swashbuckling cove. Believe me, I had rather see a first-rate burnt to the waterline than a ship's boy killed or mutilated.' Leaning over the rail he called down orders that took the frigate away from the land. 'Let us go down and look at Christy-Pallière's list with your additions,' he said. 'And may I beg you to unbuckle your breeches at the knee, leave your coat on those stunsails for the boy to bring down, and lower yourself through the lubber's hole. I will guide your feet.'

The list had been very much enriched by Stephen and Jacob's private information, and with the wind settling into the west a little south and increasing to a fine topgallant breeze they went reaching down the coast at a handsome pace. There was not a night without a fire, great or small, to larboard; and Stephen noticed that Jack and the master were more than usually exact in their calculation of distance made good, and that whenever the ships were off one of the yards Jack Aubrey was in the foretop and Reade high-perched in the schooner's rigging, gazing at the ruin with a grim satisfaction. He also noticed that the gunroom was uneasy, remarkably restrained: they knew that there was something in the intelligence line at work, something that should not be openly discussed; though Somers, an ardent fisherman, did say of the flaming carcass of a half-finished corvette, that it was more like buying one's salmon off a fishmonger's slab than catching it with a well-directed fly.

Yet the satisfaction did exist, and it reached its height off Durazzo itself, with all seven yards (counting those of the suburbs) in a blaze that lit the sky, and in which the masts and yards of a small frigate and two corvettes flamed like enormous torches.

'Well,' said Jack, 'it may not be very glorious, Stephen; but by God, your allies have cleaned the coast marvellously; and although they have lost us a small fortune in prize-money, they have saved us a world of time. There may be something to be said for your Saint George and his omens after all.'

Chapter Six

At Durazzo they stood out to sea, leaving the blaze on their larboard quarter and sailing across an uneventful sea with a fine topgallant breeze. But two days later, a little after seven bells in the last dog-watch the mild northerly wind that had brought them so far gave a sigh and faltered; and those that knew these waters well said 'We're in for a right levanter, mate.'

Jack gazed at the sky: his officers, the bosun and the older hands gazed at Jack: and no one was surprised when just before the usual moment for the pipe 'Stand by your hammocks' the Commodore took over the deck and called for preventer-stays, rolling tackles, the taking in of topgallants, the rigging of storm-jibs and staysails, and the bowsing of the guns so taut up against the sides that their carriages squeaked, all except for the brass bow-chaser that fired the evening gun.

The hands perfectly agreed with the orders, unwelcome though they were to the watch below, and they worked with remarkable speed – scarcely a word of direction, all the original Surprises being truly able seamen – partly because the larbowlins wanted to turn in after a long day and partly because they all knew how violent and sudden and untrustworthy these Mediterranean winds could be.

When at last the evening gun boomed out and the bosun did pipe 'Stand by your hammocks', the first gust of the levanter came racing across the water with a low cloud of spray: it struck the *Surprise* from astern, a glancing blow that drove her foretop deep, so that she gave a sudden peck like a horse going over a hedge and finding the ground on the far side much lower than it had expected – a movement so violent that it flung Stephen and Jacob the length of the gunroom, together with their backgammon board, the dice and the men.

'It was the all-dreaded thunder-stroke,' said Stephen.

'I am in no position to contradict you, colleague, being your subordinate,' said Jacob, 'but in my opinion it is the first blast of a levanter. And I believe Shakespeare said thunder-*stone*.'

'I do not set myself up as an authority on Shakespeare,' said Stephen.

'Nor I. All I know of the gentleman is that he had a second-best bed.'

'I was aware that being gammoned twice running had vexed you: but to this degree . . . I wonder that competitive games have survived so long, such intense resentment do they breed. Even I dislike being beaten at chess.'

Jacob, having picked up the last of the dice, was about to say something very cutting indeed, when Somers walked in. 'Well, gentlemen,' he said, 'I would not have you go on deck without tarpaulins and a sou'wester for the world. I am soused as a herring, and must shift my clothes directly.' He moved towards his cabin, and Jacob called after him, 'Is it raining?'

'No, no. It is only a prodigious spindrift worked up by this levanter – coming aboard in buckets.'

'Beg pardon, sir,' said Killick to Stephen (he rarely took notice of the assistant surgeon), 'which Mr Daniel has taken a tumble and Poll thinks it may again be his collar-bone.'

His collar-bone it was, and he was stupid from having pitched from a skid-beam to the deck, hitting his head and shoulder on a gun and its carriage. Stephen strapped him up, eased his pain, and had him carried by two strong men of his division (he was well-liked, though a newcomer) to a cot where he could lie in what peace the ship allowed, which was not inconsiderable. She had settled down to running about two points free, very fast and, apart from the racing of water along her side, very quietly; and since she was both undermanned and healthy, Daniel had an empty corner of the sick-berth. But Stephen was not satisfied with his bone, still less with his confusion and his general appearance. He sat with him until the young man seemed easier, even dozing, and then told Poll to give him as much to drink as he wanted, soup with an egg beaten up in it at the changing of the watch, and no company to trouble him with advice of what he ought to have done.

Stephen returned to the gunroom, where he found Jacob watching Somers and Harding playing chess on a heavy-weather board, the men pegging into holes. He drew him aside and said, 'You knew Laennec much better than I, did you not?'

'I believe so. We used to talk at great length about auscultation: I read his first treatise and made some suggestions that he was kind enough to adopt in the final version.'

'Then pray come and look at one of our most recent patients.'

'The scalded cook?'

'No. Mr Daniel, a master's mate. The Commodore brought him aboard at Mahon. I do not like the sound of his chest, and should like a second opinion.'

They tapped and listened, tapped and listened, trying to distinguish between the echoes they produced and the working of the ship. She was running even faster now, in the stronger wind, and the vibration of her taut rigging, transmitted to her hull by its various points of attachment, filled the sick-bay with a body of all-pervading sound, pierced by the squeak or rattle of countless blocks.

The second opinion was not much firmer than the first, but more foreboding. 'That amiable young man of yours is in a bad way, as you know very well: undernourished, meagre. I cannot directly point to an inchoate phthisis; but if a pneumonia were to declare itself tomorrow or the next day, I should not be surprised. And that contusion may well turn very ugly. We have no leeches, I collect?'

'The midshipmen stole them for bait.'

Four bells in the first watch, and Stephen remembered his traditional appointment with the Commodore and toasted cheese: he hurried up the various ladders, holding on with both hands and reflecting as he climbed that it came naturally to him now. And what was young Daniel going to do, in foul weather, with only one hand to cling by? The answer came at once: he would sit in the master's day cabin, making all the calculations necessary for fine navigation. Mr Woodbine had already said that it was like pure dew from Heaven, having a mate as clever with numbers as Newton or Ahasuerus.

For once he was early, though no earlier than the scent of cheese toasting in its elegant silver dishes: Killick peered at him through a crack in the door. Stephen had had plenty of time to reflect upon the trifling interval between the perception of a grateful odour and active salivation and to make a variety of experiments, checked by his austerely beautiful and accurate Breguet repeater, before the door burst open and the Commodore strode in, sure-footed on the heaving deck and scattering seawater in most directions. 'There you are, Stephen,' he cried, his red face and bright blue eyes full of delight – he looked ten years younger – 'I am so sorry to have kept you waiting: but I have never enjoyed a levanter half so much. It is admirably steady now, for a levanter, and we are under close-reefed topsails and courses, making close on fourteen knots! Fourteen knots! Should you not like to come on deck and see the bow-wave we are throwing?'

'By your leave, sir,' said Killick, in an obscurely injured or offended tone, 'wittles is up.' He walked in, stone-cold sober, as steady as a rock, bearing his elaborate toasted-cheese affair with its spirit-lamps burning blue, and followed by his equally grave and sober mate Grimble, bearing a decanter of Romanée-Conti. 'Which it wants eating this directly minute,' said Killick, with the clear implication that the Commodore was late, and set the dish down with a certain ceremony.

It was indeed a splendid affair, half a dozen little covered rectangular dishes poised on a stand whose lower level held the spirit-lamps, the whole made with love by a Dublin silversmith not far from Stephen's Green. But both were too hungry to admire until each had eaten two dishes, wiped them clean with what little Dalmatian soft-tack remained; then they gazed at the silver with some complacency and drank their capital wine, holding the glasses up so that candlelight shone through.

'I do not like to boast about the qualities of the ship,' said Jack, 'but touching wood and barring all accidents, errors and omissions, we ought to log well over two hundred miles in four and twenty hours, as we sometimes did in the Trades, or even better; and if nothing carries away, and if this dear levanter don't blow itself out in a single day, as they sometimes do, we should raise your Pantellaria on Friday, and the Cape Bon you mention so often. One, three, six or nine days is the rule for this wind.'

'So it is for my homely tramontane. But, Jack, do you not fear the impervious horrors of a leeward shore?'

'Lord, Stephen, what a fellow you are! Don't you know we are in the Ionian already, with Cape Santa Maria far astern and no lee-shore for a hundred sea-miles?'

'What is the difference between a sea and a land mile, tell?'

'Oh, nothing much, except that the sea-mile is rather longer, and very, very much wetter, ha, ha ha! Lord, what a wag I am,' he said, wiping his eyes when he had had his laugh out. 'Very much wetter. But leaving wit aside, another three days, do you see – if we do not waste our time stopping at Malta – should place us well west of Pantellaria.'

*   *   *

They were indeed west of Pantellaria before the levanter, in its turn, died in half a dozen sullen howls: the two surgeons contemplated the shore and the little fishing port from the taffrail. 'After long reflexion,' said Stephen Maturin, 'it appears to me that there is no great point in knowing whether the messengers have passed or not: our mission is the same in either case – to dissuade the Dey from shipping that which he does not yet possess. And with this wind Mr Aubrey assures me that nothing could have left Algiers, even if the Dey had the treasure in his care – a most unlikely event. He also states that it is extremely improbable that a houario could have survived such a tempest: a houario is not a xebec. Yet conceivably it might have taken shelter in the harbour over there,' – nodding towards Pantellaria – 'and since I think we had rather know than not know, I shall beg you to accompany the boat, which the purser is taking in, ostensibly for the purchase of horsehide, tallow, scourges and things of that kind, and ask whether there is any news of a Durazzo houario – your Italian is better than mine. And then, richer in knowledge, we can push on, passing by Cape Bon, which I long to see at this time of the year. You have no objection to climbing down into the boat?'

'None in the least, dear colleague. No one can say that my spirit is affected by six-foot waves: and by the way, what is the difference between a houario and a xebec?'

'Oh, there are so many regional variations, and without endless technical details it could not be made plain: but very roughly the xebec is longer, stronger, and most remarkably fleet. Dear colleague, here is the boat. Pray urge them to waste not a minute.'

They wasted not a minute, and Mr Candish, having bought hide and, with Dr Jacob's help, two puncheons of the famous local wine, they returned: but empty-handed as far as news of the Durazzo houario was concerned. The captain of the port, who had sold them the leather and the wine, had no word of any such vessel calling or passing, and

he very much doubted that so light a craft could have survived such a furious blow. However, he said, they need not
be afraid: there would be no wind of any kind for at least
three days, only very slight western airs, bringing a very
welcome drizzle. If the gentlemen would like company while
they lay off the island, he would be happy to send some
young women.

His forecast was perfectly accurate: they lay off the island
day after day, sometimes seeing it through the drizzle; and
the frigate's people spent their time making and mending,
pointing ropes, re-leathering the jaws of booms and gaffs,
and of course fishing over the side. The small rain spoilt
dancing on the fo'c'sle, but there was a good deal of ship-
visiting, and Jack and as many of his officers who could be
fitted round the table dined with William Reade aboard
Ringle. Jacob's forecast, however, was not fulfilled. He was
the first to admit that Daniel's thorax no longer made the
ugly noises that had alarmed them both; yet he did maintain
that the collar-bone was likely to prove long in knitting –
that active exercise such as swarming up the masts was not
to be countenanced for a moment. 'Not that I am to tell *you*
anything about a froward clavicle,' he added. 'Pray forgive
me.'

'Oh, I entirely agree with what you say,' said Stephen.
'When young fellows are returning to health, supervision is
often necessary, and when neither Poll nor the other women
nor yet his messmates are sitting with him, I shall do so. In
a sick-bay so sparsely inhabited as this, boredom is likely to
set in, growing to intolerable proportions.'

In fact the Commodore, the master, the other officers and
the inhabitants of the midshipmen's berth looked in often
enough to prevent any extremity of tedium; but the shoulder
continued painful, and after lights out, which meant no reading, he was very glad of Stephen's presence. By the time
the dreadful calm of Pantellaria ended in light and variable
breezes, often bringing rain, and the *Surprise* was working

towards Algiers, taking advantage of every favourable shift, he had quite lost his initial shyness of the Doctor.

Cape Bon was a cruel disappointment: they had passed it before the sun was up, and when the unwilling day broke at last, all that could be seen was the distant African shore to a height of twenty feet: everything above that was thin grey cloud, and although the voices of those migrant birds that travelled in groups could be heard – the clangour of cranes, the perpetual gossip of finches – never a one could be seen, though Cape Bon was a famous point of departure for some very uncommon examples of the later migrants at this time of the year.

'I hope you saw your cranes, sir?' said Daniel when Stephen came to sit with him that evening.

'Well, I heard them at least: a great harsh cry up there in the cloud. Did you ever hear a crane, John Daniel?'

'Never, sir. But I think I heard or saw most of the birds in our parts: herons quite often, and sometimes a bittern. Mr Somerville, our curate and schoolmaster, would point them out: and there were half a dozen of us, mostly farmers' sons, that he used to give a penny a nest – I mean for particular birds, sir, not any old wood-pigeon or crow. And we were never allowed to touch the eggs. He was very good to us.'

'Will you tell me about your school?'

'Oh, sir, it was an ancient old place, one long very high room – you could scarcely see the roof-beams – and it was run by the parson, his son and daughter, and Mr Somerville the curate. It did not set up for a great deal of learning. Pretty Miss Constance taught the little boys reading and writing in a small room of her own – how we loved her! And then they moved up to the great room, where there would be three lessons going on at once. The boys were mostly farmers' sons or the better sort of shopkeepers'; and in spite of the din the brighter ones had a fair amount of Latin if they stayed long enough, and history and scripture and casting accounts. I never could get ahead in Latin, but I really did shine at sums and what we called mensuration: I loved numbers even then, and I shall never forget my happiness when Mr Somerville showed me the use of logarithms.'

'Time for Mr Daniel's gruel,' said Mrs Skeeping. 'Now, sir, let me spoon it into you.' She heaved him up in his cot – an accustomed hand, and he was not a great weight – and with professional skill and rapidity fed him a bowlful, stopping only when the spoon had cleaned the sides entirely.

'Thank you, Poll,' called Daniel after her, and he lay back gasping. 'Logarithms,' he went on presently. 'Yes, but that was later, when my father had had to take me away from school, and I kept the shop while he catalogued gentlemen's libraries or went the round of the markets. Mr Somerville used to give me private lessons; and as some sort of exchange I copied his mathematical essays fair: he had a difficult hand and he made many, many corrections, while mine was tolerably neat. He lodged with us, on the first floor, as I think I said; and we were into conic sections when he died.'

'I am afraid that must have been a sad loss to you.'

'It was, sir: a cruel, cruel loss.' After a silence he went on, 'And although it sounds almost wicked to say so, it could not have come at a worse moment. Trade had dropped away most shockingly, and without his few shillings we were poor indeed. I would sit there in the shop all day, and no one would come in. I read and read – Lord, how I read at that unhappy time.'

'What did you read, upon the whole?'

'Oh, Mr Somerville's mathematical books, as far as I could: but most were beyond me. Nearly all the time it was books of voyages, as it always had been in my childhood. My father had taken over a stock of such collections – Harris, Churchill, Hakluyt and many another. I had learnt my reading in those heavy great folios. They were beautiful books, full of delight; yet nobody would buy them. People were not buying books any more, and if ever a customer appeared it was to sell, not to buy. In the days when people were buying, my father had sold on credit, long credit; but however long, the bills were not paid. And then an old gentleman whose library my father had been cataloguing for a great while and who owed him a large sum that he relied upon, died. His heirs fell out about the will, and neither side would settle my poor father's account – the court would decide who was responsible, they said. In the town it was reported that the trial would take years and that my father was penniless. Some tradesmen spoke of suing, for we owed a good deal; none liked to give any more credit. So we lived on very miserably, selling odds and ends, doing what we could. Then a London bookseller from whom my father had had several expensive great books on architecture and the like for gentlemen who had not yet settled, came down, saw how things were with us, and said he must have his money. This came at the same time as rent and taxes, and although one of the gentlemen wrote from Ireland saying that he would deal with the bill on quarter-day, nobody believed him and nobody would lend us a groat. It was clear that my father would be in a debtors' prison very soon, so I walked down to Hereford, to the rendezvous as they call it, and volunteered for the Navy: they looked rather doubtful, but men were very hard to find, so they gave me the bounty – all in gold – more than a year's living in a quiet way, our debts paid – and I sent it home by a carrier I knew well. Then the little band of pressed men and . . .'

'Oh sir, if you please,' cried Poll, 'Dr Jacob says Captain Hobden has fallen down in a fit and please would you come and look at him?'

It was clear that Jacob, though an experienced physician by land, had not served at sea long enough to make an instant and correct diagnosis of alcoholic coma, a state not uncommon in officers aboard His Majesty's ships, they (unlike the hands) being allowed to bring any quantity of wine and spirits aboard, according to their taste and pocket.

And in any event, his practice had been largely among Jews, who drink very little, and Moslems, who at least in theory drink nothing at all.

Hobden was carried by two admiring, envious seamen to his cot, where he lay motionless, breathing (but only just), his face devoid of expression apart from its habitual look of discontent. 'There we may leave the sufferer,' said Stephen. 'Or rather the sufferer to be: there is a word for the morning state, but it escapes me.'

'Crapula,' said Jacob. 'A very loathsome condition that I have rarely encountered.'

Stephen returned to the great cabin, where he found Jack dictating a letter to his clerk: and Mr Candish the purser was sitting by with a pile of dockets to be checked and countersigned. In any case it was almost time for his evening rounds: they amounted to a couple of obstinate gleets and a tenesmus, and when they had been attended to he said to Jacob, 'I shall look after Daniel's last dressing with Poll, if you like to sit with your comatose patient and take notes on pulse, rate of breathing and sensitivity to light.'

The dressing was a simple exercise, but Poll, running her hand over Daniel's shoulder, cried, 'There we are, sir!'

'Well done, Poll,' said Stephen, 'there we are indeed. Bring me a lancet and the fine pincers and we will have it out in a moment.' Poll ran to the dispensary and back. 'There,' he said to Daniel, showing him a splinter of bone, 'that will allow a quick, clean, painless healing. I congratulate you: and I congratulate you too, Poll. Now,' he went on, Poll having blushed, hung her head, and carried the old dressings and implements away, 'a little while ago you were telling me about the beauty and fascination of number: do you think it allied to the pleasures of music?'

'Perhaps it is, sir: but I have heard so little I can hardly give a sensible answer. Yet as for this splinter, sir' – holding it up – 'it may be that my bones are like shaky timber, liable to part, because I had just such a piece come out some years ago. I was in *Rattler*, sixteen, and we were cracking regardless after a French privateer out of La Rochelle that had taken two West Indiamen in the Bay: she was making for home, deep-laden, with everything she could bear, and our skipper drove the ship, drove her and every man aboard, and although our bottom was dirty from lying weeks on end in the Bight of Benin we were gaining on the chase when the maintopgallant carried away. I was aloft, and down I came. I was stunned and out of my wits for a great while, and when I came to I found my mates all disconsolate. We had lost the Frenchman of course, but *Dolphin* had snapped her up next morning and carried her into Dartmouth. She was condemned out of hand, and she, hull, goods, head-money and all, was worth £120,000 odd pence. *A hundred and twenty thousand pound*, sir! Can you conceive such a sum?'

'Only with great difficulty.'

'And since we were very short-handed from fever in the Bight, my one and a half shares as seaman would have been £768. Seven hundred and sixty-eight pound. Happily they did not tell me until I was over the worst of my wound – it was when my head was being shaved that the splinter of bone I was telling you about came through my scalp – or I think I should have run mad. Even as it was I was haunted, right haunted, by that sum. Seven hundred and sixty-eight pound. It was not a beautiful prime or anything like that: nor it was not what people would ordinarily call a fortune; but for me it was or rather would have been freedom from hard labour and above all freedom from the continual anxiety that runs through ordinary people's life – loss of employ, loss of customers, even loss of liberty. At five per cent it would bring in £38.8.0 a year, or £2.18.11d a month – a lunar month, Navy fashion; whereas even an able seaman has no more than £1.13.6d. No, it was not what would be called wealth, but it would have meant a quiet life at home, reading and going much farther into the mathematics, and sometimes fishing – I used to delight in fishing. Dear Lord, when that Paradise was lost I could not keep my mind clear of it – £768 and how many groats, farthings or penny pieces it contained – to just this side of madness: though to be sure some of it was madness too, since the fever took me every other day or so. But, Lord, sir, I have worn your kind patience cruelly, a-pitying of myself, and prating so.'

'Not at all, John Daniel: yet just tell me succinctly about naval prize-money, will you, and then I must go. I have heard of it for ever, but I have never retained the principles.'

'Well, sir, the captain has two eighths of the value of the prize; but if he is acting under a flag-officer he must give the admiral a third of what he receives: then the lieutenants, master and captain of the Marines have equal shares of one eighth: then the Marine lieutenants, surgeon, purser, bosun, gunner, carpenter, master mates and chaplain, equal shares in another eighth; while everybody else shares the remaining half, though not equally, the reefers having four and a half shares each, the lower warrant-officers like the cook and so on, three; the seamen, able and ordinary, one and a half, landmen and servants one, and boys half a share each.'

'Thank you, Mr Daniel: I shall try to keep it in my mind. At present I shall bid Poll make you comfortable: give you good night, now.'

Cape Bon had been a disappointment. Algiers and the Bay of Algiers were not. Commodore Aubrey sent one of the boys wished upon him in Gibraltar by former shipmates – a short-legged, long-armed little creature, very like an ape – to rouse Stephen Maturin at the crack of dawn and to beg him to come at once, in his nightshirt or a dressing-gown or whatever he pleased, but anyhow at once.

'Lord, how brilliant,' he cried, blundering up the ladder to the quarterdeck, his eyes half-closed against the light. Jack gave him a hand up the last step, saying, 'Look! Look!'

'Where away?'

'On the starboard quarter – about a cable's length on the starboard quarter.'

Powerful hands gently swivelled him about, his nightshirt flying in the breeze, and there he saw a fine great company of egrets, snowy white, so near that he could make out their yellow feet; and somewhat beyond them another even larger band, all flying with a steady concentration northwards, presumably to some Balearic swamp. And with the first group there flew a glossy ibis, absurdly black in this light and company, and continually uttering a discontented cry, something between a croak and a quack: from time to time it darted across the path of the leading birds with a louder shriek.

Stephen had the impression that the ibis was extremely indignant at the egrets' conduct: and indeed so late a migration, well on in the month of May, was unusual, unwise, against all established custom. Yet the beautiful white birds would not attend, and presently the ibis left them with a final screech and hurried as fast as it could to the farther group, which might, perhaps, listen to its advice.

Stephen never knew the outcome, for Jack led him to the starboard bow – the ship was ghosting along under courses and a forestaysail – and from here he beheld a vast expanse of gloriously blue sea and a great convoy of merchantmen upon it, perhaps a hundred sail of ships, British, Dutch, Scandinavian and American, gathered from Tripoli, Tunis and further east, with the two corvettes and the sloop that Jack had sent to protect them strung out to windward, while still farther off a practised eye could make out some long, low-built corsairs waiting their opportunity.

'That gives you some notion of the trade, don't you find?' asked Jack. 'Prodigious. But come over this side, and you will see another sight.' He held back the forestaysail and guided Stephen to the larboard cathead, where they stood gazing across an even deeper blue expanse of sea to the African shore. The *Surprise* had already opened the bay entirely and now the sun was lighting first the mountains behind the town and on either side – brilliant green after the spring rains – and then in a few moments the splendid topmost buildings on the tall, symmetrically rounded hill upon which the city was built. 'That is the Kasbah, the Dey's palace,' said Jack.

Minute by minute the brilliant light moved down, showing innumerable white flat-roofed houses built very close together; towering minarets; occasional alleys, barely a single street; some blanks that would probably be great squares if one could see them from above. Row after row of houses going down and down to the prodigious great stone wall, the port, the huge mole and the inner harbour.

'It is exceedingly impressive: there is a strange beauty here,' said Stephen. 'I long to be better acquainted with it.'

'Yes,' said Jack. 'And when we are a little closer I shall ask Dr Jacob to go ashore, wait on the British consul to make sure that if, in command of a King's ship, I salute the castle, the salute will be returned. And if the answer is yes, which is close on certain, whether he can arrange for you to see the Dey as soon as possible.'

'If you do not mind, brother, I had rather go myself, with Dr Jacob to show me the way. I have a note that must be delivered into the consul's own hands. You will let me have *Ringle*, for greater stateliness?'

'Of course I shall: but in that case you may have to wait for the land-breeze in the evening, to carry you out again. Algiers bay is almost always a lee-shore.'

In spite of Jack's words, it was the stately *Ringle* that bore them in, on the understanding that her jolly-boat should pull out as early as possible with the consul's answer about the salute, *Ringle* waiting at the mole for Stephen and a favourable wind.

Very fine she was as she stood in, came sweetly against the mole and moored there to the admiration of all beholders: but there the stateliness of the mission stopped. Dr Maturin had eluded the vigilance of Killick, who supposed that the two doctors were gone aboard the schooner merely to see their friends and who had taken no notice of his rusty old black coat, his breeches unbuttoned at the knee or his crumpled neck-cloth, spotted with blood from a recent shaving. Besides, Killick had had a most indifferent morning. Presuming on his status as captain's steward he had given Billy Green, armourer's mate, a shove as he went aft along the gangway, a shove that Green had returned with such force that Killick plunged between the skid-beams to the deck below, falling on two men at work there and scattering their tools; and when Killick directed a reproof at Green, who replied 'You and your God-damned unicorn's horn', they set about him with jerks and cuffs and one threatened him with a marlin-spike, calling him 'abject reptile' and desiring him to pipe down and stop his gob for an unlucky, *unlucky* son of a rancid bitch. And although the officer of the watch very soon put a stop to this unpleasantness, Killick realized that the feeling of all those present was still very much against him.

He was grieved and angry; and he would have been even more grieved and angrier by far if he had seen Dr Maturin walking along the mole with Jacob and one of the *Ringle*'s boys, walking along in the comfortable, shabby, down-at-heel shoes that had been taken from him but not hidden well enough. He was a disreputable object, with his wig awry and blue spectacles on his nose; and his companion was not much better either. Dr Jacob was dressed in rather old clothes that might belong to the east or west of the Mediterranean – a grey caftan with many cloth-covered buttons, a grey skull-cap, and grey heelless slippers.

'It is indeed a most prodigious wall,' said Stephen.

'Forty feet high,' said Jacob. 'I measured it twice, long ago, with a string.'

They entered the town through a heavily-fortified gate, and to Stephen's surprise there were no formalities: the

Turkish guards looked at them curiously, but at Jacob's brief statement that they were from the English ship they nodded and stood aside. A few narrow streets, a small square with an almond-tree, and the *Ringle*'s boy cried, 'Oh sir, sir! There is a camel!'

'Yes, indeed,' said Jacob. 'A she-camel,' and he led them round the creature, through yet another maze to a larger square: it was the slave-market, he observed in a matter-of-fact tone, but there would be neither merchants nor wares until later in the day: and the boy was to take particular notice of all the turnings they took, since he would have to find his way back alone. 'Yes, sir,' said the boy; but at almost the same moment, in spite of Jacob's assertion, they did see one weary old man, slowly carrying his chain as he walked across the market to the fountain, and this so struck the boy, who stared with all his might, even walking backwards to see more, that Stephen resolved to ask the consul to let a servant show him the way back to the mole. Another broad rectangle, and Jacob pointed out the house where he had lived. 'I shared it with a friend, the daughter of the last descendant of a very ancient family of Grey Huns: but unhappily we neither of us quite answered the other's expectations. In the corner on the left there is a shaded coffee-house, where we might well be advised to drink a cup, because our next stage is a climb of some five hundred steps almost to the Kasbah itself. Shall we walk in?'

They walked in, and after civil greetings Jacob and Stephen were given leather cushions by the side of a table nine inches high, near the front of the well-filled shop (which also sold hashish and tobacco), while the delighted boy sat on the ground. 'Perhaps the young man would prefer sherbet?' suggested Jacob. 'Oh yes, sir, if you please,' said the young man, and he drank with ecstasy, gazing at a whole train of camels that passed slowly by, laden with dates, pliable baskets crammed with dates and covered with palm-leaves.

People were now passing in greater numbers: mostly

Moors, but many black Africans, and some that Jacob pointed out as Jews of different kinds, Greeks and Lebanese. But when, having finished their second cups of coffee and another bowl of sherbet, they declined the proffered hookah and began their climb, they did not find the path at all crowded.

'Is this a Muslim holy day, or a fast, that so many people stay at home?' asked Stephen. 'I had always thought of Algiers as a teeming, densely-populated town.'

'So it is, at ordinary times,' replied Jacob. 'I think that all who can have moved into the country or the surrounding villages. I heard the men sitting behind us speak of an English bombardment as very probable indeed; and the emptiness of the markets is something I have never known before, even in times of plague.' He was already gasping when he said this, and a few steps further on he pointed to a recess and said, 'This is where I usually sit when I am going to the Kasbah.'

They all rested on the stone bench, worn smooth with innumerable weary hams, and presently the boy cried, 'Oh sir! Do you see them enormous great huge birds?'

'Certainly,' said Stephen. 'They are vultures, you know, the ordinary fulvous . . .' He stopped short, not wishing to disappoint, and added, 'But they are very splendid on the wing. See how they turn!'

'I have seen a *vulture*,' said the boy, more or less to himself, with infinite satisfaction.

Another two hundred steps and Jacob turned off right-handed. 'There is the consulate,' he said, pointing to a considerable house with a garden full of date-palms. 'Should you like to draw breath again before going in?'

Stephen felt in his pocket for the ministerial letter, heard the reassuring crackle, and said, 'Never in life: let us not lose a minute. Boy, will you wait here, sitting in the shade of a palm-tree?'

He and Jacob walked through the side-door obviously

intended for business, and in the office they found a young man sitting with his feet on the desk. 'Who the Devil are you?' he asked. 'And what do you want? Distressed British subjects, I suppose.'

'My name is Maturin, Dr Stephen Maturin, surgeon in HMS *Surprise*, and I wish to see the consul, for whom I have a letter and a verbal message.'

'You can't see the consul. He is sick. Give me the letter and tell me the message,' said the young man; but he did not take his feet off the desk.

'The letter is from the Ministry and can be delivered only into the consul's own hands. The message is equally private. If you wish you may show him my card: and he will decide whether to receive me or not.' He brought out a card, pencilled some words on the back, and laid it on the desk. The young man changed colour and said, 'I will speak to her ladyship.'

'Dr Maturin,' she cried, running in – a remarkably handsome woman of thirty-five or so. 'You will not remember me, but we met in Sierra Leone, when Peter was on poor Governor Wood's staff – we dined on opposite sides of the table – of course you shall see him – you will not mind his being in bed, I am sure – it is the hip-gout and he suffers most cruelly . . .' Her eyes filled with tears.

'Dear Lady Clifford, I remember you perfectly. You wore a pearl-grey dress and as Mrs Wood observed it became you wonderfully. May I present my colleague, Dr Jacob? He has more experience than I of sciatica and related diseases and he may have seen similar cases.'

'How do you do, sir?' said Lady Clifford, and she led them upstairs to a sadly tumbled bedroom.

'Dr Maturin, I do apologize for receiving you like this,' said the consul, 'but I dare not get up: the fit has just died away, and I fairly dread waking it . . .' He gave Jacob a civil but enquiring look. Stephen explained his presence and the Ministry's total confidence in him; he then passed the letter

he was carrying. Sir Peter smiled kindly at Jacob, said, 'Forgive me,' to Stephen, and broke the seal. 'Yes,' he said,
putting the letter by, 'it is perfectly clear. But, my dear sir,
I believe you have come to a totally new situation. Have you
had news from Algiers since the beginning of April?'

Stephen cast his mind back and after a moment's thought
said, 'We have not. Between this and Durazzo we touched
only at Pantellaria, where they had nothing to tell us, good
or bad, only that no houario had passed or touched there –
that no houario could have survived the furious wind that
struck us. Nor did we speak any ship, though Commodore
Aubrey may even now be conferring with some one of the
captains he sent to convoy the eastern trade . . . and, sir,
before going any further may I carry out one part of my
duties? The Commodore desired me to ask you whether, if
he were to stand in, perhaps with part of his squadron, and
salute the castle, whether the salute would be returned?'

'Oh Lord, yes: no sort of doubt about it, after the way he
has been playing Old Harry in the Adriatic.'

'Then may I beg you to lend me a servant to show our
ship's boy down to the mole? He is to carry the message to
the Commodore, but this is the first time he has ever left
Stow on the Wold – he sees wonders on every hand, and I
fear he may utterly lose his way.'

'Certainly. I shall send one of my guards, a discreet grey-
bearded Turk,' said the consul. He rang, and when the guard
answered he bade him take the boy down to the mole with
the note *The salute will be answered* which Stephen wrote on
a piece of paper.

'Oh, good Lord,' said the consul, carefully lying back on
his pillows, 'we have heard such tales here of Frenchmen
joining you, of Frenchmen being sunk – Algerines shockingly battered – shipyards going up in flames by the score –
the only corsairs at sea are those from very far east: all ours are
penned up in the inner harbour. But to go back to the matter in
hand: if you have had no recent news from here you cannot

169

know that the situation is wholly changed and that my influence with the Dey no longer exists. He was strangled by the janissaries, and some days later they elected their current Agha, Omar Pasha, as the new Dey. I hardly know him. His mother was a Turk, and he speaks Turkish and Arabic with equal fluency and some Greek – illiterate in all three, but by reputation a man of very strong character and intelligent: and indeed he would not have been chosen otherwise.'

'What you tell me is very disturbing. Pray, have you any news of the Allies' progress?'

'As I understand it, the Russians and Austrians are still muddling very slowly along, still separated by great stretches of mountain, river and bog: and by strong mutual distrust.'

'Do you think, sir, that a meeting with the new Dey could be arranged as soon as possible? Perhaps tomorrow?'

'I am afraid not. Nor even in the near future. The Dey is hunting the lion of the Atlas, his favourite pursuit; and the Vizier, if not actually *with* him – for the pursuit of the lion is not to his taste – will be at the nearest oasis of comfort.'

'Consul,' said Stephen, after a considering pause, 'does it seem to you reasonably prudent for a usurper to go gadding after lions within a few weeks of winning power and so leaving his capital open to the enemies and rivals that his usurpation must necessarily have brought into being?'

'It seems unlikely, even absurd; but Omar is a case apart. He was brought up among the janissaries – he knows them through and through – and although he is illiterate he was a particularly successful head of what might be called the former Agha's intelligence service. I am of opinion that he has made this journey into the Atlas to learn who among the janissaries are likely to form parties in his absence. He has informants everywhere and I am persuaded that when he judges the moment right he will silently return, summon a body of those devoted to his interest and take off a score of ambitious heads.'

Jacob had taken no part in the conversation other than by nods and smiles that showed his keen attention: but at these last words he uttered a most emphatic 'Yes, indeed.'

'Can you tell me, sir,' said Stephen, 'how much influence the Vizier may possess?'

'My impression is that it is very great. He was the equivalent of the present Dey's chief of staff and his main support, a highly intelligent and literate man with highly-placed connexions in Constantinople. Although, as you are aware, the deys have long since thrown off all but a purely nominal allegiance to the Sublime Porte, the Sultan's titles, orders and decorations have a very real value here, particularly to men like Omar: and quite apart from that Hashin has a wide acquaintance with the chief men in the Muslim states of Africa and the Levant. He is also, I may add, fluent in French.'

'In that case,' said Stephen, 'it seems to me that Dr Jacob and I should make our way into the Atlas with the utmost dispatch, if not to the Dey himself . . .'

'An approach to the Dey himself without official standing or former acquaintance would be contrary to local etiquette: may I advise a call on the Vizier?'

'Then to the Vizier, to do what can be done to prevent this shipment, which might well be fatal to our cause. Is he incorruptible, do you think?'

'I cannot honestly speak to that. But in these parts, as you know very well, a present is rarely unwelcome. I have seen him with an aquamarine in his turban. Oh, oh . . .' The consul bent forward, his face twisted with pain. They turned him on his side, took off his clothes, felt for and found the source of the spasm. Jacob was about to open the door when Lady Clifford appeared, looking extremely anxious. Jacob asked the way to the kitchen, prepared a hot, a very hot poultice, clapped it on and hurried out into the town, returning with a phial of Thebaic tincture.

'Thebaic tincture,' he murmured to Stephen, who nodded

and called for a spoon: raising the poor consul's head he administered the dose and laid him gently back.

In a little while the consul said, 'Thank you, thank you, gentlemen. I already feel it receding . . . oh Lord, the relief! My dear Isabel, I have never known so short a bout: do you think we might all have a cup of tea – or coffee, if these gentlemen prefer it?'

While they were drinking their tea there came the sound of a perfectly regular series of shots fired from great guns in the inner bay, twenty-one of them: it was Commodore Aubrey saluting the castle. Hardly had the echo of the twenty-first died away along the walls, towers and batteries of Algiers than the entire series of fortifications facing the sea erupted into an enormous, *enormous*, thunder by way of reply, one set of rounds merging into the next and a truly prodigious bank of powder-smoke drifting out over the water.

'Heavens!' cried Lady Clifford, taking her hands from her ears, 'I have never heard anything like that before.'

'It was the new Agha showing his zeal. If he had left a single piece unfired, the Dey would have had him impaled.'

'About how many guns took part, do you suppose?' asked Stephen.

'Something between eight hundred and a thousand,' said the consul. 'I was having a count made some time ago, but my man was stopped just before the Half-Moon battery, which was just as well for him, since lions and leopards are kept there on chains which the gunners know how to work but nobody else. He had reached about eight hundred and forty, as my recollection goes. I could let you have a copy of his list, if it would interest you.'

'Thank you, sir: you are very good, but I had rather not run the risk of being found with such a paper – an almost certain prelude to being impaled and then fed to the lions and leopards. Above all on such a journey as we contemplate, to view the lions on their native heath. If you are not too tired, sir, after that cruel bout of what resembled sciatica but which may prove to be something I shall not say benign but at least more transitory and less malignant – if you are not too tired, may we speak of means, destination, mules, even God preserve us camels, guards, equipment, and of anything else that occurs to your far greater experience?'

'I am not at all tired now, I thank you, after your wonderful draught, your capital poultice – which is still charmingly warm – and above all your comfortable words. But I do not think you mentioned a dragoman?'

'No. Dr Jacob has spoken Arabic and Turkish from his childhood.'

'Oh, very good,' said the consul, bowing. 'Indeed, far better. As for means, you may certainly draw on the consulate for a thousand pounds, if you think it safe to travel with so much gold. Where destination is concerned – and of course the necessary guide – we must look at a map. Horses, pack-mules, and for some stretches I believe camels, can undoubtedly be hired: I shall speak to my head groom. Guards may not be absolutely necessary, the Dey and his escort having so recently passed that way; but I should be sorry to see you set off without them.'

'May I put in a word for Turks?' asked Jacob, speaking for almost the first time. 'They may not shine as rulers, but your medium Turk seems to me a very fine fellow. I have often travelled with them in the Levant.'

'I quite agree with you, sir,' said the consul. 'According to my experience the Turk is a man of his word. Most of my guards are Turks. And now that I come to think of it, one of our people knows the nearer Atlas intimately well. When he was not working on the reports, records and correspondence here, he pursued the great wild boar, and various other creatures. And he was particularly well acquainted with the country round the Shatt el Khadna, where I believe the Dey intends to go.'

'Do you refer to the young man who received us today?'

'Oh Lord, no. The gentleman in question was secretary to the consulate. I am so sorry you had to see that youth: most of the Algerine clerks are absent, taking their families out of the city, and I had to put him at the desk. He is the son of an intimate friend, a late friend I am very sorry to say. He is nothing remotely like his father, he was sent away from school as a drunken, stupid, pragmatical ass – sent away although his father and grandfather had been there. So as his family intended him for a diplomatic career – his father had been ambassador in Berlin and Petersburg – they begged me to have him here for a while, so that he might at least learn the rudiments of the business: his mother, God bless her, had been given to understand that in Mahometan countries neither wine nor spirits were allowed, nor even beer. No, no: the former secretary of whom I was speaking was a scholar as well as a hunter and a botanist.'

'Would he come with us at least part of the way, do you think?'

'He would certainly go with you in spirit, I am sure. But a huge wild boar that he had wounded so mangled and ploughed up his leg that it mortified and had to be cut off. But he will certainly tell you of a wholly reliable guide.'

Chapter Seven

'How homely it is, how agreeably familiar,' said Stephen Maturin. They were sitting in a row on a high, grass-covered slope overlooking the range of country they had already traversed with Stephen on the left, Jacob in the middle and then the wholly reliable guide. 'The same species of cistus, thyme, rosemary, various brooms, the same sweet-scented peonies here and there among them on the screes, the same homely rock-thrushes, wheatears and chats.'

'Did the gentleman say *homely*?' asked the guide in a discontented voice. He had long frequented the consulate and his English was remarkably good; but he was so used to astonishing foreigners with the wonders of his country that a lack of amazement angered him.

'I believe he did,' said Jacob.

'In his *home* do they have those huge birds?' He pointed to a group of griffon vultures circling on an upward current.

'Oh yes,' said Stephen. 'We have many vultures, bearded, black, fulvous and Egyptian.'

'Eagles?'

'Certainly: several kinds.'

'Bears?'

'Of course.'

'Boars?'

'Only too many, alas.'

'Apes?'

'Naturally.'

'Scorpions?'

'Under every flat stone.'

'Where is the gentleman's home?' asked the indignant guide.

'Spain.'

'Ah, Spain! My fourth great grandfather came from Spain, from a little village just outside Cordova. He had nearly sixteen acres of watered land and several date-palms: a second paradise.'

'Yes, indeed,' said Stephen, 'and in Cordova itself the mosque of Abd-ar-Rahman still stands, the glory of the western world.'

'Tomorrow, sir,' said the guide, leaning forward and speaking across Jacob, 'I hope to show you a lion or a leopard – perhaps with God's blessing both: or at least their tracks by the stream Arpad that flows into the Shatt, where the Dey is sure to have his quarters.'

'We must be getting along,' said Jacob. 'The sun is very near the mountain-tops.'

They rejoined their company and, when the camels' reluctance to get up could be overcome, they moved on, following the now quite well beaten track up and over a cold pass and down to Khadna and its fields, the last village before the oasis, then the Shatt and the wilderness. Dusk was falling before they reached it and they hardly noticed the blue-clad figure of a little girl waiting outside the thorn-hedge; but clearly she could see them, and as they came out on to the straight she called out, 'Sara!'

At this a tall, gaunt camel, a particularly ugly, awkward and ill-tempered creature that had carried Stephen over a broad stretch of shale and sand, broke into a lumbering run and on reaching the child lowered its great head to be embraced. These were camels that belonged to the village and they moved off to their usual place even before their trifling return-loads were unstrapped, while the guards and attendants set up tents. Stephen and Jacob were taken to the chief man's house, where they were regaled with coffee and biscuits sopped in warm honey, extremely difficult to keep from dripping on to the beautiful rugs upon which they sat.

Jacob was perfectly at home; he spoke for the right length of time, drank the proper number of minute cups, and distributed the customary little presents, blessing the house as he left it, followed by Stephen. As they crossed the dark enclosure to their tent they heard a hyena, not without satisfaction. 'I used to imitate them when I was a boy,' said Jacob. 'And sometimes they would answer.'

The next day was hard going, up and down, but very much more of the up, more and more stony and barren: quite often they had to lead their horses. Now there were more unfamiliar plants, a wheatear that Stephen could not certainly identify, some tortoises, and a surprising number of birds of prey, shrikes and the smaller falcons, almost one to every moderate bush or tree in an exceptionally desolate region.

At the top of this barren rise, while the Turks made a fire for their coffee, Stephen watched a brown-necked African raven fly right across the vast pure expanse of sky, talking in its harsh deep voice all the way, addressing his mate at least a mile ahead. 'That is a bird I have always wished to see,' he said to the guide, 'a bird that does not exist in Spain.' This pleased the guide more than Stephen had expected, and he led his charges fifty yards or so along the track to a point where the rock fell precipitously and the path wound down and down to a dry valley with one green spot in it – an oasis with a solitary spring that never spread beyond those limits. Beyond the dry valley the ground rose again, yet beyond it and to the left there shone a fine great sheet of water, the Shatt el Khadna, fed by a stream that could just be made out on the right, before the mountain hid it.

'Right down at the bottom, before the flat, do you see a horseman?' asked Stephen, reaching for his little telescope. 'Is he not riding for a fall?'

'It is Hafiz, on his sure-footed mare,' said Jacob. 'I sent

him forward to give the Vizier word of our coming, while you were gazing at your raven. It is a usual civility in these parts.'

'Well, God speed him,' said Stephen. 'I would not go down that slope at such a pace, unless I were riding Pegasus.'

'I have been thinking,' said Jacob, about a furlong later, when the going was not quite so anxious and the oasis was perceptibly nearer, 'I have been thinking . . .'

'. . . that we are on limestone now, with a change in vegetation – the thyme, the entirely different cistus?'

'Certainly. But it also occurred to me that it might be better if I appeared as a mere dragoman. Since the Vizier is perfectly fluent in French, there is no need for my presence; and you would more readily reach an understanding, the two of you alone. As I am sure you have noticed, a man facing two interlocutors is at something of a disadvantage: he feels he must assert himself. I am dressed in such a manner that I could be anyone or anything. You will do better on your own, particularly if you conciliate his good will with the lapis lazuli turban-brooch – a very striking cabochon with golden flecks that a Cainite cousin let me have, a merchant in Algiers, almost next to the pharmacy. He told me that there was another Cainite, one of the Beni Mzab, a calligrapher in the Vizier's suite; and that is another reason why I suggest being a dragoman, no more, on this occasion.'

'May I see it?'

'I will show it you before we are received, when I pass over the consul's letter of presentation: you will be able to look at it discreetly, since it is in a little European box that opens and closes, click.'

'You wrote the letter, I believe?'

'Yes: it is in Turkish and it states that your mission is of a private and confidential nature, undertaken at the request of the Ministry. There are the usual compliments at the beginning and at the end: they take up most of the paper.'

'Very well. This is a rather more public form of intelligence service than I have ever experienced, and it will disqualify me for many other duties of the same nature: but to be sure, a very great deal is at stake.'

'A very, very great deal.'

They had reached the level ground, and now they rode in silence until a Barbary partridge took noisily to the air almost under their noses, causing the horses to caper, but without much conviction after so wearing a day. 'And surely those are palm-doves?' said Stephen.

Dr Jacob had nothing to offer apart from 'I am sure you are right.' But turning in his saddle, he added, 'Perhaps we should let the others catch up, so that we may make our entrance in a reasonably stylish manner.'

Reasonably stylish it was, the Turkish guards and their horses having a sense of occasion, and they rode through the intensively cultivated fields of the oasis, all brilliant green beneath the towering date-palms, round the central pool (with the inevitable moorhen) to a low, spreading house with barns and stables scattered about. 'The Dey's hunting lodge,' said Jacob. 'I was here once as a boy.'

An official and some grooms came out of the gateway, the official calling what Stephen took to be greetings: he also noticed a particular glance exchanged between Jacob and him – slight and fleeting, evident to no one who did not know Jacob very well and who did not happen to be looking in that direction – and then the grooms led horses and pack-mules into the stable-yard while Stephen and Jacob walked into the fore-court.

'This is Ahmed ben Hanbal, the Vizier's under-secretary,' said Jacob. Stephen bowed: the under-secretary bowed, putting his hand to his forehead and heart. 'The chief secretary is with the Dey. Shall we walk in?'

Inside the curious pillared patio, enclosed with elaborate wrought-iron screens, Jacob said something to Ahmed, who nodded and hurried away. 'Here is the letter,' said Jacob, passing it, 'and here is the little Western box.'

Stephen clicked it open, gazed with admiration at the splendid blue, the size and shape of an egg cut in two lengthways: he smiled at Jacob, who said, 'I shall leave you now. The – what shall I say? – the announcer will come through that door' – nodding at it – 'in a minute or two, and announce you to the Vizier.'

The minute tended to be a long one, and Stephen looked secretly at the stone again: he had rarely seen so true an azure; and the gold rim echoed the golden specks within the stone quite admirably. But a most unwelcome comparison welled up in his mind. Diana had possessed an extraordinary blue diamond – she was buried with it – a blue of an entirely different nature, of course, but he felt the familiar chill grip him, the sort of frigid indifference to virtually everything; and he welcomed the opening door. It showed a cross-looking very tall greybeard, his height increased by a lofty white turban, who beckoned imperiously and walked before him into a room where a middle-aged man in white clothes was sitting cross-legged on a low couch, smoking a hookah.

'The Christian,' said Greybeard, in a loud, official voice: he bowed very low and walked out backwards.

'Good day to you, sir,' said Stephen in French. 'I have an introduction to His Highness the Dey from His Britannic Majesty's consul in Algiers, but before delivering it to him and carrying out the rest of my mission, I thought it proper to pay my respects to you, and perhaps, if it is customary, to show you the letter. Since I have been told that you speak perfect French, I have left my interpreter behind.'

The Vizier rose, bowed, and said, 'You are very welcome, sir. Pray sit down' – patting the couch – 'Like you, I do in fact speak French currently: it is my mother-tongue, since one of my father's wives came from Marseilles. And it is indeed customary to show any document intended for the Dey to his chief minister. Pray smoke, if you feel so inclined, while I read it.'

Rarely had Stephen's sense of politeness been put to such

a test, but choosing the least worn of the hookah's mouth-pieces, he smoked away with every appearance of composure. Not for very long, however, for the Vizier skipped the opening formulae and the even more elaborate ending, and said, 'The letter speaks of a private and confidential mission: since the Dey invariably discusses matters of this kind with me, perhaps it would save time and many weary journeys – for I am afraid you had but a strenuous ride of it today – if you were to tell me its general nature.'

'By all means. But first may I beg you to accept this trifling token of my personal esteem.'

He laid the box within hand's reach: the Vizier opened it, and his face changed: he carefully took the brooch out and carried it to a shaft of sunlight. 'What a stone!' he exclaimed. 'I have never seen its like for perfection. Many, many thanks indeed, my dear sir. I shall wear it in my turban on Friday.'

Stephen made the proper belittling murmurs and gestures, and reverting to their day's ride he said that although physically it was wearisome, as an amateur naturalist he was amply repaid by the plants, birds, and if not animals then at least the trace of animals, large animals, that he had seen.

'Perhaps you are a hunter, sir?'

'As far as my feeble powers allow me, yes, sir.'

'So am I: though nothing in comparison with His Highness, who, as you may know, is at present hunting the lion in the Khadna valley. But perhaps, when we have discussed this matter and when you are rested, we might go shooting together. But now, sir' – with a last look at his blue stone – 'may we turn to the reason for your presence, your very welcome presence, in this wilderness?'

'Well, sir, in the first place I must tell you that it has come to the knowledge of the British Ministry that several numerous Shiite confederacies and brotherhoods along the Adriatic and Ionian coasts and inland to Serbia who support Bonaparte have combined to intervene in his favour by doing all they can to prevent or at least to hinder and delay the junction of the Russian and Austrian armies on their march to join the Allies. But to make their intervention effective they need still greater numbers of armed men: the mercenaries are well-armed, formidable, and willing; but they will not act without payment. The very large sum of money necessary has been sought throughout this part of the world and at last it has been found. A Moroccan ruler is willing to lay down two months' pay in gold, and messengers were sent to Algiers from Durazzo very recently, begging the Dey to have this treasure sent across so that they might take the field immediately. The weather has been of such a kind that they might not have arrived: but in any event His Britannic Majesty's government would be very deeply grieved indeed if any help were given to these people.'

The Vizier gazed at him with a wondering benevolence. 'Surely, my dear sir,' he said at last, 'a man of your egregious perspicacity cannot believe these wild tales? His Highness is a most orthodox Sunnite, while the agitators in Herzegovina and those parts, of whom I have heard quite often, are violent Shiites; and they have turned to a notorious Shiite sheikh in Morocco. For them to ask the orthodox Dey to help them at this point passes belief: it is as though a band of Calvinists were to beg for the assistance of the Vatican. Can it be supposed that our Dey would advance their cause, even if he had not hated Bonaparte ever since his vile conduct at Jaffa, Acre and Aboukir, and even if he were not an admiring friend of King George, whose Royal Navy has recently been so successful in the Adriatic – a King whom no Dey of Algiers would ever voluntarily offend? He will tell you so himself, when you see him; and I believe his bluff, soldier-like frankness will be even more deeply convincing than anything I can say. But come, let me call for a soothing bath and my own masseur to restore the suppleness of your limbs; and then when you are quite recovered we will have a simple meal and go shooting. I have two London guns, very beautiful, and there are plenty of palm-doves here, quite tame. Then early tomorrow I will mount you and your dragoman on decent horses and confide you to one of the Dey's huntsmen, who will take you by His Highness' private road across the mountain and down through the forest on the other side to the Arpad river that feeds the Shatt el Khadna, showing you all manner of birds, beasts and flowers, or their tracks. It is a vast game-preserve – no ordinary people are allowed into it without a pass; and those who *do* adventure are impaled. The last Dey had five youths and a hermaphrodite impaled in one session: he thought it a powerful deterrent.'

Very early in the morning Stephen and Amos Jacob rode southward across the oasis, following the very narrow paths between the crops (mostly barley, with some chick-peas). There were still many palm-doves, but this had been an exceptionally dewy night – the dawn itself was still hazy – and the birds preferred to sit tight, with their bosoms fluffed out. Still many, many doves, for the Vizier had no notion of shooting flying, and as soon as Stephen understood this, he too waited for the occasional bird to perch, peering and gazing down at the sportsmen.

The parting had been quite cordial, although it was so very early and although the Vizier looked so very worn (he had three wives, and an applicant for high office had recently sent him a Circassian concubine). He told Stephen that he had given the huntsman particular instructions to show everything that might interest a natural philosopher, including 'le club des lions'; and he sent the Dey all possible expressions of loyal devotion.

They rode on through the damp and even misty dawn, Stephen and Jacob on strong capable geldings, past mark of mouth, the young huntsman on a serviceable pony. At the beginning of the scrub country that came with striking abruptness immediately after the green of the oasis, a sparrow flew from a thorn-bush. Ibrahim wheeled his pony and called out, 'Bird! Bird!'

'He says there is a bird,' said Jacob.

'It is unreasonable to expect him to know what is common to Arklow and Algiers,' said Stephen. 'Could you perhaps desire him to take notice only of reptiles, quadrupeds, and their tracks?'

This Jacob did, but very kindly: and before they were ten minutes from the oasis, young Ibrahim had shown them the footprints of several jackals, a hyena, and the trace of a very considerable serpent, five to six feet long. 'I am almost certain that it was malpolon monspessulanus. I had one as a pet when I was a boy.'

'Was it a satisfactory pet?'

'There was a degree of recognition, and a certain tolerance: nothing more.'

The road grew steeper, winding up in curves laboriously cut into the rock and embanked: as the sun climbed the men and their horses tired, and at one particular left-handed corner pointed out by Ibrahim they were happy to turn off the road to a small platform where one of those improbable springs sometimes found in limestone flowed from a cleft, its water making a green stripe down the slope for a hundred yards and more. As they rested they saw another horseman, very well-mounted, toiling up where they had toiled; and while they were still staring, eating dates as they did so, they heard the sound of hoofs on the road higher up. The two riders passed the corner at almost the same moment: they shouted a greeting but did not draw rein. It was evident that they were the Dey's messengers.

On. Up and up, this time to the very top of the ridge, where the forest began, a fine open forest, and although the trees were somewhat wind-stunted on the brow itself, the road had not descended five minutes before it was winding through noble oaks, with beeches here and there, and chest-nuts and sometimes an incongruous yew. And presently, where the path narrowed to thread between tall crags on either side there was a gate with huts for soldiers right and left: a small open plain beyond it.

Ibrahim rode forward and showed the Vizier's pass. The guards opened the gate, saluting in the elegant Muslim fashion. On the little plain – ten acres or so of grass – the riders stopped to gaze down over the sea of tree-tops to the vast expanse of the Shatt el Khadna. The valley of the stream that fed it was hidden from view by the mountain range, rising and falling in irregular waves; but the lake itself was a noble sight, and its splendour was increased by the presence of birds quite close at hand and overhead, which added a great deal to the sense of height, distance and immobility on the one hand, and to that of a totally different essence on the other. The birds – vultures for the most part, with two more distant eagles and some trifling black kites – were far above, wholly free in the limitless sky; and the nearer group (all griffons) were in constant smooth motion, mounting and mounting in spirals on a current rising from the warm mountain-side.

'Ibrahim says that these are the stakes used for impaling,' said Jacob.

'Certainly,' replied Stephen. 'And since vultures are in general very faithful to their sources of supply, I have been wondering whether any of those wheeling above us will drop down for leavings. Not the griffons, I think: they are too cautious. But there is a bearded vulture, a friend of my boyhood, and very glad I am to see him here, together with two black vultures, those bold rapacious creatures. Do you see them?'

'They all look much the same to me,' said Jacob. 'Huge dark creatures sailing round and round.'

'The bearded vulture is the one on the far right-hand side of the round,' said Stephen. 'See, he scratches his head. In Spanish he is called the bone-breaker.'

'You have an unfair advantage with your perspective-glass.'

'He is considering. Yes, yes. He loses height. He drops, he drops!'

And indeed the great bird settled among the scattered bones beneath the stakes, pulled some bare ribs aside, seized a battered sacrum, grasped it in its powerful claws and took off with a leap, wings beating strongly, with the clear intent of dropping it from a great height onto a rock. But he was not fairly airborne before the two black vultures were upon him, one striking his back and the other brushing across his face. The sacrum dropped into an impenetrable thicket, hopelessly and entirely lost.

'That is perfectly typical of your black vulture: greedy, precipitate, grasping,' cried Stephen. 'And *stupid*. A bird with as much sense as a pea-hen would have hit him fifty feet up, and a handy mate would have caught the bone in mid-air.'

Ibrahim understood not a word, but he did catch Stephen's disappointment and frustration, and pointing away and away to the north-east he showed another high-circling flight a great way off. Jacob translated: 'He says there are two or three score mothers of filth over there, waiting for the Dey's men to finish skinning what he shot yesterday evening: but first he will show you the Shatt, which has countless red birds on it. We are obliged to go down that way, along the edge of the lake and so up the river-bank, partly because the direct slopes are very severe, and partly to avoid disturbing the deer, wild boars, lions and leopards which the Dey preserves entirely for himself.'

'Would a devout Muslim eat wild boar?' asked Stephen as they rode on.

'Oh dear me, yes,' said Jacob. 'The Beni Mzab have no hesitation whatsoever in eating him: many the exquisite civet de sanglier have I eaten among them. But he must be *wild*, you know, wild and hairy, otherwise he would certainly be unclean. And for that matter they do not observe Ramadan, either, or . . .'

'There is a Barbary falcon!' cried Stephen.

'Very well,' said Jacob, not quite pleased at having his account of the Beni Mzab neglected for the sake of a bird; and not at all pleased either by the way his saddle kept pinching the inside of his thighs.

They rode for a while in silence, always going downhill, which aggravated Jacob's discomfort. But abruptly Ibrahim stopped, and with one finger to his lips, pointed silently at two fresh round footprints on the muddy edge. He whispered into Jacob's ear; and Jacob, leaning over to Stephen, murmured, 'Leopard.'

And there indeed he was, the lovely spotted creature, sprawling insolently along a horizontal mossy branch: he watched them with a fine unconcern for quite a time, but when Stephen made a motion, a very cautious motion, towards his telescope, the leopard slipped off his branch on the far side without a sound, and wholly vanished.

On: and now that the slope was easier by far Jacob's saddle hurt him less: his good humour returned, at least in part. Yet he could still say, 'My dear colleague, you may think me crass, but where birds, beasts and flowers are concerned all I mind about is are they dangerous, are they useful, are they good to eat.'

'My dear colleague,' cried Stephen, 'I do most sincerely ask your pardon. I fear I must have been an everlasting bore.'

'Not at all,' said Jacob, ashamed of himself. And away on the left hand, at a distance they could not determine, a lion uttered what might be called a roar – a very deep lowing repeated four or perhaps five times before dying away – which gave the impression not indeed of menace, but of enormous power.

'That is what I mean,' said Jacob, after a moment's silence. 'I like to know about *him*, rather than a curious and possibly nondescript nuthatch.'

The ground was now levelling, and shortly after this they

187

wound through a grove of high, well-grown tamarisks to the shore of the lake. And when they had pushed through the last of this screen there before them, quite close to, were countless flamingos, most of them up to their knees in the water with their long-necked heads deeply immerged, but others staring about or gossiping with a sound like geese. Those within twenty yards of the horsemen rose into the air with a most glorious show of black and above all scarlet, and flew, heads and legs stretched out, to the middle. Those that remained – the majority – carried on sieving nourishment from the Shatt. Stephen was entranced. With his glass, far over, he made out the mounds of their innumerable nests, raised mounds of mud sometimes with sitting bird, and a crowd of awkward, long-legged, pale fledglings. He also saw some crested coots and a cruising marsh-harrier – a hen bird – and a few egrets; but he was uneasily aware of having prated away interminably about his treecreeper earlier in the day, and now he said no more.

But Jacob turned a beaming face towards him and cried, 'If that unspeakably glorious spectacle is ornithology, then I am an ornithologist. I had no idea that such splendour existed. You must tell me much, much more.'

Ibrahim asked Jacob whether the gentleman had seen the red birds; and when this was relayed, Stephen smiled at the youth, made appropriate gestures, and after some fumbling produced one of the few guineas he kept in a waistcoat pocket.

When Stephen had finished his disquisition on the anatomy of the flamingo's bill, on the intricate processes that enabled the bird to gain its living – its very exact requirements where salinity and temperature were concerned – its apparent neglect of its offspring, herded in groups looked after and fed by the entire community – the need for much more work, for much more information, exact information – when he had finished, Ibrahim came closer and spoke to Jacob, pointing towards the head of the lake with great earnestness.

'He says that if we do not mind making a rather muddy detour he will show you a sight that *you* will appreciate: he very rightly looks upon you as a creature of a finer essence.'

'Long may he live. Let us by all means see his sight.'

Its probable nature became evident as they approached the part of the lake where it received the river, a little delta of mud and sand that retained footmarks with admirable clarity on either side: and footmarks there were in extraordinary numbers, this being so convenient a fresh-water drinking place – jackals, deer of various sizes, hyenas, leopards, a single bear, but above all those of lions, large and even very large tracks from different directions all converging towards the deep pool where the stream ran fast between bare rocky sides to plunge into the Shatt. Here the tracks were almost wholly lions', in great profusion, mingling and crossing.

'Ibrahim says that on some evenings the lions from our side of the river come down here to drink and to meet the lions from the other side, those that live in the plain country southwards. And when they are all assembled, each side roars at the other: all of one side, then all of the other. He has watched them from that tree. He says it is extraordinarily moving.'

'I can well believe it,' said Stephen. 'About how many lions a side?'

'Sometimes as many as eight.'

'Lionesses too?'

'No, no, no. Dear me, no,' said Jacob. Ibrahim shook his head with great disapproval, but then spoke for some minutes. 'He says that sometimes a strange lioness, a lioness from away, comes roving into our part: the lionesses from here will join and attack her, roaring very like the true lions. And he says we should hurry: we are late already, which the Dey cannot bear.'

They regained the path, and as they rode Stephen observed, 'So that is what the Vizier meant by *le club des lions.* I presume lions do not climb trees, but I should be obliged if you would confirm it with this amiable youth.'

'He confirms it. Leopard, yes: lions, no.'

'Then I believe I must see this club, if time can possibly be found.'

There seemed to be time and to spare in the Dey's hunting camp, a number of small tents tucked into an unexpected and almost invisible dell some way from the river-bank and the natural road along the stream, the highway for all the creatures of the region. There were different human paths leading from it to the camp, one for each day of the week, so that the place should not become too notorious; and today being Tuesday, Ibrahim led them up through a stand of oaks, where in spite of the presence of men no great way off, wild boars had been ploughing the ground for acorns and tubers over a stretch of between fifteen and twenty acres so that it looked like a well ploughed and harrowed field.

At the guarded descent into the dell Ibrahim showed his pass again and they were led to a tent with a small heap of rugs in it, the topmost being of an enchanting diapered pattern whose colours glowed like jewels when the sun touched them.

Amos Jacob and Stephen passed their time discussing chronic diseases they had personally encountered and the measures they had taken to alleviate them at least in some degree, with estimates of their success, usually very slight or even non-existent, but on one or two occasions most gratifying and spectacular. They were deep in two extraordinary, unaccountable and *lasting* cases of remission in phthisis and tetraplegia when the chief huntsman came to say that Omar Pasha would now receive them.

They found the Dey in a fairly high state of grease and good humour. Stephen bowed and said, 'May I present His Britannic Majesty's government's greetings and good wishes to His Highness Omar Pasha?'

Jacob translated, but in Stephen's opinion not quite literally, since the name of God occurred several times.

Omar rose, bowed – they all bowed – and said he was most gratified by his English cousin's friendly message, the first he had received from a European ruler: he desired them to sit down and called for coffee and a hookah. 'I have just succeeded in putting these together,' he said, observing that Stephen's eye was keenly turned upon a beautiful pair of guns, of double-barrelled, rifled guns. 'I took the plates off to look at the sear, but for a great while I was puzzled to get them and the sear-spring back again. However, with God's help it is done now, ha ha! Blessed be the Name of God.' Jacob made the ritual response and Stephen a murmur: the Pasha looked so pleased at his success that Stephen asked whether he might look at the nearer gun.

'By all means,' said the Dey, and put it into his hands. The gun was much lighter than Stephen had expected, and it came up to his shoulder almost like a fowling-piece, a pretty solid fowling-piece for duck or geese. 'You are accustomed to guns, I find?' said the Dey, smiling.

'Indeed I am, sir,' replied Stephen. 'I have shot many and many a creature with them, partly for sport and partly for study.'

The coffee and the pipe came in; and after a longish pause in which they smoked and drank, Stephen said, 'I do not believe I have ever had better nor more welcome coffee: but now, sir, with your permission I will deliver the message that His Majesty's Ministry has entrusted to me. It has come to their knowledge that several numerous Shiite brotherhoods and confederacies along the Adriatic and Ionian coast and inland to Serbia who support Bonaparte . . .'

'Bonaparte, that son of a dog,' said the Dey, his face clouding with anger and taking on a very wicked look.

'. . . have combined to intervene in his favour by doing all they can . . .' Stephen carried on, although he knew that he had lost the Dey's attention and that he was irritating him.

'Your master must have some very weak advisers,' said the Dey when Stephen came to an end, 'very weak, if they can believe *that* after his Royal Navy has so banged and battered Bonaparte's friends in the Adriatic. I love the Royal Navy: I knew Sir Smith at Acre ... but I leave all these things to my Vizier: he understands politics. For my part I understand soldiers: soldiers and their fate. And I know that this Bonaparte must fall. Whether there is any truth in this alleged plot and whether it succeeds or fails is of no consequence: this Bonaparte must fall. It is written. He has gone beyond what is allowed and he must therefore necessarily fall: it is written.' He jerked his head and muttered, looking intensely disagreeable; but presently his eye fell on the guns once more, and with a far more amiable expression he said, 'So you are interested in animals, sir, in the hunting and study of animals?'

'Very much so indeed, sir.'

'Then should you like to hunt a lion with me? I mean to lie in wait for one tomorrow evening.'

'I should like it of all things, sir; but I have not so much as a fowling-piece with me.'

'As for that, you may choose either of these and grow used to it, shooting all through the afternoon – there is no want of powder and shot in this camp, I do assure you – and then in the evening, with your gun still warm and supple, we will walk along the river-bank in blood-soaked shoes.'

'Blood-soaked shoes, Pasha?'

'Why, yes: did you not know that blood – swine's blood, deer's blood – does away with human scent? Along the bank until we are under Ibn Haukal's crag: a few feet up this crag there is a hollow called Ibn Haukal's cave, since he meditated there for a while during his travels: it is large enough for two men and it is somewhat hidden by tall grass and plants hanging from above. Some way farther up the stream, in the same kind of rock, there is a much larger and deeper cave where this lion Mahmud and his mate have their young. Although the cubs are quite large by now he still feeds them and of course his lioness; and it is his custom to walk down to the stream to some scattered bushes near a common watering-place and there to wait for a boar or a deer or whatever offers – last year he took one of my men who was trapping porcupines. I mean to wait for him on his way home, since he carries his prey hanging to the left. This allows one to shoot him behind the right ear and perhaps to kill him with the first shot. We shall, God willing, have the kindest moon for both his journeys.'

'Indeed we shall, with the blessing.'

'So if by the end of tomorrow afternoon you are pleased with the gun, and if you feel equal to waiting in silence, scarcely even drawing breath for half an hour and then perhaps as long again for his return, let us draw straws for the first to fire.'

Straws were brought, and Omar, with barely concealed pleasure, drew the longer. He at once began showing Stephen the management of the rifle – an American weapon unfamiliar to Stephen – and when they walked into the open, first to fire some random shots into the sky and then to shoot deliberately at a candle, a lion far down, perhaps on the lake shore itself, began a series of great coughing roars that carried wonderfully on the still evening air.

The next morning Stephen and Jacob, taking some bread and mutton with them, spent most of their time on the bank of the Shatt, Jacob improving Stephen's rudimentary Arabic, Berber and Turkish, Stephen telling him the elements of ornithology, illustrated by what few birds they had at hand. Clearly there were the myriads of splendid flamingos, but very few other waders; and the odd falcon or passerine fowl did not stay long enough for anything like close observation. The flamingos however were a feast in themselves, and they showed all their phases, feeding, preening, rising in great squadrons for no apparent cause, wheeling in splendour, coming down again, dashing the surface wide, and some placidly swimming. And in the course of the day Amos Jacob grew perfectly familiar with the griffon, Egyptian and black vultures, with a possible sight of the lappet-faced bird.

But their main business was learning the nature, temper and power of the gun: Stephen shot at fixed marks far and near, and he declared that 'this was the truest, sweetest gun he had ever handled'. 'I can make no such claim,' said Jacob, 'having had so very little experience, and that only with fowling-pieces; but I did hit what I intended to hit several times, and once at a considerable distance.' He paused and then went on, 'I would not ask many people, but I am sure that you will not make game of me if I beg you to tell me the reason for these spiral grooves, the rifling, inside the barrels.'

'They give a twist to the bullet, so that it flies out spinning about its axis at a prodigious rate: this evens out the inevitable minute inequalities of weight and of surface in the bullet, giving its flight an extraordinary accuracy. The Americans shoot their squirrels, a small and wary prey, from quite remarkable distances – shoot them with the light squirrel-rifles they have known from childhood – and in the War of Independence they were the most deadly marksmen. I have no doubt that these of Omar Pasha's are squirrel-rifles writ large.'

On their way back at dusk they met Ibrahim, sent to look for them. 'Omar Pasha was afraid you might have lost your way, and that the lamb might be overcooked,' he said. 'Please to step out. May I carry the gun?'

'There you are,' cried the Dey as they came down into the dell and its scent of wood-smoke and roasting mutton. 'I have not heard you shooting this half hour and more.'

'No, sir,' replied Stephen through Jacob, 'we were contemplating a band of apes, Barbary apes, and they persecuting a young and foolish leopard, leaping from branch to branch and pelting it, gibbering and barking, until the animal fairly ran from them in open country.'

'Well, you have been able to study animals, I find,' said Omar. 'I am glad of it: there are not so many apes about, in these degenerate days. But come and wash your hands and we will eat at once, to digest before it is time to leave. Tell me, how did you find the gun?'

'I have never fired with a better,' said Stephen. 'I believe that in a good light on a windless day, I could hit an egg at two hundred and fifty paces. It is a beautiful gun.'

The Dey laughed with pleasure. 'That is what Sir Smith said about my sword,' he observed. Three men brought three basins; they washed their hands, and the Dey went on, 'Now let us sit down, and while we eat I will tell you about Sir Smith. You remember the siege of Acre, of course? Yes: well, on the fifty-second day of the siege, when reinforcements under Hassan Bey were just in sight, Bonaparte's artillery increased its fire enormously, and before dawn his infantry attacked, thrusting into the breach across the dry moat, half-choked with fallen battlements, and there was furious hand-to-hand fighting on each side of the pile of ruins. Sir Smith was with us together with close on a thousand seamen and Marines from his ships, and they were in the thick of the fight. My uncle Djezzar Pasha was sitting on a rock a little way behind the battle, handing out musket cartridges and rewarding men who brought him an enemy's head, when suddenly it came to him that if Sir Smith were killed his men would turn and all would be lost. As I brought him a head he told me to require the English officer to withdraw and he came down with me to compel him to do so, taking him by the shoulder. And while he was held, a Frenchman, breaking through the press, cut at him. I parried the blow and with my backhand took the man's head clean off his shoulders. Between us we led Sir Smith back to my uncle's station, and it was as he sat down that he took my hand, and pointing to my scimitar, said, "It is a beautiful sword". But come, let us eat: tepid mutton is worse than a luke-warm girl.'

'I had not notion that Sir Sidney spoke Turkish,' said Stephen aside to Jacob, while Omar was tearing the sheep apart.

'He was in Constantinople with his brother Sir Spencer, the minister; indeed I believe they were joint-ministers.'

When the lamb was no more than a heap of well-cleaned bones, and when Omar, his chief huntsman and the two guests had eaten cakes made of dried figs and dates, moistened with honey and followed by coffee, and when the glow of the moon was just beginning to tinge the sky behind the mountain, the Dey stood up, uttered a formal prayer, and called for bowls of blood. 'Goat, not swine,' he said emphatically, patting Stephen's shoulder to encourage him: and so, armed and red-footed, they set off, first climbing from the dell, then dropping by Wednesday's path to the stream and its almost bare, well-trodden bank. By now Stephen's eyes were accustomed to the dimness and he might have been walking along a broad highway, with Omar Pasha close before him. For so big a man he moved with an easy, supple pace, making barely a sound: twice he stopped, listening and as it were taking the scent of the air like a dog. He never spoke, but sometimes he turned his head, when the gleam of his teeth could be seen in his beard. He would have been the very model of a hunter, thought Stephen, with his silent tread and his subfusc clothes, but for the fact that as the rising moon shed an even greater light through the trees so it shone on the steel of the rifle slung over his shoulder. Stephen's was under his light cloak, its butt far down below his knee: he had lived so long in cold, wet countries that the duty of keeping his powder dry had assumed religious proportions. He was thinking of other expeditions by night for the dawn-flighting and at the same time reflecting with pleasure that he was keeping up without much effort, though the six-foot Dey had a much longer stride, when Omar stopped, looked round, and pointing to a mass of bare rock emerging from the trees he whispered, 'Ibn Haukal.' Stephen nodded, and with infinite precaution they crept up to the small, low-ceilinged cave. With infinite precaution, but even so Omar, the leader, dislodged a little heap of shale that rattled down to the path, a very small but very shocking avalanche. They were still standing motionless when a very small-eared owl, known to Stephen from his childhood by the name of gloc, Athena's owl, uttered its modest song, 'Tyu, tyu', answered almost at once by another, a quarter of a mile away. 'Tyu, tyu.'

Omar, having listened very attentively indeed for other sounds and hearing none, moved on, bent double, into the cave. They could not stand upright, of course, but the front, opening on to the stream, was quite wide enough for two and they sat comfortably, their guns across their knees, gazing down at a path that grew more and more distinct as the great moon, just beyond the full, mounted higher and higher in the sky, putting out the stars.

The air was warm and most uncommonly still, and Stephen heard a pair of nightjars churring away in their unchanging voice as they wheeled about pursuing moths far down, perhaps almost as far off as the Shatt. Brighter and brighter still, and the path just beneath, somewhat constricted by Ibn Haukal's crag, was strikingly clear, once Omar had very gently cut away some of the overhanging shrub: and on this path they saw a hyena, most distinctly a striped hyena, carefully working out a line, like a hound – their own line, in fact, the scent of their bloody shoes. And where they had turned it paused, uttered its habitual shrieking howl (Stephen noticed that its mane rose as it did so) and ran straight up into the cave. For a moment it stood transfixed in the entrance, then turned and fled, its mad

197

laugh echoing from one side of the valley to the other. Omar neither moved nor spoke: Stephen made no comment.

A long, long pause, interrupted only by the passage of a porcupine; and though the silent wait grew a little wearisome Stephen had the consolation of his watch, an elegant Breguet, a minute-repeater, that had travelled with him and consoled him for more years than he could easily reckon. Every quarter of an hour or so he would press a button and a tiny silver voice would tell his attentive ear the time. If Omar ever heard the minute sound he gave no sign; but just after twenty minutes past the hour he stiffened, changed his grip on the gun, and Stephen saw the large pale form of a lion pace swiftly across their field of vision from right to left.

The turn of the stream and its accompanying path, together with a scattering of low bushes hid him after a very few seconds: but Stephen was left the sharpest possible image of a great smoothly-moving creature, pale, and with a pale mane, even; shoulder-blades alternately protruding through a mass of muscle. A perfectly confident, self-contained and concentrated animal, between nine and ten feet long, perhaps three and a half feet at the withers (though he held his head much higher than that), and weighing a good thirty stone, with that enormous chest.

'Mahmud,' whispered Omar, smiling: Stephen nodded, and they returned to their silence. But not for very long: far sooner than Stephen had expected, away on the left there was a crashing of branches, a wild flailing about, some high desperate shrieks, a very deep sustained growling.

Now the minutes passed very, very slowly: both men were extremely tense, and if Stephen opened his mouth to draw a deeper breath, he could hear the beating of his heart.

Then at last came the sound of jackals, very usual attendants on a lion's kill: his furious snapping as they ventured too near: and after a long but extraordinarily expectant wait, the sound of movement among the downstream bushes.

Mahmud came clearly into sight on the left, carrying a heavy wild boar, and carrying it high, well to the left to free the stride of his leg. Nearer: nearer: and when he was just past the mid-point, just going from them, Omar rose and shot him, aiming behind the right ear. But though the lion fell he was on his feet again the next moment, roaring with fury. Omar shot him again and this time he fell forward twitching, no other movement.

But now his lioness was almost there. She lowered her head over him, licking his death-wound and moaning. Then she looked up directly into the cave with the men and charged straight for them in five prodigious bounds.

Stephen saw her eyes clear in the moonlight: it was a mere fair-ground shot and with real regret he killed her as she rose in her last leap.

The Dey's huntsmen knew very well that Mahmud was his intended quarry, and when in the still night they heard three shots rather than one it was clear to them that something was very much amiss. Five of them came racing down the nearest path from the camp with torches, and they found their chief and his guest guarding the lions from the jackals and hyenas, drawn by even the faintest smell of death.

By the light of a great fire they, the second huntsman and his team, skinned Mahmud and his mate, while the headman lit the Dey and his companion back to the camp, Omar most solicitously giving Stephen his hand wherever the going was a little steep.

As soon as they reached the dell Jacob was summoned from his tent and desired to translate the Dey's gratitude and congratulations, quite remarkably well-phrased and convincing. Stephen begged Jacob to say all that was proper and smiled and bowed, with gestures that disclaimed all merit: but the force of very strong emotion so recently felt but only now fully perceived was mounting so that he wholly longed for silence and his bed.

'And the Dey says,' Jacob went on, 'that a mule hardened to the task will be sent down to bring the skins up in the morning: while as for Mahmud's cubs, they are perfectly capable of looking after themselves – have already killed several young boars and two fawns – but nevertheless he promises you that they shall be given a sheep or two every week for some months. And as for the foolish tale about gold for the Shiite heretics he assures you that not an ounce, not half an ounce, shall ever pass through Algiers while he is Dey; and he will send the Vizier a direct order to that effect, in case there should ever have been a ghost or perhaps I should say an apparition of misunderstanding or incomprehension.'

Stephen nodded, smiled and bowed yet again. Omar looked kindly at him and said to Jacob, 'My saviour is himself in need of salvation: pray lead him very quietly away.' He clasped Stephen, imprinted a bristly kiss on his cheek, bowed and withdrew.

For most of the next day Stephen and Amos Jacob rode well ahead of their companions, for not only did they wish to exchange their impressions of the Dey, which was better done without the confusion of many voices and the sound of many hooves, but they also hoped that by setting a fine brisk pace they would bring the whole group to the Vizier's oasis before nightfall, in spite of having been obliged, by the farewell feast, to start their journey much later than they had wished.

At one time they thought they might succeed, for they had already travelled this road – the fact of its being known shortened it, and there were few fresh wonders to delay them – furthermore, their own conversation was particularly engrossing. Sometimes, it is true, they discussed the possible origins of the malformation in the hand that Jacob had brought his friend: 'I know that some of Dupuytren's colleagues have blamed the habitual use of reins: and perhaps there is something in it,' observed Jacob.

'Conceivably,' Stephen replied. 'Yet it was never described before Smectymnus; nor does Xenophon speak of any such complaint; and few men handled reins more than Xenophon.'

'Well . . .' said Jacob: and after a pause in which his mind clearly drifted to the more immediate subject, 'You have not yet told me your opinion of the Dey.'

'My first impression was that he was a brute, a mere soldier: a cheerful brute at that moment because he had just succeeded in some mechanical task, but perfectly capable of turning wicked, very wicked. Then, when we went down to lie in wait for the lion, his silence and his steadfast motionless endurance moved my admiration. So did his open, unstinted praise when I shot the lioness, to say nothing of his steadiness in the uneasy moments before she charged. I have, as you know very well, some smattering of Arabic and Turkish, and what he said as he helped me up the slope pleased me very much. So, to a less degree, did the set piece that you translated: no common mind, I thought, could have turned it so well. I was left with the notion of an ideal shooting-companion, very quiet, very knowledgeable, courageous of course and jovial when joviality was in place: but apart from that, not an intelligent man. Not positively stupid, like some other highly-placed soldiers, and probably quite subtle in military politics, but not in himself particularly interesting, however likeable.'

'Did the impalements trouble you?'

'I loathed them with all my soul, although they are as traditional in some parts as public hanging is in England. But it was not that which made me doubtful about my first impression: after all, sodomy is a hanging offence with us and a matter of burning alive with some others, whereas it is a joke in this country, as it was in ancient Greece. No: after a while I began to wonder whether the simplicity was quite what it seemed, as well as the apparently complete division between Dey and Vizier where foreign affairs were concerned. But you know as well as I do that an excess of mistrust and suspicion is very widely spread in our calling: it sometimes reaches ludicrous proportions.'

'Two of our colleagues in Marseilles were obliged to be shut up in a mad-house near Aubagne, each convinced that his mistress was poisoning him for the benefit of a foreign power.'

'In my case it scarcely warranted chains, a bed of straw, and flogging, but it went pretty far: when we paused to eat by the spring I went to my baggage-mule and discovered the Dey's wonderfully handsome, wonderfully discreet present, the American rifle that killed the lioness; but when I had recovered from my astonishment something compelled me to look very carefully indeed at lock, stock and barrel – both barrels – before I could thank him wholeheartedly. A man we both knew was killed by the explosion of a fowling-piece that burst when he fired it – a gift, of course.'

'William Duran. He was incautious, having to do with such a woman: but still there are limits. One cannot live in a glass globe, like that marvellous person in Breughel. For my part I thought him subtler and more intelligent than you did, for whereas with you he was necessarily dumb, restricted to the hunter, with me, obviously, he spoke a great deal and with a choice of words, particularly in Turkish, and a felicity of expression surprising in a mere soldier. But whether he is clever enough to manage the janissaries, the corsairs and his curious Vizier, I do not know. What was your opinion of the Vizier? You saw much more of him than I did.'

'A politician of course, but one not without an agreeable side. I should not trust him in any matter of importance.'

Hootings far behind them, and the blowing of a horn: they turned, and there was the best-mounted of the Turkish guards hurrying after them, the main group being a great way off.

Jacob relayed his panting words: 'He says that the others

cannot keep up: and he fears – all the people fear – that the sirocco will be with us in an hour or two.' Looking south-ward he added, 'If we had not been prating so eagerly over other men's characters I should have noticed it long before. You see that dark bar over the third mountain range behind us? That is the precursor. Presently the south-east wind will begin to blow and then the much stronger sirocco will reach us, its hot air filled, *filled*, with very fine sand. You have to have a close-woven cloth over your mouth and nose.'

'You know this country: tell me what you think we ought to do.'

'I do not believe it will be a very bad sirocco: we shall probably not reach the oasis and the lodge before dark, but I think we should press on. The sirocco often drops after sunset, and we should have some moonlight to help us on our way. At all events, I think that is better than camping unprepared in the wilderness, with little water and the ani-mals likely to be harassed by wild beasts.'

'I am sure you are right,' said Stephen: he wheeled his horse and with the other two he rode back gently to meet the band, who greeted them with a cheer. 'Pray ask Ibrahim whether he can guide us after nightfall – whether he will be able to recognize the trail where it is very faint?'

Ibrahim received the question at first with incredulity and then with as decent a concealment of laughter as he could manage. 'He says he is as competent as seven dogs,' reported Jacob.

'Then pray tell him that if he succeeds he shall have seven gold pieces; but if he do not, then he must be impaled.'

Towards the end of their journey, which grew more hor-rible with every hundred yards traversed, with the dense cloud of fine sand quite hiding the moon and making its way through protective cloth and the hot wind growing stronger, even the seven dogs faltered time and again. Quite often Ibrahim had to beg them to stop, huddled together for protection, while he cast about: but getting them to start again and to leave the slight shelter of the larger animals was another matter. He was repeatedly kicked, pinched, reviled; and he was actually in tears when a rift in the veil of flying sand showed the oasis, with the sparse lanterns of the hunting-lodge. Sparse because almost everybody had gone to bed, and apart from the pair at the main gate the only lamp still glowing was in the room where Ahmed, the under-secretary, was finishing a letter. The porters were obviously unwilling to get up to unbar the gates and open them; but Ahmed, hearing the controversy and recognizing Jacob's voice soon induced them to do their duty.

He asked Jacob whether he should warn the Vizier. 'By no means at all,' said Jacob, 'but if you could bestow these people, give them food and drink, and allow Dr Maturin and me to have a bath we should both be immeasurably grateful.'

'All these things shall be done,' said Ahmed. 'I shall rouse some servants. But when you have taken your bath I am afraid you will have to lie in my room again.'

Down, down, down into a blessed sleep: Stephen, washed clean of sand, even his hair, fed, watered, wrapped in clean linen. Sank to those perfect depths where even the varying howl of the sirocco could not disturb him.

Nothing but strong determined hands could claw him up to the infinitely unwelcome surface, but this they did, and there was the insufferable Jacob at first light asking him whether he remembered what he had told him about Cainites – insisting upon the word Cainite and even shaking Stephen more fully awake.

'Your soul to the Devil, Amos: will you give me a sup of water, for the love of God?' And when he had drunk and gasped he said, 'Certainly I remember what you told me about the Cainites of the Beni Mzab and elsewhere, the way they were created by a superior power and bore the mark of Cain.'

'Yes. Well listen now: Ahmed is a Cainite too. We recognized one another at once. He knows roughly the nature of our visit – he knows that we are not travelling for medical experience or knowledge – he wishes to be useful to us, being entirely on our side, and he offers his services.'

'Amos, my dear, you are a deeply experienced intelligence agent: tell me in all seriousness how sound a source of information he is, what kind of information he can give, and at what price.'

'A sounder source we could not wish: as for the kind of information, he has shown me a copy of the Vizier's message to the Sheikh of Azgar, Ibn Hazm, telling him to recall his caravan at once and to load the treasure aboard a wonderfully fast-sailing xebec that has already left for Arzila, a little shallow fishing-harbour in Shiite territory just north of Laraish: Yahya ben Khaled, the captain of the xebec and the most capable and fortunate corsair in Algiers, will wait there with a very strong guard until the wind comes into the west, and then he will sail, passing through the Strait of Gibraltar in the darkness, with the wind and the strong eastward current driving him at great speed, and head straight for Durazzo by the sea-lanes he knows best, the fastest.'

Stephen sat considering: then he nodded and said, 'There was no mention of reward, I collect?'

'None. I believe his offer was perfectly straightforward: but I gathered that eventually, by no means as a direct consequence of this affair, a kind word to the governor of Malta, to allow him to set up in Valetta, where he has cousins, would be welcome. It is in no way a condition: nor indeed could it be.'

'Very well. Tell me, how early do you think we may start? By the way, I no longer hear the wind.'

'It stopped at half-past four. Obviously we cannot start

before the morning prayer: it would not only be very rude but it would also look suspicious. Yet at first light I shall cause the Turkish guards to make ready.'

'How I hope this vile wind has not plucked *Ringle* from her moorings or blown *Surprise* to some leeward shore beyond Sardinia.'

The period between his getting up, washing, shaving and waiting for the Vizier to appear for the formalities of leave-taking, would have seemed intolerably long but for the fact that Stephen, walking out into what might almost be called the wooded part of the oasis, once more caught sight of his anomalous nuthatch: it was not a particularly shy bird and it allowed him to follow, discreetly taking notes, until Jacob came hurrying through the trees to tell him that the Vizier was in motion but that the Dey's present was nowhere to be found in their baggage: the Turkish guards were distraught – they begged to be told what they should do.

'I do not think that any of our escort would have dared to steal it: but it may be the resumption of a regretted gift – I know that Omar Pasha thought the world of the pair,' said Stephen. 'I am sorry for it, because I valued the rifle for its associations and for the manner of its giving. Though there are other possibilities, of course. I shall not mention the loss.'

Nor did he mention it; but a man far less subtle than the Vizier could have told from his short though civil answers that he was not quite pleased. His first voluntary remark was, 'I am afraid, sir, that we must tear ourselves from your presence at the end of this excellent cup.'

'I very much regret that I was not told of your arrival,' said the Vizier. 'I should have enjoyed several more hours of your company. But I trust you were satisfied by your conversation with the Dey?'

'Perfectly satisfied, I thank you, sir,' said Stephen, finishing his coffee and standing up. 'But now, if you will forgive me, a very long road lies ahead. Let me first make the fullest acknowledgement of your remarkable hospitality, and then allow me to beg that you will transmit all my due respects to His Highness and my thanks for his kindness.'

Chapter Eight

A long road it was and a weary, deep in fine sand wherever there was shelter, while the gardens on the outskirts of Algiers, when at last they reached them, were desolation itself, with greenery all hanging limp, shattered and seared, but for the most part blown right off to lie in withering heaps. And from an outward turn on the mountain road which gave them a clear view of the port and both harbours, it was clear to Stephen's searching telescope that *Ringle* was not there, snug against the mole. Nor was she in the offing: he barely had the heart to search the horizon for the larger, more conspicuous sails of *Surprise*, yet he did so for a full minute before clapping his glass to with disappointment.

'My dear Amos,' he said some time later, 'may I beg you to settle accounts with our guide and these good Turks, to give them a farewell feast at whatever place you judge most fit, together with a present, and then to join me at the consulate. I can see the roof and flagstaff from here.'

Jacob looked doubtful, but he agreed and they parted at the next forking of the road. Stephen could hardly have missed his way, in spite of the anxiety, reasonable and unreasonable, that kept welling up in his heart, for this was the mare's own ground and she increased her pace to a pleasant amble, threading her way through the increasing number of asses, camels, oxen and horses until she brought him to the gate, gave him time to dismount, and then walked off to her own stable.

In spite of his anxiety Stephen had noticed an air of excitement in the city as he rode well into it: groups of people, talking louder than usual, gazing about, making gestures whose meaning escaped him – so many people that sometimes they almost blocked the way, and the placid mare had to push through: no harsh words, however, excitement overcoming all other emotions. It is true that Stephen, who had retained his sirocco headgear, did not look at all out of the way.

He was, however, at once recognized by the unfortunate young man in the outer office, who begged him to sit down – he would tell Lady Clifford at once.

'Dear Dr Maturin,' she cried, 'how very glad I am to see you. Did you have an unspeakably horrid ride? I am afraid so. A really shocking sirocco like that makes you long for the Yorkshire moors.'

'Certainly: but may I ask how Sir Peter does?'

'Oh, very well indeed, I thank you – I have never seen such a change in him – no, nor known a better pill. I take two myself, one in the morning and one before bed. But will you not come and see him? He keeps his room, because he has a great deal of work and people are such a bore: besides, his chief secretary is sick.'

The consul sprang up, not indeed quite like a lion, but very much more briskly than might have been expected in a man so recently crippled by what looked very like an exacerbated sciatica. 'Dr Maturin,' he cried, taking both Stephen's hands, 'how very much obliged I am to you and your colleague for your precious remedies. I have scarcely thought about that shocking pain these last three days; and – forgive me, my dear – such a benign and healing purgation. Sit down, sit down, I beg. You must have had a cruel hard ride of it. Did you meet two or three squadrons of horse on your way back?'

'No, sir.'

'They must have taken the lower road. But tell me, how did your journey go? My dear' – to Lady Clifford – 'you will excuse us, will you not?'

'Of course, of course; and if either of you could do with a pot of tea, pray touch the bell.'

'First,' said Stephen, having opened the door for her, 'may I ask what has become of the schooner *Ringle*? I have news of the very first consequence that I must communicate to Commodore Aubrey.'

'Alas: in the last stages of that frightful blow, the Commodore, signalling from an immense distance, called the schooner to him. I gathered from those who had been talking to the corsairs who had managed to get in that a ship of the Royal Navy was dismasted and badly damaged, and Aubrey needed the schooner to help save her and tow her – presumably to Mahon. I am very sorry to give you what is, I fear, very bad news.'

'It is bad news, about as bad as can be, without some special dispensation. Let me tell you about my mission, and you shall judge. Dr Jacob and I reached the hunting-lodge in the oasis: as you had told me, the Dey was not there but pursuing lions farther on in the Atlas. But as you had foretold, the Vizier *was* there: I therefore showed him your letter and explained my errand – he is perfectly fluent in French, by the way. He said that the rumour was completely unfounded, putting forward the religious differences and the Dey's hatred of Bonaparte: finally he suggested that I should speak to Omar Pasha himself and hear his even more convincing denial. This I did, now speaking through Jacob, and the Dey too said it was great nonsense – he reviled Bonaparte and spoke of his necessary downfall. He also spoke of his admiration for Sir Sidney Smith and the Royal Navy; and he invited me to lie in wait with him for a lion the next evening, using one of a very beautiful pair of rifles that he had recently acquired. Nothing of political consequence occurred until the next day when he did indeed kill the lion, but only with his second barrel, so that when the wholly unexpected lioness charged he was unarmed: I shot her dead, at very short range. He was kind enough to say many flattering things, and he said that he should send the Vizier a direct order that no gold should pass through Algiers; and on the return journey to the hunting-lodge, looking by chance in my baggage I found the rifle I had used concealed under my spare shirt. A little later the sirocco began to blow. It rapidly increased in strength and we only reached the hunting-lodge very late: the Vizier was already in bed. Dr Jacob was lodged with a former acquaintance and, I think, fellow-Cainite who showed him the copy of a letter from the Vizier to Sheikh Ibn Hazm –'

'The ruler who was to provide the pay for the Balkan mercenaries?'

'Just so. A letter requiring him to recall his caravan and load the treasure aboard one of the Dey's xebecs at Arzila, just south and west of Tangier: the xebec was already on its way and the captain's orders were to receive the treasure and repass the Strait by night with the strong eastward current and a favourable wind, steering for Durazzo with the utmost press of sail – it is the fastest xebec in all Barbary. This is the information that I wished to give the Commodore so that he, who knows the Strait so well, might intercept the vessel.'

'I am very sorry indeed that you should have found the Commodore out of immediate reach. I am also very sorry to tell you that later this evening or perhaps tomorrow a new Dey will be proclaimed, Omar Pasha having by then been strangled by the executioners sent to the Khadna valley with those squadrons I mentioned earlier – strangled as his predecessor was strangled. He impaled one youth too many. An error in his calculations that I had not reckoned upon.'

Sir Peter touched the bell: the tea appeared: and when Stephen had drunk a sip he asked, 'Do you suppose the Vizier was privy to this usurpation?'

'I have no doubt of it at all. In the first place they were wholly incompatible: the Vizier despised Omar Pasha as an illiterate brute and the Dey despised the Vizier as a cotquean, in spite of his numerous harem, his collection of guns and his status as an important shareholder in the larger associations of corsairs. Furthermore, the Vizier *privately* admired Bonaparte and *privately* stood to receive a huge commission on Ibn Hazm's gold. But even in so small a court as that of Algiers privacy, real privacy, scarcely exists. I can do favours on occasion, and I have a number of voluntary informants.'

'I do not think I know the word cotquean,' said Stephen.

'Perhaps it is rather out of use now, but we lived in a remote part of Yorkshire and my grandfather often used it – most of his neighbours were cotqueans, particularly those that did not choose to hunt the fox or hare. He meant that they were somewhat effeminate, given to embroidery and probably to sodomy – little better than Whigs.'

After some moments of reflection Stephen said, 'I grieve for Omar Pasha. He had some excellent qualities; he was truly generous; and I did him a shameful injustice.'

'Come in,' called the consul.

'Sir,' said the messenger, 'you told me to warn you the moment the schooner was seen. Moussa believes she is just hull-up in the north.'

'Shall we go and see?' asked Sir Peter. 'I have a telescope on the roof.'

'Will your poor leg bear you?'

'It has done so ever since the *Ringle* vanished.'

The roof, like almost all the others in the city, was whitened against the heat of the sun with tiles or lime-wash, and the mass of them gave the impression of some superhuman bleaching-field; but Stephen's whole attention was fastened upon the fine stout telescope that stood on a bronze tripod weighed down and steadied by pigs of lead: beside it stood a black boy in a scarlet fez, smiling with triumph.

Sir Peter hurried over, bent double against the wind but moving even more nimbly that when he had climbed the ladder, and inwardly Stephen swore to abide by no obvious diagnosis for the rest of his life.

'She is certainly fore-and-aft rigged,' said Sir Peter. 'But this damned wind does so blur the image. Come and look: here is the focusing knob.'

Stephen peered with lowered head, cupping his eye with both hands. The air was indeed horribly troubled. A little whiteness came, grew almost clear, then utterly dissolved in shimmer.

'I wish I had a smaller eyepiece,' said Sir Peter. 'This atmosphere will not cope with such a magnification.'

'I have her,' cried Stephen. 'I have her . . . but alas she is not *Ringle*. She is a craft with a lateen; and she is losing ground on every tack.'

'I am so sorry,' said the consul. 'So very sorry: but at least it shows that some hopes of approaching exist. Let us sleep on that, and conceivably the morning will find her snugly in her berth by the mole.'

'Sir Peter,' called a head at foot-level, the speaker standing precariously on the wind-shaken ladder, 'Dr Jacob sends his compliments and could he be received?'

'Sir Peter,' said Stephen, 'I ask your pardon for interfering, but my colleague, though an excellent physician (*God forgive us both* he added mentally) and linguist, is no mariner. Pray let us go down and speak to him in safety.'

'By all means,' said the consul, and he gave Stephen a hand over the dreadful gulf between the parapet of the roof and the ladder-head.

'Sir Peter,' cried Jacob, starting up, 'I do beg your pardon for this intrusion, but I thought you would like to know that the lot has fallen on Ali Bey.'

'Not on Mustafa? I am amazed.'

'So was he, sir: and I fear it is the bowstring for him – he was led away. But I ventured to come in this informal manner to tell you that Ali is to be proclaimed immediately after the evening prayer.'

'I am very much obliged to you indeed, Dr Jacob. And as I said, I am *amazed*: of all the candidates Ali was the most in favour of the Allies and opposed to Bonaparte. Perhaps I had misread the situation . . .' He pondered, and then went on, 'And I should be still more obliged if you and Dr Maturin would go on my behalf – it is still generally understood that my health keeps me withindoors – to be the first to congratulate the new Dey. We have all the proper ceremonial garments here. And after that I hope you will both stay with Lady Clifford and me until the wretched south wind dies enough for your ships to come in. These blasts are very rare, but once they have set in doggedly they usually last six or seven days. Though now I come to think of it, I shall go with you. I shall take a stick and you two will support me: that will be a capital stroke.'

Jacob glanced at Stephen, saw assent in his eye, and having coughed he said, 'Sir, we should be very happy to support you, as being your known physicians. But as for your exceedingly kind and handsome invitation, for my part may I be allowed to decline? Having uttered all the necessary words of congratulation, I should like to retire to an obscure lodging-house near the Gate of Woe, a house in which some of my less presentable Algerine and Berber friends would excite no comment, whereas they might well compromise an official residence.'

'By all means,' said the consul. 'And Mr Maturin shall do just as he pleases – dining and spending the night with us, and walking about with you by day, meeting your no doubt very interesting friends: and I am sure watching barometer and the horizon with as much zeal as Isabel and myself, or even more . . . the divan will take place at about seven, I suppose?'

'Just so: within the half hour following the proclamation.'

The city, in a state of intense yet still somewhat restrained excitement, grew wonderfully calm for the evening prayer – almost nothing but the voice of the south wind in the palm trees – but the last pious words were barely said, the little prayer-carpets were hardly rolled, before the enormous roaring blast of the Algerine batteries saluted the sky; and as the last echoes died away thousands upon thousands of janissaries and of all those citizens who valued their well-being bawled out the name of Ali, competing with countless harsh trumpets and with drums of every pitch.

The city now settled down to open merriment and joy and endless conversation across the narrow streets or the full width of the few great squares; and Sir Peter's coach and four made its slow but discreetly magnificent way to the palace. Here the consul's physicians were handed out, gorgeous in their robes, and they supported Sir Peter into the council-chamber, where the new Dey greeted him – the first representative of any foreign state to appear – with great kindness, sending for a particular deeply-cushioned seat for him, and listening with grave satisfaction to Jacob's fluent, sonorous and no doubt elegant Turkish congratulation, interspersed with Persian verse and proverb. An excellent speech and above all one that did not last too long: when it was finished, and when Stephen had presented the ritual sabre, the Dey returned thanks, calling the blessing of Heaven and peace on King George. He then clapped his hands and four powerful black men carried Sir Peter in his padded chair to the carriage amidst a triple blast of trumpets sustained beyond anything that Stephen had heard in his life.

By this time it was dark and the steady horses made their way through fireworks, cheering crowds, bonfires with children leaping over them, and great numbers of muskets being fired into the air, the smoke alas still racing northward, perhaps even faster than before.

'Lord,' said Stephen, as he and Jacob, having changed into more everyday clothes, walked downstairs to dinner at the consulate, 'such an overwhelming wealth of colour, light, noise and emotion I do not think I have ever known before: nor had I known that there were anything like so many people in all Africa Minor. Yet in spite of the dreadful underlying anxiety about *Surprise* and *Ringle* – the dreadfully swift passage of time – I do not find that the tumult has quite destroyed my appetite.'

'Even if it had done so, I believe my news would deal with the situation. Sidi Hafiz, whom I have known these many, many years, told me that great masses of the Russian horse, foot and artillery were blocked by floods in Podolia: the vanguard is waiting for them, so that the dangerous proximity – the time when our Assassins, our Bonapartist Balkan Moslems, can strike at both, causing hopeless confusion, ill-will, delay, mistrust and the like – is postponed for at least a week. This came in a wholly reliable overland message from Turkey.'

'Thank Heaven for that,' cried Stephen. 'I have been watching the calendar, seeing this wretched month advance so briskly . . . and every change in that vile moon's shape has wrenched my heart.'

'You have indeed grown much thinner these last days.'

'I shall eat like a lion tonight, however. A whole week gained! Thank you so very much for telling me, dear Amos. Perhaps they will give us mutton.'

Lady Clifford's dinner did indeed include mutton: boiled mutton in the English manner, with caper sauce. It was well enough in its way for those used to such dishes (and after several other delights it was followed by a really stout, solid pudding, of which the same might be said), but it could not really compare with the tender lamb, roasted or grilled on skewers in Jacob's obscure quarters near the Gate of Woe. Stephen ate there daily when he was not staring at the horizon or walking about Algiers with Jacob; but in the evening he returned to the consulate to dine with the Cliffords. It was on one of these days, these as it were free days which a kind fate had added to their calendar, that Jacob and he were passing through the now active, reanimated slave-market when Jacob, catching sight of an acquaintance, begged Stephen to wait for him. By heredity Jacob was a jewel-merchant, and the profession, still slumbering in his bosom, was always ready to awake: he had retained not only an intimate knowledge of gem-stones but a fervent love for some of them, and he wished this acquaintance to exchange a small, exquisite jasper bowl for some few of the paper of moderate diamonds that he habitually carried, very well hidden, to provide for such a deal. 'I shall not be long,' he said. 'Let us meet at the blue-domed coffee-house, there in the far corner.'

'Certainly,' said Stephen; and he was wandering slowly through this ultimate unhappiness and desolation, rendered just tolerable from being so customary, a fact of every day, like a cattle market, when he heard a voice lost in misery say, 'Oh for the love of God,' in Irish: not at all loud, with no strong emphasis. He turned and saw two small children, a boy and a girl, ugly, dirty, and thin. They were far too young for the usual chains, but they were tied together, left arm to right arm, by a piece of string.

The cheerful merchant called out to Stephen, first in Arabic, then in a mostly Spanish lingua franca, that he should have them for a trifle – they were perfectly healthy and in a very few years, if fed moderately, they would be capable of severe labour: even now, ha, ha, they could be put to scare crows, and they could always be used for pleasure.

'I shall speak to them,' said Stephen, and this he did. They were twins, said the boy, Kevin and Mona Fitzpatrick, from Ballydonegan, where their father worked for Mr Mac-Carthy: they had gone to Dursey Island with Cousin Rory in the boat for crabs: somehow with the great wind and the rain from the north the boat came adrift while Rory was with his sweetheart and they were swept out to sea. In the morning the corsairs, the Moors, took them aboard. They had been raiding along the coast but they had brought away only one man, Sean Kelly: and the gentleman there – nodding at the merchant – had sold him yesterday. Sean had told them that the people of Dungarvan and somewhere to the north had killed two dozen Moors.

A person with a somewhat bookish, secretarial look – a person whom Stephen might well have seen among the new Dey's retinue – spoke privately to the merchant, who listened with obvious respect: and when he had gone Stephen said, in the usual indifferent horse-coper's tone, 'I should like to know what kind of a price such goods fetch in this city.' The merchant replied, 'Four guineas for the boy, sir – the usual redemption fee – and I will throw in the girl for the honour of your custom.'

'Very well,' said Stephen, feeling in his pocket. 'But you must give me a receipt.'

The merchant bowed, wrote on a piece of paper, sealed it, received the coins, cut the piece of string, and formally passed the children over with the customary blessing and a second bow. Stephen returned the civility, told the children that he had bought them, and bade each take a hand. This they did without a word, and he led them across the market to the blue dome.

'Amos,' he said, 'do you think that the people of this house would have something suitable for children? I have just bought these two.'

'Have they teeth?'

'Kevin and Mona, have you teeth?'

They nodded very gravely, and showed them: fine healthy teeth, with the gaps usual at their age.

'Then I shall call for yoghurt, sugared, and soft bread. Pray what was the language in which you spoke to them?'

'It was Irish, the language spoken by many if not by most of the people in Ireland.'

Jacob waved his hand, gave his order, and asked, 'Do these children speak no English?'

'I will ask them when there is a little food in their bellies. They might weep if they were questioned before.'

How it vanished, the yoghurt and the great soft flap of bread: within minutes the children looked far more nearly human. And on being asked, after a second helping, Mona said that although she did not know much, she could say most of a Hail Mary. Kevin only hung his head.

'Do you think that kind woman by the Gate of Woe would wash these children, clothe them in modest decency, and even brush their hair?'

'Fatima? I am sure of it. She might find them shoes, too.'

'I doubt they have ever worn shoes.' He asked them and they both shook their heads. 'Not even for Mass?' Renewed shaking, and a hint of tears. 'I know what might answer very well,' said Stephen. 'Those shoes we call espardenyas, made of sailcloth with soft cord soles and ribbons to attach them. Are they to be had, do you think? I should not like to carry them to the consulate barefoot.'

'Certainly they are to be had. At the southern corner of this very square they're to be had.'

In these shoes (red for the one, blue for the other) they hobbled with ludicrous pride to Amos Jacob's dubious lair: by the time they reached it they were walking quite easily and their starved little faces were more nearly human, even ready to smile. Fatima, a capable, intelligent woman, looked at them with more sorrow than disapproval: after a longish pause she brought them back washed, clothed, brushed, fed yet again and almost unrecognizable, but perfectly willing to be friendly.

'They are brisker by far,' said Stephen '– do you notice that the sound of the wind is less? – but they will never walk up all those infernal steps. Would there be carriages to be had, do you suppose?'

'Certainly there are carriages to be had, and I will send Achmet for one, if you wish.'

'Pray be so kind.'

'And certainly I have noticed a lessening in the perpetual roar: it clenched one's innermost man, diaphragm, solar plexus, pericardium into a hard knot that is now perceptibly looser. If we take a carriage, we shall have to go a great way round to reach the consulate, and for two thirds of the journey we shall be gazing over the sea . . .'

Sea there was, a vast extent of white-flecked sea with its horizon growing more and more distant as they rose: but the whole of it was still empty even by the time they reached the consulate. Stephen left the wondering children with Jacob under the palms and walked in: he was told that Sir Peter was at a consular meeting, but smiling at the news he sent his name up to Lady Clifford.

'Oh Dr Maturin,' she cried, 'I am so sorry Sir Peter is not at home: he is at one of those odious conferences that go on and on for ever, and all to no purpose.'

'I grieve for him, upon my word,' said Stephen. 'But my errand is rather to you than to him. I bought a couple of children this morning in the slave-market, a boy and a girl, twins, of I suppose six or seven. Although they do not speak a word of English beyond the Hail Mary they are literally distressed British subjects. They were picked up by an Algerine corsair that had been raiding the Munster coast – picked up in a drifting boat, brought here and sold. May I beg you to shelter them for two or three days, while I make arrangements to send them home?'

'Dr Maturin,' she said without any change of expression or tone that he could detect, 'I wish I could oblige you, but children are my husband's aversion, his absolute aversion: he cannot bear them.'

'I am told that it is often the case with men.'

'It is like some people with cats: he cannot tolerate them anywhere in the house. But if, as I suppose, from their origin and from what you say, they are Roman Catholics, then I believe the Redemptorist Fathers are the people to apply to.'

'Many thanks, your ladyship,' said Stephen, rising. 'My compliments wait on Sir Peter.'

Outside, cheerfully greeted by his slaves, who showed

him a palm-frond torn from the tree, he saw with great satisfaction that Jacob had retained the carriage. 'I came on a fool's errand,' he said. 'Lady Clifford does not choose to house the children. I was truly astonished at her frankness.'

'Were you, though?' asked Jacob, looking at him curiously. 'Nevertheless, we shall be perfectly happy at our lodging-house: but I am sorry for your disappointment.'

It was a disappointment, however, and it shook his faith in his own judgement to a remarkable degree. He sent a note excusing himself from dinner and spent a pleasant evening feeding the children – ingenuous little creatures – with Fatima. Jacob was away, visiting a Lebanese cousin who also dealt in gem-stones, though on a much larger scale, and in negotiating loans. Coming back when Stephen was in bed, he asked him whether he was asleep. 'I am not,' said Stephen.

'Then let me tell you that my cousin has had news that Ibn Hazm's caravan began its return only yesterday. It is difficult country and they will need ten days to reach Azgar, let alone the little port whose name escapes me.'

'Arzila, I think.'

'Arzila indeed: so with our blessed days of grace, I believe we have a fortnight and to spare.'

'That is very good news indeed: I rejoice.'

'And Abdul Reis, the head of one of the corsair groups, says that the wind will diminish tomorrow. If we like to see some of his galleys we should be welcome at the inner harbour, but quite early in the day, because if the wind does as he thinks it will, he may set out for Sardinia before noon. There are advantages in being well-seen by the Dey.'

'Certainly. Listen, Amos: did you ever read an author who said "Never underestimate a woman's capacity for jealousy, however illogical or inconsistent or indeed self-defeating"?'

'I do not think so: but the notion is fairly wide-spread among those who think of men and women as belonging to two different nations; and who wish to be profound.'

Nevertheless, Lady Clifford's behaviour puzzled Stephen, and until he fell asleep he turned and re-turned it in his mind, with no satisfactory answer at all. He was awakened at dawn, not by any of the usual noises of a disorderly house nor by Dr Jacob's steady, persevering snore, but by a little girl's voice in his ear, asking whether there were any cows to be milked.

There were not, but there was water to be drawn with Fatima's help, faces to be washed, prayers to be said, and a perfectly delightful breakfast to be eaten – bananas and dates amazed the children – in a little hidden court behind: soft bread toasted on the brazier that at some distance kept the coffee warm – toasted and spread with honey. 'Are you not cold, children, with nothing but shirts?' he asked.

'Not at all; and they are not just ordinary shirts but proper clothes: Achmet, though quite old, has nothing else,' they replied. 'Here is the other gentleman. Good morning, sir: God be with you.'

Jacob gave them a Hebrew blessing, drank a great draught of coffee, and said to Stephen, 'When you had gone to bed, a parcel came for you. I did not choose to wake you, but there it is in our room. I shall bring it down as soon as I am more nearly myself. How very much better these children look after a night's sleep: you could hardly mistake them for half-starved apes any more.'

In a little while, his good nature returning, Jacob fetched the parcel, forwarded from the consulate: hardly a parcel in the western sense – no paper, no string, but a sombrely gorgeous robe lapped about with silk scarves enveloping the rifle with which Stephen had killed his lioness. Attached to it was a letter with the Vizier's elegant explanation of a mistake among the people of the baggage-train, his well-turned apologies and his hope that if the loss had been mentioned to his present Highness, the return might also be noticed. And after the European signature came a far more beautiful passage of Arabic. 'Please would you read this for me?' asked Stephen.

'It is a blessing, a series of blessings on you and yours, mentioning many of the attributes of God, the Merciful, the Compassionate . . . My impression is that the Vizier was so sure that his friend Mustafa would be elected that he could do whatever he chose to do with impunity; and that he has now delivered himself to you, bound hand and foot.'

Stephen considered, nodded, and then, bringing out another paper he said, 'And may I beg you to read this as well?'

'It acknowledges receipt of four English gold coins of adequate weight in payment for two young Franks, male and female, warranted virgin: it is dated, sealed and signed in due form.'

'Thank you: I did not want them to be snatched away, reclaimed: they have had quite enough to bear as it is.' He looked with intense admiration at his rifle for a while and then asked when they were to meet Abdul Reis, the corsair.

'We could go whenever you choose. The inner harbour is only a few steps from the Gate of Woe.'

'Then the children can come too. I shall confide this to the good Fatima's care' – tapping the wrapped-up gun – 'and then we can go.'

The street was extremely narrow and the balconies almost touched overhead: parts of it were encumbered with sheep, goats, horsemen, and Algerine children playing a game that required a great deal of running and screeching. Many of them looked remarkably like Mona and Kevin, who were of the black-haired Irish, and they wore the same kind of tunics. Then, working past three heavily-laden and exceptionally ill-natured camels, Stephen, Jacob and the children were suddenly through the gate, and there was the great sky above them and the sea stretching away and away, wind-whitened still, but much less so. And just this side of its northern limit, *Ringle* beating in for the shore, just visible from the inner harbour's wall, and recognizable to one who knew her very well.

The children shied extremely at the sight of the galleys that filled the inner port; they fell silent, and each grasped one of Stephen's hands. The Reis, a formidable great red-bearded figure, was markedly affable to Jacob, showing him the arrangement and the ordering of his handsome craft: he would almost certainly set out for Sardinia when the sail-maker brought the new lateen.

'They do not mean to row, then?' asked Stephen, when this had been explained to him.

'Oh no: they only use their oars when the wind does not serve: at present it serves perfectly for any voyage to a little north of east, to north itself, and a little north of west, particularly as the seas are diminishing every half hour.'

'Dear Amos, pray ask him whether that vessel on the horizon that is turning so valiantly into the wind will eventually reach this port.'

Jacob's question to the Reis was interrupted by the coming of the coal-black sailmaker with two pale Sclavonians, lightly chained but heavily burdened; but eventually, when the new lateen was bent to its long, long tapering yard, Abdul looked out to sea, smiled at the sight of her coming about so briskly on the larboard tack, and said, 'The little American schooner – I have seen her before, the frigate's tender: yes, with the wind lessening like this, she may get in by moonrise – in the early part of the night at all events.'

Stephen said, 'Jacob, if I do not mistake, she will soon be almost exactly in the galley's path, steering for Sardinia: if the Reis would put us aboard her I will give him any sum you think proper. These few hours are so very precious.'

'I am so nearly certain of it that I shall hurry back, settle with Fatima, and bring our belongings,' said Jacob. He made the request, with joined hands, received an amiable smile, and hurried away.

Orders, cries, in much the same peremptory tone usual in the Royal Navy but sometimes with an additional Moorish howl; and as soon as Jacob, helped by Achmet, had put their meagre luggage aboard, the galley began its smooth glide towards the harbour's mouth: the silent children stood pressed against Stephen's side, for although this was not a raiding voyage with the galley full of boarders but an ordinary mercantile carrying and fetching of goods, the diminished crew was still made up of right corsairs, for whom an habitual brutish ferocity of expression was as much a part of their equipment as the knives and pistols in their belts.

The open sea. The Reis put the helm amidships, loosed the sheet and attended to Jacob's further explanation. His red beard opened in a laugh and he said, 'If your friend will guarantee that the schooner will not fire upon us, I will put you aboard for the love of God.'

When this was relayed to him, Stephen bowed repeatedly to the Reis and said to Jacob, 'Could I climb on to some eminence and wave, let us say a handkerchief, when we are nearer, to show our peaceable intent?'

'By all means, if you can find a suitable eminence and remain firmly attached to it in spite of all this heinous pitching.'

Stephen gazed about the unfamiliar rigging: there was a sort of box abaft the masthead, but there seemed no way up to it but levitation. The shrouds, to be sure, had ratlines so that one could climb, as on a ladder, but there was a shocking gap between the topmost ratline and the box, practicable perhaps for an ape or a hardened corsair, but not for a doctor of physic. 'I shall stand in the prow, watching with my pocket-glass, and when we are close enough, I shall make antic gestures.'

The bows of a galley running before the wind did not prove much of a vantage-point, particularly as the children, who would not be left, tangled themselves in the woolded bumpkin; so all three wedged themselves fairly comfortably along what forward rail the galley possessed, and Stephen showed them the wonders of his little telescope. This occupied them until the two vessels were so close that he could distinctly make out William Reade's gleaming steel hook holding him to the starboard shrouds of *Ringle*'s foremast. Stephen inwardly prayed that nothing might go wrong now, and waved his handkerchief: the young master's mate standing behind the schooner's captain with a much more powerful glass, instantly reported this and Reade waved back. Stephen told the children to stand up – their presence would explain the situation – and only by the grace of God did he prevent them from tumbling into the sea as the galley pitched. However their good stout shirts held fast and he hauled them in, gasping and ashamed.

The tedious hours that had dragged by with so little apparent gain since the morning suddenly hastened their pace – faces could be seen and recognized, voices heard. Stephen hurried aft, untied his parcel, wrapped the gun in some shirts and a pair of long woollen drawers and clasped the Vizier's gorgeous robe to his bosom. As the two vessels kissed gently together, the Ringles made the galley fast and thrust across a brow for their unreliable surgeon, who, before venturing upon it, crabwise with a child in each hand, presented the splendid garment to Abdul with a flow of heartfelt thanks, translated by Jacob.

'Why, sir, and here you are!' cried Reade, heaving him in-board. 'How very happy I am to see you, and how happy the Commodore will be. He has been fairly eating his heart out in Mahon. Good-bye, sir,' – this to Abdul Reis – 'and many, many thanks to you and your beautiful galley.'

These last words and the Reis's reply were lost as the two vessels separated, *Ringle* heading for Minorca and the galley for Sardinia, but they went on waving until they were out of sight.

'These children,' said Stephen, 'are Mona and Kevin Fitzpatrick, from Munster – Mona, make your bob to the Captain: Kevin, make your leg.' This in Irish. 'And corsairs picked them up in a boat off the coast, carried them back and sold them in the slave-market here. I bought them, and I mean to send them home in the next ship commanded by a friend and bound for the Cove of Cork. As soon as we are aboard *Surprise* Poll will look after them: but where can we stow them here? And what can we feed them on?'

'Oh, we have plenty of milk, fresh eggs and vegetables – well, fairly fresh, we having beaten into this hellish wind so long: but edible – and as for sleeping, we will sling a cot in the cabin: these two will fit into it with room to spare.'

'Perhaps they could now be given something in the galley, and be shown the heads. I perceive a certain uneasiness familiar to me from my youth.'

'By all means,' said Reade. 'Do they speak English?'

'Scarcely a word; but they have picked up a surprising amount of Arabic,' said Stephen, looking at Jacob, who nodded.

'Then I shall pass the word for Berry: he has children of his own and he was a slave in Morocco for some years.' The word was passed, the children led away by a kindly seaman, rather old; and Stephen said, 'But may I be forgiven, William: first things first, for all love. Tell me about *Surprise* and the Commodore.'

'The coffee is ready, sir: should you like to drink it in the cabin?' asked his steward.

'Certainly. Doctors, shall we go below?' He collected his wits as he poured the coffee, and then said, 'Late in the afternoon of the day that horrible blow began the Commodore was far out in the offing helping a disabled ship – *Lion*, totally dismasted but for about ten foot of the mizen – and we could just distinguish his signal calling us out. So we slipped moorings, struck topgallantmasts down on deck, roused out our heavy-weather canvas and cleared the harbour. Very soon we were reduced to a storm forestaysail and a few other scraps. When we arrived, guided by minute-guns, we could scarcely see fifty yards for the sand and the flying spray, but we did make out that *Surprise* had managed to pass *Lion* a tow to get her head round a little so that she might recover some of her wreckage and set up a jury-rig to give her at least steerage-way. I passed under his lee for orders, and while he was telling me what to do, a heavy Dutchman, part of a scattered convoy, came hurtling down under little more than bare poles, saw us at the last moment, clapped his helm a-lee, severed the tow and struck *Surprise* just abaft the starboard cathead, carrying away her bowsprit, heads, her forefoot, much of her gripe and starting God knows how many butt-ends.'

They listened, amazed: they both knew enough of the sea and of that particular blast to have some notion of the appalling situation of the three ships in question. They shook their heads, but said nothing.

'It is difficult to believe that we survived those God knows how many days, but at least *Ringle* could carry and fetch, and we were all fairly well supplied. And luckily the weather, though as foul as can be imagined, was not cold: luckily, for all the beds aboard *Surprise* had to be stuffed into those shocking started butts, where the sea came pouring in for the first two days, in spite of all the fothering in the world. The bows of sharp-built craft are very, very hard to fother. It was a rough time, with the pumping alone; and I have never seen so much grog drunk with so little effect. And the people, at least our people, behaved very well: never a cross word. In time *Lion* did manage a tolerable jury-rig, enough to give her five knots; the wind and our leaks grew a little less wicked; and we limped into Mahon on Tuesday morning, making a perfect landfall. We landed our wounded – strains, hernias and falling blocks, mostly – the Commodore had *Ringle* surveyed – they pronounced her fit – we took some stores aboard, and with the wind veering just enough to let us out of Mahon he sent me off to fetch you, while he and all the shipwrights who could be spared from *Lion* laboured on repairing *Surprise* right round the clock. We went with a heavy heart – heavier still when the wind shifted right back into the south and we thought we should never see Africa again. Nor did I think I should ever again bless a southerly gale, though this one is all a man could wish.'

Indeed it was now the kindest breeze, and late the next morning it wafted them up the long, long inlet to Port Mahon, where the naval yard echoed with the caulkers' mallets thundering upon the *Lion*'s hull. But out in the fairway there rode *Surprise*, apparently as trim as ever she had been, with her captain in a boat under her newly-painted bows telling his joiner just where to place the last rectangles of gold leaf on her upper forefoot.

As soon as he was aware of the *Ringle*'s presence he sent his joiner up the side, spun the boat about and pulled rapidly across the harbour. He was in the plainest of working clothes, but the Ringles had seen him from afar and he was received with all the ceremonial honours that any commodore has a right to, and with much more pleasure and good will than most.

'A very hearty welcome to you all,' he cried. 'I never thought to have seen you so soon, with a full gale so steady in the south.'

'Nor you would not have seen us, sir,' said William Reade, 'but for an uncommon blessing. We could make no headway at all – turned and turned just in sight of Algiers, losing ground on every tack the last day or so; but a corsair galley came racing out full before the wind, her lateens hare-eared on either side; and she was carrying Dr Maturin and his slaves, and Dr Jacob.'

'Doctors,' said Jack, shaking their hands, 'how very glad I am to see you. Come back to the ship with me, and we will all have dinner together – some guests are coming, among them the Admiral, and we have been preddying her fore and aft.'

'Mona,' said Stephen, 'make your bob to the Commodore: Kevin, make your leg.'

Jack bowed to each in return, and said, 'These are your slaves, I presume?'

'Just so,' said Stephen. 'May I be allowed to take them with us and confide them to Poll?'

'Of course you may,' said Jack. 'William, if you bring *Ringle* alongside, I think it would be better than in and out of boats.'

It was very like a home-coming, and as he gazed about the spotless deck, the impeccable exactitude of the yards and the gleaming paint, to say nothing of the extreme brilliance of every piece of metal that could be induced to shine, Stephen felt that he might have been aboard the frigate fresh from Sepping's yard and Madeira, lying within the New Mole and waiting for the visit of the Commander-in-Chief and Lady Keith, rather than on a vessel that had undergone a battering so severe that she very nearly went down with all hands. It was true that Jack Aubrey looked twenty years older and quite thin, that the traces of extreme hard labour and fatigue were evident on most of the faces – the smiling faces – that he saw, and that the grey, bowed figure that approached, touched his hat, and said, 'I give you joy of your return, sir,' remained unrecognized until he spoke.

'Killick,' he cried, detaching himself from Mona and shaking his hand, 'I hope I see you well?'

'I ain't complaining, sir; and you look tolerable spry, if I may take the liberty. Which I have laid out your decent clothes in the bed-place.'

'Must I change?'

'You would never wish to bring discredit on the barky, with all that filth.' Killick pointed to some odd patches of rifle-oil here and there. 'The Admiral is dining aboard.'

Stephen bowed to the inevitable and said, 'Killick, please do me another kindness and take these children to Poll with my compliments – beg her to wash, brush and rig them in a suitable manner, feed them on whatever is appropriate, and above all be very kind and gentle with them. They do not speak any English yet, but Geoghegan will interpret.'

'Kind and gentle, sir?' He sniffed, and added, 'Well, I shall give the message.'

Stephen explained all this to the children: but he doubted that they, with so many new and extraordinary experiences, sights, so many strange people, even partially understood his words. However, they did each give Killick a hand and followed him to the after hatchway, from which they cast back a wan and anxious look.

He found Jack and Harding looking most attentively at the new accommodation-ladder, shipped for their illustrious guests. 'Jack,' he said, 'forgive me, but I must have a word with you. You will excuse me, Mr Harding?'

In the cabin he went on, 'I have been bursting with my news – there was not a single fit moment aboard the *Ringle*. As you know very well, one of the prime objects of our voyage was to prevent gold reaching the Adriatic Muslims.' Jack nodded. 'The then Dey agreed not to let it pass by way of Algiers: but he has been murdered and betrayed: the gold is now aboard a very rapid vessel in the port of Arzila – is now or very soon will be aboard. This vessel, a galley, as I recall, is to attempt the passage of the Strait by night with a favourable wind. Is it reasonable that we should lie here, inactive? I knew the facts in Algiers, and it almost killed me, being unable to tell you because of that cruel south wind, and the days passing, passing.'

'How well I understand your pain, dear Stephen,' said Jack, laying a hand on his shoulder. 'But you must recollect that these same southerly gales have been blowing elsewhere, even far west of the Canaries. They have kept almost all shipping on the west coast of Spain and Portugal in port, and even stout, new-built ships of the line did not attempt the Strait and its wicked lee-shore until last Monday. Your Moorish galley or xebec would never, never have ventured out in such seas. Take comfort, brother. Drink up a little glass of gin to restore your appetite, and enjoy your dinner.

The Admiral is coming, and his politico, and your friend Mr Wright – he has often asked after you.'

'You relieve my mind wonderfully, Jack.' Stephen sat breathing deeply for a while: he looked so pale that Jack poured his gin at once, added a squeeze of lemon, and urged him to get it down in little sips before he changed.

Before the glass was empty someone knocked at the cabin door. It was Simpson, the ship's barber, with a fresh white apron and jug of hot water. 'Simpson, sir,' he said. 'Which Killick thought the Doctor might like a shave.'

Stephen ran his hand over his chin, as men will do on such occasions – even Popes have been known to make the same gesture – and he acquiesced. It was therefore a smoothed, brushed, and quite well-dressed Dr Maturin who stood there on deck, just before the appointed hour, behind the Commodore, his first lieutenant and the officer of the Royal Marines, all equally smooth and all in their splendour, blue and gold for the sailors, scarlet and gold for the soldiers. As the more conscientious clocks of Mahon prepared to strike the hour, Admiral Fanshawe stepped from a coach, followed by his secretary and political adviser; and before he set foot on deck, hats flew off, the bosun sounded his call and the Marines presented arms with a perfectly simultaneous crash.

Some time after this, an aged, shabby gentleman wearing the clothes of another age and followed by two porters carrying a copper tube wandered hesitantly towards the accommodation-ladder: mounting it with some difficulty, he said to the officer of the deck, 'Sir, my name is Wright: Captain Aubrey was so kind as to invite me, but I fear I may be a little late.'

'Not at all, sir,' said Whewell. 'May I show you the way to the cabin, and unburden your men? Wilcox, Price, come and take this tube, will you?'

'You are too kind,' said Mr Wright, and he followed Whewell aft. But the two porters would not be unburdened:

they carried right on with their tube, entering the already somewhat crowded great cabin with their tube and thrust it across the table, regardless of cloth, glasses and silver, saying loud and clear, 'One and fourpence, sir, if you please.'

'Eh?' cried Mr Wright, from the midst of his conversation with the Commodore and Dr Maturin.

'One and fourpence, or we carry it away.'

Harding whipped round the table, gave them half a crown and in a low, very, very vicious tone desired them to get out of the ship. Killick and his mate Grimble, together with the more presentable gunroom servants, smoothed the snowy cloth, rearranged the glasses and silver and watched as Mr Wright, wholly unconscious of inconvenience, untimeliness and fuss, unsealed one end of the tube, gave the other end to the Commodore to hold, and withdrew the gleaming narwhal's horn, perfect in its curves and spirals, without a hint of repair. 'I cannot detect the slightest join,' cried Stephen. 'It is a masterpiece. Thank you, sir: thank you very much indeed.'

All this, to the bitter grief of the Commodore's cook, had delayed the beginning of dinner quite shockingly; but in time they were all seated. Jack at the head of the table, Admiral Fanshawe on his right, then Reade, the Marine officer, the Admiral's secretary, Harding at the foot, then Stephen with Mr Wright next to him; then came the Admiral's political adviser and lastly Dr Jacob – a pretty large party for so small a frigate, but with the table set athwartships and the guns trundled into the coach and the sleeping-cabin it could be done. And done it was, with great success: the news of the horn's perfect restoration, of its being in an even finer state of beauty than before – Mr Wright, with his delicate burrs and buffs having given it the gleam of fine old ivory – spread rapidly through the frigate: the ship's luck was aboard again. Killick's unattractive, shrewish face beamed once more, his messmates (he had very nearly been expelled from their society) smiled, winked and nodded at him in the cabin and slapped him on the back as he travelled to and from the galley.

Good humour is a charmingly infectious state anywhere, particularly aboard a ship that has recently had a very rough time of it and that is now in port, moored fore and aft. Conversation at table very soon rose to a fine volume of sound, and Mr Wright had to strain his quavering old voice to give Stephen an account of the many mathematical calculations and even advanced physical studies in a current of strongly-flowing water, to determine the effect of the narwhal horn's spirals and tori on the animal's progress, all to no effect – to no effect *yet*: but so important a process must have a function, almost certainly a hydrodynamic function, and either plodding science or one of those beautiful intuitions – or perhaps Mr Wright should say *sudden illuminations* – would give the solution. Harding and the Admiral's secretary agreed very well; and although the Royal Marine found it difficult to get beyond 'An uncommon fine day, sir' to William Reade on his left, they somehow discovered that they had both been at Mr Willis's school together when they were little boys; and from that moment on, except when common good manners required that they should say something to their other neighbours or drink a glass of wine with an acquaintance on the other side of the table, it was a series of 'Old Thomas and the mad bulldog, of how kindly the maids would hand out yesterday's cold suet pudding from the back windows of the kitchen, of the famous thrashing Smith major had given Hubble'. The Admiral had known Jack time out of mind, and they had a great deal of naval news and recollection to exchange, while Jacob and the politico got along reasonably well together, once they had established a neutral ground on which they could speak with no fear of compromising anybody at all and where no unguarded word could do harm.

'God love us,' said Joe Plaice, taking his ease on the quarter-deck, a little abaft the wheel, 'what a din they do make, to be sure. You would think it was the snuggery of the William at Shelmerston of a Saturday night.'

'Never mind, mate,' said his cousin Bonden, 'the port decanters are just putting on the table, and once they have drunk the King, they will be quieter. They have eaten two whole sucking-pigs, which weigh on the stomach.'

There was indeed a pause after all present had murmured 'God bless him' and drunk their wine; and when the talk had regained a moderate pitch Jacob said to the politico, 'I believe my colleague is anxious to have a word with you.'

'And I with *him*, as you may imagine: we have had hardly any news from the other side since the sea went mad.'

In a reasonably subtle manner which other people – their neighbours and the servants standing behind their chairs – would not understand, they arranged for a private meeting somewhat later in the day: but their professional cunning was cast away entirely, when the party came to an end and the Admiral quite openly asked Stephen to come with him and speak about his experiences on the Barbary coast and the present state of affairs in Algiers itself.

This he did, in as plain and straightforward manner as he could, and Admiral Fanshawe listened gravely, with close attention, never interrupting. 'Well,' he said when Stephen had finished, 'I am sorry for Omar Pasha: he was a likeable ruffian. But that is one of the risks a Dey must run: and from the political point of view I think the Commander-in-Chief will think that we gain from the change. Ali Bey has always been more in our favour than otherwise, and many English merchantmen have had reason to be grateful for his moderation, and indeed his kindness on occasion. But I am afraid you must have had but a weary time of it, over there.'

'Well, sir, that too is one of the risks of my calling: and I did see some very glorious spectacles in the Atlas. The only thing I really did regret, and regret most bitterly, was the spectacle of *Surprise*'s tender trying in vain to beat against that shocking wind when I needed so desperately to bring my news to Mahon. Yet even that extreme vexation of spirit faded when Captain Aubrey assured me that the same blast must necessarily have confined the Moorish galley to her port, so that my anguish had no real basis.'

'It was a shocking blast indeed. All the East India and Turkey ships were blocked in Lisbon, and Lord Barmouth only just managed to get into Gibraltar.'

'Lord Barmouth, sir?'

'Why, yes: he has superseded Lord Keith, and it is to him that you will have to address your report.'

'Lord Barmouth,' cried Stephen, startled out of his usual equanimity. 'Oh yes. I remember Lady Keith telling Captain Aubrey that her husband did not wish for a long tenure, but that they should retire to a house near the Governor's cottage until the weather in England grew more tolerable. But I had not expected it so soon. Nor had I expected Lord Barmouth.'

'You are displeased, Dr Maturin?' asked the Admiral, smiling.

'I beg pardon, sir,' said Stephen. 'I have not the slightest right to an opinion on the matter: but I did know that Lord and Lady Keith had a long-standing friendship for Captain Aubrey, and I had hoped that the Admiral would do everything possible and impossible to reinforce his scattered squadron, to make the capture of the Arzila galley more probable.'

'Oh, I am sure that Lord Barmouth will do his utmost,' said Admiral Fanshawe. 'But as you know, the forces at his disposal are precious thin on the ground. Still,' he said, rising after a pause, 'I do wish you the best of success; and at least you have a fair wind for your voyage.'

Chapter Nine

This was the kind of sailing that Stephen liked: with a gentle breeze a little north of east the *Surprise*, with her tender under her lee, made a steady four and a half knots under all plain sail or a trifle less, with a pitch and roll that he scarcely noticed. At first he had wondered at the absence of kites – of royals, studdingsails in all their interesting variety – and the frigate's placid advance had vexed him to the soul, until reflection told him that Jack Aubrey understood his profession as well as any man afloat; that he was perfectly well acquainted with the relative positions of Arzila and Gibraltar; and that his plans must take the moon into consideration – no corsair commanding a galley ballasted with gold was going to attempt the passage of the Strait when she was full or anything like it. Yet still it grieved his unreasoning part (no inconsiderable part of the man) when topgallants were taken in at the setting of the watch.

This evening he had come on deck for a breath of fresh air, leaving the sick-bay (rather fuller than usual with the diseases often produced by so much shore-leave and by some cases of military fever) in Jacob's care, and he sat on a coil of rope right forward. He could hear the children hooting and screeching in the maintop, for the midshipmen and the hands indulged them extremely: they were picking up an extraordinary amount of English, and so far they had done themselves no serious injury. Yet as he sat there pondering his mind was very much less concerned with them than with the new Commander-in-Chief at Gibraltar. Admiral Lord Barmouth – his family name was Richardson – had been a famous frigate-captain, with several brilliant actions to his credit. Jack Aubrey was now a famous frigate-captain, and one or two of his actions were perhaps even more brilliant. Early in his career Jack had served under Captain Richardson as a master's mate in the *Sybille*: they had disagreed from time to time, never seriously but enough for Captain Richardson not to ask Jack to follow him when he moved to his next command, a heavy frigate in which, with a consort of almost equal force, he destroyed a French ship of the line on the coast of Brittany. Jack was sorry not to have been present at the battle, but that did not prevent him from taking young Arklow Richardson aboard a command of his own and even rating him, in his turn, master's mate – a senior midshipman. Yet in young Arklow all the sides of his father (now Lord Barmouth) that Jack had disliked were reproduced on a larger and more offensive scale; in the severe naval discipline of the time even a master's mate could be rude, cruel and tyrannical, and Arklow made full use of his opportunities. To some extent a captain is obliged to support his officer, and reluctantly Jack reproved, stopped grog or imposed some other small punishment.

But presently it became obvious that Arklow had no intention of attending to his captain's often strongly-worded advice: more than that, there was not a single able seaman aboard who did not see that Arklow differed from his father in being no sailor. When this was established beyond a doubt Jack got rid of him; but he did so in such a tactful manner that the youth, the very well-connected youth, was very soon a lieutenant. Then he was given command of a vessel of his own, where he could flog as much as he chose: not unnaturally his people mutinied, and the case against the young man was so flagrantly obvious that he was never employed again.

Barmouth did not openly hold this against Jack Aubrey – they were members of the same club in London and they exchanged civil words when they met; but the powers of a

Commander-in-Chief were very wide indeed, and if *Surprise* reached Gibraltar in anything but perfect condition, Barmouth might very well order another, wholly undamaged frigate to undertake the interception of the galley.

Indeed, *Surprise* had not been wholly surveyed and passed at Mahon: how this had come about Stephen could not tell for certain, but he supposed that Admiral Fanshawe, who was aware of the urgency and who was very fond of Jack, had taken his word for the frigate's perfect health. This supposition was much reinforced by the quite unusual activity of the carpenter, his mates and crew, who were busy all day and even after lights-out in the filling-room, right forward and far down, and in the forepeak, hammering, sawing, fitting and driving great wedges. Stephen had pointed out that this was not all that could be wished for, so near the sick-berth; but observing Jack's embarrassment, his uneasy and probably false assertion 'that it was nothing, and anyway it would soon be over', he had not pressed the subject, the more so since Jacob happened to be with them at the time, tuning a fiddle he had bought in Mahon, so that they might attempt Haydn in D major.

The carpenter too was oddly reticent, as though there were something improper or even illegal about the work in the forepeak and its neighbourhood, a near-furtiveness that took refuge in technicalities – 'We'm just setting the hawse-pieces and bollard-timbers to rights' – and Stephen was wondering how far down in the carpenter's chain of command this attitude reached when a small pair of calico drawers were flung down at his feet and Poll cried, 'No, sir: no for shame. There is that heathen Mona running about mother-naked but for her Algiers shirt: and she has thrown down her drawers – I have tried to teach her shame and so has Mrs Cheal; but it is no good. She just says "No English, ha, ha," lays aloft and throws her drawers to the wind.'

'I am very sorry for your trouble, Poll, my dear,' said Stephen. 'But I will tell you what I shall do. Barret Bonden is a good creature, and a capital hand with needle and thread. I shall beg him to make her a pair – two pair – of a number eight sailcloth trousers, tight at the top, broad down below and the seams piped with green. Once she has them on, she will never throw them off, I warrant you. The same for her brother Kevin too.'

Poll shook her head. 'When I think of all that good calico, the cutting, the measuring and the fine stitching – look at these flounces! I could find it in my heart to have her whipped and put in the black hole with biscuit and water.'

The trousers were indeed successful: in both cases they were a cause of sinful pride and they never came off, but hid the children's shameful parts day and night, except when they went to the head; furthermore they promoted such a degree of agility and daring that on any idle day, with light airs coming from all points of the compass – a make-and-mend day too, with most of the hands busy with thimbles and shears on the forecastle or in the waist of the ship – Kevin, on his way to the mainmasthead, discerned a sail in the west, bringing up a little breeze of its own. Partly out of mother-wit and partly because he could not remember the English for west, he climbed the remaining few feet and told Geoghegan, the lookout, who had been watching a couple of tunny-boats far astern, but who now hailed the deck. 'On deck, there. On deck. A sail three points on the starboard bow.' Then some time later, 'Frigate, sir, I believe.' Pause. 'Yes. *Hamadryad*; and she is making sail.'

'What joy,' said Jack to Stephen. 'That will be Heneage Dundas out of Gibraltar. I have not congratulated him yet on his new ship: we will ask him to supper – a pair of fowls, and there is still plenty of sucking-pig. Killick, Killick, there. Pass the word for Killick.' And when his steward arrived, with his invariable look of ill-usage and a denial of anything, anything at all that might be alleged against him, 'Killick, freshen some champagne, will you?'

'Which we ain't got none, your honour,' said Killick,

barely containing his triumph. 'Not since the Admiral dined aboard. Oh dear me, no.'

'Some white Burgundy, then: and let it down in a net on a twenty-fathom line.'

There was no white Burgundy either; but Killick was capable of relishing a private victory too, and he only replied, 'A twenty-fathom line it is, sir.'

'Now, Mr Hallam,' said Jack to his signal midshipman, 'Once the usual signals have passed, pray invite Captain Dundas and Mr Reade to supper. Doctor, should you like to come up into the foretop to watch *Hamadryad* make sail?'

It was not really a very dangerous ascent, nor lofty, and Stephen had been known to go even higher, entirely by himself, but he had so often been found clinging by his fingernails to improbable parts of the rigging that Jack and Bonden exchanged a private look of thankful relief when they had successfully pushed and pulled him up into the top through the lubber's hole.

Though the foretop was of no great height it gave them a splendid view of the western Mediterranean: they were a little late for some of the phases of *Hamadryad*'s increase of sail, but still there were many delights to come: studdingsails aloft and alow on either side of fore and mainmast, of course, and even royal studdingsails, which was coming it pretty high, as Jack observed – then a skysail above the main-royal – 'and look, look, Stephen,' cried Jack, 'the audacious reptile has flashed out a skyscraper – do you see? The fore-and-aft affair above everything: take my glass and you will make out its sheet. Did you ever see the like, Bonden?'

'Never, sir. But once when I was aboard *Melpomene* in the doldrums we spread a sail above the royal: though it being square we called it a moonsail.'

This prodigious spread brought *Hamadryad* within pistol-shot of the little *Surprise* before dusk. She clapped her helm a-lee, swung round in an elegant curve, spilt the wind from her sails, furled her wings, and sent her captain across the narrow lane in his barge, as neat and trim as the Channel fleet. 'My dear Hen, how do you do?' cried Jack, receiving him on the quarterdeck with a hearty shake of his hand. 'You know Dr Maturin and all my officers, I believe?' Captain Dundas made his round of civilities. 'Come below,' said Jack, 'and let us have a whet – you must be mortal parched after such a frantic spread of cloth. What did you make?'

'Only a span above eight knots, even with all our washing hung out to dry,' said Dundas, laughing. 'But it did please our topmen.'

'It certainly amazed all ours – amazed and impressed. Sherry, or a draught of right Plymouth gin?'

'Oh, gin, if you please. Two of our victuallers were stove on the Berlings in that shocking southerly blow and we have not had a drop since then – they happened to be carrying it all. Did the wind reach as far as you?'

'Yes: and as far as Alexandria, I believe: a truly wicked blast. But tell me, Hen' – pouring him a stiff tot and speaking with an affectation of casual unconcern that deceived neither of his friends – 'what has Lord Barmouth in the way of frigates?'

'None at all,' said Dundas. 'Some battered seventy-fours, a sixty-four-gun ship, some indifferent sloops, and of course the flag. But *Hamadryad* was the last of the frigates. The rest have been sent to Malta and eastwards: though indeed he is to be reinforced in two or three weeks, or perhaps earlier. They too were much delayed by the weather, carrying the C-in-C's new wife, and had to put back into Lisbon.'

Jack drank his own sherry with satisfaction and they sat down to a remarkably copious supper. Picking up his fork he said, 'Did you say that Lord Barmouth was remarried? I heard nothing about it.'

'He was, though. To Admiral Horton's remarkably handsome young widow. It is her absence that makes him crosser than usual.'

Jack nodded vaguely, and in the pause between the pair

of fowls and the sucking-pig he asked, 'Did you wait on Lord Keith?'

'Yes, I did,' said Dundas. 'I had a message for him from my father; but I should have gone in any case. I have a great respect for the Admiral.'

'So have I. How was Lady Keith?'

'As lovely, and kind, and learned as ever: she was good enough to ask me to dinner, and she and the chaplain of one of the seventy-fours prattled away about some peculiarities of the Hebrew used in the Jewish community on the Rock.'

'Do they indeed use a colloquial Hebrew?' asked Stephen. 'I had always supposed that they kept to their archaic Spanish.'

'From what I gathered they spoke Hebrew when Jews from remote countries appeared – countries where Arabic or Persian took the place of Spanish. Rather as those more learned than I am use Latin when they are in Poland or, God preserve us, Lithuania.'

'As I remember,' said Jack, 'they meant to take a house somewhere near the Governor's cottage.'

'Just so: Ballinden. It is a little higher up, but somewhat closer to the town. A charming place, with a prodigious view of the Straits and a fine garden kept by a Scorpion: perhaps rather large for them and I am afraid the apes are a nuisance at times. But they both seem very happy there.'

'Bless them,' said Jack, raising his glass. 'They were both most uncommon kind to me.'

Pudding came on almost as soon as they had drunk the Keiths' health, a fine honest naval pudding of the kind that Jack and Dundas loved, and to which Stephen (unlike Jacob) had become inured. 'Thank you very much,' said Dundas, refusing a second piece, 'and I am afraid I must . . .' Before he could utter the words 'tear myself away' the *Surprise*'s bell struck eight times, the cabin door opened and the midshipman in charge of Captain Dundas' barge said, 'Sir, you told me to . . .'

'Very true, Simmons,' said Dundas. 'Jack, thank you many, many times for a splendid supper; but if I do not speed on my way, I shall be flogged round the fleet. Gentlemen' – bowing to Stephen and Jacob – 'your servant.'

All was over, the table cleared, all but for the brandy. Jacob had said good night, and a curious silence filled the cabin.

'Seeing Dundas hurry off in such a dutiful, truly naval fashion,' said Stephen, 'puts me in mind of an indiscreet question that I have often been tempted to ask you: and since after all I too am essentially concerned in our voyage, I shall venture upon it now. If Heneage Dundas is in danger of being flogged round the fleet for dillying and dallying on his way, may you not run the same risk, when at last your snail's pace brings you to Gibraltar and the Commander-in-Chief, who is not your very closest friend?'

'Stephen,' said Jack, 'I dare say you have noticed that the moon changes both her shape and her hours of rising and setting from time to time?'

'Indeed I have – a most inconstant orb. Sometimes a mere sickle facing left, sometimes right; and sometimes, as I have no doubt you have observed yourself, no moon at all. The dark of the moon! I remember you once landed me on the French coast at just such a time. Yet I am no great lunarian: a priest in the County Clare explained her motions to me, but I am afraid I did not fully retain his words.'

'He did persuade you that it was a regular process – that the changes could be foretold?'

'I am sure he did, at least to his own satisfaction.'

'It is the case, I do assure you, Stephen: and the very first appearance of the new moon at certain seasons is of the utmost consequence to Jews and Muslims. Now you are aware that the commander of the Arzila galley must be either the one or the other – almost certainly a Muslim – and in any case a sailor. Furthermore he is presumably a sailor in his right mind, so wind and weather permitting he must necessarily pass through the Strait at the dark of the moon or as near as ever he can get to it, a night that he can foretell as well as we can. So seeing that both he and I think alike, I hope to give him the meeting somewhere south of Tarifa.'

'To be sure, that puts a different complexion on the matter.'

'Furthermore, I have no wish to lose any spars by cracking on, nor to lie there day after day under the eye of a Commander-in-Chief who dislikes me. He is a very distinguished sailor, I fully admit; and his reputation as a fighting captain was very high indeed; yet as a flag-officer he has been less fortunate . . . It is very odd, but there is something about the Admiralty board-room table that has a sad effect on some of those who sit there, sensible men who can club-haul their ship off a roaring lee-shore or take a huge Spanish beauty like the *Santisima Trinidad* and remain perfectly civil and unassuming until this point, this board-room table. It is not invariable, but I have served under some who, on becoming a Sea-Lord, above all *First* Sea-Lord, who suddenly swell up into creatures of enormous importance, who have to be approached on hands and knees, and addressed in the third person. No. Lord Barmouth will have a monument in the Abbey with a great many fine actions engraved upon it; but he is perfectly capable of doing a dirty thing, and I should rather make my obeisance a very short time before the dark of the moon and then go about my business, looking as much like a distressed merchantman as possible.'

It was a good plan; it kept the ship from the wear and tear of a hurried passage, so that (apart from other considerations) she should be entirely ready for the eagerly-expected meeting. But it was based on the false assumption that the Commander-in-Chief should be sitting in Gibraltar.

He was in fact exercising the vessels under his command, the ships of the line to port, the sloops and minor craft to starboard, in line abreast; and well behind them sailed a numerous convoy of merchantmen.

This surprising armada was reported, bit by bit, from the masthead as the morning cleared, starting with the foremost division of sloops; and Jack had time to spread more canvas, much more canvas, to the north-east breeze before the hail came down: 'On deck, there. On deck: flag two points on the starboard bow.'

Fortunately the *Surprise* was in a high state of cleanliness – decks already dry from the swabbing – guns as neat as a paper of pins – all hands reasonably well turned out and necessarily stone-cold sober; but this did not prevent Harding, Woodbine and the Royal Marine officer from fussing about the ship or Killick from overhauling the rear-admiral's uniform that Jack wore, on formal occasions, as commodore.

The day cleared. The signal midshipman and his yeoman watched the almost continual stream of hoists running up aloft as Lord Barmouth put his fleet through a variety of manoeuvres and expressing a variety of comments, mostly unfavourable. At last *Surprise*'s number appeared, together with *Commodore repair aboard flag.*

Bonden and his crew already had the barge clear for lowering down and the moment he saw Jack emerge from his cabin in the glory of number one scraper, presentation sword and a large quantity of gold lace he gave the word and the boat glided down, instantly followed by bargemen and a master's mate at the tiller. 'As soon as we are a cable's length away,' said Jack to Harding, 'start the salute: and I am sure you will never forget a couple of spares in case of a misfire.'

With this he ran down into the barge, and as usual Bonden shoved off, saying to his crew, 'Row dry, there; row dry.' And when they had pulled just a cable's length, the *Surprise* began her salute to the Commander-in-Chief, seventeen guns: for this was the first time she had met him in office. After the seventeenth *Implacable* replied, but hesitated slightly after the thirteenth as though doubtful of Jack's right to more, though his broad pennant was clearly to be seen – hesitated until some angry voice roared from the quarterdeck, when the remaining two were fired almost together.

The captain of *Implacable*, Henry James, an old shipmate, received Jack kindly as he came aboard: the Royal Marines presented arms, and the flag-lieutenant said, 'May I take you to the Commander-in-Chief, sir?'

'I am happy to see you, Mr Aubrey,' said Lord Barmouth, half-rising from behind his desk and giving him a cold hand.

'So am I, upon my word,' said Sir James Frere, the Captain of the Fleet, whose grasp was much more cordial.

'But I do not quite understand what you are doing in these waters. Pray sit down while you tell me.'

'My Lord, the previous Commander-in-Chief gave me a squadron with orders to proceed to the Ionian and Adriatic and – having seen the trade on its way – to put an end to Bonapartist ship-building in those parts, to persuade some French ships to come over to the Allies and to take, sink, burn and destroy those who would not. An emissary from Sir Joseph Blaine also spoke of the Ministry's concern at reports of a Muslim confederacy's intention of preventing the junction of the Russian and Austrian forces marching westward to join the British and Prussian armies, or at least to delay it long enough for Napoleon's superior numbers to crush each of the Allied states separately. This move on the part of the Muslim group however required the enlistment of a large number of mercenaries; and they had to be paid. The money was to come from a Muslim state on the confines of Morocco, and it was expected to travel by way of Algiers: our intelligence people eventually put an end to that and it is now to come by sea, through the Straits, as I have told Lord Keith in repeated dispatches, not knowing that he had been superseded. Perhaps I should add that Sir Joseph also supplied my political adviser with a local expert, a gentleman perfectly fluent in Turkish and Arabic, who was of the great-

247

est value: with his help we detached one French frigate, destroyed two others, and burnt a score of yards together with the ships they were building.'

'Yes,' said the Admiral. 'I have heard something of it; and I congratulate you on your success, I am sure ... ('How he banged them about!' murmured Sir James.) Have you prepared a report?'

'Not yet, my Lord.'

'Then you can come back to Gibraltar with us and let me have it there as soon as possible. You spoke of your political adviser and his colleague?'

'Yes, my Lord.'

'I should be obliged if you would send them both across to confer with my politico. And Aubrey, although Lord Keith gave you quite a handsome squadron, it has melted away, for convoy duty and the like. What is that schooner you have in company?'

'She belongs to my surgeon, sir, and she acts as our tender.'

'Well, she is a handsome little craft, but she don't amount to a squadron; so perhaps it would be more proper if you were to strike your broad pennant and revert to a private ship.'

Jack had intended to ask the Commander-in-Chief whether there was any news of the French or Allied armies, but these last words were so clearly meant to be disobliging that he merely took his leave. On deck, however, he found *Implacable*'s captain, who said that although there were rumours of the wildest sort, such as a rising in Ireland and a French invasion of Kent, he had heard nothing authentic except for the soldiers' exasperation, frequently expressed, at the Russians' slowness.

Jack nodded with satisfaction and then said, 'Lord Barmouth has ordered me to send my surgeon and a politico across: they are amazingly gifted linguists and very learned men, but neither has much notion of coming up the side of a ship, and was you to rig a bosun's chair, I should take it kindly.'

Back in the *Surprise* he took off his finery, struck his broad pennant, told Harding to follow the flag into Gibraltar, and sent for the log-books. He and Adams were still establishing the bases of his report – obviously with great gaps that only Stephen and Jacob could fill – when they heard the boat's return, the anxious cries, and the children's piping 'Welcome aboard, dear Doctors, welcome oh welcome aboard!'

Coming below, Stephen looked attentively at his friend, deep in papers, and said, 'You are low in your spirits, brother.'

'Indeed I am. For your own ear alone, I am very much afraid that we are going to be baulked of our galley – pipped on the post – done brown. In my simplicity I told the Commander-in-Chief that she was coming up by the Straits and that I meant to intercept her. I let it be understood that I was still acting on the orders given me by Lord Keith; but I fear I may be set aside and the chance given to some more favoured man.'

'Be easy in your mind, my dear,' said Stephen in a tone that carried great conviction. 'Jacob and I have just been talking with the Commander-in-Chief and his politico, then with the politico alone – Matthew Arden, a very intelligent man, very highly influential in Whitehall. The Ministry regard this as an exceptionally important theatre of war and they have sent one of their best brains, a man who has refused high office, very high office indeed. He is also a close friend of Lord Keith's, who would be mortally offended at having his evident wishes set aside. Arden and I have known one another these many years: we have never disagreed on any important point, and this time again we got along together exceedingly well. Furthermore, I am happy to say that for all his domineering manner, Lord Barmouth is in awe of Matthew Arden . . . you are drawing up an account of our little campaign, I see . . . heavy going, heavy going:

I must give you some remarks on Algerine politics and my sojourn in Africa. But I do wish you could have heard how Arden exulted at your doing in the Adriatic, and how he obliged the Commander-in-Chief to acknowledge that the elimination of that particular danger was a most important feat ... No, no, Jack: courageous though Lord Barmouth quite certainly is, I do not believe for a moment that he would dare to use you ill in these circumstances.'

'How very kind you are to tell me all this, Stephen,' said Jack. 'From anyone else I should scarcely have regarded it, but from you ...' He threw aside the pen he had been chewing, walked across the cabin, took up his fiddle and played a wild series of very rapid ascending trills that vanished quite out of hearing. Then he sat at his desk and with another pen he quickly drew up several lists, sent for the gunner and asked him for a state of the ship's powder and shot. 'I can tell you quite exactly after five minutes' look round the magazines, sir,' said the gunner.

'Very well: then you fill in the figures to top us up where I have left room, and take them along. Here is a guinea to sweeten the usual palm for reasonable dispatch. Then there is this, also for the ordnance wharf.'

'Blue lights and red,' murmured the gunner, slowly going through the list. 'We do have a few, but it's as well to be sure they are fresh. Then extra-high Congreves: I don't think I know about them, sir.'

'They are white star-bursts, and on occasion they can be very useful. Half a guinea for all the fireworks together would be about right, I believe?'

'Oh, very handsome, sir; and I make no doubt I shall bring them back myself.'

When this interview and a few others that showed the trend of Captain Aubrey's mind were over, Stephen said, 'And I shall be getting some medical stores: we are sadly short of portable soup; and, since that unfortunate lingering in Mahon, blue ointment. Tell me, Jack, am I right in supposing that we shall have four or even five days longer here than you had wished?'

'No: you are quite right.'

'Then shall you wait on Lady Keith?'

'Of course I shall. And on the Admiral too.'

'Please may I come with you?'

'By all means. Queenie speaks of you so pleasantly.'

On the day of the visit Stephen went ashore early, bought a new wig at Barlow's and searched through the entire market until he found a pot of lilies-of-the-valley in just-opening bud. Returning he gave Mona and Kevin a square of chocolate calculated for solid jaws and iron stomachs; yet though they thanked him prettily they neither ate nor moved but stood gazing up in something between wonder and alarm. At last Mona said, 'You have *changed your hair.*'

'Never mind, my dear,' he replied. 'It is only a wig.' He took it off to show: and both instantly burst into tears.

'Dear Lady Keith,' he said as they sat in the parlour overlooking her fine garden and the Strait, with misty Africa on the far side, 'do you remember the first time you ever saw a man without his wig?'

'No. Papa always took it off when he was teaching me to swim at Brighton, and I was so much concerned with splashing that I did not remark the change, or scarcely: a rapid moult indeed, but a perfectly natural one.'

'I ask because my two children – children that I bought in the slave-market at Algiers – a boy and a girl, twins – wept most bitterly when I took mine off this morning, and could not be comforted.'

'Poor little souls – there are those damned apes again: Jack, pray bang on the window, will you? – how old are they?'

'Just losing their milk-teeth. An Algerine corsair took them off the Munster coast and I mean to send them back to their parents, peasants in a village I know. I hope to find a King's ship bound for the Cove of Cork.'

'There should be no difficulty: I shall ask the Admiral. But what do you mean to do with them in the mean while? If you are ordered to sea, for example? Ordered to the West Indies?'

'I had hoped to find a suitable, kindly family, to keep them until a suitable, kindly man-of-war should carry them home, with a letter to a priest I know in Cork and a purse to take them to Ballydonegan in an ass-cart.'

'Do they speak English?'

'Very little, and much of that little rather coarse: but it is wonderful how the infant mind absorbs a language through the ears.'

'Well, if you like to entrust them to me, I shall tell our Scorpion, our chief gardener, to put them up: he has a good wife, quite a large cottage, and only grown-up children. He speaks English, Rock-English, and he is a good, decent man. In any case I shall look after them.'

'How deeply kind of you, Lady Keith: may I bring them up later today?'

'Please do. I shall look forward to seeing them. But tell me now, Dr Maturin, what did you see on the Barbary Coast, in the way of birds?'

'Some way inland there was a vast saline lake crowded with flamingos and a large variety of waders; vultures all the usual kinds; the brown-necked raven. Among the mere quadrupeds there were hyenas, of course, and an elegant leopard. But what would really have pleased you was an anomalous nuthatch.'

'Dear me, Maturin,' cried Lady Keith, who was particularly attached to nuthatches, 'anomalous in what respect?'

'Well, you instantly see that he is a nuthatch, though an absurdly small one: but then you realize that he has almost no black on his crown, that his whole mantle is more nearly blue than is quite proper, that his tail is even shorter than that of other species, and that his voice is more like that of a wryneck than . . .'

The description was cut short by the Admiral bursting in with the cry 'Oh those hell-damned apes – they are at it again'. But his indignant voice changed when he saw the visitors. 'Why, Aubrey! How very welcome you are – you too, Doctor. Lord how you stirred them up in the Adriatic! Your earlier dispatches came to me of course; and they gave a great deal of pleasure in Whitehall. And I do hope you will both give *us* the pleasure of your company at dinner on Saturday.'

'Should be very happy, my Lord: but I have not yet quite finished carrying out your orders. I hope to have done so a little after the new moon, and then we are entirely at your disposal.'

The sound of a carriage – of another carriage – the voices of two different sets of callers. Jack and Stephen took their leave and by good luck they were able to skirt round the newcomers, all gathered in a knot on the gravel drive exclaiming at the extraordinary coincidence of the arrival *at the very same moment*!

They walked back to the town, and as they went along the quays Stephen noticed the daily Tangier hoy – it might almost have been called the ferry – rapidly filling with Moors, Gibraltar Jews and some odd few Spanish merchants. Jacob was among them, in a caftan and a skull-cap, wholly inconspicuous; Stephen made no remark at the time but he was not surprised at finding a suitably obscure note from his colleague saying that he was crossing to see some people who might have some quite valuable jewels to sell: but later, as he and Jack were supping to-gether he said, 'I believe Jacob is not officially on the ship's books?'

'No: I think he is carried as a supernumerary, without victuals, wages or tobacco.'

'Who feeds him, then?'

'Why, I suppose you do: at any rate everything he eats or drinks or smokes will be stopped out of your pay to the last halfpenny and with the utmost rigour.'

'I find that I have been giving my life's blood to a parcel of hard-hearted mercenary rapacious sharks,' said Stephen with a rather forced smile.

'Exactly so. And the children you bought in Algiers have each a docket on which every dish of pap is charged against you, together with the earthenware pot they broke. This is the Navy, after all.'

'So I do not suppose he would be flogged or put in irons for absenting himself without formal leave?'

'No. In such cases we have a punishment known as keel-hauling. But do not let it distress you: the victims often survive – well, fairly often. But I am so sorry: this really is not the time to be facetious. I am afraid you must be missing your children cruelly. They were engaging little creatures. I do beg your pardon.'

'I miss them, I admit, though Lady Keith was so very good and kind: in better hands they could not be. But I do miss them, and when they fully understood my betrayal they howled most pitifully. Yet my grief was somewhat lessened by their fascination with the apes that gathered round, by their continuing suspicion of my seriousness and by the cheerful laughter that reached me when I was quite far away, nearly at the bottom of the hill, watching two intertwined serpents, rising in the air almost the whole of their length in an amorous clasp.'

'Oh sir,' cried a messenger from Mr Harding, 'please could the Doctor come and look at Abram White? He has fallen down in a fit.'

Abram White was in fact quite ill – comatose, bloated, heavily contused – yet this was not really a question of apoplexy nor yet of epilepsy. For reasons best known to himself he had brought three concealed bladders of rum aboard, to drink slowly, privately, with delectation. But believing himself detected by the ship's corporal he had done away with the evidence of his crime by swallowing the whole pot-full, had choked, and had pitched down the fore-hatchway. He lay pallid, insensible, only just breathing, with a barely perceptible pulse.

Yet Stephen, after some years at sea, was quite used to pallid insensible seamen, and when he had made sure that Abram's limbs, spine and skull were unbroken, he pumped him out and had him carried to the sick-berth. He was perfectly well and going about his duties by the time Jacob came back. If anyone had noticed his absence it must have been thought official or medical – a spell at the hospital or the like – for his return excited no comment at all, particularly as he had again changed his clothes.

He found Stephen counting glass-hard slabs of portable soup and he said, 'I do hope my sudden disappearance did not prove inconvenient? I had sudden word of a friend the other side of the water.'

'Not in the least. I hope the voyage was worth the displacement?'

'You shall judge for yourself: on the other side their notions of security are contemptible and I have my information from no less than three concordant sources.' They were speaking French, as they generally did when there was anything of a medical, private or confidential nature; but now, even so, he lowered his voice: 'The Arzila galley is at present in Tangier, loaded, very heavily manned and as heavily armed as a galley can be: two twenty-four pounders in the bows and two in the stern, with a fair amount of musketry when she proceeds under sail. The guns are said to be particularly fine – brass, very exactly bored, with truly spherical and accurate round-shot. Yahya ben Khaled, who is in command, means to pass the Strait, unless there is a very strong east wind in his teeth, on Friday night, a night of complete darkness, to make straight for Durazzo, deliver his gold – he has given his parents, wives and children as sureties – take his tenth part and return, using his great strength against all the merchantmen he finds.'

'It is a bold stroke.'

'Indeed it is. Murad Reis is very well known for his bold strokes, his bold and almost invariably successful bold strokes. He always helps Fate as much as ever he can, and this time he has hired two smaller galleys to act as decoys, one sailing close to the African shore and one in mid-channel, while he, lying under Tarifa, makes his dash along the European side.'

'Amos,' said Stephen, 'I am inexpressibly gratified by your news. Will you come and repeat it all to Captain Aubrey?'

'Certainly.'

Jack listened to him gravely, his face gradually assuming the look of an eagle, one of the larger eagles, that sees its prey at no great distance.

'Dr Jacob,' he said, shaking his hand, 'I thank you very heartily indeed for this piece of intelligence – this matchless piece of intelligence, as I believe I may call it. So if the wind has anything of west in it, Murad Reis sails on Friday, lies under Tarifa until I presume the turn of the tide a little after midnight and so makes his attempt. Clearly we must be ready for him.' He reflected. 'And there is this to be said,' he went on. 'If there is so much indiscreet talk in Tangier, and if an account of it can come over so quickly, we must suppose that any indiscretion on our part may go over to the other side of the Strait with the same speed. Now I shall stop all shore-leave, of course; and since by tomorrow morning we shall have all our supplies, the only thing that could betray our intention of sailing is the carrying of our sick ashore. I am ashamed to say that I do not immediately call the sick-list to mind.'

'Oh, as to that,' said Stephen, 'we only have a couple of obstinate poxes and a hernia, and those I can hand over the rail to my old friend Walker of *Polyphemus* late on Friday evening.'

'Very good, very good indeed: so by the time any fool chooses to blab, we shall with God's grace be well out at sea.'

Chapter Ten

Captain Aubrey and his officers spent that afternoon going along the Strait in *Ringle*, very carefully surveying and in places sounding as they went; and at one point, far to the westward, they met two heavy frigates, *Acasta* and *Lavinia*, with whom they exchanged numbers: both had obviously suffered much from the weather, and both were still pumping without a pause – strong, thick jets flying to leeward.

Out and along the Strait, the familiar skyline memorized even more firmly, and back in the late afternoon: and speaking privately to Stephen in the cabin, Jack said, 'Now that it belongs to the past, Jacob's piece of intelligence, so whole and perfect, seems to me to be too good to be true.'

'Whole and perfect, to be sure. But I believe it to be true. Jacob and Arden are the only two men in this matter of intelligence for whom I would lay my head on the block.'

'In that case, dear Stephen, I shall shift my clothes, pull across to the flag and either ask for an interview or leave this note.' He passed it and Stephen read *Captain Aubrey presents his respectful compliments to Lord Barmouth and on account of very recent intelligence most urgently begs leave to sail this evening: he takes the liberty of adding that his political adviser is wholly of the same mind.*

'Very well put, Jack,' he said.

Jack smiled and called, 'Killick. Killick, there. Plain coat, decent breeches; and tell Bonden I shall need the barge directly.'

The barge received him and took him across the smooth water to the flag, where, in reply to the hail, Bonden called

'*Surprise*'. After the formalities of the reception of a post-captain Jack said, 'I am sorry to trouble you again, Holden, but I must either see the Admiral or have this note conveyed to him.'

Moments later the flag-lieutenant returned, begged Captain Aubrey to come this way, and brought him to the great cabin, where Lord Barmouth, looking ten years younger, received him with a cordiality he had never known before, though the Admiral had always been known as a temperamental man, moving from one extreme to another. 'As for this note,' said the Commander-in-Chief, 'how happy do you feel about your source of intelligence?'

'Happy enough to stake my life upon it, my Lord,' said Jack. 'And Dr Maturin is of the same opinion.'

'Then you shall certainly go. But Aubrey, I had no idea that you were a childhood friend of my wife's – indeed some sort of a cousin. *Acasta* came in this afternoon, bringing her at last, in blooming health in spite of the weather – she is a splendid sailor – and as she had a package for Lady Keith we went straight over to their place. They very kindly kept us to dinner – just an impromptu scratch dinner, the four of us – and I do not know how your name arose but it very soon became apparent that both the women had known you ever since you were breeched and even before: they had followed you from ship to ship in the Gazette and the Navy List, and when they put a foot wrong, as in the date of your appointment to *Sophie*, Lord Keith put them right. In the end it was decided that we should ask the Keiths and you and Dr Maturin – Lord Keith has the highest opinion of him – to dine with us aboard the flag tomorrow. But I fear this request of yours may put it out of your power.'

'I am afraid it does, my Lord; but I am very sensible of your goodness, and I am sure Maturin will say the same.'

The Admiral bent his head, and went on, 'Now as to the request, do you feel entirely confident of your agent's intelligence?'

'Entirely so, my Lord: should commit my ship and myself to the hilt; and Maturin agrees.'

'And the occasion is urgent?'

'It could not be more so, my Lord.'

'You must go, then. But Lady Barmouth and I will be very happy to see you both and the Keiths on your return.' He rang the bell and told his steward to bring the old, old, very old brandy. When it came he filled their glasses and drank 'to *Surprise* and her success'.

'This is famous brandy, upon my word,' said Jack; and after a pause he went on with a certain embarrassment, 'I never had the honour of serving under Admiral Horton and being very often out of England I never heard either of his marriage or his death.'

'He married Isobel Carrington just after he was given his flag.'

'Isobel Carrington!' cried Jack. 'Of course I should have thought of her when you spoke of Queenie and her. Isobel and Queenie! Lord, those names bring back such delightfully happy memories! I shall very much look forward to paying my respects to Lady Barmouth. And I thank you most heartily for your permission to sail, my Lord.'

The Commander-in-Chief gave him his hand and they parted on better terms than Jack would have believed possible.

Aboard *Surprise* again, and in ordinary working clothes, he called for the carpenter and said, 'All things considered, Chips, which do you think our fastest, most weatherly boat?'

'Oh, the blue cutter, sir, without a doubt: the blue cutter, with Mr Daniel at the helm. He can coax her an extra half-point nearer the wind, and an extra half knot.'

'Very good: pray run an eye over her, and if anything is wanting let Mr Harding know: the gunner will give you some blue and red lights and some star-bursts.' Then directing his voice over the still water he called, '*Ringle*: Mr Reade, we shall be moving out into the Strait very soon, so if you have any women aboard they had better go ashore directly. And when we are well clear of the mole, I should like to have a word with you.'

How easy it seemed, the quiet departure of the two vessels a little after the evening gun: scarcely an order was needed, and scarcely any were uttered: long-practised hands coiled down the familiar ropes, hauled the bowlines as the ship left the mole and made all fast with scarcely a conscious reflection. But Jack did check the customary hoisting of the top-light; and he called for only one single stern-lantern. The Surprises winked at one another and jerked their heads in a very knowing fashion: they were perfectly aware that something was up, and presently they knew just what that something was.

Jack called William Reade to join him and his officers on the quarterdeck. 'Gentlemen,' he said, 'you are all perfectly aware that this voyage was undertaken in order to discourage Bonaparte at sea: but it also had another side. From the landward point of view Napoleon's supporters in Bosnia, Serbia and those parts believed that if they could prevent the Russian and Austrian armies from joining the British and Prussians, he would be able to defeat each of the Allies separately, piecemeal. For this intervention they had to hire a large number of Balkan Muslim mercenaries: we stopped the Dey of Algiers letting the money pass through his country, but now it is on its way by sea from Morocco in a large galley that means to run through the Straits tonight. According to our intelligence the galley intends to lie under Tarifa until the turn of the tide, and then, the wind being favourable, to run through the Straits. And if the breeze fails him, then to row: they can make seven or even eight knots for a burst. And then again there is the advantage of the eastward current. The captain of the galley, a well-known, active corsair, has hired two others to act as decoys, one on the African side and one in mid-channel. We shall take no notice of them, but make steadily for Tarifa, *Ringle* to larboard and Mr Daniel in the blue cutter to starboard, each three cable's lengths abeam of *Surprise*. The first to sight the galley will send up a blue light if the enemy is to starboard, red if to port, and a star-burst if the galley is right ahead.'

'Blue to starboard, red to larboard, white if right ahead,' they murmured, and Reade went back to his command, while the blue cutter was lowered down.

No moon, but a most splendid wealth of stars – Orion in his glory, great Vega blazing on the larboard quarter and Deneb beyond; a little forward of the beam, both bears and the Pole Star; Arcturus and Spica on the starboard bow: and had the foresail not been in the way, Stephen would have seen Sirius, but he was shown Procyon. Then on the larboard bow Capella, low down but still brilliant, and both Castor and Pollux – 'Castor is a glorious double,' said Jack, pointing them out to Stephen. 'I must show him to you in my telescope when we are at home.' Then raising his voice a little, 'Mr Harding, I believe we may shorten sail a little,' for the faint wafts of vapour – they could scarcely be called cloud – beneath the stars were now some five or even six degrees more southerly than they had been when first he had started pointing them out to Stephen. The breeze was certainly backing, and if it went on at this rate the *Surprise* would certainly be well to windward of the galley by the time they reached Tarifa. Furthermore, if Jack waited for the turn of the Atlantic tide there was a strong likelihood that the galley would begin her run; and although she could sail half a point nearer the wind than a square-rigged ship, once the corsair was a little way into the Strait, *Surprise* would even more certainly have the weather-gage and an encounter could not be avoided.

No moon, of course; but the suffused starlight gave a practised eye a fair view of the Spanish skyline – Punta Carnero, Punta Secreta, Punta del Fraile, and Punta Acebuche were all astern: Tarifa was not far off.

'Topsails alone,' said Jack quite low; and some of the way came off the ship.

'Four knots and two fathoms, sir, if you please,' said the midshipman in charge of the log, murmuring low.

There was a steadily mounting sense of crisis aboard, and for some time now the quartermaster had sounded the bells only with his knuckles. Almost no talk or even whispering along the deck, where the guns were already run out and the slow-match smouldered in the tubs.

It was Daniel in the blue cutter who first saw the galley, inshore of him and already under sail, two fine lateens sheeted well in and rounded with the breeze. He sent up a blue light and its lasting effulgence showed the enemy clear, the sea, and its own smoke, still more distinctly drifting from the south.

The galley was not quite as deeply engaged in the Strait as Jack could have wished, but she lay pretty well: pretty well, indeed. He signalled *Ringle* to pick up the cutter and follow him, then spread all the canvas the *Surprise* could carry in this moderate breeze, increasing as it backed, and he hauled her as close as ever she would lie.

The galley, seeing that she had been detected by perhaps as many as three men-of-war – possibly with others towards the eastern end warned of her approach – abandoned all hope of racing through the channel, struck her sails and took to her oars, steering into the eye of the wind.

The frigate's great spread of white sail showed clearly enough in the starlight for Murad Reis to chance a long shot with his larboard chaser when the galley was head-and-stern in line with *Surprise*: the heavy guns could not be traversed: they had to be aimed by means of the vessel that carried them, and he moved the rudder with an expert hand.

A long shot: but the combination of good aiming, excellent bore and powder, and the toss of the sea caused the twenty-four pound ball to strike the second gun of the *Surprise*'s starboard broadside, killing Bonden, its captain, and young

Hallam, the midshipman of the division. Once the gun had been secured Jack ran the length of the battery, checking the captains' pointing – though indeed the low-lying galley was but the faintest blur – urging highest elevation and then, on the rise, he cried, 'Fire!'

Even with his night-glass in the maintop he could not make out for sure whether the guns had had any effect: but after a few more distant exchanges in which the *Surprise* received only a harmless, spent ricochet, it seemed probable. At all events, after twenty minutes the galley's pace seemed to slacken, either because of damaged oars (terribly vulnerable to broadside fire) or because that first dash had exhausted the rowers.

While his glass focused on what was almost certainly the galley (for their courses were convergent) Jack ordered a forward gun to fire, and in the flash he distinctly saw her making sail.

She was fast, and her lateen rig gave her the advantage on a wind; but in their present positions and with the breeze still backing steadily, any attempt on her part to cross the frigate's bows or stern before the changing wind made it quite impossible would expose her to at least three or four unanswerable broadsides: a galley, however heavy, well-handled and however dangerous her bow- and stern-chasers, could not stand broadside-to-broadside combat with a man-of-war mounting fourteen twelve-pounders a side, apart from chasers, swivel-guns in the tops, and musketry, to say nothing of much stouter timbers.

There was no possibility of boarding, either, without the certainty of being raked fore and aft several times before coming alongside; and although Murad Reis had boarded and taken merchantmen heavier than *Surprise*, the truly naval speed and efficiency of her broadside convinced him that the attempt would not answer and he turned to the only other alternative – that of outsailing her (a galley could be very fast in a reasonably smooth sea with a following wind) and so of casting an eastward loop at the end of a very long run, thus, perhaps, regaining the weather-gage and freedom.

The morning sun, rising over Africa, showed the galley almost exactly where Jack had expected her, about two miles away westward: her two lateens out on either side making the most of the topgallant south-west-by-south wind: and so they ran all that pure cloudless day, and even the next, when sea, wind and current were almost exactly the same. But the extreme tension of that first day, when every man, woman and boy tried to urge the frigate on with clenched stomach muscles and extraordinary zeal in racing aloft or doing anything that might possibly increase the vessel's speed, diminished to the extent that the people went about their ordinary duties – cleaning decks, stowing hammocks, directing the fire-hoses high into the sails to help them draw a little better, eating their breakfast and the like – without perpetually breaking off to look at the chase. One boy even went to tell Stephen of a curious bird, a brown-faced booby; and Stephen and Jacob were much less often disturbed in their favourite observation-point right forward, by the starboard cathead. They had little or nothing to do in the sickberth that could not safely be left to Poll and Maggie. Jack was as active as any of his officers in drawing the last ounce of thrust from the breeze; and in any case Jack was disinclined for any other occupation whatsoever. He was, of course, very thoroughly acquainted with sudden death, but this time he felt the loss of Bonden, an admirable sailor, and of young Hallam, the son of an old shipmate, very deeply indeed.

This day was most uncommonly hot, and the next, a Monday, hotter still: Jacob, in the most natural way in the world, put on a turban, and Stephen, without much urging, a knotted white handkerchief. 'This might go on for ever,' he observed before dinner, settling down on his coil of rope.

'To be sure, these two long wakes and the infinite quantity

of sea have something of the look of eternity,' said Jacob. 'Or of dream. But for my part I do not think it can last much longer. I have been aboard an Algerine corsair and a Sallee rover, and since their chief aim is to take by boarding, they are usually very full of men. Furthermore, unless they intend the raiding of a distant coast – which is not the case here – a mere dash down the Straits and so to Durazzo – they rarely carry much in the way of provisions. Then again, when the galley was using its oars at such a pace I observed the quite exceptional number of rowers: all these mouths have to be fed.'

Eight bells: the hands were piped to dinner, and they were still chewing or smelling of rum or both when they came hurrying back forward to see how the chase lay now. 'What is your opinion, Tobias Belcher?' asked Stephen, speaking to a grey-haired seaman from Shelmerston, a shipmate on former voyages and a member of the Sethian community, renowned for truthfulness. Belcher looked and considered, and in time he replied that 'there was something not wholly Christian about this here weather.'

At this point the gunroom steward came to warn the doctors that dinner would be on table directly, so they hurried off with nothing more precise than a vague apprehension. The *Surprise*, on reverting to a private ship, had lost her Royal Marine officer, but still with the three lieutenants, the master, the purser and her two surgeons, it was a fine full table, with a great volume of talk about the probable outcome of the day – a volume cut dead just as the pudding came in, by a magistral crash right forward, the impact of yet another ricochet from one of the galley's stern-chasers.

Now, under the blazing sun, there began a curious form of sea-warfare: a slight strengthening of the breeze reached the frigate first and brought her within range of the galley's chasers; but since the vessels were not directly in line, the galley, in order to aim these guns, had to shift her helm, exposing some of her quarter. This danger increased with the wind, which brought *Surprise*'s foremost guns, trained right forward, into play; with the further peril that she might put her helm hard over, showing the galley the whole of her flank and sending a hundred and sixty-eight pounds of round-shot into the galley's relatively fragile timbers.

Both captains, the one right forward, the other right aft, watched one another most intently, trying to detect the slightest change and to counteract it. Jack had all his forward guns manned, of course, to give nothing away by movement; and when a favourable gust had brought the frigate perhaps fifty yards nearer he said to Daniel, in charge of the forward guns to larboard, 'Mr Daniel, I am going to put the helm a-lee and fire the bow-chaser: the moment she goes off, fire as they bear.' He stepped to the port bow-chaser, a beautiful brass gun of his own, a nine-pounder: it was already at what he judged the right elevation, and kneeling to the sight he cried, 'Helm a-lee: handsomely, now!' And as the galley's stern came just into view he fired. The ball skipped from the enemy's wake and through her after-lateen, while at the same time the three foremost broadside guns sent splinters flying from the galley's stern; but they too struck only on the rebound. Very shortly after, the gust that had brought the frigate nearer, reached and favoured the corsair, carrying her out of range.

'By God, it's hot,' said Jack: he turned and drank from the scuttle-butt, imitated by all hands.

And so it went, burning day after burning day; and now even the moonlit night sky seemed to radiate heat. Day after day, with each doing all that human skill, ingenuity, craft and malevolence could do to destroy the enemy, neither gaining any decisive advantage though each wounded his enemy – wounded him, but far from mortally.

If Jack and Adams his clerk had not kept the ship's log-book – the exact record of positions, distances made good, variations in the wind, observations on the weather, natural phenomena – he would scarcely have known that it was a

Wednesday – the first Wednesday in June – when at last the wind failed them entirely, and standing in what trifling shade the limp sails could offer they watched the galley ship her oars and pull, still westwards, towards what might have been a cloud on the horizon, if this pitiless sky would have suffered even a single cloud.

This day Stephen had three cases of sunstroke, and Jack, by way of prevention and diversion, had a sail lowered over the side – all the edges well clear of this shark-infested water – a truly shocking number of sharks – leaping in himself to encourage the crew, but finding, alas, precious little refreshment in the more than luke-warm tide.

Neither surgeon saw fit to join the splashing throng, and seeing that they were quite unwatched, Stephen undertook to guide Jacob up into the maintop, from which – the ship having swung with the current – they could see the galley with a telescope borrowed from the gunroom. It was not a very perilous ascent, but Daniel and three midshipmen, stark naked, ran up the side and into the rigging to give them not only advice but active, expert muscular heaves at moments of crisis.

From the top, Maturin sent them back to their water with many thanks and the assurance that they should be able to make their own way down with no more help than the force of gravity: and after breathing for a while he went on, 'Amos, I believe you have never been up here before.'

'Never,' said Amos Jacob, 'but I am very glad to be up here now – Lord, what an expanse: and Lord, how near the galley seems. She is in active motion. May I have the telescope? Oh God . . .' he added in a tone of utter disgust. 'But I had foreseen it.'

He passed the telescope. The breeze had filled the galley's sails, and the corsairs were throwing many of their manacled rowers overboard.

They watched in a wholly disgusted silence: and then Stephen leant over and called, 'Captain Aubrey, the galley has the wind. She is sailing towards the island we can see from up here.'

For the cloud had become island, a conical island hollowed out on the near, the eastern side.

Jack was with them in a moment, dripping wet. 'I have heard of their doing that, to save food and water,' he said. And after a silence, 'I do not know that island. But then we are right off any known tract of the sea.'

'I believe I have seen it on an old Catalan map in Barcelona,' said Stephen. 'And as I recall its name is Cranc, a crab.'

'The breeze is joining us,' said Jack, and he gave orders for all hands to come aboard: within minutes the frigate was alive again, her sails full, her bow-wave mounting. And well before the hellish sun dipped down at last, they were in with the Island Crab. There was not a hand aboard who had not seen one of the rowers – slave or unransomable captive – thrown screaming into the sea, the bloody sea, and there was not one who did not hate and loathe those that did it.

The island was presumably of volcanic origin, an eruptive peak that had then blown out its east side, leaving a shallow lagoon with a high wall broken only by a narrow channel through which the sea flowed in and out. From the tops they could see the galley moored under the rock wall near the entrance, close to a battered mole and some derelict buildings. She was entirely sheltered from anything but mortars: and the frigate possessed no mortars; nor could she enter such shallow water to use her guns.

The gentle topgallant breeze carried her round the island, surveying and sounding as she went, clean round with only a single tack: deep water, no apparent reefs, almost no vegetation on the land, no sign, no sign at all of water: nor, to Stephen's astonishment, of sea-birds. On the west side, under quite steep cliffs, there was a little grey-green strand.

Jack had himself rowed to it, with Stephen: and as they

walked on what sand there was, Jack observed that this was high tide; that the surf must be very severe indeed on this side, after a strong westerly blow; and that he hoped Stephen had found some interesting creatures in that cave.

'I found something more interesting still,' said Stephen. 'A total absence of life. Well into June and not a nestling petrel even. No birds, no bird-lice, no feather mites. And I tell you what it is, brother: there is an uneasy smell in that rock, those fissures – pray thrust your nose into this one. I am no chemist, God forbid, but I very much suspect the presence of a poisonous emanation. That would account for the near-absence of vegetation, even in June.' He mused, and while he was musing Daniel came and said to Jack, 'Sir, we have a hand in the boat, McLeod, who was in *Centaur* in the year four: he says the position here is very like what it was when Captain Hood took the Diamond Rock. He was a Saint Kilda cragsman in his youth, and he helped to get the guns up the cliff.'

'It had not struck me,' said Jack, 'but the situation is indeed very like. Yet could he really carry a line up that cliff? McLeod,' he called, and the tall, middle-aged seaman, a recent draught from *Erebus* in Gibraltar, came up, awkward and embarrassed. 'Do you think you could take a line up that cliff? Right up that cliff?'

'I think so, sir,' said McLeod in his halting English, 'with a little well-tempered hand-pick, and a stout peg with a block to send me up another twenty-five fathom. This is no so steep as Diamond Rock, but it is softer, and may be false at top.'

'Should you like to try? If ever it grows too false you may come down with no shame – it is only an attempt, a trial.'

'We hauled up twenty-four pounders,' said McLeod, not quite following him.

'Let us shove off at once,' said Jack, and he led the way to the boat. They pulled back at a great pace, helped by the current and buoyed up by recollections of the Diamond

Rock, that most uncommon feat – back to *Surprise* as she lay so moored that her broadside would shatter the emerging galley on the starboard side if ever she ventured out, while *Ringle* would do the same to larboard.

The bosun roused out coils of the strongest white line; the armourer blew his forge to an incandescent heat, fashioned wedges with eye-holes for the blocks, forged and tempered a little hand-pick, one head a beak, the other a hammer, under McLeod's supervision.

They were still too hot to hold as the boat pulled back, though in the mean time McLeod and his cousin had sewn tight sailcloth climbing shoes.

'In the Pyrenees I have pursued the izard, God forgive me, who dwells in the highest peaks,' said Stephen, standing with his hands behind his back, watching McLeod's ascent, 'but never have I seen such climbing. He might almost be a gecko.'

It was indeed an extraordinary spectacle, that stalwart twelve-stone man moving up the almost perpendicular lower cliff, fissured to be sure, but from below apparently smooth; and when he reached a more craggy stretch where he could rest and then drive home his peg and make fast his line, all hands cheered amain. He tossed down his ball of twine for the next coil and so, heaving it up and putting the coil over his shoulder and carried on, faster this time, up to the middle height, while his cousin Alexander, making use of the first line, made his way up. In a surprisingly short time they were able to look cautiously over the top, the whole lagoon open below them.

Now, while bold but less wholly intrepid hands chipped footholds along the line of the first rope and beyond, began one of the most elaborate cat's cradles that Jack had ever seen: although it was nothing to the aerial railway of the Diamond Rock, it was the bosun's seventh heaven, and presently all was ready to send a nine-pounder cannon up, sliding along a steep messenger to a point where it commanded the lagoon: and if a nine-pounder would not answer, then two fourteen-pounders could not possibly be denied.

By night the *Surprise* came round at low tide, when the water was too low for the galley to attempt the outward passage from the lagoon. And offshore, in excellent holding ground, she dropped two anchors and then sent hawsers ashore. They rose by means of powerful tackles past the various staging points to the very summit, where they were made fast to a complexity of stakes and hauled taut by the ship's capstan. 'Chaser away,' said Jack, and his personal nine-pounder was made fast to the messenger, slung below it by iron hoops. At the cry of 'Handsomely, handsomely, now,' the hands at the uppermost winch, under the command of Whewell, began to turn: the long hawsers, spliced end to end, stretched, sighed, grew more rigid, and the gun began its smooth progress up along the messenger. The gun, its emplacement, its munitions, represented a prodigious amount of labour; but as the sun rose, lighting the lagoon, with the galley up against its mole, nobody was in the least fatigued.

Jack knew his gun intimately: the distance was nothing much for a well-bored chaser – a little over a furlong – but as he told Stephen – who with Jacob, had been carried up like parcels – he had rarely fired at such a downward angle. 'I shall just try one or two sighters,' he said, 'aiming at those dilapidated houses. Run her up, shipmates.' The gun thumped against its emplacement: Jack shifted the wedge still farther, glared along the sight, made one more trifling adjustment and clapped the linstock down, arching his body to let the recoiling nine-pounder shoot back under him. While the team swabbed, cleaned, reloaded, rammed home the wad and ran her up again, he stood fanning the smoke and smiling with satisfaction: the shot had gone right home. And the Moors were swarming about the galley and the mole like startled ants.

They were corsairs, men of war: they very quickly grasped

their situation, their hopeless situation, and they seized Murad Reis, manhandled him along to the end of the mole nearest the cliff, tied his hands, forced him to kneel and called up, 'Our sins on his head. Our sins on his head.' With a single blow one of the corsairs cut Murad's head clean off, held it up to the watchers on the cliff and cried, 'Our sins on his head. Give us water and we shall be your slaves for ever – you shall have the galley: you shall have the gold.'

Some were drinking the blood, but most were gazing up, holding out supplicatory hands.

'Will you answer, Dr Jacob?' asked Jack.

'It would wholly compromise my position,' said Jacob. 'Let us wait a little. I believe they have some other resource.'

They had: some moments later a dozen almost naked powerful seamen, deeply sunburnt, scored with whip lashes but recognizably white, were pushed forward, and their leader, squaring up to the cliff, called out in a hoarse Port of London voice, 'God bless King George. Which we are British subjects, taken out of the *Three Brothers*, *Trade's Increase* and other craft: and should be very grateful to your honour for a drop of anything wet. Amen.'

'Hear him,' croaked the others. 'Right parched we are. Drinking piss this last week.'

'Listen,' said Jack in his strong, carrying voice. 'You take the Moors' weapons and pile them at the end of the mole, tie their hands, and I shall signal the schooner to send in a boat full of fresh water and something to eat.'

The British subjects uttered a hoarse discordant cheer; Jack fired three or four times at random to keep up the tension; and the weapons came piling up on the mole.

Just off the lagoon the Surprises, overflowing with satisfaction and wit, carried out the small heavy, heavy, wonderfully heavy little chests from the galley to those places deep in the *Surprise* where their weight would be most useful as ballast. The Moorish prisoners, reasonably fed and watered, were stowed in the cable-tiers. They were, at least for the time being, very low in their spirits: indeed morally destroyed: but Jack had seen strange surprising changes in men freed from mortal danger: he reckoned with the resilience of the human spirit, particularly the maritime human spirit; and having, with his officers, fixed the ship's position with the utmost accuracy he set her course for the nearest point in Africa, where he meant to put them ashore.

For the moment however he and Stephen were breakfasting in comfort, gazing with some complacency at the island Cranc. 'Jacob tells me,' said Stephen, 'that in Moorish Arabic the place is now called Fortnight Island. It had been a moderately prosperous fishing and corsair port – dates, carobs, pearl oysters, coral – hence the mole and the ruins – until the time of, I think, Mulei Hassan; but then a new eruption destroyed the few springs, broke the aqueducts and cisterns and slowly liberated that noxious vapour we observed. It seems that you can breathe it for fourteen days with nothing but headaches and gastric pains; but on the fifteenth you die.'

'I beg pardon for interrupting you, sir,' said Harding, 'but you desired me to tell you when all was aboard. The last chest has just been handed down.' As he spoke his usually grave face spread in a most infectious smile: that last case, carried staggering by strong men, weighed well over a hundred and twelve pounds, and Harding, though not an avaricious or grasping man, knew just how many ounces of that mass belonged to him as prize-money.

Patriotism, promotion, and prize-money have been described as the three masts of the Royal Navy. It would be illiberal to assert that prize-money was by any means the most important, but as they left the flat shore north of Ras Uferni in Morocco, where they had at last disembarked their prisoners after a tedious voyage with contrary winds, it was certainly the subject still most frequently discussed.

'If you people will sail the galley into Gibraltar with us,' said Captain Aubrey to the slaves, 'You shall share as able seamen.'

'Why, thankee, sir,' said Hallows, their spokesman. 'We take it uncommon handsome: and I promise we shall do our duty by your prize.'

'That's right,' said his mates, and indeed they handled the galley very well. But they did think it part of their duty to run alongside the frigate on three separate occasions, begging the officer of the watch to shorten sail. 'There are too many eggs in this one basket to risk anything at all,' was the usual formula, thought to be both conciliating and witty.

Jack was on deck the last time they did this, and he said, 'Hallows, if you do not keep your station I shall turn you ashore,' with such conviction that although they very nearly came within hail to tell the frigate that there was an enormous great fire on the very top of Cape Trafalgar, they thought better of it and kept the news for *Ringle*.

Indeed there were fires all along the European side of the Straits, exciting unspeakable wonder aboard the three vessels: but the sight of Gibraltar itself ablaze with innumerable bonfires, the harbour filled with ships dressed over all, bands playing, trumpets blowing and drums beating madly checked all conjecture, and *Surprise*, having made her number, wafted silently to her usual place, with her companions.

'The flag-lieutenant, sir, if you please,' said a midshipman at his side.

'Give you joy of your splendid prize, sir,' cried the flag-lieutenant. 'By God, you could never have timed it better.'

'Thank you, Mr Betterton,' said Jack. 'But pray tell me what is afoot?'

The flag-lieutenant stared for a moment, and then he gravely replied, 'Napoleon is beat, sir. There was a great battle at Waterloo in the Low Countries, and the Allies won.'

'Then it is I that give you joy, sir,' said Jack, shaking his hand. 'Have you any details?'

'No, sir. But the courier is arrived and the Commander-in-Chief will have them. When your number was reported he bade me remind you of your engagement: Lady Barmouth has taken the coach to fetch the Keiths.'

'Please tell Lord Barmouth that Dr Maturin and I shall be charmed to wait upon him, above all on such a day.'

'There you are at last, Aubrey,' cried the Commander-in-Chief, obviously overcome by the events and obviously somewhat flushed with wine. 'Doctor, your servant, sir: very happy to see you. So here you are at last, Aubrey, and with a thundering great prize at your tail. Give you joy, of course . . . but the fellow must have led you a most infernal long chase?'

'He did indeed, my Lord. He went to ground in an island I had never heard of, called Cranc, an island with a very shallow but sheltered lagoon – too shallow for *Surprise* – and I had to winkle him out by a kind of Diamond Rock caper, getting a gun up a five hundred foot cliff to fire down on him.'

'Well, I am sure it was very creditable and I congratulate you of course; but I wish to God you could have done it under any other Dey of Algiers – this one has cut up very rough indeed – says it was *his* galley and everything in it – sent me a furious note and swears he will take it out of our merchantmen if there is no restitution, compensation and the rest of it.'

'But my Lord, the galley fired on us first. That made him a pirate and fair game.'

'That is not what the Dey says.'

'Is the word of an upstart Dey who was never there and who knows nothing about it to be taken against that of a sea-officer who was there and who does know all about it?'

'. . . under any other Dey,' repeated Barmouth. 'My politico takes the gloomiest view of the whole situation, and so I fear does the Ministry. They have a special commission out there, half a dozen men of the first distinction, to discuss the possibilities of a treaty, Ali Bey having always been so much in favour of England . . . Was it a very large sum of money, Aubrey?'

'I cannot say, my Lord: it was in the form of very small gold ingots, about the size of the upper joint of one's finger. But there was one chest that must have tipped the scale at eight stone or more.'

'A hundredweight . . . how many chests were there?'

'I did not count, my Lord.'

'Well, if there were only eight, my flag-officer's third would have amounted to about five thousand. It fairly makes me tear my hair . . .' Jack was tempted to say that he was not acting under Barmouth's orders at all, but carrying out Keith's, which were still valid. However, he kept his mouth shut: Barmouth muttered under his breath for a while; then, recollecting himself, he said, 'But in course it is far worse for you; and how you will ever explain it to your people without a bloody mutiny I cannot tell. But hush, the Keiths have just arrived.'

The door opened and in walked the ladies – very fine ladies indeed, glowing with happiness, victory and all their best jewels, followed by Lord Keith. 'Jack!' cried the one, and 'Dearest Cousin Jack!' the other; and both kissed him most fondly.

With the utmost affection and the happiest look he said, 'Queenie and Isobel, Isobel and Queenie, how very delightful it is to see you both together, and in such glorious looks, my dears.'

'Do you remember . . . ?' cried the one, and 'Do you remember . . . ?' cried the other, until the Commander-in-Chief broke up the unseemly group, insisting in no very urbane or even civil tone, that their guests should be seated.

He took one end of the table, with Queenie on his right and Arden, his political adviser (only just not late and still pale with emotion) on his left; Isobel Barmouth the other end, with Lord Keith on her right and Cousin Jack on her left.

The politico had been detained by some further details of the great battle or rather series of battles, and these he related with a fair degree of precision; but after that the conversation languished. There had been a very, very great deal of emotion that day, and both admirals were feeling their age. Queenie and Stephen rambled along pleasantly about the island; but then she, having tried to move the Commander-in-Chief from his only too evident ill-humour, fell silent, imitated by Stephen. The only people really enjoying their meal were Jack and Isobel. Isobel was much younger than Queenie: the cousins were indeed much of an age and when they were adolescents there had been a certain degree of ambiguity about the nature of their friendship: now that ambiguity was distinctly more evident. Isobel was in fine voice and very high spirits; and it was evident to Stephen, on the other side of the table, that they were holding hands under the cloth.

She was, he reflected, something of a rake: a very pretty rake. And it was not improbable that her cross old husband was aware of it, for when her cousin had said something that moved her to an indecorous fit of laughter, Lord Barmouth straightened in his chair and called down the table, 'Aubrey, I have just been thinking that now you have nothing to do with the Navy, you might be well advised to slip your moorings and sail off to survey the Horn and plumb the depths of Magellan: the inhabitants may prove grateful, and I am sure the young ladies would welcome such a very amusing companion.'

This was said in such a tone that Isobel stood up at once: she and Queenie paced into the drawing-room, leaving an abashed group of men standing there, all at a moral disadvantage.

The servants were by no means unaccustomed to this, and the port very soon made its appearance; it had gone round three times when a servant asked Stephen whether Dr Jacob might have a word with him.

Stephen excused himself and found Jacob in the hall. 'I beg pardon for disturbing you,' he said, 'but the forerunner of an Algerine delegation brought me the news of Ali Bey's deposition – he was strangled in the slave-market – and since the news of the French defeat reached Algiers earlier than Spain, the new Dey, Hassan, is sending these people to congratulate the Commander-in-Chief, to announce his accession, and to annul his predecessor's absurd claim on the captured treasure; but he should like the galley back, as a symbol of his office, and he would be most grateful for an immediate loan of two hundred and fifty thousand pounds to consolidate his position in Algiers.'

'What you say fills me with ease,' said Stephen. 'Yet since the Commander-in-Chief, Lord Keith, the politico and Captain Aubrey and nobody else are in there, I believe you should relate all this to them.'

'Very well: and I have the head of the English mission with me to substantiate what I say. Shall I fetch him?'

'Not if it would take ten minutes. This news must be eaten hot.'

'Very well.'

Stephen led him in. 'My Lord,' he said to Barmouth, 'may I introduce my colleague Dr Jacob, a gentleman very well known to Sir Joseph Blaine?'

'Hear, hear,' said the politico.

'Of course you may,' said Barmouth. 'How do you do, sir? Pray take a seat. May I offer you a glass of wine?'

'My lords and gentlemen,' said Jacob, bowing over his port. 'I must tell you that one of our most reliable agents in Algiers, accompanied by a member of the Ministry's special commission, Mr Blenkinsop, has just told me that tomorrow morning a delegation from the new Dey, Hassan, will arrive to congratulate His Majesty on the defeat of Bonaparte, to announce his own accession, and to settle a point at issue

– the Algerine galley and its alleged cargo. He waives his predecessor's absurd claim, and although he should like the galley back as a symbol of his office, he fully acknowledges that its commander, in firing first, deprived all persons other than the captain of His Britannic Majesty's ship of any claim to its contents. He should however be most grateful for an immediate loan of two hundred and fifty thousand pounds to strengthen his present position – a loan very soon to be repaid.'

There was a silence: then the Commander-in-Chief said, 'Dr Jacob, we are very grateful indeed for your good news and your early warning – at least we shall be able to receive these gentlemen in a suitable manner. Lord Keith, you are the senior officer present: may I ask your opinion?'

'My opinion is that we should welcome this approach most heartily . . .'

'Hear, hear,' said the politico. Stephen and Jack, being parties concerned, said nothing; but Jack at all events felt a spring of delight rising in his heart.

'. . . and,' went on Lord Keith, 'since I was concerned with Captain Aubrey's orders in the first place, and since I know the little ways of the prize-court through and through, I propose taking this case before them at once, and then desiring the dockyard to give the vessel something in the way of gold leaf to make her a more presentable present. As for the Dey's loan, I am obviously no longer in a position to speak of the colony's finances, but I have no doubt that the Ministry would consider it a very reasonable outlay.'

'Hear, hear,' said the politico.

The Commander-in-Chief only nodded; but his mobile face, recently so very sour and ill-natured now shone with an inner sun: in the course of these last few minutes his flag-officer's third part of Jack's share of the prize, so recently despaired of, had returned as a solid, very beautiful fact.

*   *   *

280

Lord Keith was a good friend to Jack Aubrey: very early in the morning he had surprised the swabbers at their task and within minutes there were a score of barrows alongside the *Surprise*: under guard they wheeled the massy little chests to the premises of Gibraltar's three substantial goldsmiths, who reduced the whole to tested ingots of a stated weight well before the Algerine ship came in with its delegation and a present of full-grown ostriches.

Jacob was present at the various ceremonies, but Jack and Stephen were wholly taken up with other things – Jack with persuading the officers, warrant-officers, steady petty officers and seamen to have at least two-thirds of their prize-money sent home, and with storing the ship for the first leg of his voyage; while Stephen did much the same for his department, as well as writing a very long coded report to Sir Joseph.

The ceremonies, it appeared, went off very well, particularly the state appearance of the loan on silver salvers: but in the evening, with the Algerines gone to the sound of guns, drums and trumpets, when the Keiths came down to say good-bye, accompanied by an over-excited Mona and Kevin, barely to be restrained by their nursemaid, Jack and Harding found to their grief that they had not been able to keep all their people sober.

It was none of it very gross, and even Queenie had seen a drunken sailor: yet even so Jack was relieved when the moorings were cast off and *Surprise*, dropping her foresail, glided free of the mole.

'God bless,' called Queenie; and 'Liberate Chile, and come home as soon as ever you can,' called her husband, while the children screeched out very shrill, fluttering handkerchiefs. And at the very end of the mole, when the frigate turned westward along the Strait with a following breeze, stood an elegant young woman with a maidservant, and she too waving, waving, waving . . .